IN A CERTAIN LIGHT

Also by Karen Brownstein

MEMORIAL DAY

IN A
CERTAIN
LIGHT

Karen Brownstein

PaperJacks LTD.

TORONTO   NEW YORK

PaperJacks

IN A CERTAIN LIGHT

PaperJacks LTD.

330 STEELCASE RD. E., MARKHAM, ONT. L3R 2M1
210 FIFTH AVE., NEW YORK, N.Y. 10010

G.P. Putnam's Sons edition published 1985
PaperJacks edition published February 1987

This is a work of fiction in its entirety. Any resemblance to actual people, places or events is purely coincidental.

ISBN 0-7701-0501-7
Printed in Canada

For
My cherished teacher, mentor and friend
HOWARD M. TEICHMANN

Chapter One

"They want you to do it on television," was what Jenny Roo's agent had said on the telephone.

"Do what?" Jenny had asked, turning off the electric typewriter on which she was typing her weekly column for the *Trib*, and trailing the extra-long cord to the Mr. Coffee pot she kept in her study.

"What you do," Burger said. "Come on up to the office Friday, and we'll talk about it." Burger was not a man for long telephone conversations, especially not when he liked the person on the other end of the line. And he liked Jenny Roo. "Think about it, Jennifer. You're a whole lot prettier than Andy Rooney or Jack Anderson and they're talking big-league money. Maybe I'll even buy you a sandwich. Come at lunchtime."

"I see my mother on Fridays."

"Tell her to call Rent-a-Daughter this week. See you Friday."

So here was Jennifer Golman Roo, thirty-four years

ed, the mother of a street-
ter from whose lips fre-
ond that which appeared
ving in from Westchester
ttan to find out what "doing
it on tele   about.

Questions floated in her head like tiny bubbles, making
her slightly tipsy behind the wheel. She opened the sunroof to let the cold February air clear her head, and sang
to herself, "One day at a time, girl . . . just one day at a
time." It was a ridiculous lyric, she thought as she drove
the easy curves of the Hutchinson River Parkway, and if
anyone ever discovered that she had composed it herself, this slightly torchy country-western ballad, her
career as a columnist was over. Still, the song was comforting to her, and in the nine years since the words had
first come into her head she had found herself humming
it often. Her cornpone tranquilizer, she called it privately.
"Things will turn out fine, girl . . . if you take just one
day at a time."

"Garbage," Jenny informed the forested roads of
Westchester County that shaped her view. "The woman
is driving to what may be one of the most important
meetings of her career, and how is she preparing for it?
By opening up her sunroof in February in New York City
and singing out cornball garbage."

By her own description Jenny was a "soft
journalist." Schooled in objectivity, educated in the
skills of dispassionate reporting, she had been trained
into wariness of her own instincts.

"You're a cornball by nature," her feature-writing
professor had caustioned her. "Tender, merciful, compassion oozing out of every pore on your young body.
Try to toughen up, girl. There's nothing wrong with
compassion. Compassion can be your strong suit, Jenny.
Provided that you keep it in check. All of that sensitivity
should inform your work, but the moment you find

yourself shedding tears into the keys of your typewriter, you're lost. Trust me."

She tried to. To toughen up. To stop crying at weddings. To give up singing in the shower, to quit reading love poetry by candlelight. And if she felt the chills coming on when a boy and his lost puppy were reunited on the eleven-o'clock news, she changed the channel. Was it the offhand advice of a well-intentioned teacher that had changed her, she wondered, or the cruelty of her marriage? It didn't matter, she told herself as she drove; it had been years since anyone had called her a cornball.

On the contrary, her weekly column at the *Trib* was the space in which she was regularly rewarded for forging the oozing mush of sentimentality into the hard tarnished amalgam of reality. In *The New York Trib* Jenny had been granted a public space for the sole purpose of exposing what she had called the "goop" of contemporary society. When a major publisher had anthologized her first two years of columns in a volume called *Natural Ingredients*, he had paid her what he considered to be the ultimate compliment to a female newspaper columnist: "Jenny," he said, "you are a young Erma Bombeck with guts."

"Naw," Jenny had replied while signing the contract for the book advance. "She's a lot funnier than I am. But I bet that if you stripped Erma naked and got her stoned before she sat down at the typewriter, she'd write a lot like me." And that afternoon she had written a letter to Mrs. Bombeck thanking her for having paved the way. A sincere letter of gratitude in which Jenny had struggled to omit any reference to dirty laundry, peanut-butter-and-jelly sandwiches, or sagging anatomy.

The letter had never been mailed. Today Jenny could remember that letter and that day with perfect clarity. It was the day her husband had tried to strangle her. Not for the first time, but — in Jenny's memory — the worst time.

Paul had known for weeks that his wife was about to be paid more money than he had earned in ten years as a playwright, simply, as he put it, "for collecting yesterday's newspapers." But on that night, when they were alone in the kitchen of their apartment on West Fifty-fourth Street; when their baby, Rachel, had been lullabyed to an uneasy sleep, he had held the check to the light and feigned a kind of vague surprise. "Fabulous," he had said, breaking the stony silence that had reigned throughout the evening. "Just fabulous, Jennifer," he had said, counting the zeros with exaggerated awe. "You're really something, aren't you, Jenny?" he had whispered as he refilled his glass from the open bottle of scotch that had become a fixture on their kitchen counter. "Best little hack on the block." With that fixed smile leering at her over the rim of his glass.

He had once been so beautiful to her, Paul, so very beautiful. On the day they had met at the writers' seminar in New England the sap had flowed in her as if she were one more Vermont maple ready for tapping. "Syrup," she remembered telling her best friend Nina Croft when she came back to the city. "I take one look at him and you could pour me like syrup." Paul was a playwright, a playwright with black curls and eyes like honey-dipped coals. So what if her mother thought that he dressed funny with the floppy hats and the beat-up tennis shoes? So what if he thought that journalism was the garbage dump of "real" writers? He was beautiful. Every word he wrote, spoke, or whispered had thrilled her. They were married in the woods, two hills away from where they had met. She wore snow boots and a bridal gown, her mother wore a borrowed full-length mink coat, and on their wedding night he covered Jenny with pure maple syrup and licked her clean.

She should have known then that sticky sheets make only a mess, not a marriage. When his third play, the one that had taken him six years to acquire backing for, opened and closed in one night, the theater was so far off Broadway that the cab fare to get them back to their apartment had been more than twenty dollars. The genius playwright was too broke to pay the babysitter Jenny had hired for Rachel on what was meant to have been their glory night. "Come by tomorrow, kid, and my wife will take care of you," he had muttered. It seemed to Jenny that those were the last sober words she had heard him speak.

Had it started with Rachel's birth or with her pregnancy? Or was it before that? Sometimes she couldn't remember. Her pregnancy had been confirmed in February, months before Mother's Day, and riding the Madison Avenue bus home from the obstetrician's office she had been euphoric. She rode with her hands resting on her lap, imagining the tiny being that was miraculously harbored within her. She would save the surprise for Mother's Day, she decided. Paul she would tell tonight, of course, but the news that each of them were to become grandmothers she would save for Minna, her own mother, and for Paul's mother, Clara, until she actually showed. A fabulous Mother's Day gift, welcome beyond all others.

She carried this happy fantasy with her as she transferred to the crosstown bus that would take her home to the West Side. Walking, she stopped at the bank to cash her paycheck from the *Trib*, and with a giddy sense of fairytale adventure she splurged on cheap champagne and flowers. At the butcher shop where she normally bought only ground beef and chicken because everything else was beyond their budget, Jenny chose the pinkest sirloin steak Mr. Antonelli had in his case.

"Somebody gonna have a celebration," he sang as he trimmed the meat for her. "Somebody's gonna have something special tonight." Jenny stood on her tiptoes to watch him work.

"Can you keep a secret, Mr. Antonelli?" she whispered, although there was no one else in the shop.

"Sure I can. Of course I can."

Jenny leaned farther over the counter and tested the magic words. "I'm going to have a baby," she breathed, expecting that those buoyant words would rise like bubbles, that they would now hang from the ceiling like the brightly colored posters advertising fresh turkeys and honey-baked hams.

"Ah, Mrs. Roo," Antonelli had said, wiping his hands on his apron and coming around the meat case to pump her hand, "that's wonderful news. The best! A baby, that's really something. When is it coming, your bambino?"

"Oh, not for a long time," she had confided. "I just found out today."

"You tell your hubby yet?"

"No, no. I'm going to tell him tonight."

"Ah, that's how come you buy the steak. Oh, he's gonna be so happy, Mrs. Roo. I remember when my missus tell me about the first one coming. Like yesterday, I remember. This is the first one, right?"

"That's right," Jenny had said.

"Ah, he gonna go crazy he be so happy."

But he had not been happy. He had chewed the steak with a stiff jaw that made the silence in their small kitchen seem all the more awkward. When he had downed the last of the champagne and had fortified himself with three glasses of scotch, Jenny spoke. "I thought we were agreed. I thought now that I had the raise and your play was going so well, I thought . . . I thought . . ."

"What did you pay for the steak?"

"What?"

"The meat!" he said, suddenly springing up from his chair and picking up the broiling pan that lay on the table. "How much did you pay for the goddamn meat!" he thundered.

"I don't know," Jenny had said. "What difference does it make?" She was suddenly nauseous, her body drenched with cold sweat.

"What difference does it make! Listen to you, Mrs. Got Rocks! What difference does it make? You think you're going to be eating like this for nine months? Do you! There are going to be doctor bills! Hospital bills! Ah shit!" he exploded, knocking the pan to the floor.

There was grease spattered all over the linoleum of the small kitchen. Jenny had taken her napkin and kneeled down to wipe the floor, afraid to look up. Afraid to see the twisted rage in his face, the pitiless cast of his hard eyes.

"Do you know what you are, Jenny? Do you know?" he had said, refilling his glass. "You're sloppy! You're so damn sloppy you can't even remember to use your diaphragm!"

"That's not true," Jenny said, crawling toward the shelter of the space under the kitchen table. "We were agreed. Paul, dear, please . . ."

"Don't 'Paul dear' me!" he shouted. "You're not my mother!" He pounded his fist against the table. "Who needed this, Jenny? Tell me! Who needed this! I'm not even finished with the first act of *Hillside* and you're buying steak. Who needs it!"

"We can afford to splurge once in a while," Jenny had said in a small, unsteady voice. A voice she prayed carried reason.

"We? We!" Paul yelled. "There is no we! There's you! There's just you! You're the big shot around here!" And then he was dragging her out from under the table, pulling on her hair, his face a demon mask of fury. "I'm not there yet, goddamn you! I'm not ready for this!"

She had run for the bedroom when he let go of her hair, and slammed the door behind her. The closet. That was where she had hidden from him. The tiny dark closet. How many times had she stood frozen in that airless space, her teeth clenched around fabric, her mouth stuffed with a shirt sleeve so that the screams in her throat could not escape her lips? How many times? Lying crouched on the floor, her head splitting with the effort of holding that door closed. Her muscles screaming with the pain of holding on, holding on.

"I need time!" he kept yelling that night. "I'm not ready!" And then, at last, she heard the slam of the bedroom door. And the muted slam of the front door. And she knew that he was gone. She had lain on the floor of the closet that night, her arms trembling with the effort of holding that door closed against him, her legs leaden, her face pressed against the dusty rug that offered the closest thing to comfort in that dark and suffocating space. And she had run her shaking hand across her belly and prayed for the safety of her child.

As she prayed now.

By the time she had been offered the weekly column at the *Trib*, he had already lost four jobs in advertising, two in press agentry, and it was clear that he was becoming an alcoholic. Sometimes Jenny could not remember which had come first — the booze or the beatings. It seemed to her that they had come together, bound in one obscene package. In the two years during which his failures mounted, her successes compounded. She felt as if they were locked in some sort of terrifying elevator. If she could make it to her floor at the top, if she pressed the up button hard enough, she could get off the elevator without Paul making it crash.

Now, driving along almost a dozen years later, with the Hudson River flowing its undaunted course beside her, she winced at the piercing irony of words he had spoken on one of their earliest dates.

"You don't drink, do you?" Paul had asked her earnestly after the first time they had made love.

"Writers mustn't drink, you know. Booze is death to writers. Playwrights especially. Eugene O'Neill could have —" She had silenced him with a kiss.

"Not to worry," she had told him, "I don't even like the taste. And besides, I'm not a writer. Not the way you're a writer. I'm just a light-weight Jewish girl who has a way with words."

"Yeah, right," he had said, stroking her small, firm breasts, "and so is Lillian Hellman."

Oh Christ, she thought to herself as she drove past the Cloisters, a child could have read that message. A child could have seen what was coming.

But not Jenny. Jenny was in love and Jenny was married to a genius. And geniuses were temperamental. And that first time he ever abused her she was sure, on immediate reflection, that she had provoked him.

She had been over this ground again and again. Every therapist she had ever seen, every group session of battered women she had ever attended, had demanded this information. "The First Time," they called it, giving it a whispered romantic inflection that Jenny thought perverse. "Can you talk about the first time?"

Yes. She remembered now.

The first time was a morning in October, 1974. It was easy for Jenny to chronicle the details of timing because she was pregnant; for the nine months of carrying Rachel she had been obsessed with the passage of time in a way she had not known before. Oh yes, Doctor, it was definitely October because that's when the morning sickness was at its worst. And that's when Paul had been struggling hardest with the second act of his play, *Hillside.* And that was the morning she had had the audacity to turn her back on his proud reading of the final scene, and throw up into the kitchen sink.

"Jesus!" he had roared, grabbing the manuscript from the table where they had been having coffee.

"Jesus, you could have waited! It was only three more lines until curtain! You could have fucking waited, Jennifer!"

She had tried to speak, tried to talk past the nausea, and the tears, and the crash of the coffee cup against the wall beside her. "I can't help it," she had tried to say, gagging on the words, "I can't help it." She had run the cold water.

"You're damn right you can't help it!" he had yelled, grabbing a length of her dark-brown hair and twisting her to face him. "You never could help it! You don't have it in you to help it. All you have inside of you is you! You!" Pulling her by the hair until her back was arched over the rim of the sink, her skull knocking against the cold porcelain. "You! You're so goddamn full of yourself!"

Full of yourself. Hours later, when he had phoned from some bar in SoHo, sobbing with remorse, choking on contrition, the words were still in her head. *Full of yourself.* She had pictured a round, brightly painted nesting doll, its wooden belly swollen, its glazed-enamel face her own face. Herself, this doll. His hands twisting her doll-self in two, dividing her, *crack!* to reveal another, smaller but otherwise identical version of herself. Inside herself, inside herself — until his long white knuckled fingers came to rest on a self so tiny it was smothered between his thumb and forefinger. Smothered, yes, that was the self he sought. The self that could be divided no further. The self that birthed no progeny. No progeny, no likeness, no life. The self that he could press beneath his thumb until it became what it had once been: wood pulp. Gussied up with paint, enlarged by replication, pregnant with sameness.

She became convinced that she bored him. That the sensitivity he needed to do his best work was being destroyed by the banalities of her pregnancy. After all, she told her friend Nina as they shopped the baby departments of Lord & Taylor, Bloomingdale's, B. Altman, "how can a man who's applied for a grant from the Shubert Foundation, who's one act away from breaking into the magic circle of Broadway, take an interest in booties and baby blankets? It would be absurd."

"The man," Nina had said quietly, "is going to be the baby's father." It had taken years for the words to penetrate.

Maybe Nina had said it too quietly. Maybe the morning in October had stood for too long as an isolated incident. Maybe Jenny had such a fine way with words that she was able to talk herself out of the truth with more artful self-deception than the average victim of battering. But the fact was that circumstances seemed to enfold her in a structure of realities so complete she could not see through any window.

The increased frequency of his drinking binges, the mounting incidents of his anger, the abuse, the unprovoked beatings and the savage verbal attacks — all of it could be explained away by any mass-circulation women's magazine. It was all so obvious that, briefly, she had considered writing the article herself. The man was suffering from an overblown case of baby envy. *Classic,* Jenny told herself, perfectly normal, utterly standard. Sure. The creative energies that she had once poured into her own work and still maintained a reserve of to contribute to Paul's writing were now being expended in behalf of her baby, Rachel. Paul was jealous. That was all it was. Simple jealousy.

It was normal, her obstetrician told her, perfectly normal. If the obstetrician had just once in all of those postpartum visits asked her to roll over; if he had just once seen the bruises that ran up and down her spinal column, perhaps the denial would have ended sooner. But he hadn't, he hadn't asked her to roll over. He hadn't seen.

It was Nina who saw, who saw first. On a two-week vacation at Fire Island, an oceanside celebration Nina had paid for because *Hillside* was finished at last — and because if there was one thing better than having a best friend who giving, loyal and nonjudgmental it was having a best friend who was all of those things and rich besides — Jenny ran out of excuses for not putting on a bathing suit, for not cavorting on the beach with Nina and Paul and the toddling Rachel.

Alone, in an extra bedroom facing the ocean, she had sat at the typewriter wearing gauzy caftans that hid the ugly yellow and purple bruises that marbled her flesh. Resisting Nina's taunts that she was a workaholic.

"Are you crazy?" Jenny had laughed, still trying to believe that she was telling the truth. "You want me to come out and get sand in my pants and third-degree burns on my skin instead of sitting here and waxing wise and witty on the subject of female drug abuse? Listen, rich kid, *Redbook* magazine is paying me one thousand dollars for this piece and we need the money. What are you offering for an appearance at the water's edge?"

"First of all," Nina had said as she kicked the door closed behind her and advanced toward her seated friend, "I am not a rich kid. Second of all," she had giggled as she reached for the hem of Jenny's flowing cover-up, "I think you're just embarrassed by ugly stretch marks and matronly boobs and you're turning into a very boring house guest! Now if you don't get out of this tent and into a bathing suit by yourself, I'm going to strip you right here, right this very minute!" And with that she had ripped the thin fabric from the neck to the hem in one bold stroke.

"Oh Christ!" Nina whispered, so stunned by what she had uncovered that her voice was barely audible. "Oh baby. Oh sweet Jesus, what's happened to you!" With the torn garment still in her hands she had backed away from the naked horror story of Jenny's body.

The bleached white light of sea and sky had poured through the open window, a pitiless beam of illumination, highlighting old bruises, dark and cold as sea mud, and more recent violations, tender welts of pink where blood swelled beneath Jenny's flesh. She had sat in the chair facing the beach and tried to shield herself from Nina's horrified stare, tried to will away the wild arhythmic heartbeat that pummeled her from within.

"How?" Nina kept saying. "How?" Her panting made the question into a kind of chant. "How, Jenny, how? Please tell me how."

Nine years later, driving to her appointment with her agent, making up the lyrics to some crazy country-western ballad, Jenny saw the scene once more, astonished all over again that she had somehow found the courage to answer Nina's question with the truth. It was a lifetime ago, that day at Fire Island. The woman who had cowered naked at the typewriter was someone else. Someone young, and stupid, and afraid. And as she sat stalled in crosstown traffic she recognized that she was no longer quite so young, and definitely not stupid, but still afraid.

If she had not opened the mailbox before leaving her house this morning, she might have gotten away without knowing that quite so clearly. It had been nearly two years since Paul had sent her the last newspaper clippings — the carefully cut-out stories about men who kidnapped their own children from mothers who had sole custody.

The mailings had begun about a year after he had moved to California. They always came the same way, in thin brown typewriter-addressed envelopes containing only the clippings and a small handwritten note that never varied: "For your files." Never a return address, but always postmarked Los Angeles, California.

Over the last year, free of such brown envelopes, Jenny had grown into the habit of opening her mailbox the same way most people did, casually. An automatic gesture as reflexive as putting her key into the door. She had grown so relaxed that she barely noticed when Rachel got to the mailbox before she did. These days the mail carried rewards, she reminded herself. Fan letters and royalty checks. Party invitations. She had tossed the brown envelope into her desk drawer unopened this morning and left the house. Forget it, she had told herself. He's three thousand miles away. This is too good a day to be spoiled.

"Too good a day to be spoiled, girl," she sang in a tentative soprano voice as she sat behind the wheel. It had that same cornball ring as "One Day at a Time," it would make just as good a country ballad. But by the time she had crossed Broadway she gave it up. The rest of the lyrics just wouldn't come now.

Toughen up, she told herself.

Chapter Two

"So," Steve Burger said as he stepped around his cluttered desk to wrap Jenny in a bear hug, "your mother agreed that you could play hookey today? She didn't write you out of her will?"

"No problem." Jenny forced a laugh. "I'm still first in line for the waxed fruit *and* the world-class Tupperware collection."

He gave her an extra squeeze, kissed her chastely on the forehead, and motioned for her to sit down. Too bad, Jenny thought as she looked for a chair that wasn't heaped with file folders, loose papers, books. Too bad. She liked Burger's hugs, she looked forward to them. She could count on one hand those men in whose arms she felt truly safe. Three were related to her by blood, the fourth was Nina's husband, David Kalish, and the fifth was this blustery man who, when he grinned, seemed to have hollows in his cheeks, his dimples were so deeply carved. He was doing it now, grinning at her.

"So," he said, "you got my letter on *Natural Ingredients?* Fourth printing. Not bad, sweetface."

"I put it on my bulletin board. Hallowed space, right between the pediatrician's home phone number and Minna's chocolate-cake recipe." Humor, Jenny reminded herself. Humor, if she could somehow summon it, was what might get her through this day. Might.

"Cute," Burger said, "but not lovely. Did you tell Mama Minna that if you play your cards right, not only will she keep company with her daughter on Fridays, but also on Tuesday nights?"

Jenny sighed. "No, I didn't discuss that with her. Frankly, Burger, you didn't exactly swamp me with details."

"Put your coat back on, Jenny, and we'll walk over to The Palm, get us a steak, and I'll cross your eyes with details."

Jenny gasped in mock horror. "You're kidding, Burger. Please say you're kidding. You're actually going to pop for a steak?"

"Never mind," said Burger, pushing back his chair. But it was true that after twenty-three years in the representation business, he was not an agent for picking up client tabs.

Long ago, Burger had decided that if there was a choice to be made, it was always wiser to put the dazzle in the deal than to have it melt away in the client schmear. In the early days of his agency this had been a simple, economic decision. He could not afford fancy office space, and his client lunches were mostly delivered in brown paper bags catered by the delicatessen around the corner. More than one of his earliest contracts carrried the stains of hot mustard and french-fry grease. And, although today his current client roster read like *Who's Who in Media*, and he was undisputedly one of the most powerful agents in the country, that decision still held. Only now, of course, the maintenance of a low overhead was seen as professional wisdom. Before, he had been merely poor; now he was shrewd. In the beginning, his office furnishings were tacky; now he was a man of eclectic taste.

"Just one preliminary question," Jenny said as he helped her on with her raccoon coat. "This TV offer? Is it local or network?" It was a question that had been sitting on top of her brain like a teetering granite boulder ever since Burger had phoned. If she was going to be seen only in New York, perhaps she would consider it. But if it was network, then it was no go. Paul Roo was living in California, a world away. He had some vague involvement with a Los Angeles theater group. It had taken her much too long to put three thousand miles between them for her to suddenly appear weekly in his Los Angeles living room. Who knew what bombs that might set off? Divorce or no divorce, today's mail had carried a red-alert warning she could not ignore. She was not about to risk even a televised appearance in his world. Frequently she gave thanks that her column was still not syndicated in Los Angeles.

"Local," Burger said matter-of-factly as they entered the elevator and rode down to Madison Avenue. "But listen, Jennifer, New York City is not exactly Dubuque, Iowa. There is no bigger local market. And furthermore, you come on a little rough for late night in the boonies."

The sunshine that greeted them at street level was a mirror of Jennifer's relief; she felt warm and comforted as they started across town. It was turning into one of those rare crystalline days in New York's otherwise wet, gray February. Reprieve, Jenny thought as she trotted along in her high-heeled boots, trying to keep Burger's no-nonsense pace among the lunchtime throngs. Reprieve. For her and for the throngs of people who seemed less hurried, less frantic than usual as she walked among them.

"Ever notice," she panted at Burger, "that when the winter temperature in this town rises, the hostility index goes down?"

"What?" he chortled as he crossed Forty-ninth Street against the light.

"Never mind," she said. It was a column idea, too good to be talked away. *There are days in New York and there are days. Friday was such a day. A day when the people who ordinarily push and shove their way to Maalox during lunch hour were whistling "I Love New York."* She filed it for future use under the imaginary title "Worm in the Big Apple Goes Underground," and thought about what it would be like to deliver her material to an audience, flesh-and-blood people, instead of typing it into a word processor in Scarsdale for reception in the *Trib*'s computer in Manhattan.

Feed me, Burger, feed me details, she thought as she caught his arm to avoid the three whistling Puerto Rican boys who threatened to block her path with their chirping obscene flattery.

"You see," Burger said as he bulled through their ranks, "Andy Rooney doesn't get that kind of appreciation."

"I bet in her salad days Barbara Walters got it."

"Forget it, kiddo. You're not there yet," Burger said as they entered the restaurant and pressed through the wall of bodies that crowded the length of The Palm.

"Oh yeah?" Jenny hollered as she followed him through the crowd. "Where do you take Barbara Walters for lunch?"

"Anywhere she wants to go!"

"You have reached the Kalishes' answering service. We regret that we are unable to answer your call at this time. But if you'll leave your name and number, Nina or I will get back to you as soon as possible. By the way, research shows that a lot of people are intimidated by these machines. Don't you be one of them. At the sound of the tone, just give it hell.''

Jenny held on, laughing in spite of herself. David Kalish was not a man for punch lines, and he could butcher a story to its entrails, but he was a master at putting people at ease. Jenny waited for the tone.

"It's me, you two. Get the hell home! I've got big news and no one to share it with. I need counsel, advice and a shot of your infamous aged bourbon. Hurry home, damn it!"

How often she had heard divorced women say that one of the worst things about being alone was that there was no one there to share the good stuff that came your way. No one to rush home to with your great news. No one to just grab you on the spot and hug you for your small triumphs. No one to pour the wine and hoot for your major accomplishments. Now, as she hung up the telephone and paced around the silent, empty house, Jenny felt the chill of that particular breed of loneliness.

Rachel had gone straight from school to her piano lesson, and from there to her bimonthly Friday-night sleep-over with Patience Wasserman. More than once Jenny had wanted to ask Judy Wasserman how she could have done that to her daughter, hung a name like that on a kid. *Patience Wasserman*. What chance was there in life for a girl who had a joke for a name? She herself had been only twenty-one years old when she married onto the slippery ground of being called Mrs. Roo. It had seemed to her that people stood around waiting for her to recite Housman's "With Rue My Heart Is Laden" at her own wedding reception. More than one copy of *A Shropshire Lad* had been among their wedding gifts. Only years later did she open it to discover that the poet had presaged an epitaph for the death of her marriage:

> *And many a peer of England brews*
> *Livelier liquor than the Muse,*
> *And malt does more than Milton can*
> *To justify God's ways to man.*
> *Ale, man, ale's the stuff to drink*
> *For fellows whom it hurts to think.*

Jenny cracked two eggs into a bowl and cautioned herself against such memories. Paul Roo was in Los Angeles. She had not heard his voice in nearly a decade. Who knew if it still hurt him to think? That was not her business, she thought as she sliced mushrooms for her solitary celebration dinner. Not her concern. Absently, she picked up the grater that lay on the butcher-block kitchen counter and attacked the cheese for her omelet. Oh, wouldn't he have what to say about her television offer? Wouldn't he adore a go at her small triumph? A chance to script her success with thundering malevolence and scorn. "Well, well, well," he would say. "Look what our little hack has achieved now. Print isn't good enough for her enormous talents anymore. Now it's television too. Jenny the Queen of the Boob Tube." She turned on the kitchen radio, so clear was the sound of his voice as he might spit the words.

"Screw him," she whispered under her breath. And before she carried her dinner into the living room she poured herself a glass of champagne left over from New Year's Eve.

"Celebration," she told the cat who curled beside her on the sofa. "Celebration."

Midway through her second glass, Jenny decided that she had swallowed enough champagne to fuel her resolve, and she sprang up and headed for her desk so suddenly that the startled cat took refuge behind the sofa.

The brown envelope that had arrived today was barely sealed, and its contents, Jenny saw, was one small story

from a back page of *The Los Angeles Times*. In other
envelopes like this one Paul had sent her long stories
that began on the front page and continued on another,
but the clipping she now held in her hand was no more
than four column inches. She read it where she stood.
Her eye counted five paragraphs as she read with
quickening speed the story of a noncustodial father in
Los Angeles County, a reformed alcoholic, who had
sued his ex-wife for joint custody of their two sons five
years after their divorce — and won. Jenny could not
believe it; there had to be more.

She shook the envelope in her hand for the rest of the
story, but nothing fell out. Not even the usual handwritten note. Her first response as she forced herself to
slowly reread the story was to do with it what she had
always done with such mailings in the past — tear it
into small pieces and throw it and the brown envelope
away. To thwart Paul's dictum that she store the dread
he hoped to summon with these mailings. She purposely
kept no file of these clippings, telling herself that she
could not risk Rachel's discovery of such terrifying
stories. But this, this small article that she held in her
hand, was no grisly kidnapping story; it was a cold,
dispassionate report of a legal suit. Maybe it did belong
in someone's file.

"Call someone," she urged herself. "Get this on the
record," she instructed the empty room.

She picked up the address book that lay on her desk
and opened it to the page where her attorney's phone
number was written. She stood looking at the phone
number for a long time before she realized that it was
much too late at night to call anyone. And certainly not
at his home. And certainly not because her malicious ex-
husband was playing with her head again. That's all it
was, she told herself, more mind games. It was one
thing to have suffered his physical abuse, she
understood, and another to let him torture her mind.

She was through with that. She had been through with that for nearly two years. She tore up the article and the envelope and went to bed. It was too good a day to be spoiled.

It was four o'clock in the morning when the phone rang. Jenny Roo reached a warm hand out from under her pillow, knocked a half-full mug of Sleepytime tea onto the floor, and picked up the receiver on the seventh ring. She had never been rung into wakefulness without expecting to hear Paul's voice.

"It's over, Jen," David Kalish's voice said quietly. "You're not going to be a godmother quite yet. Nina lost the baby."

Jenny pushed herself up on one elbow and waited for the jolt of sudden wakefulness that is supposed to accompany bad news delivered after midnight. When it did not come, she sank back onto her pillow and cradled the receiver in her neck.

"How?" Jenny said as she reached for the switch on the bedside lamp. "When?"

"It doesn't matter how it happened," David said in a voice so low it was barely audible on the telephone line, a four-o'clock-in-the-morning voice. "It only matters that it has happened."

Again, Jenny thought. It has happened again. A third miscarriage. Three strikes. Out. Retire the side. "Do you want me to come?" she asked. She was awake now, mopping up the tea and knowing the answer.

"Listen," David said. "I can't tell you what to do. It's the middle of the night, you'd have to leave Rachel alone. It could certainly wait until morning." He sounded as though he were being choked from behind. "I can't tell you what to do," he repeated. This time his voice broke.

David Kalish had been Jenny's friend from the day he had confided to her his desire to marry Nina. There was little she would deny him.

She pulled underwear out of a drawer and grabbed her pantyhose off the foot of the bed. "I'll be there in half an hour, David, no problem. Rachel is sleeping at a friend's. Mount Sinai, right?"

"Right."

"Klingenstein Pavilion, right?"

"The lobby," David croaked. "Same as the last two times."

"Gotcha," Jenny said, "half an hour." She had nearly hung up when she heard David's voice, this time stronger, more his own. "Jenny? Jenny, listen. You're really one hell of a friend, you know that? I mean that, Jen. One hell of a best friend. I don't know what —"

"Save it, dear heart," Jenny interrupted. "Go and take care of your wife."

Driving along the black, deserted roads of Scarsdale, Jenny sat back and thought about David's words: "One hell of a best friend." Why, she wondered as it registered that she had driven this route twice already today, did it always seem to require trouble for friendship to be appreciated? Still, in all of the years she and Nina had been there for each other, no one had ever kept a score card. What was a middle-of-the-night ride into the city? Nothing. A little hand-holding, a little philosophizing, a few carefully chosen words meant to soothe the disappointment. Big fat deal, Jenny thought as she came fully awake. For nine years, Nina had kept all of her terrible, her ugly secrets. There was no way, ever, to repay that act of loyalty. So what if they were the kind of friends who fought and made up on a weekly basis? Nina had never let her down.

David Kalish was not in the lobby of the hospital. Jenny found him instead in an empty visitors' lounge on the labor floor, one of those hospital waiting spaces which are always brightly lit. No matter that it was nearly five o'clock in the morning and still dark as death in Central Park across the street, lights blazed everywhere.

Lamps burned, overhead fluorescent bulbs hummed, and in the bright artificial stillness the squeak of a nurse's rubber-soled shoes was as chilling as fingernails scraped against a chalkboard.

He was slouched backward in a brown lounge chair, his arm bent across his face as if to block the articial light, the night's events, and all the world from his sight when Jenny found him.

"David," she said softly, "I'm so sorry. So genuinely sorry."

He rubbed his hands across his eyes and stood slowly to embrace her, smelling of fear and anger and stale men's cologne.

"Hard to find the justice, isn't it?" he whispered against her cheek. His own face was wet with tears. "Hard to come up with answers."

"There are no answers," Jenny said, stepping back and stroking the crisp gray hairs at his temples. "Not easy ones, anyway. I learned that a long time ago, my friend."

"Yeah, well, you traipse around this town seeing a new specialist every month for two years, you kind of believe one of them is going to come up with something like an answer," he said. His blue eyes squinted at her from swollen sockets.

"Yes," Jenny said, her hands still trying to smooth the lines of grief from his face, "I suppose you do, David." There was little more she could say without sounding like a parody of one of her own columns. That was the trouble with having a gift for words: she could come up with a dozen ways of decribing the pain she saw in this man's face, but not one of them could erase it. "Want to walk a little? Maybe take me in to see Nina?"

"No," he said, taking her arm. "I was just in there. She finally stopped fighting the medication and fell asleep. She'll be out until noon. Let's walk."

Fifth Avenue and Ninety-eighth Street were deserted except for the security guard at the entrance to the hospital, and the absence of traffic, of noise, of any movement save their footsteps sent a shiver through Jenny's body.

"It's cold," David said, putting his arm around Jenny's shoulders as they walked south along Fifth Avenue. "You should have worn a warmer coat." David himself was bundled into a three-quarter-length nutria trench coat.

"I dressed in a hurry," she answered, looking across the street to where one of New York's homeless, illuminated by the glow of a streetlight, lay snoring beneath a pile of newspapers. Nice, Jenny thought. Nice to know my words can bring comfort to someone. In her imagination, it was the *Trib* that lay across the shoulders of the sleeping vagrant, her column that protected him against the cold.

"You know what worries me the most?" David was saying. Of course she knew. What worried him the most was that he wanted a baby more than any man she knew, and now he was convinced that he could not have one.

"What worries me the most is that she has no plans."

"What do you mean, she has no plans?" Jenny said as they crossed Ninety-first Street. She was glad now that she had worn her old tennis shoes. Four empty cabs had already cruised past without David hailing one of them. This would be a long walk. Long, cold, dark. "Of course she has plans. I'm supposed to have lunch with her next week, David."

"Yeah, well, don't hold your breath. When the bleeding started yesterday, I put her to bed and she asked me to check her calendar again. She circles the dates of her periods with red ink. I guess she wanted to recheck her timing. Anyway, that's not the point. When I gave it to her, she opened the drawer in her night table and took out an eraser. One of those artgum things she uses for her collages. And she just started erasing everything. As if there were no future if we lost this baby. Just sat up in bed rubbing it all away. March, April, all the way through May, she made the pages blank. There were tiny grains of pink rubber all over the sheets. She just sat there, not saying a word, Jenny. Erasing. Just erasing." He shook his head, as if to free himself of the image. Jenny walked silently beside him.

Blank pages. Emptiness, Jenny thought. Weren't we a clever little species with all of our modes for expressing our angers, our disappointments? Paul had done it with his fists. Nina did it with an eraser. She herself had found release tonight in destroying printed words by ripping them into small disposable pieces. She wondered, as she watched him in profile, how David Kalish found release. And then she looked quickly away from his face.

"I need to go," she said, stopping suddenly on the deserted pavement. Across the street the formidable stone columns of the Metropolitan Museum of Art stood as shadowy inscrutable witnesses to the intimacy growing in the dawn light. "We both need some sleep, my friend. I'll see you about noon."

"Walk with me a little more," David said softly, "and then I'll send you back to your car in a cab."

"Sure," Jenny said as he tightened his arm around her, and again, even in the open air, she could sniff his stale men's fragrance and smell his loneliness.

"Just so we're in agreement, Jenny. Just so we both know how damaging it would be for her to have nothing to look forward to, no plans."

"Right," Jenny said as she moved out into Fifth Avenue to hail a cab. "Plans are very important, I agree." She stood on her tiptoes to quickly kiss his cheek before she opened the door to a yellow Checker that had been briskly cruising the sleepy avenue. "I'll call Nina as soon as she's ready and we'll make some plans. Something frivolous, okay?"

"That would be wonderful," he said and moved to kiss her, but she was already in the cab.

It wasn't until she was back in her own house that she remembered how this endless day had begun. With the mail. With the brown envelope. All the way home she had pondered the scene of Nina's erasing her calendar. To Jenny, the wonder was not so much in Nina's action, her denial of the future, as in David's concern for that action. Imagine, a man who cared so much about a woman that even her erasures had significance for him. In her absorption with the the workings of David's mind, Jenny had forgotten her own plans. Her appointment with Burger. Her future as a television commentator. All of that had been shaken loose from her thoughts by the envelope from Paul and the sleep-shattering phone call from David.

She checked the locks on all the doors and windows and set the alarm. The sight of the lone half-filled wineglass on the coffee table reminded her now that her own future might hold surprises. She carried the glass upstairs with her. "Very important to have plans," she said as she brushed her teeth before the bathroom mirror. God, she looked terrible. Only the flush from her cold cheeks gave life to her face. "Here," she said, lifting the half-full goblet of flat champagne to her lips and rinsing her mouth with it, "here's to my plans." And then, with day breaking outside her bedroom window, she crawled into the cold bed she had left behind and fell into a sour sleep.

Chapter Three

"I can't stand it," Nina Kalish was saying. "It's like being married to Baby Jesus. Picture yourself the daughter-in-law of an absent God the Father and a bigoted Blessed Mother, and maybe you'll understand what I'm talking about, Jenny. I want out, and out means only one thing."

It was March now, and for the third time since the last miscarriage Jenny had to remind herself that when one's best friend talked about divorce, all one could do was listen. Even if one thought her best friend was temporarily demented; even if one thought that David Kalish was the last of the twenty-four-carat husbands left in America. One listened.

"The man is obsessed," Nina said as she settled herself in the restaurant booth and absently picked up a menu. "All he thinks about are babies. Babies and old people. Nothing in between." She laid down the menu. "I'll have the onion soup," she told the waiter.

Jenny laughed out loud. "Nina, my gorgeous Gentile friend, in Manny's Deli you don't order onion soup. In Manny's Deli you order mushroom-barley or you skip the soup." Humor was not real toughness, Jenny knew, but sometimes it passed as the real thing.

"Please bring me onion soup," Nina repeated to the waiter. "Just ignore my friend, the soon-to-be-famous TV star." The waiter did a double take and disappeared.

Nina Croft Kalish and Jennifer Golman Roo had been friends since the sixth grade at the Ethical Culture School on Central Park West. At fourteen they had shared crushes and pilfered lipsticks and a box of tampons that Jenny kept in her locker for the blessed day when her late-blooming friend would finally join the club. They had been friends, for so many years that neither of them still wondered how long the bond would hold.

At fourteen they had wondered about nothing and dreamed about everything. Boys and men, colleges and careers, faraway places whose names were so hard to pronounce you knew that they had to be exotic just by the way your tongue felt as it linked the syllables together. Marjorca. Guatemala. Aix-en-Provence — God, but the world was enormous and slick and sweet and so full of possibilities. Like an ocean, the possibilities. You could dive in head first and surface anywhere. You could touch the sky and pull down any star and make it your own. You could fly to outer space like the Apollo astronauts. You could be Natalie Wood and you could touch Jimmy Dean's face in *Rebel Without a Cause* or you could write words as wonderful as Dylan's. "The answer, my friend, is blowin' in the wind." It was all blowing in the wind — the answers, the possibilities, the dreams. Only now Natalie Wood was dead and Jimmy Dean was dead, and Bob Dylan, not satisfied with the first time around, had made himself born again and then again. Jenny sensed that both of them sometimes wished that they could do that, make themselves born again.

"Wait a minute," Nina said as the soup was placed in front of her. "It's not just babies and old people that bewitch my husband. Scratch that. He also spends a great deal of time thinking about dead animals." Maybe it was the way she arched her brows to emphasize the irony, or maybe it was the sense of loyalty Jenny felt for David, but the fact was that Jenny couldn't listen anymore. Best friend or no best friend, she had heard enough.

"You know what?" Jenny said as she watched the cold sleet spatter against the restaurant window, "you're amazing to me, Nina. Stupefying, really. How could one woman, the one woman who kept her head screwed on when everyone else I knew was losing hers and blaming it on men, have suddenly grown so boringly bizarre?"

"That's a contradiction in terms," Nina said, holding back her thick chestnut hair so that she could bring the soup spoon to her lips. "Boring and bizarre are antithetical. You better watch that stuff when you're in front of the camera next month."

"Stick it, Nina!" Jenny scoffed. "I didn't volunteer for this assignment. You invited me, remember? You came to me and asked for my opinion. So here it is: I think you're screw-loose, Nina. I think you're late for the train. And, by the way, there's melted Gruyère cheese stuck in your hair. How's the onion soup?"

Nina laid her soup spoon carefully beside her plate and looked directly at her friend. Her face was composed inside that luxuriant frame of hair, nearly as serene as it had been in the bridal portrait printed in the Sunday *New York Times* four years earlier. Only at the outer corners of her eyes, where the fiery brown had gone soft and liquid, was there any hint of pain, of beseechment.

"Please, Jen," she whispered, "please try to understand. This time I mean it." And before Jenny could respond she was up and off to the ladies' room.

By the time she returned to the table, her face looking more composed, Jenny had thought of a new argument, one she hoped would appeal to Nina the individualist. Nina the nonconformist.

"The thing about divorce," Jenny said as she finished the last of her mushroom-barley soup with a satisfied smack of her lips, "is that it's so common, so nonexclusive. So boring." And here she held the word in her throat the way Rachel did when she rolled her eyes and told her that meat loaf was *borrrrring*. "When Paul and I split up it was still an original idea, still worth a nod. But now it's right there on the life list. Go to college, get a job, get married, make a baby, get divorced. Your basic seek-create-and-destroy mission. Everyone's doing it."

"We haven't created anything," Nina countered in a chilled tone that matched the leaden sky visible from their table. "And furthermore, you're wrong. Not everyone is doing it. There has never been a divorce in David's family. Kalishes do not divorce. Kalishes do not quit on things." Her chin trembled ever so slightly as she spoke this last, as if a toothache had suddenly erupted.

"Is that a direct quote?" Jenny asked, still smiling because no comment had been made about her own divorce. Its specific circumstances. You see, Jenny told herself, if enough time passes, private tortures become lumped statistics.

"Oh you bet it's a direct quote! Direct, determined, and frequently repeated." Nina avoided Jenny's eyes as she said this, dipping her spoon into the lukewarm soup and mindlessly stirring the translucent onions at the bottom of the bowl.

By whom? Jenny wanted to ask. Frequently repeated

by whom? Surely not by David Kalish. If ever a man was deaf to the disharmony sounding about his ears, it was David Kalish. Ask David what he thought about his marriage, and he would tell you that it was made in heaven, a union certified by the angels. Except for Nina's failure to bear him a child, David was much given to celestial imagery in describing his wife. Even her first miscarriage, Jenny remembered, he had tried to defend in heavenly terms. She had a sudden memory of Nina languishing in the peach and gold bedroom on Fifth Avenue after the first miscarriage. And there was David, mixing Jenny and himself Bloody Marys at the wet bar in the library.

"Look at it this way, Jenny," he had said, smiling, with the tomato juice can in his hand. "A miss is God's way of fixing his own mistakes. Every now and then He screws up. You know, like General Motors recalling all of those cars because they had faulty tire rims or something. But the terrific thing about God is that He wouldn't let those cars go out of the showroom in the first place. Somebody could get hurt driving them. You'll see, Jennifer, we'll make you a godmother yet."

It would have been pointless, Jenny knew, as she studied her friend's silent distracted spooning of the soup, to have told David that God sometimes screwed up and didn't fix things. That damaged fetuses came into the world each day, that birth defects and tire trouble were not in the same category of screw-ups. Not when he was trying so hard to keep Nina from sinking into such blurry depression.

She had been only seven weeks pregnant that first time. A less serious woman might have called it a late period and hopped right back into bed to try again. A less serious woman might have even enjoyed the trying. But Nina *was* serious, Jenny knew. A Methodist at Sarah Lawrence, she had chosen philosophy for her major, and, unlike the scores of liberal arts degree holders who were basically unemployable in the affairs of the world, Nina had used her education. She found a job at the Guggenheim Foundation reading grant proposals. It was astonishing to her colleagues that someone so lovely looking, so clearly social as Nina Croft could get her kicks from reading endless pages of research material. She was not yet a final decision-maker, far from it; but in her own mind, judgment flowed like wine. She got drunk on it. Which Ph.D. in sociology really deserved to be funded for his study of early adoloscent drug abuse in Connecticut? Who among the host of applicants in biochemical research was truly worthy of a Guggenheim grant?

"Heady stuff," David had said to her on their first date, "controlling all that cash." They had gone to see Cliff Gorman in *Lenny*. "An uptown first date," Jenny had called it.

"Oh," Nina had said, blushing in the theater lobby. "I don't get to control it. I just get to think about it and pass on my thoughts. But you're right, it is heady stuff."

And so was David Kalish heady stuff. Thick dark hair showing gray at the temples, shoulders that wouldn't quit, and the most compellingly soft mouth she had ever known. And all of this packaged with more good taste, expensive tailoring and gracefulness than she had ever encountered in one man. But it was not the looks that had won Nina. She was too much a beauty herself to be daunted by men who were merely handsome.

"He cried, Jenny!" Nina had exulted when the two friends met for brunch the following Sunday at Jenny's apartment on West Fifty-fourth Street. Paul had taken Rachel to the park and they were contentedly alone. "I don't mean that phony glazed look some guys give you when you walk out of a revival of *Casablanca*. You know, that macho Bogey wet look. These were real tears, Jennifer. When the curtain went down on *Lenny*

Bruce slumped on the toilet seat with the needle still in his arm, he just sat there and let the tears fall. And when Cliff Gorman came out in his bathrobe, just wasted from that utterly draining performance, David stood right up and cheered like everybody else in the house and never even took out a handkerchief, never even tried to hide it. And then, and this is really the best part, instead of making it into a big deal — "where should we eat, Nina? What would you like Nina?," that garbage dialogue — instead he just took my hand in his and we start to walk and he didn't say anything at all. Just held my hand and walked. And when we wound up at Pearl's, where he tried to pretend that they didn't know him instead of making a big deal out of the fact that they obviously did, he didn't say another word until the egg rolls came. And then he spent the next two hours talking about self-deprecation in Jewish humor. It was unbelievable! He'd read all this comic theory when he was at Yale, and he remembered it, could talk about it with such ease, such — he's a lawyer, right? You told me he was a lawyer?"

Jenny had rearranged the scrambled eggs on her plate. Let her go on, Jenny had thought. Not now.

"Anyway, I'll bet I've had dinner with four dozen lawyers since college, and not one of them could ever get past Woody Allen in the ha-ha department. They tell two Wall Street jokes, try out one slightly extended sex gag just to test the waters, and call it quits. David can do hours on the subject of comedy. He appreciates that Lenny Bruce was the tormented flip side of the comic temperament. David said that if Lenny Bruce hadn't been so wracked with Jewish guilt he never could have —"

"David is a furrier," Jenny had interrupted.

Nina had set her coffee cup hard against the scarred oak table. "That's not funny, Jennifer," she said too loudly.

"It may not be funny, kiddo, but it's the truth."

Poor Nina, she had looked dazed, as though someone had punched her right between the eyes. She blinked at Jenny in the smoky kitchen, tried to make out if there was even the slightest hint of a smile on her friend's twitchy mouth. "You told me he was a lawyer," Nina blurted, confusion making her voiçe brittle. "You said medium height, good-looking, a lawyer. I remember distinctly."

Jenny had poured more cream into her coffee and avoided Nina's accusing stare. When at last she had spoken she had leaned across the table and peered into her friend's troubled eyes. "Tell me the truth, kiddo. If I had told you I know this terrific guy, a marvelous conversationalist, a heavy-duty thinker and a hunk besides," and here Jenny had inhaled deeply, "and he's got two hot tickets to *Lenny* for Monday night, and, oh, by the way, he's a furrier — would you have gone out with him?"

"You lied to me," Nina had said tonelessly. "You deliberately lied to me."

"With reason," Jenny said quickly. "A white lie, a half-lie actually. He did go to law school for a while, I think. Anyway, that's not the point. Answer the question. If I had told you he's a furrier, would you have agreed to meet him?"

Nina had gnawed on a piece of cold raisin toast that lay on her plate. It was her turn to stall for time. "The point is that you're my best friend, I have trusted you since forever, and you lied to me."

"I said, Nina Croft, that if I lied, it was with reason. Good reason. And the reason is that because you have been my best friend for as long as I have been yours, I know that you're a goddamned snob when it comes to this sort of thing! If I had told you the truth you would have hung up on me and missed meeting a man you were raving about just ten minutes ago. True or not true?"

Nina had not answered. Instead she had asked for another screwdriver and not until after she had had a good hard taste of the vodka did she speak. "True," was all that she had said.

And now, four years later, Jenny was thinking, the truth was crying out like the endangered species that it was. She would like to have told that to Nina — that the truth, like personal freedom, is an endangered species. Nina with her philosopher's slant and her seat on the board of the New York Zoological Society.

Hadn't Nina herself been the first to call attention to the irony of a furrier's wife sitting on the zoo board?

"What do you wear to the Zoo Ball?" Jenny had chided her. "A cloth coat? A Pat Nixon special?"

"The Zoo Ball is in July," Nina had answered with a straight face. "Balenciaga. I wear Balenciaga."

Ah Nina, with her perfect replies and her perfect husband and her perfect duplex condo on Fifth Avenue and her perfectly off-the-wall notion of chucking it all.

"This is the third time I've heard about it, pal, and I still don't get it. Run it by me again, Nina. Quickly. I've got a new babysitter to interview at three o'clock."

"What happened to the student from the junior college? I thought she was working out fine?" Nina asked.

"Yeah, fine. Until I found her trying to turn Rachel on to grass. An eleven-year-old with a joint in her fingers. Can you imagine? Oh, to be a single career mother in New York," Jenny sang with false gaiety, and then she turned her attention to the bagel, cream cheese and lox platter that kept her coming back to Manny's Deli when her friends wanted to lunch at the tonier Continental restaurants in the neighborhood. Maybe once she was on television she would have to give up Manny's. It was hard to imagine Dan Rather lunching here.

Nina took a tentative bite of her overstuffed pastrami on dark rye and spit it delicately into her napkin.

"I can't," she said with a finality that confused Jenny. "I try, but I can't." She looked around the noisy restaurant as if in search of someone, anyone, who could explain it. "I can't eat the food. It's too heavy. I try. I keep opening that copy of the *Love and Knishes Cookbook* his sister Marilyn gave me at my kitchen shower, and I think, this time I'll get it right. This time the soup won't be greasy and this time the matzoh balls will float like water lilies. But I can't. I just can't. And I can't summon new tears every time a terrorist's bomb explodes in Israel, and I can't turn myself inside out to be what I am not! I can't, Jenny." There were tears welling in her eyes and she furtively dabbed at them with her napkin.

"Sugar," Jenny said, reaching across the Formica table for her friend's hand and holding it firmly in her own, "Nina dear, I am a member of the tribe, born to it, and I couldn't cook a decent matzoh ball to save my life. But that's not why Paul and I were divorced. That's not why Paul beat up on me. And that's not a reason to end your marriage. There are a thousand caterers in this town who could supply you with award-winning matzoh balls at any hour of the day or night and you can afford to use any one of them. Don't try to tell me this is about chicken soup and potato pancakes. No way. Now, if what you're trying to say is that you're uncomfortable for having married outside your faith, okay. All right, I can buy that. But, Nina, I have been there, as they say, from the beginning with you, and I don't recall you ever breaking down the doors to get inside the Church. What I do recall, and quite distinctly, is a rather intellectual disdain for orthodoxy of any kind. Yes?" She squeezed Nina's hand. "Now tell me the real reason."

Nina took her hand from Jenny's and began to tear the dark bread of her untouched sandwich into small square pieces with silent concentration. The way I tear up newspaper clippings and brown envelopes, Jenny thought watching her. Even Nina didn't know about those bizarre mailings.

"The real reason?" Nina said, avoiding Jenny's eyes. "The real reason is that he's just too damned good. Okay? Does that make sense? Will that do? Or does that explanation mean I get on the next express bus to the funny farm?" She bit her lip and that was the beginning. Her entire face was suddenly contorted by the effort it had cost her to speak those words. "I'm going to cry, Jen," she said, pulling her pink angora hat down over her ears and slipping her arms into the quilted down coat the hung over her shoulders. "I'm going to blow, my friend. In public. Let's get out of here! Now!" And with that she was up from the booth, out the door, and onto the icy street before Jenny could respond.

Jenny grabbed the check and, ignoring the "Please pay cashier" directive stamped on it, threw a twenty-dollar bill on the cluttered table.

On the slick ice-covered sidewalk of Sixth Avenue, Nina was pacing, her body shivering as she traced and retraced her steps.

"I'll get us a cab," Jenny said. "Hold on, kiddo." She stepped out between two parked cars, stuck two fingers between her teeth and whistled down a yellow Checker that was parked down the block.

"My place or yours?" she asked when they were settled in the warm tobacco-drenched air of the back seat.

"Oh sweet Jesus," Nina whispered, "not mine."

Chapter Four

The front door was open when Jenny got home from her shopping trip the next day, a Saturday, and Rachel, all bristling fifty-three inches of her, stood blocking it with her hands planted firmly on what would someday be her hips. But for now, the best that she could do was to screw her delicate child-features into a well rehearsed mask of indignation.

"And where exactly have you been?" she asked, refusing to allow her mother entry. Her defiance was all the more disconcerting to Jenny because her daughter's voice was so perfect an imitation of her own voice when she was hurt. She pressed her lips together to hold back the smile.

"I suppose you forgot that you promised to drive me to the shopping mall at three o'clock. I suppose you don't care that I have been waiting here since exactly one o'clock, which is when you said you'd pick me up for lunch." Rachel's voice dropped in pitch here, but picked up volume. "I suppose you know that there's absolutely nothing to eat in this entire house except yogurt and moldy French cheese? I suppose you know that Grandma has called about sixty zillion times bugging me about absolutely everything. And that Nina is going totally crazy needing to talk to you. And David called twice. And Burger called. And even though by then I was completely ready to kill you, I remembered to call him *Mister* Burger." She had tried to say it all in one breath, and her small face was flushed scarlet with the effort. She turned her back quite suddenly, whether to draw breath or hide tears of frustration Jenny could not tell, but either way Jenny hugged her from behind and whispered "Sorry" into her daughter's long fragrant hair.

"Really, Rach, I'm very sorry."

"Yeah? Well, guess what, Mom. While you were gone I changed the secret password," Rachel croaked, awkwardly pulling away from Jenny's embrace, "and sorry doesn't work anymore." Rachel stomped up the stairs to her bedroom and closed the door, leaving her mother alone with the discomfiting words.

Jenny sank down onto one of the bottle-green velour sofas that faced each other in the living room and ran her hands through her newly fashioned hairdo. You had to hand it to the kid, she thought with a mixture of pride and wonder. At eleven, her daughter could do what she herself had been incapable of doing until she was twenty-five: turning her back on apology. What did that take? Poise? Self-esteem? Or just plain guts? Where had her child learned so soon what it had taken her so many years of agony and punishment to figure out? Sorry doesn't work anymore.

Sorry, Paul would say when his rage was spent. Sorry, when he was drenched with remorse, pickled in contrition. When the beating was over. When the damage was done. It was Paul's password. Paul's way of graining reentry when she had sworn to herself that this time she would bar the door. This time she would not accept it. This time she would call the police. This time would be the last time.

For Rachel there would never be a first time, Jenny had prayed from the night she had wrapped up the sleeping child and stolen out of the apartment on Fifty-fourth Street. She had taken so little with her that night. Only her typewriter, one suitcase, and the telephone number of the West Side Women's Shelter tucked into her handbag. She had never visited the shelter — only called, and even then she had never used her real name. What sort of credibility would her column have if the news that Jenny Roo was an abused wife appeared on page 26 of the *Trib*?

But by the time that night had come, there was almost no part of Jenny's body that had not known his uncontrolled rage. No limb uninjured, no organ unpunished. Merciless blows to her head, frenzied punches to her breasts, her back, her belly. Only her face, where bruises might have advertised his desecration, was safe from his fists. It seemed to her that when she remembered those years, and God knew she tried not to, the pictures always came to her in black and white. Paul's black eyes glittering from a face white with fury. Herself, usually dressed in black because light colors might be too easily seen through. "My daughter the writer," Minna would say mysteriously, her message unclear to Jenny. "Always with Gypsy earrings and the black turtleneck sweaters."

And behind a white door at the far end of the apartment on Fifty-fourth Street, Rachel. Tiny Rachel. Diapered in white, asleep on white sheets, guarded by a huge stuffed White Rabbit.

"We'll start her off with Lewis Carroll," Paul had said the night he had carried in the towering package from F.A.O. Schwarz. "*Alice in Wonderland*. A great beginning for her. Wit, fantasy, plenty of conflict, tons of symbolism. All the right stuff." That was before. That was during a good time. A time between her pregnancy, when she was convinced that he might understandably loathe a body so distorted, and his screaming accusations that she was neglecting him to favor that "mewling infant, that she-wolf." A time long before she understood how sick he was. A time before he had threatened Rachel.

"He could have broken every bone in my body and left me for dead," she had told the counselor on duty at the shelter that night. "But not Rachel. Not my baby."

Until that night, the threats against the baby had all been verbal. "Damn it, Jenny, I'm trying to work in here!" he would holler in the middle of the night. "If you can't shut her up, I will!" "God damn it, Jenny, I'm hungry! Get that kid out of the bathtub before I drown her in it!"

But on that night he did more than snort and stomp and scream obscenities. On that night, when she had turned away from him in bed, saying Rachel had a fever of 103 and the pediatrician had warned her to be alert to a developing ear infection, he had stormed into the white nursery, snatched Rachel from her crib with one hand and pushed open the fourth-floor window with the other.

"You want to see how to make a baby's fever drop, Jenny? Watch this!"

That was the night she left him. That was the night she had packed up her sick baby and her injured self and sought shelter.

"You may have saved two lives tonight, Mrs. Roo," the counselor told her.

"One," Jenny had whispered. "One will be enough. Rachel's."

"Hey, Mom! You going to return those calls, or what? I need the phone." The voice that carried downstairs to

Jenny had lost its petulant edge. The scene was over, Jenny guessed.

"You can use it," Jenny called, lifting the bundles she had dropped on the floor of the hall when she came in. "But first come have a look at my new wardrobe." Lightness. That's what we need around here, Jenny thought as she stood there. Jokes, new wardrobe — lightness.

Rachel met her at the top of the stairs and took the biggest of the boxes out of her hands. She really was a good kid, Jenny thought. Eleven-year-old girls were supposed to have scenes with their mothers. She had no real complaints with her daughter.

"Is all this stuff for TV?" Rachel asked when the bags and boxes were laid out on Jenny's bed.

"Yup. A whole new me."

"So who picked the clothes?" Rachel asked as she opened boxes and examined their contents. "You or what's-her-name?"

"Alicia, honey. The wardrobe coordinator's name is Alicia," Jenny said, trying to stifle her own mixed feelings about a complete stranger selecting what she, Jenny, was going to wear in front of millions of people.

Rachel, now warmed to the task, continued to rifle the splendid bazaar of dresses, suits, blouses, scarves, jewelry and other accessories that lay on the bed. "Wait a minute," she said in a suspicious voice, "how come there's nothing red in all this stuff? Mom? You love to wear red. You look great in red. So how come there's nothing here that's red?"

Jenny sighed. "Because, Rach, the anchorman likes red, too, and he was there first."

"A man is going to wear red?" Rachel giggled. "Are you kidding, Mother? What kind of newsman wears red? What is he going to say — 'Good evening, I'm Santa Claus and now for the late news . . .'? Be serious, Mom."

"Well, not bright red, Rachel. But he does like

burgundy, and burgundy clashes with red. So, no red on Tuesday nights. It's no big deal, I can wear it every other night of the week. How do you like the new haircut?''

"It's okay. It's a little mixed up, though." Rachel opened a shoe box from Lord & Taylor and peeked inside. "These are terrific. They going to show your feet on the tube?''

"No." Jenny laughed. "I just liked them. What do you mean my hair's a little mixed up? What's that supposed to mean?''

Rachel stood up and walked a full circle around her mother, surveying her from every angle. "Well," Rachel finally said, "it's like the guy couldn't exactly make up his mind. The front is all short and kind of punk, you know. That's okay. But the back, well, the back is all poufy and stiff. You know, kind of like Grandma's. I mean, it's like from the front you look like a kid. A cute kid. But from the back you look like the kid's mother.''

"That's so the studio lights won't shine through. The back has got to be smooth. You turn on the six-o'clock news tonight and you'll see. All the women on TV are smooth in the back.''

Rachel filed this nugget of inside intelligence with the rest of her privileged information about television production. By now she figured she could blow away any slumber party from here to Larchmont with all that she knew. Even Lisa Altheimer, whose mother was dating some anchorman from ABC, didn't know about smooth in the back. Would she be impressed! Not to mention that her mother was getting all these new clothes, the hairdo, *and* a whole new makeup job from Pablo all at the station's expense.

When Jenny had told her about the possibility of her going on television, the first thing that had come into Rachel's mind was a picture of her mother, seated in front of the typewriter in the study, chewing on her pencil, wearing jeans and tee shirt with no bra. It wasn't that her mother looked bad with no bra. Actually, Rachel was hoping to look a lot like that herself, and the sooner the better. It was just that the idea of all her friends, the boys especially, being able to press a button and tune in her mother's nipples, for God's sake, was a little creepy.

"Can you wear this stuff anytime you want, or just on TV?" Rachel asked, holding a creamy silk blouse with a high stand-up collar against her sweatshirt and jeans and examining herself in Jenny's full-length mirror.

"I don't know, sugar. I forgot to ask. Why?"

"I just wondered. Just curious." It was Rachel's theory, fully endorsed by Patience Wasserman, that Jenny was really a very pretty, almost sexy lady. The only reason she didn't date more was that she went around looking like such a schlep most of the time. And now here was the American Television Company stepping into the picture to change all that. It was almost as good as the fairy godmother waving the magic wand over Cinderella.

"So when can I tell everyone?" Rachel asked for what seemed like the fifty-first time that week.

"I told you, Rachel. When the countersigned contracts come in the mail. Then it's official. Then you can tell."

"Anyone? I can tell anyone I want?"

"You can take out an ad in *The New York Times*. You can write it across the garage door in magic marker. And you can even tell Lisa Altheimer!"

"What about Dad?"

Jenny's hands felt suddenly cold. Quite cold. "What do you mean, what about Dad?"

"Well," Rachel said, examining her full-length profile in the mirror with what passed for total absorption, "you said I could tell anyone I wanted. I was just wondering, since he calls me on Sundays usually, and today is Saturday, if I could tell him tomorrow." She did a small pirouette in front of the mirror so that now she could view herself from the other side. "Do you think I need a training bra yet?"

"No!" Jenny said too loudly.

"No, I don't need a training bra yet; or no, I can't tell Dad you're going to be a TV star?"

"I am not going to be a TV star!" Jenny snapped. And furtively she began to stuff all of the clothes, the shoes, the scarves and jewelry she had been unpacking back into their bags and boxes. "I am simply going to go on doing what I have been doing for years. Only now, instead of just writing stories for newspapers, I'm also going to read my stories on TV. Okay? That's all it is, Rachel. Once a week I will look into a camera and read out loud. Just like when you're having language arts with Mrs. McDonald and she calls on you to stand up and read aloud. Got that, Rach? No big deal!"

Rachel flopped down on the bed and looked up at her mother. "Right. Yeah. No big deal," she repeated tonelessly. "Boy, are you weird, Mom. Two minutes ago you told me it was news that belonged in *The New York Times* and now you're telling me that it's just like language arts with Mrs. McDonald? Tell me that isn't weird, Mother?" She turned her head on the pillow, away from Jenny.

"That isn't weird, Rachel." Jenny said, sitting down on the bed beside her daughter and turning Rachel's face so that she was forced to look at her. "That isn't weird. Look at me, baby."

"How come you don't want him to know?" Rachel said, her hazel eyes wide open, her head cocked, every part of her small body tensed for the information of Jenny's answer.

"I didn't say that I don't want him to know," Jenny said, stroking Rachel's hair. Time, damn it. Why was there never enough time to think through her answers to

Rachel's questions? Why did her child's insights have to come so unexpectedly, popping up like some ugly jack-in-the-box surprise, catching her off guard? Making her seem foolish, weird. She had wonderful, carefully prepared answers to all the questions Rachel never asked. How come you got divorced? We stopped making each other happy, we stopped being nice to each other. How come he never comes to see me? Because some people can love better from a distance than up close. But she never asked those questions. Maybe some child-wisdom in her already knew the answers. Maybe in an environment where divorce had grown so commonplace that every school emergency form, every summer-camp registration sheet left space for "name of parent child resides with" or "primary custodial parent," such questions were gratuitous. Instead she asked questions Jenny could not answer.

"How come, Mom? If it's no big deal, how come you don't want him to know?"

Jenny tossed her head from side to side in a motion meant to lighten her answer with a feigned ignorance. "Well, sugar, he might not like the idea so much." That is not a lie, Jenny thought as she watched Rachel's mouth pucker into disbelief. I am not lying to her, I am telling her the truth. The fact that Jenny could see the next question coming did not make it any easier for her to answer.

"Why not? Why wouldn't he like the idea of you being on television?"

Because it is fuel, Jenny thought. Because it is fuel for a fire she could never be wholly certain had been put out. Because when you were dealing with a keg of dynamite like Paul, none of the rational answers were good enough, strong enough. Because, as so many doctors, psychologists and social workers had taught her, the cures for Paul's sickness could never be absolute. At best, they were clinical.

Clinical, it was a such a tidy, antiseptic word. A word

that made her think of a laboratory full of test tubes. Paul, Paul's personality filled a giant test tube. It had been examined, manipulated, and experimented with by all the best researchers, and still the results of their work were inconclusive. The best that they could do was to report on the current state of the mixture. What they had told her eighteen months ago, when he was released from the outpatient program at Glen Crest in California, was that as measured by their tools the component parts of Paul's personality seemed to be in balance. As long as she remained three thousand miles away from him, as long as she did not introduce some new components into the mixture, he would remain stable. "What does that mean?" she had asked the lawyer who informed her of Paul's release from the rehabilitative outpatient program. "Some new component?"

"It means that a psychiatric review board has determined that Paul can handle things as they are now without posing a threat to you or anyone else. That as long as things stay as they are, you're quite safe, Jenny. The circumstances to which he has been resolved are the circumstances that exist now: you have sole custody of your child, you live in the state of New York, you work for the Tribune Corporation, you have brown eyes, you're single —"

"That means I can never remarry?" Jenny had asked at once. Not because there was anyone begging for her hand in marriage, but because she had, at that time, just begun to see a successful widowed doctor, the first man she had felt comfortable dating for a long, long time. "That I can never move to Kansas City? Never change jobs?"

"No, no," the lawyer had answered. "It means that if you are comtemplating some major life change, it might be wise to get in touch with some professional on the West Coast. That's all. Just don't spring it on him. He doesn't do well with surprises."

"You mean if I'm thinking about packing up Rachel and joining a commune on Tahiti, I better make sure I don't leave a forwarding address, is that it?"

"Jenny," the lawyer had said in a tone that made no effort to hide his exasperation, "don't be cute. You are free, white and twenty-one. Go out and live your life. It's once around, Jennifer. Go for it!"

Go for it, Jenny had repeated to herself that day and many days since. Just make sure, when you're up there on the tightrope, and the spotlight is on you, and the crowds are hushed, that you don't slip. That you don't try to grab the gold ring too fast, that you don't lose your balance. That you don't fall into the center ring and rattle the tiger's cage.

Rachel was turned on her side now, propped up on a an elbow, waiting for an answer.

"I think he wouldn't like me to be on television," Jenny began hesitantly, "because it would make me a little too public."

"Too what?" Rachel said, dropping to the floor and arching her body into a back bend she had lately mastered in her gymnastics class at the Y.M.C.A.

"Too public," Jenny repeated. "Too out there. Too exposed to the masses."

"Oh, I get it," Rachel said, going from the back bend to a full split before Jenny could monitor the response on her daughter's face. "You mean like some loony could see you on TV and fall madly in love with you. And some night when we're both sound asleep he could come and break in through the sun porch and climb up the stairs and hold a gun to your head. Or stick a knife in my ribs unless you agreed to make love with him on *The Channel Ten News?*"

Jenny felt as though her head were detaching from her body, as though the air in her lungs could not make it to her mouth and she could not breathe.

"Jesus!" she gasped. "How did you come up with a

story like that? Where did you ever get the imagination!"

"Simple," Rachel said as she stood up to face her mother and give her what seemed a totally artless grin. "My parents are both writers. It's in my genes, you know."

Jenny sat down on the bed and massaged her forehead. There was a kind of hissing sound in her brain, as though someone had turned the gas on. "In your genes," she repeated tonelessly.

"Yeah, right," Rachel said, turning for the door. "And besides, you're all wrong about Dad. He thinks your being on television is really terrific."

Jenny froze. Something cold and hard as ice was exploding in her chest. "You told him?" she whispered, the words wrapped in chill vapors of disbelief.

"Last week. Last Sunday's telephone call. You said only the Kalishes and family could know," Rachel beamed. "And you told Grandma, so I told Dad. That's the only family we've got, right? Anyway, he said it was a terrific surprise and he was really happy for you. So you see, you had it figured all wrong. And about the loony, Mom?"

"Yes," Jenny croaked. "What about him?"

"Well, first of all, we have an unlisted phone number. And second of all, in all the time you've had your picture in the paper and you've being doing public appearances, if he were out there . . . I figure he would have come for us by now."

"Got it all figured out, haven't you?" Jenny said, willing herself to sound calm.

"Yeah. Just about." Rachel grinned. "Listen, don't you have a bunch of calls to return? I mean Grandma's probably called Missing Persons by now, and Nina sounded really, well, disturbed, if you know what I mean. You better call her, Mom."

She was nearly out the door when Jenny summoned the strength to call her back. "Not so fast, whiz-kid! If you told your father a week ago, what was all that charade about 'Can I tell Dad?' What was that, Rachel? Why did it take a week for you to be honest with me?"

Instinctively, Rachel backed away from the anger in her mother's voice, but almost as quickly she came forward and stood directly in front of her at the foot of the bed. "I didn't lie," Rachel said boldly. "I just waited. "That's all I did." There were tears beginning to well in her hazel eyes, and her chin began to quiver, but she held her ground. "What's so wrong with that?"

"Nothing," Jenny said quietly, her breath coming more freely now. "I would just like you to tell me why you waited."

"Because," Rachel said, blinking back the tears, "because sometimes, Mother, you are weird."

Two months before Jenny Roo was scheduled to become a New York television celebrity, her former husband was looking forward to a debut all his own. *Pennydance*, a play he had pushed and poked and dreamed out of the stubborn Smith-Corona typewriter he had carted with him when he fled to Los Angeles, was having its first full-cast rehearsal tonight.

Paul Roo paced the empty lobby of the Burgess Theater on Melrose Avenue and chain-smoked. By the end of the first act, he figured, he would probably be out of cigarettes. Maybe out of luck too, he told himself as he lit still another of the small black filterless smokes. Maybe out of playwriting altogether. And maybe, he thought with an anxiety headache so strong it made his teeth ache, out of the fool's notion that this play was, at last, his one-way ticket to sanity. His passport to credibility. A genuine, money-in-the-bank success that even he could believe in. Standing there in the lobby, the script rolled up tight in his fist, he tried not to think about how *Pennydance* had come into being.

What difference did it make, he told himself, that the

initial idea for this play had come to him while he was a
patient at Glen Crest? While he had walked the lush
California grounds, an attendant never very far from
view. A shrink always waiting in the wings to pick his
brain and examine the debris. Never mind all that, he
told himself. Some terrific babies had been swaddled in
dirtier linen than his. Theatrical history was replete with
successes born of the playwright's misfortunes. Full of
examples of genius set free by pain, misery, madness,
rotten luck.

Paul threw the butt of his cigarette on the cracked tile
floor of the theater lobby and crushed it with his heel.
He laughed out loud. Genius. What a joke. He wasn't
even close. Not even in the ball park. At best, he'd written a lousy little two-act diversion that the critics would
see through like gauze. No, he stopped himself. Not like
gauze, that was the wrong word. Gauze was flimsy, but
not all that easy to tear apart. There was a better word
than gauze. Cheesecloth. Yes, cheesecloth. That was it,
that was the word the critics would use in *The Los
Angeles Times.*

Paul Roo, the unknown miscreant from New York
whose program notes list him as Brooklyn born, has
brought a flimsy piece of cheesecloth, titled *Pennydance*, to the Burgess Theatre. The playwright Paul
Roo (also known as the alcoholic Paul Roo, the wife
beater Paul Roo, and the absent father Paul Roo)
would do better to send it back to the mother he
abuses with language in *Pennydance*. Better to have
Mama use this cheesecloth for wrapping her strudel
dough than to have her baby boy parade it as drama
to Los Angeles audiences. If her strudel weighs as
light as her son's talent, Mama Roo has a smash hit.
Her son, alas, is another story.

He could picture the words, the space they would fill

on the newspaper page. "Christ," Paul had muttered to himself as he banged his way through the heavy theater doors to the darkness of the street, "give yourself a break, an intermission!" He had thrust his hands deep into the pockets of the Burberry raincoat he had purchased especially for tonight, and walked away from the theater.

At nine o'clock on a Wednesday night the Los Angeles streets surrounding the Burgess Theater were empty. Nobody walked in Los Angeles anyway. Paul had the streets to himself. Aimless, he passed no one as he walked; so there was no reason to keep his head down and his eyes averted. But he did.

For nearly thirty years Paul Roo had felt his life to be an indelibly scripted black comedy. He had even described it that way, in those very words, to the legions of psychiatrists, psychologists, social workers and assorted mental-health professionals who had struggled with his demons, and failed. An indelibly scripted black comedy.

They were all alike, Paul had once thought, these men and women of good intent who fought his furies with science and lost. Whether they were upscale private doctors paid for with his inheritance money — an irony that did not escape Paul, since he considered the funds to be blood money from his dead father, a father who had gone to his grave leaving Paul a legacy of confusion and guilt and hatred so thick he could feel it on his tongue — or they were low-budget counselors in clinics where he played poor. They all had this in common: before they failed, before they passed him along, before they set him loose with his demons still intact, they all complimented him. They all had read his plays and they all said he had talent. *Talent*. These people were educated, Paul told himself, cultured. They could not have escaped Shakespeare, Chekhov and Ibsen while studying Freud and Jung. They must know something.

Their judgments must certainly be informed. He did not know what they wrote about him in their little notebooks while he lay on their couches, or what they scribbled on their yellow legal pads as he spoke. But he knew what they had said to him. They had said he had talent.

Such praise, he had realized early on, was more curse than blessing. It mean that without throwing a single punch, without raising a weapon, he could render the doctors impotent. He could do it with words. With words he was in control. With words he could make mincemeat, crap, out of any shrink who probed too close to the wounds. Words were his stock in trade, after all. His strong suit. His ace in the whole. And what was all this therapy, all this analysis, all of this tortuous road leading nowhere, but words? The words he chose to speak and the words he carefully selected for silence.

And what of the words spoken to him? The words that were meant to examine, explore, uproot and destroy his demons, words Paul viewed as an effort to beat his subconscious at its own game — what were they to Paul? For a wordsmith like Paul Roo, the words of the doctors were like soft clay in the hands of a child. He could take their words and mold them like Silly Putty, so that no matter what words the doctors spoke, Paul could bounce them back faster than the experts could toss them off. And always he had sent the words back to them transformed, prettier — reshaped to his own purpose. With wit and cunning and an unquenchable passion for language — a passion his doctors agreed was rooted in self-destruction, a passion they noted as bigger and stronger than his instinct for survival — Paul Roo could vanquish any head-shrinker who dared to take him on. Until he had met Phil Gruber.

Even now, with his play aborning just blocks from where he walked, with his hopes soaring through the yellow haze of the Los Angeles night sky, the horror of memory cracked and moaned and exploded in his head.

"Intermission," he whispered to himself to chase away the dark visions of his agitated brain. "Intermission."

Chapter Five

"One day at a time, girl," Jenny sang against the hard spray of her morning shower a week later. "Just one day at a time." It wasn't working. The lyrics were not calming her and the melody offered no solace. Usually she loved Sundays, the free-floating, unhurried pace of a day that answered only to impulse. But this day, Jenny thought as she lathered her small, taut body, had an agenda that advertised trouble.

First there was the dread anticipation of a long-distance phone call from Paul, a call that had failed to come last Sunday. And even though Rachel had spent the intervening days pretending not to notice that her father had missed calling her, in the rhythm of Jenny's days it was a missed beat that thundered. She understood that by not calling he was more than ignoring her new career plans, he was spitting on them. And how like him it was to send her this silent message through the most vulnerable of conduits — Rachel. How typical of him to wound where he could draw the most blood.

And Burger. Then there was Burger calling her every other day to ask if she had received the countersigned copies of her contract with the American Television Company. His prodding was gentle, but increasingly she sensed that she had somehow disappointed him. Not in any notable way, but perhaps by showing less enthusiasm for the whole project than he had expected.

"I'm waiting, Jennifer," he said to her last week. "I'm waiting, ATC is waiting, nearly all God's children are waiting, and not only do you not show up for a look-see at the set they're building especially for you, you beg off for lunch with the show's executive producer and all I get is that sweet voice of yours stalling me like I was an unwelcome suitor. You go on the air in five weeks, cookie. What gives?"

"I'm sorry, Burger, I —"

"Forget sorry, Jennifer. Sorry is for kids. Do you know what bothers me about this behaviour? Besides that it's unprofessional and makes for bad business? What bothers me is that it's not like you. In all the years I've represented you, I never heard a complaint until now. You don't miss deadlines, you don't holler, and you keep writing better every year. For a whole bunch of years you've been a lily, Jennifer, an agent's dream. And now, when we get you the kind of TV plum that most print journalists drool for, you start turning up your nose. Be straight with me, Jenny, sweetface. Have you got second thoughts?"

"No, no," she had assured him. "Nothing like that. It's just that I've had a lot on my mind these past few weeks."

"Like what?" he had asked a little nervously, a little troubled.

"Like my best friends are considering divorce."

"Welcome to the world, Jennifer," Burger had sighed. "So what else is new?"

"No, you don't understand. They really are my best friends. And they really are misguided, you know, Burger. They belong togeth —"

"Hey, Jenny. Leave that stuff to Dear Abby, will you? You've got your own beat, and it's not marriage counseling. Now what else is on your mind? Talk to me, Jennifer."

My mother, she was tempted to answer. My weird mother. My mother and her categorical refusal to even discuss moving out of her apartment. My mother and her alternately angry and tearful accusations that I want to bury her alive in New Jersey. "Bury me alive" — those were Minna's words. Words uttered when she was her lucid, independent self. When she was not forgetting to lock her door at night. When she was not failing to refrigerate the milk or get dressed before she went outside. How good it would feel to Jenny to unburden herself, to talk. To tell all of this to someone who was willing to listen. To talk about brown envelopes and news clippings to someone who, unlike her friend Nina, would not turn the fragile sharing of a confidence into a fast game of emotional one-upmanship. *My problems can lick your problems.* But Burger hated long phone conversations, Jenny reminded herself. And besides, she owed him. She really owed him.

"Listen, Burger," she said, "I won't say I'm sorry. Okay? My eleven-year-old child already clued me in to the futility of that response; but I really will try to shape up. All right? When I make the time to think about this opportunity, I'm honestly excited. Really. And I know, Burger, I mean I never forget, who I owe it to."

"Oh Christ," Steve Burger had laughed on the other end of the line, "I already gave you the lily tag, quit trying to gild it, Jennifer." And suddenly his voice took on that laconic, paternal monotone she loved him for. "A week from Saturday night. Eight o'clock. The Four

Seasons. A few well-chosen TV types, your new media buddies, want to play cut and paste with you over the goose-liver pâté. Be there. And please, sweetface, as a personal favor to me, don't get yourself involved in other people's problems. Not now. Save the juice for your work, okay?"

"Okay," Jenny had answered. He was right. Paul's mailings required no response save that she ignore them. And there was nothing more she could do for Nina and David anyway. They were grown-ups, or what passed for grown-ups these days, Jenny thought grudgingly. And as for her mother, she had scheduled the next week with a slew of interviews for private home-care companions. And maybe she would also take a trip to the West River Home in New Jersey with David Kalish, who sat on the board of directors there, whose success with Kalideoscope furs had allowed him to endow an entire wing of the main building. There was no reason not to be agreeable. "Hey," she said, just as Burger was about to end the conversation ,"what do I wear to the Four Seasons?"

"A bra," Burger had answered. And then he had hung up.

Jenny tried, as she toweled herself dry, to clear everything problematic from her head and just let the day find its own focus.

Sundays were supposed to be Family day, or what passed for it in Jenny's meagerly populated household on Cherry Hill Lane. Fourteen Cherry Hill Lane. When Jenny had bought the place three years ago she had thought that the address alone guaranteed that she would never run out of material for her column. "Supremely suburban" was how she had described it to her editor. "It's no mansion, but it's got three bedrooms, a magnolia tree, a microwave and a colossal mortgage. It's even on a cul-de-sac street. Any day now

I expect to see a station wagon taking root in the driveway.''

Yet for all of her Manhattan-bred disdain for the trappings of her new setting, she had found herself remarkably comfortable in the house itself. And when her Manhattan friends wondered aloud why a single career mother would trade the possibilities — ah, that lovely vague code word among the unattached — *possibilities* of the city for the flaccid complacency of the suburbs, Jenny almost always cited Rachel as the answer. But it was not just her child who seemed to thrive in their new setting.

On the day they had moved in, Jenny had run her hands over the bare white walls and touched beginning. In these rooms there were no ghosts. No jagged holes had been punched into these walls, no blood-stains clung to these carpets. And no child had ever been dangled from these windows. In spring, forsythia bloomed outside these windows. Soft grass grew here. The microwave oven worked and Jenny learned to use it. She went to the supermarket in her jeans and bought tulip bulbs to force in her freezer. Here, she had told Nina, she was relearning the meaning of comfort.

And it wasn't as if her whole life were lived in Scarsdale. At least three times a week she managed to be in Manhattan. On Tuesdays she often delivered her copy personally, enjoying the slightly mad bustle of the *Trib*'s editorial offices. On Fridays, fortified by her dual self-indulgences, chocolate-dipped strawberries from Krön Chocolatier and a manicure from Ilana, she visited her mother. Oh God, her mother. Occasionally she sat still for a pedicure as well, but only on those Fridays when she found herself uanble to face the sad realities of Minna's mental decline. On those Fridays, she let her feet soak a little longer.

On Saturdays, she saw to it that Rachel did not miss the cultural advantages of city life. Concerts, art ex-

hibits, craft fairs. Theater matinees. Ballet matinees.
Rachel had begun to refer to 2 P.M. on Saturdays as
"educational feeding time." But there were rewards for
her mother as well. "It is common knowledge in this
town," Jenny wrote in her column,

> that on a rainy Saturday afternoon more telephone
> numbers get exchanged amid the dinosaur bones at
> the Museum of Natural History than at any singles
> hangout on the East Side. If there is any justice in the
> world and the study of anthropology maintains its in-
> tegrity, a thousand years from now visitors to the
> museum will pass through a large hall displaying
> stuffed single parents.

And Sundays were Family Day. No matter that of the
people who showed up for brunch on Cherry Hill Lane
with any frequency, only Minna qualified literally as
family; that was the working title for what took place.

"Will you make me French braids?" Rachel asked
this Sunday morning as Jenny walked barefoot into the
kitchen wearing a short white eyelet bathrobe and smelling of soap and an excess of Norell dusting powder.
"Will you, Mother?"

"In a minute," Jenny answered as she began taking
cut limes out of the refrigerator for David Kalish's
Bloody Marys. "In just one minute."

"What smells in here?" Rachel wrinkled her slightly
pug nose and sniffed around the oven.

"Bread," Jenny said as she wrapped the quartered
lime wedges in plastic wrap and set them on the tray
with the Tabasco sauce and the pepper mill.

"Bread?" Rachel repeated, slapping herself on the
forehead with exaggerated dismay. "You're baking
bread?"

"What? Is there an echo in here or something? I said
I was baking bread."

"Whatever happened to bagels and onion rolls?" Rachel said, as if these were the names of her two favorite kittens.

"I felt like baking bread."

"Oh my God! It must be the television thing. You think we're the Waltons, or something? Want me to have John-boy run out to the henhouse and bring in the fresh eggs? Huh, Mama, do you?" Rachel batted her dark eyelashes at her mother.

"You know what, Rachel? One of these days, Rachel, one of these days . . ."

"I know! I know! Pow, right in the kisser. Jackie Gleason. *The Honeymooners.* Nineteen fifty-seven."

"Nineteen fifty-eight," Jenny corrected. God, she loved her kid.

"So what's the big deal with Nina? I heard you on the phone last night. They could probably hear you in Yonkers, actually, the way you were hollering. You guys mad at each other?"

Jenny feigned sudden interest in the contents of a large copper pot on the stove.

"Well, are you?" Rachel probed.

"Not exactly mad," Jenny said dryly. If her face said more, if the puffiness of her eyes and the drawn line of her mouth gave a more explicit answer, it was lost on Rachel. No, not exactly mad. "Why don't you do me a favor and set the dining-room table, Rachel?"

Allowing for the fact of Nina's conspicuously vacant chair at her usual place between David and Minna, by the time everyone had finished off the last of her Quick'n Easy Salmon Mousse Jenny surveyed her dining-room table and decided that this morning's brunch was going surprisingly well. No one, not even Rachel, had pumped David for any detailed explanation of his wife's absence beyond his mumbled announcement that they had been out very late last night and

Nina was just too tired to come. "She barely made it through *Saturday Night Live*," David had announced.

But what with the high marks for her home-baked bread and the genial conversation between David and the Wasserman family, Jenny began to relax, to feel more expansive. Maybe it would be a pleasant Sunday after all. Even Minna was behaving herself.

"Fabulous meal, Jenny," Greg Wasserman said as he pushed his chair back from the table. "And it's a glorious day out there. What do you say, everybody? Let's hold off on the coffee cake and take a brisk walk to the park to work off all this good cooking."

Jenny tried to hide her disappointment as everyone got behind the idea and trooped for the front door. Only Minna lagged.

"I'll stay and help Jenny clear these dishes," she said with motherly consideration. No one argued.

"So?" Minna asked, the moment she and Jenny were alone in the kitchen loading the dishwasher. "What's his name?"

"Whose name?" Jenny asked, bewildered by this break in what had been a companionable domestic silence shared with her mother.

"Your new fellow," Minna chuckled. And then she winked and did a small pirouette with the wet sponge she was holding aloft. "Your new beau?"

"What new beau?" Jenny said, laughing at the sight of her mother dancing across the kitchen with a dripping sponge in her hand. For all of her mental confusion, Minna, with her headful of tight white curls, her voluptuous little body, and her button nose, still looked more like someone who should be bouncing around a tennis court in suburban New Jersey playing in a seniors tournament than moldering in a home for the aged there. "There is no new beau."

"It isn't nice to lie to your mother," Mina said as she attacked the frying pan with an SOS pad. "A cute new hairdo? Eye shadow on Sunday morning? Who do you think you're fooling here, Jennifer?" She reached over and with a wet soapy hand felt Jenny's back. "Aha! I thought so! The whole time we were sitting at the dining-room table, I kept looking at your white silk shirt and thinking maybe, maybe I'm wrong, but I think my daughter may actually be wearing a brassiere under that shirt. And it may actually have lace on it! So whose is it, anyway? Vassarette? Lily of France? Bali? No! Don't tell me." She put her wet hands on Jenny's shoulders and turned her so that she was facing into the light that came through the kitchen window. "I got it!" she said, staring at Jenny's breasts with studied concentration. "Sweet Nothings. By Maidenform. Front closure, no underwire. Let's see it!"

"Mother!" Jenny hollered, backing away with her arms folded over her chest. "This is not a dressing room at Macy's. You are not the lingerie department manager anymore and this is not Herald Square! This is my kitchen, and there are people about to walk in that door! What will Rachel and David think if they walk in and find me half naked in the kitchen? What will the Wassermans think?"

"Wasserman?" Minna said, wiping her hands and smiling broadly. "That's the fellow's name? Wasserman?"

"Mother," Jenny said with forced composure and genuine sadness, "there is no new fellow. The Wassermans are Rachel's friend's parents. You had brunch with them just now."

"Of course," Minna said sheepishly as she turned away to fold the linen napkins that lay in a soiled heap on the kitchen table. "Of course I knew that. Patience. Patience Wasserman, right?"

Jenny smiled. "That's right, Mother." She would unfold the dirty napkins before she put them into the washing machine later, after Minna had gone home. At the same time she would take the dry, blackened apple cake Minna had baked and forgotten to take out of the oven, and toss it into the garbage.

"All of it, Mother — the hairdo, the eye shadow, and the bra — is for my Tuesday nights on television. I was just practicing this morning."

"What kind of television?" Minna asked with genuine curiosity. "What's this about television?"

Jenny had told her all about it three times before. Now she told it for a fourth time, trying to give the news of her impending television career the same enthusiasm she had felt for it when she said it the first time. Minna listened intently, her small face beaming with maternal pride as Jenny recited the details of her contract with Channel Ten.

"Oh sweetheart!" Minna said, hugging her when Jenny had finished this fourth telling of the news. "I'm so proud, I could bust! Imagine? Television! Jenny Golman, my own daughter — on television!" And then her smiling face turned suddenly thoughtful. "But, Jenny," she asked in a whispered voice as she looked over her shoulder, "what will Paul have to say about this TV business of yours?" She had asked exactly the same question in exactly the same concerned whisper every time Jenny had told her the news. On each of the other occasions Jenny had steeled herself and offered a long painful narrative explaining that she and Paul had been divorced for a long time, that Paul now lived in California and had no interest in her life. But each time she had delivered this brutal monologue Minna had responded as if she were learning about the divorce for the first time, and the ensuing scenes had cost each of them so much pain, so much emotional exhaustion, that Jenny had vowed not to repeat it.

"Paul thinks it's a terrific idea," Jenny said now, painfully aware that she was repeating Rachel's words and lying at the same time.

"Oh, I knew he would see it that way." Minna grinned. "He's so sensitive, that husband of yours."

Jenny bit her lip. Tomorrow, she told herself as she heard the front door open and lighthearted rational voices came to her from the hall, tomorrow she would call David at his office and privately ask him to drive her out to the West River Home for the Aged Tomorrow. Without fail.

Chapter Six

Three days later Jenny woke up before daylight, and as she lay wide-eyed in the center of the double brass bed she knew that no further sleep would come. All of the nervous anticipation that had been suppressed by sleep now surged through her body in wave upon wave of restless energy. Quickly, she threw of the warm antique quilt that Nina had given her for Christmas and ran down the dark hallway to turn up the thermostat. It seemed to her that she had only just now turned the thermostat *down*, one of her favorite techniques for summoning sleep being to make the empty bed more inviting by chilling the air around it.

Through Rachel's open doorway she glimpsed the curled heap of her sleeping child and heard the faint sounds of rock music that lately had become her preteen daughter's lullaby of choice. The digital clock-radio in Rachel's room glowed with the illuminated time: 5:13. Jenny folded her arms to ward off the cold and headed down the stairs to brew coffee. If ever a day was worthy of a head start, it was this one.

Measuring the dark aromatic beans for the grinder, she visualized this day, March 16, as the white rectangular space on her desk calendar that held the words "Minna — West River," and she saw that her hands were shaking. Against the growling motorized roar of the coffee grinder, Jenny silently recited the reasons why this day had come. The good, logical reasons for putting her mother into a home. No, Jenny thought, as she spooned the dark grind into the sleek German coffee maker, not for putting her into a home, for *considering* putting her into a home.

No one, David Kalish had promised her, would expect her to actually decide today. No one was going to ask her to sign anything on this visit. "Just come on out and have a look," David had said. "I think you'll be pleasantly surprised." Jenny expected no pleasant surprises; she knew West River. Paul's mother had died there. She would be satisfied, she told herself, if someone, anyone, would just listen to her reasons — her hard ineluctable reasons — and tell her that it was all right, that what she was considering was all right. That a woman who twice during the last month had needed to be resuscitated by paramedics because she has fallen asleep with the gas burners on should no longer live alone. That a seventy-one-year-old woman who would pause in midsentence, look furtively around Jenny's dining-room table, and say about a husband who had been dead for twenty-six years, "You know, Papa's very late getting home tonight; he must have missed his train. And I don't see Paul either. Where have all the men gone?" was no longer able to maintain her own apartment.

In its beginning stages, Minna herself had refused to believe that this was happening to her. That her own blood, her own arteries, should betray her. For months she had accused Jenny of rearranging her furniture, of changing her phone number so that friends could not call, of stealing her mail, of upsetting her routine.

"You forgot the Golden Farms sour cream again, Jenny? Is it so terribly difficult to remember?" she would ask, accusation making her voice brittle. Golden Farms Dairy had gone out of business the year Jenny graduated from Sarah Lawrence. Mother, Jenny would want to shout, why don't *you* remember? It was no use, Richard Eisenstat, the earnest bearded gerontologist had said. Screaming, hair-tearing, denial — none of them were of any use.

"This," he had said to Jenny when she visited his office at New York Medical Center, "this is the one we can't seem to lick. This is senility, Jenny."

Too soon, Jenny had wanted to shout at the pleasant white-coated man sitting behind the big mahogany desk. Too soon!

The West River Home was in New Jersey, so for the sake of expediency Jenny had arranged to meet Nina and David Kalish at an underground garage on the Upper West side, a midpoint between Scarsdale and the Kalishes', and then ride in one car to West River. But when Nina locked the Porsche and slid into the passenger seat of Jenny's white Toyota, she was alone.

"Where's David?" Jenny asked, trying to keep the uneasiness from her voice. The garage was cold and damp and it had been David, after all . . .

"Not coming," Nina said without expression. "He's not coming."

"What do you mean he's not coming? He's the one who talked me into this in the first place. Where is he?"

Nina chewed silently on her lower lip. "I don't know. What difference does it make?"

Jenny gripped the steering wheel. "It makes a lot of difference," she said, making no effort to hide her

frustration. "A whole lot of difference. Moving my
mother into West River was his idea, not mine. If it were
up to me, I'd get her home care, a paid companion.
Anything but stashing her in some institutional hellhole
in bloody New Jersey! She could come out to Scarsdale
and move in with Rachel and me, she could —"

"Bullshit!" Nina interrupted. "Pure, Grade-A bullshit,
and you know it, Jennifer. And if your beloved David
were here, he would say the same thing. So if you're
finished with the hysteria sequence, I suggest you put
the key in the ignition and get us on the road before you
say something you'll regret."

Jenny forgot David's absence and drove in silence,
her mind wandering over the dense, sad facts of life that
marked the route of her mother's decline. It was
pointless to fantasize that if she had not been an only
child, if there were a brother or sister with whom she
could share the weight of this decision, it would be an
easier one to make. Furthermore, Minna had been
widowed when Jenny was eight years old, so it wasn't as
if she had to convince some stubborn protesting father
that what she was doing was the sensible, the responsible course of action. No, she and Minna and Rachel
were all the family each of them could claim, and until
recently that had seemed enough.

For years Jenny had thought that some special (probably female) god had spared her from the clichéd
mother-daughter conflicts that informed the lives, the
popular fiction, and the nightmares of women of her
generation. When the feminists among her friends uttered the tired line "I can handle sex now, if only I could
deal with my mother," Jenny smiled politely and silently
gave thanks that her adoring, quick-witted mother was
the singular exception.

There had been times when she had found herself
consciously emulating Minna, determining her own
decisions, her words, her acts by speculating on what

her mother would do in the same set of circumstances. That was how deeply she admired her mother. Only in her life with Paul did such borrowing fail her. Not until after the divorce did Jenny recount to her mother the true measure of violence her married life had been. And then, with the horror, the rage, and the self-deprecation for not having figured it out sooner turning her face purple and her body limp, Minna had stuck her fist in her mouth, cried silent tears, and held her arms wide to her only child.

Driving on the lower level of the George Washington Bridge, Nina sitting silent and sullen beside her, Jenny thought back to the night she had called Minna from the women's shelter, asked her to care for Rachel for a while, and then at last revealed where she was, what had happened. The horror stories of Paul's abuse had poured out that night. She had spoken in long, unbroken streams of stories she had bitten her lips bloody to keep from telling her mother before now, pausing only to ask every now and then, "Mother, are you there?" And then, not waiting for answer, she had described yet another attack, another set of bruises to be camouflaged by the high necklines and the long sleeves that were the staples of Jenny's wardrobe. Minna had listened, Minna had breathed, but, except to punctuate Jenny's terrible monologue with the words "I'm here," she had not spoken. When Jenny was finished, when she stood at the pay phone in the upstairs hallway of the shelter, out of coins to drop into the box, out of energy to go on, when all of it and everything she had was spent, Minna had asked only one question: "What can I do?" "Be there," Jenny had replied at once, "just be there for me, Mother."

"I'm here," was all that Minna had said. It had been enough — that singular voice, that one rock-solid source of unconditional love. But now, now when Minna could no longer remember that Jenny was divorced, let alone why, Jenny understood that the rock had shattered.

It had all happened so fast. One day Minna had been as wise and clearheaded as anyone, managing her life as efficiently as she had managed the Lingerie Department at Macy's, and the next she was a parody of old age. It wasn't fair, Jenny thought. Look at Nina's mother. Marjorie Croft marched around Bergdorf's wearing perfect little hats and well-coordinated designer clothes, advising the saleswomen that business would surely improve if someone were employed by the store to be certain that all of the mannequins in the Fifth Avenue windows had "fuller bosoms and always wore gloves." Okay, maybe that was a little strange, but hardly cause for alarm. Hardly cause to be put away in New Jersey. And what about David's mother?

Nina had been right about one thing — her mother-in-law was a bigot. Rose Kalish had never yet missed an opportunity to wound her Gentile daughter-in-law, and she was no Madonna when it came to her own daughters either. David's older sister, Marilyn, was too fat; the younger sister, Vicky, was too dumb. And every twinge of bursitis was cause for an emergency gathering of her children.

"Close," she would whisper into the telephone at all hours of the night. "I'm very close. I can feel it. I'm not saying you should come this minute, but it's my left arm, darling, and you know what that means. Not that I would be around to see it, but I would hate to think of you kicking yourself for not getting here in time." The wonder of it was that they came. All three of Rose Kalish's children would roll out of bed and head for West End Avenue, where they would inevitably find their mother snoring contentedly in her bed. "Marilyn," she would say, blinking at all of them, "maybe David would like a cup of coffee. And when you fix mine, be sure to remember the sugar."

But Rose Kalish was about to move into West River. And oh yes, Jenny reminded herself, there was Mr. Waldheim too, Jenny's white-haired neighbor who roamed the Westchester County shopping malls all day long and complained about Jenny's dog, though she and Rachel kept only two gerbils and a cat as pets. Well, he wasn't crossing the Hudson River so quickly, either. Mr. Waldheim had a wife. A twitchy little woman who rang doorbells to deliver homemade banana-nut muffins and smooth over her husband's blunders. It wasn't fair. Jenny could hardly come face to face with anyone past the age of seventy without measuring their situation against her mother's — and always, it seemed to Jenny, always Minna suffered by the comparison.

"We had a fight," Nina was saying as Jenny rolled down her window to pay the George Washington Bridge toll. "Not an argument, Jenny, a real fight. I ended up wanting to punch him." It was the first time that either of them had spoken since Jenny had pulled out of the underground garage, and Jenny, still preoccupied with thoughts of her mother, wasn't sure that she had heard right.

"What are you talking about?" she asked, edgy.

"David," Nina said matter-of-factly. "I'm talking about David. You wondered why he isn't going with us, so now I'm telling you. We had a fight. Make sure you stay to the left as we go over the bridge, for the turnpike. And then get off at Exit —"

"I haven't forgotten, Nina," Jenny said. "Clara Roo died there."

Nina sat quite still in the passenger seat, a study in contrition. She glanced at Jenny from the corner of her eye. "I'm sorry, Jen. That was stupid. Of course you know the way. But I swear, you won't recognize it since David's taken over. Furs are just a sideline since he got into old people. Actually, it was Clara's death that started the whole thing."

Jenny wasn't listening. Jenny was sitting behind the wheel thinking that if Clara Roo had lived another year, another six months, she would have gone to her grave with the terrible knowledge that her only son, her Paul, her genius, her jewel, was a wife beater. How was it that so gentle a woman could have spawned so monstrous a child? She would like to have asked Clara that. That and about fourteen other questions, the answers to which might have illuminated all of the darkness that surrounded Paul. Did his father beat him? Did his father beat you? Ever? Ah, what was the use? It was too late to ask. Clara was gone. By the time her tombstone had been unveiled, a ritual year after her death, Jenny had stood at the cemetery alone. Paul was in California, and the divorce had been final for six months. Whatever questions were left unanswered by his mother's death Jenny would have to uncover for herself. She shook herself behind the wheel, a small shudder to blot the past, and turned her attention to Nina.

"Once he saw that place," Nina was saying, "once he got an eyeful of how utterly grim life was for those old folks out there, he was obsessed. Just totally and absolutely obsessed."

Jenny did not respond. She thought that if a man had to have an obsession, doing good was not such a bad choice. As bewitchments went, caring for old people certainly beat alcohol, greed, and hell-raising. And it was a country mile better than beating up women.

Nina's voice kept taking her by surprise today, it seemed. She was talking now. Talking fast, and without her usual well-bred modulated tones. "I tried to tell him last night. That I wanted a divorce, I mean. That I had had it. That all this pressure to make babies was making me insane, but he wouldn't listen. I want to go back to work, I told him. I want to do what I'm good at and quit trying to accomplish something three infertility specialists have made clear I'm not good at. He wouldn't listen. Do you know why? Because he wanted to talk about your mother instead. About how Minna and some woman named Fanny, Flora, something with an F, would be well suited as roommates. How they had so much in common. Can you believe it? I'm fighting for my life and he wants to talk about nursing-home standards of roommate compatibility. *Compatibility*, for Christ's sake! Wait until he hears from my lawyer. I'll teach him compatibility, frigging Boy Scout!''

There were times when Jenny, confused and angry herself, thought that she could begin to understand the impulse for violence that had shattered her marriage. It was an impulse that lay, belly deep, in everyone. Jenny felt it now, bubbling up to her throat as she gripped the steering wheel and shifted into fourth for the open road. Nothing, Jenny thought, would help her poor friend Nina more than a thrashing. Someone grabbing her by the shoulders and shaking sense into her.

How was it possible that a mind like Nina's, a mind that could handle Aristotle and Spinoza, didn't have the smarts to recognize how lucky she was to be married to David Kalish? How could a Phi Beta Kappa from Sarah Lawrence be so bubble-brained? Jenny bit her lip to silence the question.

"He's developed a real thing for broken hips and dentures," Nina was saying now. "If he had his way, they'd all be covered with chinchilla comforters when they got tucked in at night."

"That's enough!" Jenny hissed as she crossed three lanes of traffic and skidded onto the side of the road before she came to a stop on the emergency shoulder of the New Jersey Turnpike. "Get out of the car, Nina," she said tonelessly, her eyes fixed on the rearview mirror.

"What?"

"Nina," Jenny said, "I can't listen to this anymore. I really can't. Please get out of my car."

Nina looked out the window of the Toyota. There was barely a shoulder to the road in this place. They were miles from a gas station, a toll booth.

"This is a rotten joke," Nina said, touching Jenny's arm.

"It is not a joke, Nina. Either stop badmouthing a perfectly wonderful man or get out of my car and tell it to someone else! I can't listen to it anymore. Look, there's an eight-wheel semi coming up behind me. If you move fast enough, you may get lucky."

"Are you nuts?" Nina asked nervously as she pulled her silver-fox coat around her. "It's beginning to snow out there. You're not actually planning to abandon me here in the middle of nowhere, are you?"

"The New Jersey Turnpike is not the middle of no-where," Jenny said, still avoiding her friend's gaze. She punched on the windshield wipers. The snow was begin-ning to stick.

"Jenny?" Nina laughed nervously. "I don't think you're seriously suggesting that I hitchhike, are you?"

"Why not? You used to do it all the time from Sarah Lawrence into Manhattan. We both did. We were pretty good at it, as I recall." Jenny turned off the engine.

Nina sank back against he seat. "Do you know what I think, my friend? I don't really think you want to do this to me. What I really think is that this TV prospect is making you just a little crazy, and maybe — since we're so close — you're taking it out on me."

Jenny slumped behind the wheel. "That's terrific, Nina. That's really astute. You're a lot of good things, kiddo, but you're a lousy street shrink. Why don't you just cut out the armchair analysis and get out of the car."

Nina sat up very straight in the passenger seat and looked directly at Jenny. "Jenny," she said in a voice that was strong and laden with breeding, "I don't think that would be in your best interest."

Jenny clenched her teeth. If this was what she thought it was, blackmail, she would throw Nina out of the car and abandon her forever. She had other friends. Sensible friends. She worked at making her voice come out calm and steady, in spite of the pounding in her head. "What does that mean, Nina? Exactly what does that mean?"

Nina, her hands trembling, lit a cigarette and inhaled deeply. "It means that West River has a waiting list that is two years long, that you have a mother who needs continuing care you are in no position to provide, and that through the good graces of my foolish husband we are on our way to West River to circumvent the waiting list." She crushed out her cigarette and turned to face Jenny. "Now if you'll put the car in gear we can get on with this happy little field trip."

Jenny laughed, the thin, uneven laughter of surprise. For several heart-stopping moments she had thought that Nina had a much more potent trump card. That reference to the television job had really thrown her. For terrible moments she had held a fantasy in which Nina, with all of the dark secrets of Jenny's past that she was privy to, had approached the Channel Ten station manager to suggest that her first segment, the premier appearance of Jenny Roo on Channel Ten, be devoted to an hour-long documentary on battered women. "Honestly," Nina had said in Jenny's terrible fantasy, "it's perfect material for her."

"That's it?" Jenny chuckled. "You want to save your skin by sacrificing my mother's? That's your best shot? For that you studied Aristotle?" Her laughter was edged with hysteria. "Answer me, Nina! Is that what you want? Is that the exchange rate among friends these days? Is it? Tell me, Nina? Tell me what you want!"

"I want a divorce!" Nina exploded. "I want out! I want to stop pretending that a baby means as much to me as it does to him! It doesn't!" she sobbed. "It doesn't!'' She bent over in the seat now, her body heaving, her words disjointed. ''He gives me everything . . . jewelry . . . kindness . . . fancy trips . . . expensive doctors . . . patience. Oh God, for the patience alone I could kill him! And the one thing — the only thing — he wants from me . . . *I can't give him!*'' The small car seemed to rock with her keening. ''I can't give him a baby,'' she cried softly. ''I've had every diagnostic test in the book. My uterus has been dyed, X-rayed, and cultured. I've been tested for diabetes, anemia, liver abnormalities, and even syphilis and gonorrhea. My chromosomes have been studied, my endometrium has been biopsied, and they've put me to sleep and had as good a look at my equipment as state-of-the-art medicine can get — and still, still I've had three miscarriages. Don't you think that's enough!'' she cried. ''Enough! If I were a piece of fur, Jenny, an animal, David would have thrown me away without a second thought.'' She took a handkerchief from her purse and blew her nose. ''Do know what I am, pal?'' she whispered hoarsely. ''I'm damaged goods.''

Who isn't? Jenny wondered. Nina. Minna. Herself. ''Listen to me, my friend,'' Jenny said. ''If you hold each of us up in a certain light, we're all damaged goods in one way or another. The trick is to avoid that light. The trick is to make your own light.''

She kissed her friend's wet cheek, put the car into gear, and drove back onto the road. At the next exit she got off the turnpike, paid her toll, and with a few simple turns she was headed back to New York. West River was not for Minna, she had decided. Not while there were so many ghosts on the road between here and there.

Chapter Seven

The slim brown envelope Jenny held in her hand was no ghost. It was of this world, Jenny chided herself as she took it from the mailbox. This world. The world she had been absent from while the turbulent events of recent days — interview with home-care companions for Minna, promotional segments taped for Channel Ten, and countless unproductive sessions with Nina — had so completely engulfed her in a sea of preoccupation. The simple, routine tasks of her life had been accomplished with a robotic efficiency, as if someone else had broiled the chicken, shopped for Rachel's new sneakers, and written her column. Jenny had been somewhere else. Absent, preoccupied, not paying attention. Out of it.

"Sloppy," she now scolded herself as she closed the mailbox at the end of her driveway and walked up the path to the house. "Stupid and sloppy." In the shuffle of all that activity, something had been lost: vigilance.

How quickly, with Paul's reminder in her hand, it now came back to her. For all of her efficiency, her purposeful efforts in behalf of others, she had lost touch with the most demanding need of all — her own responsibility to be watchful. And here was Paul to remind her, she thought as she sank down on the floor of her tiled foyer and wrapped her bathrobe more tightly around her. Paul, calling her away from ancient ghosts and summoning her to current dangers. As if to compensate for her lapse in judgement, that lost time, she quickly ripped open the envelope now. There was no news clipping in this envelope, no black-and-white challenge to her security, she saw as she unfolded an informal piece of pale-gray stationery embossed in bold black letters with the name "Paul Roo." An check in the amount of one hundred dollars nestled in the fold of the brief handwritten note above Paul's signature.

Jennifer —

Recent good fortune allows me to mark Rachel's birthday this year. As I am ignorant of both the tastes and the needs of girls approaching their twelfth year, I leave it to your judgment to choose something suitable. Please let her know that it came from me.

Paul

Jenny got up off the floor, telling herself it was the cold tile that was chilling her.

He never sent Rachel gifts. The phone calls, the brief weekly phone calls that came on Sundays, were his only acknowledgment of the fact that he had fathered a child named Rachel. And even those calls were unreliable. There were long Sundays that passed with no call at all. And now this, Jenny thought as she tore the letter in two and inspected the check. It was drawn on a California bank and made out to Jennifer Roo. Because he was ignorant. Because he had enjoyed recent good fortune. Jenny pieced the letter together and read it again, searching for clues to his purpose. Had he known that civility would confound her? Had he labored to achieve that effect? There was nothing he had ever sent to her in all these years that did not advertise his motive, and the motive had always seemed clear to Jenny. The news clippings were meant to frighten her, to threaten her, and they had succeeded. They were bizarre menacing reminders of his presence in the world. "Hold your breath, Jenny, I'm still here," was how she had always interpreted the message of those mailings.

From time to time Rachel would ask, with what Jenny saw as innocent curiosity, nothing more, "What should I say to Daddy about his letter? He keeps asking me if you got his letter and I don't know what to say. What kind of letters does he write to you?"

"Short ones," Jenny would say offhandedly, hoping to avoid any futher discussion of a topic that served only to terrify her.

"Short ones about what?"

Jenny made up answers for Rachel. What real answers could she offer her child? Could she tell her that her father's envelopes concealed the thinly veiled workings of a sick mind? That each time she opened another of Paul's wicked, manipulative letters her body tensed for danger just as it had when he was physically threatening her. She could feel that tension now.

His words, damn him. His sick demented words.

Once, after he had tried to strangle her with the telephone cord, he had come home to her two days later in one of those fits of sobbing remorse, begging for her forgiveness. This time she had steeled herself and held him away from her, avoiding his tearful, drunken embrace.

"Don't!" she said when he reached for her. "Don't

touch me, Paul. I can't be with you when you're like this."

"Like what?" he had mumbled, his arms still held wide to her.

"Drunk," she had whispered, the tension, the fear gnawing at her bones. "On your knees like some kind of strung-out supplicant. Crying for forgiveness, whining like a child — 'I'm sorry, oh Jenny baby, please, oh please, Jenny, I'm so sorry.' I can't talk to you when you're this way. You're an adult, Paul. I want to talk to you like one. You're a writer, you're so full of words! Give me some. Please! Give me some adult words so that we can talk about this."

"Talk about what?" Paul had mumbled, drawing a pint of scotch from the pocket of his soiled trench coat.

"About that," Jenny had said, gesturing at the bottle. And then, with trembling hands she had unbuttoned her blouse to reveal the vicious red ring of bruises that circled her throat. "And about this."

Paul had looked away and taken a long pull on the bottle. "Words!" he had shouted. "You want words, baby?" His portable typewriter was sitting on the table next to where he stood. He picked it up now, and the liquor bottle slid from his hand as he rammed the machine hard against her body.

"Here, Jenny! Here's words! A bellyful!"

And now this. First, stories about fathers who abducted; then stories about fathers who reopened the wounds of old custody battles; and now this. Judgment. He was leaving it all to her judgment.

She sat at her desk with the envelope in her hands and twirled it from one side to the other. Judgment. He was waiting for it. A hundred dollars' worth of judgment. On the back of the envelope she saw there was a handwritten return address in Venice, Calfornia. Judgment came quickly. She stuffed the check and the torn note back into its envelope, resealed the flap with library glue, and then marked it "RETURN TO SENDER" in capital letters so big they nearly obscured the original address.

She had an appointment at Channel Ten. She would mail the envelope on her way to the city.

"Levity," the neatly bearded man in the wine-colored silk suit was saying as he paced behind Jenny's chair in the small conference room at Channel Ten, pausing occasionally to pat her back. "Wit and levity, Jenny. That's what these guys are paying you for, sweetheart, and that's your ticket, your informing focus." He leaned around to catch the expression on Jenny's face. To make certain that those words, "informing focus," had registered.

"Who is Fred Howcroft?" Jenny had asked Burger when she received the call from Channel Ten summoning her to this meeting. "I thought I had already met everyone I'd be working with at the station."

"Howcroft is a consultant, sweetface. A media consultant. News departments all over America pay him big bucks to polish up their half hour so that it outshines the competition. He's the originator of the informing-focus principle."

"The what?" Jenny had asked, stifling a giggle.

"Informing focus," Burger had repeated tonelessly. "That's media-babble which freely translates: 'Let's change our format and do something original, but not too original.' Just do me a favor and go to the meeting, be a lily, listen to what Howcroft says, and then forget about him."

"Now, then," Fred Howcroft was saying as he pulled out a chair and sat down opposite Jenny, "when I say levity, I don't mean four minutes of stand-up comedy. No, no, Jenny, no laugh-till-it-hurts stuff from you. You leave that to the late-night folks you lead into with the news. Got that? What we're looking to you for, sweetheart, is four minutes of helium, a little lightness to leaven all that bad news that's being delivered in the same half hour. See what I mean?''

"Certainly," Jenny said as her thoughts strayed to the Polish immigrant she had interviewed yesterday at Minna's apartment. Irma Swatinsky. The rawboned former nurse's aide had impeccable references from everyone she had ever worked for, and senility was her specialty, she had told Jenny on the phone. She carried letters from physicians to prove it. She was clean and strong, she could drive, and she told them that she could also "cook microwaves."

"I have only one mistake in character," the otherwise self-confident Irma had declared to them.

"What's that?" Jenny had asked nervously.

"I like to, how you say, make fun."

"What?"

"Make jokes. I like to laugh."

Minna had grinned. "Me too. You're hired, Irma."

"No jokes, no punchlines, just helium. Certainly I see what you mean," Jenny said to Fred Howcroft now. She pictured herself as a red balloon floating freely across the exposed pipes of the television studio. "I can certainly relate to that," she said with a deadpan seriousness that seemed to delight Howcroft.

When he smiled he flashed the best bridgework Jenny had ever seen. "Wonderful. That's really wonderful, Jenny. You have no idea how many anchor and weather people I deal with who in their heart of hearts would rather be Johnny Carson than Smilin' Stan the Weatherman. It's a genuine pleasure to be dealing with a true professional who knows her limits."

Jenny smiled. "Oh Fred, if there's one thing I know, it's my limits." *With rue my heart is laden*, she added to herself.

Jenny was waiting in the driveway when Rachel came riding down Cherry Lane on her bike that afternoon.

"Hi," Rachel said as she came to a one-handed stop at Jenny's feet. "What's up?" Her face was flushed with the effort of pedaling up the inclined street and she was slightly breathless. "How come you're waiting for me out here?"

"Well," Jenny said as she reached over and brushed the bangs out of Rachel's eyes, "I was wondering what your homework situation is."

"Two math problems and a spelling list. Which I've already memorized," Rachel panted. "Why?" It was not her mother's habit to ride herd on her schoolwork.

"Well, I have a terrific idea, then. Remember that day we were supposed to go shopping at the mall together and I messed up and forgot?"

"Sure, the day you came home with all that new stuff for you. And the haircut. What about it?"

"Well," Jenny said, "suppose we make up for lost time."

"Like how?" Rachel said as a slow smile began to light her face.

"Oh, suppose we start at Lord & Taylor, and work our way through every junior department from here to Connecticut."

"A spree?" Rachel whooped. "A real shopping spree?"

"That's what I had in mind," Jenny said. "How fast can you park that bike and get in the car?"

"Watch me!" Rachel said.

"I don't get it," Rachel mused as she sucked up a forkful of fettucini at dinner that night and looked over at the empty chair that held all of her purchases. "Two skirts, new jeans, three — I can't believe it, three — sweatshirts, and practically a whole wardrobe of Esprit. And it's not even my birthday yet. I just don't get it. How come you're buying me all of this, Mom? I mean, it's not that you aren't always generous, you're not cheap or anything, but this is — well, this is like terrific and weird at the same time. You must have spent a fortune on me tonight. How come?"

Not a fortune, Jenny thought as she buttered a piece of crusty Italian bread, but a lot more than a hundred dollars. "Because you're my favorite daughter," she said. "How is that for a reason?"

"I'm your only daughter," Rachel groaned as she twirled the noodles around on her plate and grinned. "I'm your one and only."

"I know that," Jenny said. "I know that."

Oh dear God, how well I know that.

Chapter Eight

"How many people?" Rachel yelled into the kitchen. "Is your bald doctor friend coming again?"

"He has a name, Rachel," Jenny said as she abandoned the cheese platter she was preparing and poked her head into the dining room. "His name is Michael and I would appreciate it if you would use it."

"Okay," Rachel said as she stood with the place mats poised above the dining-room table, "Is your bald doctor friend named Michael coming?"

"Not today," Jenny said, taking a deep breath. What was there not to like about Michael Gurzony? she wondered. "He's on call at the hospital this weekend. Set five places."

"Five?" Rachel repeated, her fine eyebrows arching with surprise. "Who's not coming this morning? Is it Grandma?"

"It's Nina," Jenny answered quietly as she set the silver tea service that had once belonged to Minna on the table.

"Again? What's going on with her?" Rachel asked as she flipped five place mats onto the worn table.

"Nothing is going on with her," Jenny said carefully. "She's just not feeling up to brunch this morning. And Rachel? I would very much appreciate it if you would pretend that you didn't notice when David arrives by himself later."

Rachel stood very still as she considered this strange request.

"Okay," Rachel finally answered. "But just tell me one thing. Is this about the miscarry? Is she staying home because she's still sad about the dead baby?"

Jenny put her arms on her daughter's shoulders and turned her around so that she could look at her face. How much Rachel had looked forward to the birth of Nina's baby. Not only did the prospect of a new baby satisfy her unnamed yearning for family, Jenny knew, but to an only child it offered up the coveted prize of status: someone to be bigger than. Someone to flex for. Someone to whom she could say, "What do *you* know, stupid? You're just a kid." Her question, phrased as it was, was not so much an inquiry after Nina's state of mind as it was an expression of her own, Jenny guessed.

"Sweetheart," Jenny said softly. "It was not a dead baby. It was a damaged fetus. It was, well, Rach, sometimes God makes a mistake and . . ." what had David's words been that night at the hospital? ". . . and before it's too late, he fixes it." That was a lousy paraphrase, Jenny knew. Rachel deserved a better explanation than this. Maybe later, when she herself better understood Nina's feelings, she would be able to offer it to her.

"You ought to tell her that, Mom. Maybe then she'd come over today," Rachel said solemnly.

"I don't think so, sugar. So will you do that, please? Will you pretend that you don't notice when David comes in without her?"

"Sure," Rachel said, a small smile lighting her face. "If you'll make me French braids."

When someone rang the doorbell repeatedly at nine-thirty, a full hour and a half before anyone was due for brunch, Jenny continued to tear lettuce for a Caesar salad and assumed that the insistent bell-ringer was one of Rachel's friends. Probably Patience Wasserman, Jenny mused, having run out of the virtue for which she had been named. Her spirits really were picking up, she noted happily as Rachel sped for the door.

Nice, Jenny thought as she pried the key from a tin of anchovies and began to roll off the top, nice how some things — anchovies in their tins, marshmallow Easter eggs in bright-pink foil, lemon drops in boxes lined with waxed paper — had not changed their packaging. Had not been heat-sealed or plastic-wrapped into a fancy new container. Perhaps she would talk about that on television. About packaging. She could work in her ideas about a lot of things with that one word. Fashion addiction, cosmetic surgery, consumerism — they were all possibilities. No, wait. Skip consumerism; the station already had a segment that treated that topic. But there were pine coffins, and Christmas cookie tins, and a million other containers that carried meaning from one generation to the next without being changed. Open-ended light-bulb cartons, cellophane strips on cigarette packs. She loved it when this happened, when ideas bounced whizbang swish in her head. Such mental fertility made her feel buoyant, almost high. She abandoned the anchovy fillets and headed for the study to make notes.

As she passed the opened French doors to the living room, her bathrobe flapping open behind her and her mind set on packaging, she stopped suddenly. "David!" she panted, pulling the short white robe around her nakedness. "What are you doing here so early? I'm not even dressed, I didn't —"

"Sit down, Jenny," David Kalish said in a tone she had never expected to hear from him. Distant, imperious. "Sit down and talk to me." His eyes, usually so clear, so level in their gaze that they summoned implicit trust, now beat and twitched in bloodshot sockets.

Jenny sank onto the bottle-green velour sofa opposite him and silently signaled Rachel, who was greedily watching from the doorway, to disappear.

"What's wrong, David? Is there something wrong? Where's my mother? I thought you were going to pick her up? David! Has something happened to my mother?" Oh God, oh please, God!"

"Minna's fine, Jenny. I called Irma and told her brunch was off." That same voice, that same unyielding tone.

Jenny ran her fingers through her newly layered haircut, a nervous gesture, a stall to keep herself calm. "Why," she asked softly, "why would you tell her that?" She had the disquieting feeling that she was sitting opposite a stranger, someone she had never seen before. It was the same dark complexion, the same broad shoulders, shoulders she had leaned on; the same sharp jaw, the same fullness in the lower lip. But it was as if she were drawing a composite, filling in the blanks the way a police artist might, hoping to supply enough details to stumble upon recognition. "Why would you cancel my brunch?"

He did not answer. Instead he swallowed the ice in his glass and got up to pour himself another shot of vodka from the rolling brass tea cart she converted to a bar when she entertained.

Jenny stood and walked up behind him. Confused, flustered, all thoughts of columns and TV shows flown from her consciousness. "There's Bloody Mary mix, David. Limes. Should I get you some limes?" Nine-thirty in the morning and he was drinking straight shots of Stoly. Oh Jesus.

"Jenny!" he said, whirling on her so quickly that she flinched. "Where's my wife?"

"Nina?" Jenny whispered in astonishment. "Where's Nina?"

"Don't screw around with me, Jenny!" he hollered suddenly. "You know where she is! If anyone knows, it's you. Now talk to me, Jenny. Please." Up close, his skin was mottled, doughy.

"I swear to you, David, I don't even know what you're talking about. I thought she was with you. I talked to her last night. About ten. Ten-thirty. I thought she was calling from home." Jenny went back to the sofa and sat on its edge.

"She wasn't calling from home, Jennifer. She's left home." David fell into the space beside her and held his head in his hands. "She's gone, Jenny."

"What do you mean *gone?*" Jenny said. "What gone?"

"Just what I said. She's gone, missing." His knuckles were white with the pressure of his hands rubbing against his temples, but his voice was low, almost inaudible. Gone was the imperiousness from his voice, vanquished by the difficult truth he was telling.

"Missing," Jenny repeated tonelessly. "Missing?"

"Yes, and so are half of her clothes, all of her jewelry and her pocketbook." He recited this as if it were a litany, one he had already chanted many times this morning.

Missing. Jenny closed her eyes against bizarre visions of what that word meant. Nina, her perfect body lying black and bloated at the bottom of the East River. Her long legs dismembered in a bloody car trunk on Staten Island. Brutalized. Dead. Missing. "Oh Lord, David! Have you called the police?"

"I don't need to call the police," he said, taking his hands from his eyes and looking at Jenny as if she were the crazy person here. "Why would I call the police?"

And here he began to speak very slowly, "No one hurt her, Jenny. She left on her own."

"How do you know that?" Jenny asked softly. "How can you assume that?" God, she had thought he was smarter than that.

"Because her damn furs are still hanging in the closet. Because there's not a goddamn piece of silver missing! Because nothing of mine has been touched."

"Circumstantial," Jenny said lamely. "Purely circumstantial." And then, all at once, it was clear to her. David wasn't stupid. David was a very bright man who was shouting out denial. *Denial* — boy, couldn't Jenny write the primer on *that* technique. *This is not where Paul hit me, this is where I slipped getting out of the bathtub.* "I think you should call the police right now, David," she said gently. "I don't think you should delay another minute." She stood up and started for the kitchen.

"Hold it!" David said, grabbing her shoulders and holding her in front of him. "Jenny," he said, "Jenny, you're a great friend. No lie!" In a voice like a wounded animal. "Everyone should have a friend as loyal as you. But let's not play any more games, okay? Can the crime-reporter stuff, will you? Nina left a note, Jenny. Nina left a note! Nina has walked out on me. Now I want you to talk to me. Please!" So gently that she hardly knew it, he sat her back down on the velour sofa and talked directly to her. "You're her best friend, Jenny. She confides in you. Please don't deny it. You may not know exactly *where* she is, but I'd bet everything I own that you know who she's with. Who is it, Jenny? Who? And don't jerk me around."

Jenny blinked. There was the quality of undeniable masculine demand in his tone, and she instinctively recoiled from it. "There are no other men," Jenny said, crossing her arms in front of her, "at least not that I know about." There were men who tried, Jenny knew.

Men who phoned Nina and suggested lunch, a drink. Foolish men who were captivated by the heady mix of beauty and intellect that Nina Kalish flashed at dinner parties and charity balls. For brief moments these men had held Nina in their arms in candlelit grand ballrooms all over town, tightened their grips on her willowy back, and waltzed into fantasy. But that was all it was, Jenny knew, fantasy. Nina had told her so. And besides, David was always there waiting. Tuxedo-clad, nursing a drink, waiting for some bedazzled schnook to waltz her back to his side, clap him on the back, and tell him what a lucky son of a bitch he was to have her. "There are no other men," Jenny repeated stolidy.

David said nothing, but reached into the breast pocket of his hounds-tooth jacket and pulled out a folded piece of taupe-colored paper that Jenny recognized as Nina's personal stationery. "Really?" he said as he unfolded the letter. "Well, then, what's this supposed to mean?" His darting eyes scanned the handwritten page, found the line it sought. " 'In time you will come to see that I am damaged goods and that you are far better off without me.' " David paused. "Huh, Jenny? What is that supposed to mean? *Damaged goods?* What is that?"

Jenny swallowed hard and stared at the lilac bushes that were coming into bloom outside the living-room windows. That, she thought, is pain. That is the self-inflicted wound of one woman denying her own worth, eating herself up alive.

"He's too good to even complain, Jenny," Nina had told her in New Jersey last week. "Too good to even hint that I'm less than he bargained for. But I see it, Jen. It's in his eyes when he looks at Rachel. It's in the droop of his shoulders when he stands at the window and stares out at the kids playing in the park across the street. And I can feel it every time we make love. It's no way to live."

"I think," Jenny said, reaching out a tentative hand to stroke David's face, "that 'damaged goods' means that she can't give you the baby you want. That some lab test came back and found her wanting. Some sort of chromosomal imbalance, or something. But it certainly doesn't mean that she's run off with someone, that she's cheating on you. David."

"Mmm."

"David, why don't we both just sit tight and wait to hear from her? Okay? I know there are problems, but welcome to the world, my friend. I'll bet she's holed up in some midtown hotel right this very minute, trying to figure out a way to make it up to you."

"Jenny," David whispered, pulling her to him and hugging her hard, "from your mouth to God's ears." But to himself he said that a woman who wanted to make it up to him wouldn't have packed up half of her clothes. Wouldn't have left so obvious a note. It was hard to think that Jenny was flat out lying to him, but women stuck together. You couldn't grow up a male with two sisters without knowing that. And even with her warm, soft body cuddled against him, even with her skin smelling so fresh beneath the white robe, he believed that Jenny was holding something back. Something important.

Chapter Nine

If David Kalish had not left Jenny's house in such a flurry of despair, he still might have been there twenty minutes later when Nina phoned from John F. Kennedy International Airport.

"Where in God's name are you going?" Jenny demanded the instant she recognized the background noises at the airport — the amplified voices announcing flight departures, paging passengers. "Where, Nina?"

"I can't say right now." Nina's voice seemed very loud against the background din. "But I need to see you before I go. Can you get out here and meet me at the Aer Lingus ticket counter?"

"You're going to Ireland?" Jenny asked, incredulous.

"Of course not," Nina said. "But neither is anyone else we know. It's the perfect place to meet."

Jenny moved a curious Rachel out of the room with a series of hand gestures that said "Beat it, kid," quickly tallied the years of their friendship, factored in the time and distance from her house to the airport in Queens, and told Nina she would meet her in an hour and a half. "Maybe two hours if the Jets are playing preseason exhibition at home and I have to deal with the traffic to Shea Stadium."

"They're not playing at home," Nina said. "They're at Cincinnati. I checked. "I'll see you in an hour and a half at the Aer Lingus ticket counter."

"Please deposit twenty-five cents," the recorded voice of the operator interrupted. "Your three minutes are up."

"You're a real friend," Nina was saying when Jenny heard the click of disconnection.

And you, my dear pal, Jenny was thinking as she shuffled Rachel off to the Wassermans' and began the long drive to the airport, are a real nut job.

"There's a cop out there hassling me," Jenny shouted as she bounded through the glass doors opposite the Aer Lingus ticket counter. "Should I park or what?"

"I don't know," Nina called, leaving a huge pile of luggage in the middle of the crowded terminal area to run and meet her. Underneath the carefully applied makeup and the huge sunglasses which gave her the look of the fugitive, Jenny saw her friend's pale face as a grossly contorted mask of confusion. "Yes, Okay. Park. I'll wait here," Nina said.

In the huge labyrinthine parking area Jenny tried to rehearse a speech that she hoped would sound to Nina like good sense offered without judgment. The kind of speech Nina herself had made to Jenny that long-ago day at Fire Island when she had torn away the flimsy fabric of the caftan that hid Jenny's worst secrets. The kind of no-nonsense advice she had offered Jenny when she gave her the phone number at the West Side Women's Shelter. "I've researched them all," Nina had assured her. "This place is the best."

Nina, Jenny thought as she circled the garage with mounting frustration, was good at that stuff. She knew how to research, prioritize and formulate. "Real sensible, my friend Nina," she said to herself as she put her car in reverse to make way for a green Pontiac that was pulling out of a space she quickly zipped into. Nina the Logic Queen. But the question was too obvious to avoid: if she was so logical, what was she doing at Aer Lingus? Just keep your mouth shut and listen, Jenny cautioned herself as she entered the International terminal building.

"I'm going to keep my mouth shut and listen," Jenny announced when they were finally seated at the corner table in one of those excessively dark cocktail lounges that line the broad corridors of airports, offering nervous or weary travelers an oasis of Naugahyde and Formica. "You do the talking, my friend."

Nina pushed her sunglasses to the top of her head and took a small sip of the gin gimlet that sat untouched in front of her.

"Try to understand this," she said as she toyed with her glass. "Some women should not be mothers. True or not true? Some women have babies for terrible reasons and they wind up being lousy mothers. Isn't that right?" Nina did not wait for an answer. "Remember, Jenny? You once did a column about unwed teenage mothers. Those girls who refused to give their babies up for adoption because they believed that the baby was the only one who would ever love them unconditionally. And love them forever. Do you remember that, Jenny? Do you remember that piece? All of the interviews you did with pregnant kids who were waiting for their real live dolls to be born?"

From the corner of her eye Jenny could see three men in business suits sit down at the bar and look pointedly at their table, the only one occupied so early on a Sunday. In the dim light of the lounge she could not tell what they looked like or if they were actually staring, but she could clearly hear the joke they were telling. "This virgin gets beat up by a cowboy," the tallest man was saying, "and as he's getting back up on his horse he says to her . . ."

"Jenny, are you listening to me?" Nina demanded.

"You are not a pregnant teenager," Jenny said too loudly. The men at the bar laughed out loud. One of them hooted, but Jenny did not look up to see which one it was. She sat with her hands in her lap, her fingers laced tightly, and tried to concentrate on Nina.

"That's not cute and it's not friendly and you're missing the entire point," Nina was saying. "I'm talking about David, not about me."

"Get to the point," Jenny sighed, "and then I'll get friendly." The men at the bar had turned their attention to the wall-mounted TV set, where the marathon Sunday orgy of sports programming she remembered from her years with Paul was in progress. Basketball and downhill ski racing, Jenny remembered. Those were his favorites.

"Okay," said Nina. "Here's the point. David is like those girls you once wrote about. He wants a baby for all the wrong reasons. He wants a baby he can name after his father. A baby who unlike him will start at Yale and finish at Yale. A baby his father would be proud of. A baby who won't grow up and spend his life among dead animal skins. Come on, Jenny, you've heard him tell that awful story about his father's ghost showing up in his bedroom after the funeral and shaking his head like he was saying no as many times as I have by now. My Lord, he tells it often enough! Every time he drinks too much. Every holiday — Christmas, Passover, Chanukah, Easter, it doesn't matter if it's his holiday or mine. He just gets looped and before anyone can stop him he's into the ghoulish tale about the ghost of his father. About how when he rides to West River he feels like his father is with him." Nina leaned back in her chair as if she were a lawyer who had just offered a brilliant summation to a jury of one.

"So what?" said Jenny, unimpressed. "I think that's perfectly normal. Holidays do that to people. They eat too much, they drink too much, and they get a little sloppy. A little sentimental. And they remember the dead. You know what? I was eight years old when my father died, and every Fourth of July I still think about him. Especially now that Minna's fading from me. He used to take me, carry me actually, to the Brooklyn Bridge to see the fireworks. It was spectacular! When I think of those explosions in the sky now, I can see the shower of colored sparks from the Roman candles a lot more clearly than I can see his face, but I still remember him. What's wrong with that, Nina?"

"There's nothing wrong with that," Nina said quickly. "That's normal. But David's memories are . . . damn it, Jenny! He wants a baby to take care of his unfinished business with the dead, and that's a lousy reason to want a child! A very sick reason to want a child."

"And you?" Jenny said, feigning interest in the bowl of mixed nuts that sat untouched on their table. "What about you? Do you think taking off like this makes you Miss Mental Health?"

"Me!" Nina cried out. "I'm not the one with the ghostly obligations. David is! He's the one with the problem!"

Jenny carefuly picked three cashew nuts out of the bowl and slowly arranged them against the length of a cocktail straw that lay on the table. She thought they looked like new leaves on a small twig. And then she leaned across the table and told Nina she was full of shit.

She thought that she had said it quietly, but the cheering and foot stomping from the three men at the bar made her realize she must have shouted it. Even the bartender was applauding her. Cretins, Jenny thought as she felt the heat in her face and knew that she was blushing. Morons! Armchair macho men who told jokes about virgins and probably pushed their wives around because it made them feel like heroes. But look at how they needed to put away a fifth of scotch to get the courage to board a plane. Christ, but she had a lot she could tell them! "Uh, fellahs," she said, smiling sweetly, "you just missed a great hook shot by Julius Erving. How about getting back to the game and minding your own business."

"No problem, little lady," the tall one said, the self-appointed spokesman. "We were just admiring your style. Not a whole lot of good-looking women out there who know how to call a spade a spade. Here's to you, honey," he said, tossing off a shot glass full of scotch.

"Great," Nina whispered angrily. "You really pick 'em, Jennifer."

"What is that supposed to mean?" Jenny shot back.

"Nothing," Nina said. "Forget it. Anyone who can attract that kind of attention while telling her best friend she's full of shit — well, what can I say, little lady?" She raised her own glass and held it steady in the space between them. "Here's to you," she said, swallowing the drink before she stood up and ran out of the lounge.

Jenny was too stunned to move at first, and in the time it took her to gather her wits and run out after her Nina had disappeared.

The wide endless corridors of the International terminal building were crowded with travelers now, and as Jenny sprinted among them she seemed, except for the wild look in her eyes, no different from anyone else who was late for a flight. How could she possibly find Nina here? There were miles of corridors, hundreds of departure gates. That Nina had left her bags with Aer Lingus meant nothing, Jenny told herself as she nearly collided with an Indian woman who walked sedately in her sari, both arms dragging hand luggage. Nina could be anywhere.

Jenny scanned the boarding area for Air France as she ran by its gates. A tall blond woman in a dark mink coat. Long hair. Seen only from the back. Was that her? Was that Nina? Nina had carried no coat, Jenny remembered as she ran on past where the signs read "Air France" and began to say "Alitalia." Rome, Jenny thought. Nina loved Rome. She stopped running and looked hard at five Alitalia gates. Impossible, Jenny told herself when her heartbeat began to slow down. Nina wasn't going to Rome or Paris or anywhere. Not without her bags. Sensible Nina would no more get on an airplane without her luggage, with just what she had on her back and the money she carried in her purse, than she would fly to the moon. Yes, Jenny thought, but sensible Nina doesn't ordinarily run away from me in public places either. Sensible Nina, Jenny thought as she began to run again, sensible Nina has gone 'round the bend. Rational, prioritizing Nina could be swallowing pills in any one of the rest rooms Jenny was passing. She could be smashing glasses in the TWA Ambassadors Club.

How long had it been since she had ridden with Nina on the New Jersey Turnpike and heard her call herself "damaged goods?" Heard her say that it was her own abnormality that made her want to leave David. A week ago? Ten days? she asked herself as she ran. And now here she was saying it was he who had the problem. He who needed help. Oh God, Nina was confused! Ten days ago she had said she wanted to go back to work, to do something she was good at. There had been some sense in that, Jenny had agreed at the time. Maybe if she were back in her old job at the Guggenheim Foundation she might forget all the pressures to have a child and relax enough to actually have it happen. Jenny thought all this as she ran in and out of rest rooms spaced at fifty-yard intervals along the endless corridor. Nina was in none of them.

In an empty passenger lounge just opposite the SAS counter, the last of the boarding areas along this walkway, Jenny sat down to catch her breath and to try to figure out what to do next. There was a part of her that had run out of patience for Nina Kalish weeks ago. A part that wanted to button up her trench coat, get into the car and drive back home to salvage whatever was left of this day she normally shared with her child. And there was another part, the part that wished that she could somehow hand Nina a prescription, a slip of paper that Nina might redeem for peace and understanding, the way Nina had pressed the slip of paper with the West Side Women's Shelter phone number into Jenny's hand years before. While the two disparate parts, each offering in its own voice to instruct Jenny in what to do next, debated in her head, a third voice, amplified and metallic, sounded. "Jennifer Roo. Jennifer Roo. Please pick up the nearest white courtesy phone."

Jenny's skin tingled with cold sweat, and for a few seconds her vision blurred. Then she stood up and walked slowly to the SAS ticket counter.

"I've just been paged," Jenny told the blond airline clerk behind the desk. "Where is the nearest white courtesy phone, please?" A chill ran through her body and she raised the collar of her trench coat.

"You're Jennifer Roo, aren't you?" the clerk asked with the melodious Scandinavian lilt in her voice that matched her clear Danish blue eyes. "I recognize you from your picture. You go on the tube soon, yes? On television?"

"Yes," said Jenny, who was always flustered by recognition. "But first I really must answer my page. The white courtesy phone? Where is it?"

"Just past the phone booth to your left," the smiling

young woman told her. "You're much smaller than I thought," she was saying as Jenny ran for the phone.

No one spoke on the line of the white phone for what seemed to Jenny an interminably long time. "May I help you?" a cheerful airline voice finally offered into the silence.

"This is Jennifer Roo. I was just paged." And I also just lost my best friend, ran a marathon, and caught a glimpse of my television future, Jenny felt like adding.

"One moment, Ms. Roo." Jenny rubbed her wet palms together. "Here it is. You are to meet a Mrs. Kalish at the TWA domestic ticket counter. She is waiting there. Have you got that, Ms. Roo?"

"TWA domestic?" Jenny repeated uncertainly. "That can't be right. That's in another terminal building, isn't it?"

"I don't know, Mrs. Roo. I don't know where you are speaking from."

From the moon, Jenny wanted to say. I have left reality behind and I am flying to the moon with my crazy friend Nina. I'm speaking to you from a white courtesy phone on the moon.

"I'm near the SAS counter," Jenny said, "in the International terminal."

"Well, then, yes, Ms. Roo," the voice said pleasantly, "you will have to leave that building and go to the building where TWA domestic is located."

"Where is that?"

"South," the voice answered. "South of where you are now. I think there's a bus," the voice said.

The bus took fifteen minutes to circle the airport's perimeters, and by the time Jenny came through the doors opposite the TWA domestic ticket counter her hair was blown wild and her jaw was clenched with anxiety. Not only had the stopping and starting of the bus at every airline along the route made her nauseous again, she had no idea what Nina was going to say to her.

What she did say when Jenny spotted her sitting in a lounge chair beside the door, her full-length mink coat draped elegantly over her shoulders and her gloved hand holding a ticket voucher, was, "I'm sorry I left you like that. Without saying goodbye."

Jenny grimaced as though Nina had just told a tasteless but passably good joke and sat down beside her.

"I see you're holding a ticket voucher," Jenny said as she brushed the hair out of her eyes. If there had ever been a more strained silence in the twenty years of their friendship, she could not remember it now.

"That's right," Nina said.

"Where are you going?" Jenny asked.

"Chicago."

"Really?"

"Really."

"What's in Chicago?" Jenny said, struggling to keep her voice casual.

"A job," said Nina.

"Oh," Jenny said, "a job." A job in Chicago, a husband in New York, and suitcases on their way to Dublin. "That makes sense," Jenny said. "What kind of job?"

"I'll be reading grant proposals for the Chicago Urban Foundation. It's actually a pretty good job considering how long I've been on the shelf."

"How did you get it?" Jenny asked in the same toneless voice in which she had been speaking. Her legs ached from her marathon run through the airport.

"Through somebody I used to know at Guggenheim."

"That's nice."

"I think so."

"And, uh, how long have you known about the job?"

"Thursday, three days ago. That's when they called me and offered me the job."

Jenny inhaled. "What are you planning to tell David?"

"The same thing I told my mother. That there's an infertility specialist in Chicago who's got an experimental treatment no one in New York is practicing yet."

"Is that true, Nina?"

"Yes," Nina said in a voice so emotionless she might just as well have answered no.

"It's cold in Chicago," Jenny said.

"I know that. That's why I took my coat out of the luggage before I checked it through. My coat, my gloves and my boots," she said, sticking her legs out so that Jenny could see that she had boots on her feet now.

"That was certainly sensible," Jenny said.

"That's what I thought," Nina said. And then they fell into a fit of giggles so loud and uncontrolled that people all around them turned to stare.

"Why Aer Lingus?" Jenny said, gasping for breath.

"I told you," Nina said. "Because no one we know goes to Ireland." She stood up and reached for a worn oxblood leather briefcase that lay beside her chair.

"Remember this?" she said as she held up the case and began walking toward the departure area, Jenny at her side.

"Of course I remember it," Jenny said. "I gave you that briefcase the day you got the job at the Guggenheim Foundation."

"Remember what you wrote on the card?" Nina asked as she paused to check a video screen for her gate number.

"No," Nina said. "But if it was something stupid I'd rather you didn't remind me of it now."

"Gate Seven," Nina said. "It wasn't stupid at all. The card said, 'You're a serious woman with a serious job and you deserve a serious briefcase.'"

"Profound," said Jenny, rolling her eyes.

"I thought it was. At least then I thought it was."

They were approaching the security machines, and Nina paused and put her hand on Jenny's arm. "You don't need to go to the gate with me," Nina said evenly. "Honest, I can take it from here."

"What about the details?" Jenny asked.

"All taken care of." Nina tried to smile. "I've withdrawn a thousand dollars from my Citibank account — that should cover me until I can open an account in Chicago. And the Foundation keeps a furnished apartment downtown, so really all I have to worry about is work."

"What about the infertility treatment?" Jenny asked softly.

"That's the doctor's business," Nina said dryly. "Let him worry about it." But for all her glibness, Jenny saw that Nina's fingers were crossed as she said this.

Jenny sighed. She had it all figured out, Nina did. Within thirty-six hours she had managed to analyze her husband, go to the bank, pack nine suitcases and consult a medical specialist. She was, Jenny thought, entitled to her confusion.

"I don't know about you, my friend," Jenny said, "but any minute now I expect you to wipe that enigmatic Mona Lisa smile off your face and break into an off-key chorus of 'I've Got to Be Me.' "

"I would do that," Nina said as she hugged Jenny hard, "but there are two things I don't do in public. I don't cry and I don't sing."

"I cry," Jenny said.

And most of the lonely way home she did.

Chapter Ten

Rachel had secrets, an arsenal of private information and beliefs she held in constant readiness. If the arbitrary adult world in which she mostly functioned should turn suddenly hostile and strike without warning, Rachel considered herself well armed for her own defense. With no brothers or sisters to count as allies, she viewed her stockpile of covert information and personally researched intelligence as her only weapon.

For example, last Tuesday night when David Kalish was over for dinner, Rachel had seen him kiss her mother on the back of her neck as he carried out the garbage. Twice. Once when he was going out and once when he was coming in. The back of the neck was not, she was positive, where friends kissed each other. Rachel had no idea what to do with this information; she only knew that thinking about it made her legs feel as though they were made of Jell-O.

Tonight, on the eve of her twelfth birthday, she sat

cross-legged on her girly canopied bed and examined her collection of secrets the way she had once arranged and rearranged her family of stuffed animals and her assemblage of music boxes. Her mother was out with some TV people, and Mrs. Forester, the dried-up old-lady babysitter who had been hired to keep Rachel company, as her mother delicately put it — because Rachel abhorred the idea that there was any connection between herself and a baby — was asleep in the den downstairs. It was a perfect time to take the locked gray metal file box out of her lower left-hand dresser drawer and examine the three-by-five lined index cards that held her most personal opinions. The file box, she had explained to her friend Zoë Benz who kept a white leatherbound diary with a miniature combination lock, "is better than any diary because if you change your mind about something you don't have to rip it all apart. You can just tear up the card and write a new one."

For example, during the two weeks that Nina had been gone, Rachel had written seven different cards on the subject, each positing a different opinion about where Nina was hiding out and whether or not she would ever return. The current card, revised last Tuesday night after Rachel had stood silent witness to the kiss-on-the neck episode, held that Nina was gone for good.

Until recently, Rachel would have shared that opinion with the world, or at least with her mother. But not now. A child of words, outspoken and possessed of a fertile imagination she described as "genetically inherited" lest anyone think her merely childish, Rachel had lately grown silent.

"It's a stage," she told her mother when Jenny questioned her uncharacteristic reticence. "I'm just gearing up for adolescence, Mother. Would you try not to worry about me so much."

"I don't worry about you," Jenny had lied. "I just think. And one of the things I think about a lot is you. But it's not worry, it's just that I'm thinking."

And so am I, Rachel wished that she could tell her. Believe me, so am I. But she kept this and other secrets to herself, struggling to keep their dimensions within the three-by-five frame that held them.

The one true secret that could not possibly be written down or contained was that she was planning to change her name. Neither a whim nor an angry impulse, it was, she thought, the most grown-up decision she had ever made. Tomorrow, in honor of her birthday, she was going to make a public announcement to her mother and her grandmother.

"Rachel Roo is a stupid name," she had already declared to her friends. "It makes me sound like I'm a stripper or a centerfold. Or some kind of marsupial. I really hate it." What she had not told her friends, not even Patience, the painful secret she had kept locked in the metal box, was that her father had not called her in nearly four weeks. So why should she have to go around carrying his stupid name when he couldn't even find the time to call her? Why? Just because her mother was smart enough to divorce him didn't mean that she was smart enough to get rid of his name. Golman, Jenny's maiden name, was a perfectly good name. Why couldn't she be Rachel Golman from now on?

Her father had abandoned her, she told herself at night when she drew the sheets up under her chin and thought about all of the orphaned heroines she had ever read about. He didn't care one whit about her. He had lied during that last call when he said that he might just surprise her and show up one day to buy her a Coke. It was his idea of a joke that she should listen at the living-room window for the sound of strange car engines and watch in the schoolyard for men with black eyes and curly hair. A cruel tease. Didn't he know that she was too old for teasing? Didn't he know that? Didn't he count the years?

Besides, if her mother continued to date that balding doctor guy or she kept spending so much time with David Kalish and he kept kissing her on the neck and Nina really was gone forever, there was a chance that Jenny might change her name first — leaving Rachel alone, stranded with the ultradumb name of Roo. The possibility that her mother would someday remarry was one of her most fervently held opinions. Part dream, part dread, it was Rachel's best-guarded secret.

There were other secrets which floated more loosely through her daydreams and seemed for the time being of less consequence to her. Her grandmother, for instance, who was not yet pinned down as an index card but who definitely inspired thought.

It was Rachel's current theory that her grandma Minna had redistributed her love in much the same way that Rachel had chosen to redistribute the books in her bookcase, giving the biggest shelf to Judy Blume books now and thinning out her collection of horse stories. It was that way with Minna's love, Rachel believed. She seemed not to be so crazy about Jenny anymore, and it appeared to Rachel that all of that leftover unused love for Jenny was being lavished on her.

She did not know exactly what to make of this, but lately there were delicate little bracelets (on which Minna pointed out the tiny 14K stamp), leatherbound books, and expensive French cloisonné music boxes waiting for Rachel when she went to visit her grandmother. There was nothing particularly wrong about receiving these unexpected gifts. Other girls at her school had grandmothers who took them to lunch at special places like the Bird Cage at Lord & Taylor and then let them charge practically the whole store. And there was a boy in her class who had traveled around the entire world with his grandparents plus his own private tutor so that he wouldn't fall behind in the fifth grade while he was off in places like Hong Kong or Melbourne. That was just the way things were with some grandparents. Except that Minna had always been — well, different than that.

When she was a little kid, Rachel could recall, so young that her father's vague face still floated through those memories, she would go to Minna's apartment and there would be a glass jar of hard candies on the buffet in the dining room. She was allowed to choose two on every visit, and, apart from her birthday and Chanukah, that was about it. That Minna offered only red-and-white peppermint swirls and cellophane-wrapped butterscotch nuggets didn't mean that Rachel hadn't always loved her grandmother and known that her grandmother loved her; it was just that she had grown up not expecting much from Minna in the present department. And now, here were these fancy-wrapped boxes suddenly showing up on the dining-room table when what she was expecting was a marathon gin rummy game and maybe some oatmeal-raisin cookies from the bakery on the corner. What was most disconcerting to Rachel was the exclusivity of this sudden generosity. All of the presents were for her; there was nothing for Jenny, Minna's own daughter. And even that wasn't the whole thing.

There was the way Minna was always looking up from the treasure trove on the table lately and saying to Jenny, "So? Don't you have something better to do while I visit with Rachel? A date, maybe? An appointment with what's-her-name who does your feet?" It was just so obvious that she didn't even want Jenny around anymore. So her mother would leave them alone for a few hours while they mostly watched the soaps, and Irma — the thin Polish woman who had moved in with her grandmother and whose face made Rachel think of skeletons on Halloween — would appear suddenly to inquire, "Mrs. Golman, you want? You need?" Actually, Rachel thought that was okay. That was almost nice. What troubled her was the way her grandmother kept locking her up in the bathroom with the see-through plastic shower curtain and slipping her ten-dollar bills. And the way she then made her promise not to tell Jenny.

"Our secret," she would say, taking the folded bill from the pocket of her housedress. "Do you want to try my talcum powder?" And then, no matter what Rachel answered, she would sprinkle talcum powder on her and call it fairy dust. As if she were the fairy godmother in "Cinderella" and Rachel was Cinderella herself and the absent Jenny was just a wicked stepdaughter.

The whole scene at her grandmother's apartment made Rachel nervous, but the worst part, the part that kept slipping into her dreams and was too big to be contained in a metal file box, was the strange look on her mother's face when she would walk back into Minna's apartment after she'd been out. A look like she was in some kind of pain but there was no way to figure out where she hurt. That strange sad look made Rachel wonder if one day her mother might stop loving her the way Minna had stopped loving Jenny. That was the worst thing about grown-ups, Rachel thought. It wasn't hypocrisy, which was what Patience contended when she caught her father snorting coke in the garage after he had just delivered lecture number two zillion on the dangers of teenage drug abuse. And it wasn't even that they broke promises. Or that they made you do things that were ridiculous and when you questioned them they gave answers like "Because I say so." That was not the worst thing. The worst thing was that when it came to something as important as love, grown-ups were unreliable.

"Rachel? . . . Rachel? . . . Ray-chill!" the slobby old babysitter called from the bottom of the stairs.

"What?" Rachel hollered in exasperation. The

woman's name was Forester. Mrs. Forester. Rachel thought it was the perfect name for a woman who looked like a tree stump.

"Turn out the light like a good girl, Rachel. Time to go to sleep," the old tree stump yelled up the stairwell.

"Too lazy to climb the stairs," Rachel mumbled. "And too fat. Yech, grown-ups."

Rachel gathered up the note cards that had slid all over her slippery satin bedspread and put them back into the metal box. Her mother had once loved her father, but no more. And even though he had never once in all those weekly phone calls actually said so, she supposed that her father had once loved her mother. But obviously that had ended, too.

Sometimes a man and a woman just stop loving each other and . . . That's how they explained it, grown-ups did. That's how they told their children about divorce, legal custody, and the world splitting in two. Those were the words that they used.

It was the best they could do, Rachel supposed. But they were special words — specific, as her English teacher would say — meant to apply to couples. Maybe they could be used to explain why Nina had gone away; maybe Nina had just stopped loving David. But what about mothers and daughters? What about Minna no longer loving Jenny? What were the specific words for that? And what could explain a father who had stopped loving his daughter even the little bit it took to make a phone call?

She put the locked file box back into her dresser drawer and decided to skip brushing her teeth. What was the point? Every time a kid got the speech about a man and a woman who had stopped loving each other, they got the line about how that didn't change anything for the kid. *But that doesn't mean that we're going to stop loving you. Oh no! We'll always love you, sweetheart. Nothing can change that.*

Bullshit, Rachel thought as she wiggled under the

covers and pulled the soft edge of the blanket close to her face. Lies and bullshit. Things did change that. The trick, she decided as she punched her pillow into a tight ball, was to figure out what things. What made love come unfixed? What attached children to their parents and what made the attachments come apart? She fell asleep thinking that maybe when she was twelve she could figure it all out, but not tonight. Tonight she was eleven. Just a kid.

The phone in the den rang seven times before it roused Mrs. Forester, and even when she held the receiver against her slightly deaf right ear she was sure that she was dreaming. The loud, menacing music that blasted from the phone was just like the music the McFarland boys for whom she babysat after school played on their tapes. It was mean music, she thought. Mean raucous music that assaulted even her dreams. She fumbled for her eyeglasses, as if clarity of vision could also smooth sound.

"Mrs. Roo's residence," she announced against the din. The news was on the TV screen, she saw. That meant it was after eleven o'clock. The only people who made phone calls after eleven o'clock were thoughtless people. Mean people. Maniacs. "Speak up, why don't you?" she demanded.

In the library of the actress Jessica Meir's Beverly Hills home Paul Roo kicked the door closed against the noise of the live band playing on the terrace and cupped his hand around the phone. "I'm sorry. There's a party going on here. I want to speak to Rachel." He gripped his glass of club soda on the rocks and tried to pretend that he was as drunk as everyone else who was here to celebrate the overwhelming success of his new play, *Pennydance*. It wasn't working. The glass was sweating, and he was sweating, and he had never felt more coldly sober.

"Who is this?" Mrs. Forester demanded. The world was full of lunatics. All you had to do was read the papers to know that. And some of them used the telephone to spread their evil lunatic messages. Who but a lunatic would call a child at this hour? She sat up very straight on the sofa. "Who are you to be calling Rachel in the middle of the night?"

Damn it! Paul thought. In all the years since he'd been in California he'd been accommodating the three-hour difference without flaw. Tonight, when it mattered the most, tonight he'd screwed up. "Listen," he said as calmly as he could, "this is Rachel's father. I'm calling long distance and I forgot the time difference. I know it's late, but I'd appreciate it if you would ask Rachel to come to the phone." He inhaled deeply and wondered how many more things he might screw up before he got this right.

"I most certainly will not," Mrs. Forester shot back. "Rachel is sound asleep, and furthermore, for all the years I have been caring for her I have never heard mention of her father. So far as I know, there is no father. You could be anyone."

It was a lie that she had cared for Rachel for years. Actually this was only the second time the agency had sent her out to Mrs. Roo, but someone had to stand guardian to the innocent child asleep in her charge. Someone had to protect the young and the helpless in a world full of lunatics. Wasn't it lucky that Evelyn Forester was on the job tonight to do just that. How grateful Mrs. Roo would be for her vigilance. She might even register her appreciation with a very generous tip. Not that that was necessary. Certainly not. Mrs. Forester saw her duty and did it. "Good night," she said emphatically and hung up the phone with a satisfying smack of the receiver.

Paul held the dead line in his hand and thought that if that woman, whoever she was, was in his presence instead of three thousand miles away in New York, his "cure" would have been seriously tested. He hung up the phone and loosened his tie. A month ago, he would have gone outside and hunted down Phil Gruber, the psychiatrist who not only had been responsible for his changed behaviour but had also been the first backer in the deal to finance *Pennydance*. Gruber was out there somewhere partying, celebrating the success of the previews with the rest of the backers. He could find him if he chose to. He didn't. He hung up and redialed the number.

The phone caught Mrs. Forester in the kitchen, rummaging in the refrigerator. Ice cream, she had learned from a recent magazine article, was a comfort food. Interesting, that description. Comfort food. It was not her habit to indulge herself in other people's kitchens, no matter how they encouraged it, but certainly her rattled nerves deserved solace of some kind. That maniac caller had been very troubling indeed. So when the phone rang, Mrs. Forester was scooping cherry-vanilla ice cream into a cereal bowl and her anger against the caller was mightily increased for having been interrupted.

This time Paul would allow her no opening, no chance to speak first. The phone clicked against Paul's ear, and before she could even breathe he spoke. Very quickly. Very sharply. In a voice not his own. "I am calling from Arizona to wish my niece a happy birthday. Is she at home?"

Mrs. Forester automatically licked the spoon she held in her hand and thanked the Lord and the Westchester Agency for placing so competent a woman at 14 Cherry Hill Lane this night. A woman of such quick-wittedness, of such well-practiced composure. Uncle indeed! She swallowed a spoonful of ice cream and spoke with a chilled mouth.

"No," said Mrs. Forester, "I am afraid she is not. And if you really were who you say you are you would know that the child's birthday is not until tomorrow. You maniac! You telephone slime! It's not until tomorrow!'' She slammed the phone down, and with the self-satisfied delight of one who has earned generous reward she added more ice cream to the already heaping bowl. Lunatic. Long-distance lunatic!

The ice cream had melted to the creamy consistency she liked best, but before she turned off the kitchen light and carried the bowl back into the den she took the phone off the hook. That would fix him. Father! Uncle! Lunatic!

Chapter Eleven

Jenny Roo excused herself from the dinner table at the
Four Seasons, where her network hosts were finishing
the last of their cognacs while their glossy wives were
making whispery, uninspired small talk with her date,
Michael Herzony. Doctor Michael Herzony. It was
unlikely, Jenny thought as she stood before the mirror
in the spacious ladies' room and slowly freshened her
makeup, that Michael would enjoy her absence. She had
left some very bright women at that table, and one of
them, the blond wife of Art Kronigsberg, her show's
director, had been launched on the subject of unnecessary female surgery — hysterectomies, radical
mastectomies and such — when Jenny left the table.

As a surgeon, the forty-nine-year-old doctor could
more than hold his own in any medical debate; she had
heard him do that last month when he had introduced
her to colleagues of his at New York University
Hospital. But the well-fed and equally well-oiled com-

pany in which she had left him were not his peers. They were media types, and even their women, who were as well schooled in the bait-and-lunge interview technique as they were in choosing their expensive clothes and their yoga classes, seemed to take pleasure in grilling the uninitiated. Jenny, who had spent some time on their well-greased roasting spit herself this evening, attributed this fierce instinct for interrogation to the nature of their husbands' business careers.

News programming was at once the bane and the promise of every television station's existence. Good or bad, the ratings and the revenues generated by the news division of any station held an importance that could not be overstated. And it wasn't just the Dan Rathers and the Roger Mudds who stood in the epicenter of all this broadcast fear and trembling. Local stations, especially those owned and operated by the network as Jenny's New York station was, felt the tremors, too. What had her hiring at Channel Ten been, after all, if not the finger-in-the-dike attempt to shore up the station's crumbling ratings as the tides rose for the competition? No wonder they were nervous out there in the main dining room.

If she bombed next Tuesday night, if her polished patter and her provocative renderings of life in the sleepless city failed to capture an enlarged Tuesday-night audience, she could just send back the new wardrobe and go back to being what she was — a nationally syndicated newspaper columnist who sat braless at her typewriter in the sheltered anonymity of Westchester County. But not those guys. If the well-publicized and expensively purchased arrival of Jenny Roo at the Channel Ten News Team failed to rouse sleepy New Yorkers from their warm beds and didn't woo them into turning the dial away from NBC, CBS, ABC or their favorite cable station, their flawlessly groomed heads could roll. Not to mention how much failure might impact the relationships their women held with Halston, Jenny thought without malice. They were, she knew, very vulnerable women. And even as she held that thought and applied her newly purchased lip gloss to her mouth, she could hear the distant echo of Steve Burger's words: "You know what separates you from the other slice-and-dice female columnists in this country, Jenny? Generosity, that's what. Before you go in for the kill, you always manage to salute the target."

Those women, Jenny thought as she licked at the unfamiliar slickness of her lips, deserved better recognition than a salute. From time to time she had considered writing a column on wives of men who held precarious jobs, and she kept these ideas filed. Women who shared their lives with firemen, poets, test pilots, stunt men and aeronautical engineers were already on her list. Under the subheading "Early Heart Attack Candidates" she would tonight go home and add television news executives. Tomorrow, she decided, she would begin research on the Mesdames Rather, Mudd, Brokaw and — no. She stopped herself.

Those women, if in fact they existed, were charter members of a long-suffering club; they were entitled to whatever comfort their privacy could grant them. Just think what might have happened if someone had had the temerity to stick a microphone under Paul Roo's nose and ask him for a few well-chosen words on the subject of Jenny's career. Jesus! Just the thought was enough to set her teeth on edge. And once again, as she had almost every day of her life since he had left New York, she thanked God and every lucky star in the three thousand miles of sky that separated them, that he was gone.

The fact that he had not called Rachel for so long was more comforting to her than she could ever say. It was obvious that Rachel suffered for his silence, but Jenny was warmed by it. Where other divorced women took comfort from their former husbands' continued devotion to their children, Jenny wished only that Paul would somehow vanish. There was nothing Rachel needed from him, nothing he could give her that was good. Her judgment in returning his check had been sound.

She examined her face in the mirror. Even the freshly applied makeup could not hide the pallor that thoughts of Paul summoned. It was as if, she sometimes thought, those years had drained her, left her bloodless and somehow dry.

Quickly she snapped closed her evening bag. Knock it off, she chided her mirrored image. That was a million years ago. *Michael.* You ought to be thinking about Michael. And going to bed with Michael. And falling in love with Michael. But not necessarily in that order, she corrected herself as she headed back to the table with no further inspection of her own image.

"Talk to me," Michael Hurzony said as he filled Jenny's glass with white wine in the kitchen of his brand-new Larchmont town house later that night.

She had been here only once before — on their first date when they were on their way from Scarsdale to Manhattan and he asked if she wouldn't mind stopping. The sixty-three-acre complex of expensive detached buildings had just been completed and he wanted to check out what the interior decorator he had hired had accomplished so far.

Following him up and down the freshly painted and papered empty four levels, she had heard him wonder out loud if he would ever be comfortable here. It wasn't just the problem of moving his old things into so contemporary a space, he told her. There was nothing in the rule book that said antiques couldn't furnish a room with a slate fireplace and track lighting. And it wasn't the high-tech kitchen that threw him, either. "If I can find my way through the human abdominal cavity, I can surely master a microwave oven,'' he had said. "It's more the . . . the *context* of such a place,'' she remembered him saying.

She had known at once what he had meant with that dry word. Singles. That was the context here. A developer who had installed four swimming pools, six lighted tennis courts, three indoor racquetball courts, and a party room with a wet bar and a bandstand was not exactly courting families. No, 101 Hightop was not going to be populated with boisterous children who would tear up the eleborate landscaping. Its rolling lawns would not be the repository of bikes or Big Wheels. Its street-level garages were meant to shelter only the Porsches, the Fiats, the Maseratis and the Mercedeses of the young members of the Me Generation who had succeeded in keeping Me as their number-one priority — and the well-maintained Sevilles and Mark IVs of the comfortably retired seniors who still played frozen-smiled, color-coordinated mixed doubles on Saturday mornings.

Michael, he had said that night, felt no kinship with either group.

Coming through the front door tonight, she had seen that it was true. A Bukhara rug seemed to float in the otherwise empty living room. A massive, slightly worn Chippendale dining-room set crowded the small skylit dining room. And where there ought to have been soft plushy towels to match the chic wallpaper of the entry-level powder room, there was a pile of medical journals and a roll of Scott's paper towels instead.

"Talk to me, Jenny,'' Michael Hurzony said again as he refilled her glass. It was after midnight, Jenny noted on the futuristic stainless-steel wall clock she supposed the decorator had chosen. The babysitter sent by the Westchester Agency got time and a half after midnight, she reminded herself.

"I am talking to you.''

"About nonsense."

"Tax shelters are not nonsense. The science curriculum at Rachel's junior high school is not nonsense. What would you rather talk about?"

"You. What you're thinking, what you're feeling." Michael Hurzony was a widower who would be fifty years old in May. She had met his wife at the Scarsdale Public Library two years ago when they were both asking for the same book, and she had liked Joan Hurzony enough to break a strict private rule and invite her to have lunch. It was one thing to plant tulip bulbs and another thing to plug into the suburban "Let's have lunch" syndrome, Jenny believed. But Joan Hurzony was a well-considered exception that proved her rule.

They had lunched maybe three or four times over the next year before Joan confided that on the day she had met Jenny in the library she was there to take out books for a hospital stay during which she would undergo an exploratory operation.

"Exploratory?" Jenny had repeated, her mouth full of Chinese chicken salad. "Looking for what?"

"What you would think if you were inclined to think the worst," Joan had said evenly.

Jenny remembered that she had suddenly fixated on the texture of every ingredient in the salad. The creaminess of the mayonnaise, the crunchy hardness of the celery bits, the chewiness of the shredded chicken.

"And . . . ?"

"And they found it."

Five months later she was dead. The first time Jenny had ever seen Michael Hurzony was at his wife's memorial service.

"I'm telling you what I'm thinking," Jenny answered with an acute awareness of the game-playing that was going on here. "With the additional income that will be coming in from the television work, it's only natural that tax shelters should be on my —"

"Enough!" Michael interrupted. "I won't push it."

"Push what?" Jenny asked, taking a long swallow from the glass of wine. Soon the glass would be empty and her head would be empty and she and this decent person who had been buying her dinners and theater tickets and an occasional piece of costume jewelry for the last few months would be alone in the shiny unused kitchen with the knowledge that they were, after all, a man and a woman for whom a soundless bell was now tolling. The fact that Jenny insisted on paying for some of the tickets and some of the dinners did not change that.

"I'm going to be fifty years old next month," Michael said solemnly. "I haven't slept with a woman since Joan died. Haven't wanted to. I look at naked female bodies every day of my life. Not all of them turn out to be sick, you know. And some of them are very attractive. But none of them make me forget I'm a doctor. Yours does. You do. You make me forget a lot of things, Jenny. Do you know what someone once said about turning fifty?" he asked as he pulled her to her feet and brought her trembling body to him. "They said that fifty was the youth of old age." He kissed the top of her head and ran his hands over her back. "The youth of old age. Hmm? I like that. I like that appraisal."

"It has a nice balance," Jenny mumbled against his shirt.

"So does the Statue of Liberty, but I wouldn't want to snuggle up to it," he said before he kissed her, before he took her hand and led her out of the kitchen.

The Statue of Liberty? Jenny thought as she stalled at the bottom of the stairs that led to the bedrooms of the town house. *So does the Statue of Liberty?* It was not the sort of riposte she expected from Michael. Someone she knew might have said that, used that kind of unsettling comparison. But not Michael. She couldn't say who it was, but it was definitely someone else. From Michael she expected careful handling and uninspired dialogue.

"It's late," she said, taking her hand from his and stroking his face. "I have a new babysitter, and tomorrow is Rachel's birthday, and —"

"And you don't want to sleep with me," he finished for her, his voice low.

"You're wrong, Michael," Jenny said as she stood back from him and took in the broad chest and the clear-eyed gaze and the pure vision of plainclothed strength she saw in him. "But it would take me years to explain why you're wrong." Years, she thought, to tell you that only twice since Paul have I trusted my body to a man, and twice I regretted it. Twice I've felt nothing but terror. Twice I've pretended pleasure when what I felt was panic. You would be the third. Three strikes. Out. Retire the side, Nina would say. If Nina were here. "You're wrong. But I can't tell you why."

"Because of Joan?" he asked in what seemed to Jenny a voice both understanding and hopeful. "Because you knew her? Beause you were her friend?"

Jenny shook her head. "No," she answered, "it has nothing to do with Joan. I wish I were that noble."

"Then it's because there's someone else. Some other man?" And now there was no missing the meaning in his tone — it was regret. He sat down on the bottom stair as if the thought of a rival were too much to stand against.

"No," she said softly, kneeling beside him. "Not in the way you mean.

"Look," she said, standing up to banish self-pity, "it's a very long story. A very long and very complicated story. One that has absolutely nothing to do with you." She saw by the stricken look on his face that she had chosen her words badly. Again she dropped to her knees beside him. "Well, of course it concerns you, but I mean that there's nothing personal in it."

Oh Jesus, she was making it worse.

Michael grimaced. "Sometimes," he said, rising to his full height and studying the slate tiles of the foyer hall where they stood, "I am called upon to do a very delicate and specialized operation. It requires that I remove a foot from a mouth." He walked to the hall closet and took out their coats. "I'm actually pretty good at it. Care to make an appointment?"

"Yes," she said as they walked out of the town house, not touching, and got into his car, "I would like to make an appointment. A real one. One that would give me enough time to . . ."

"To what?" he asked tonelessly.

"To explain."

He sighed. "How's Tuesday night?"

"I go on the air Tuesday night." The Hutchinson River Parkway was very dark at this hour.

"Wednesday night," he said dryly.

"Wednesday night I work against the Thursday deadline for my column."

They drove the rest of the way to Scarsdale in silence.

Just as Michael turned off his ignition in Jenny's driveway and began to move closer to her, she suddenly realized whom he had sounded like with that corny line about snuggling up to the Statue of Liberty — Steve Burger, her agent. She found herself smiling into Michael's perfunctory kiss. It wasn't that thinking of Burger made the kiss seem any sweeter. It was only that it made her feel safer.

Chapter Twelve

On Sunday morning, having slept badly and not enough following her awkward parting from Michael Hurzony, Jenny woke Rachel and told her they were going out for pancakes. She was to get up and get dressed immediately.

"What happened to Family Day?" Rachel muttered into her pillow. "What about Grandma?" Before Jenny could frame an answer Rachel had closed her eyes and burrowed more deeply under her covers.

"We'll see Grandma later," Jenny said. "Right now I want you out of this bed, out of your pajamas, and into the shower!"

"Shit," Rachel breathed into her pillow.

"What was that? What did you say, Rachel?"

"I said 'Shit,' " Rachel hollered. "Shit! Shit! Shit!" For as long as she remembered having birthdays, Rachel had always been invited to design her own. What kind of cake, how many children, favors or no favors. A clown or a puppet show. And in more recent years, a movie or a slumber party. It was always her day, her decision. But today, when she was practically a teen-ager, her mother was yelling orders like some Marine drill sergeant. "I don't want go out for pancakes on my birth-day." There, it was said, just in case her weird mother had forgotten what day this was.

"Why not?" Jenny asked, flustered. She had spent a good portion of the night trying to figure out ways to defuse this day so that it could be held safe for Rachel. Ways that would keep all of her own will-Paul-call-or-won't Paul-call worries from spoiling her child's birthday.

It was too late to burst through her daughter's bed-room door with a hearty "Wake up, kiddo! You're twelve! Today's the day!" Too late to dummy up the hearty good cheer and shimmering visions of a boundless future that were supposed to infuse childhood birthdays. Once on Jenny's own birthday, Minna had awakened her with a cake, all of its candles blazing in the gray morning light of her small bedroom. She was younger than Rachel then, her mother already widowed, and she had thought, breakfasting on sugary store-bought birthday cake and ginger ale, that she had the best mother in New York City. It was too late for that, Jenny knew. Exhausted, she sat down on the edge of Rachel's bed.

"I thought that you were crazy about the blueberry pan-cakes at that place on Edgewood Avenue."

Rachel refused to open her eyes. She sucked in air and blew it out of her mouth so fiercely it was as if exaspera-tion had a taste she could not abide. "Not blueberry. Chocolate chip."

"Okay, then," Jenny said matter-of-factly. "Chocolate chip." Her head ached, her back hurt, and her legs felt numb with fatigue.

"Chocolate is bad for my skin. I don't eat it anymore." And then a silence as petulant as her words. "In case you haven't noticed."

Jenny ignored the sarcasm, too weary from lack of sleep and a head weighted with troubling thoughts of slim brown envelopes to explore what might be at the root of this sniggering behavior.

"Well, when you decide what you'd like for breakfast on your birthday, let me in on it," she said with forced patience. "I'm going back to bed for a while."

Rachel mumbled something unintelligible into her pillow before she turned her back on Jenny and feigned the even breathing of deep sleep. The only word that Jenny could make out was "phone." She tiptoed from the room as if she believed that Rachel really was asleep.

Stretching out on her own unmade bed, her hand stroking the comfortable bulk of the folded Sunday *New York Times* that lay beside her, Jenny thought that it would never end — Paul's brutality. In one way or another she would always be at the mercy of his demons. Hadn't he managed to destroy this day, his child's birthday, as cruelly as if he were actually here, delivering blows? There was a child in that bed down the hall who wanted desperately to have her father, to hear his voice. He knew that. He had to have known that or he wouldn't have called last night — so late last night. When he knew she'd be sleeping. When he hadn't called her in weeks. Sadistic, she had decided long ago, was not too strong a word.

It hadn't helped of course, that the babysitter's histrionic report of the phone calls had reached its highest pitch with words like "maniac, monster, criminal." "He was drunk, Mrs. Roo. Whoever that maniac, that obscene telephone criminal was, I'd bet my boots he was pie-eyed besides."

Mrs. Forester was a sloppy self-important woman who had left a sticky trail of melted ice cream from the kitchen to the den. Nevertheless, she had managed to intercept a phone call that Jenny was sure, by the lateness of the hour and the drunkenness of his voice, Paul had intended for her, not Rachel.

What had he wanted to say to her after so long a

silence? It was a question too frightening to summon answers — only more questions. What drunken words had he wanted to hurl across three thousand miles? With what hideous voice could he have spoken more loudly in her ear than the voice of her own fear of him had shouted in her head last night at Michael Hurzony's townhouse?

She had feelings for Michael. Tenderness, respect, and even a physical desire to know what such solid strength might yield in bed. But could she ever dare to count love among those feelings? No. No, the lonely, patient man who had wanted to make love to her last night could now be added to the list of men who had been left to mistakenly believe that Jenny had rejected them — when in fact they were innocent victims of Paul's. For all of the brave words she was able to put on paper, for all of the verbal agility with which she was able to write about feelings, to communicate intimately in the public space of a daily newspaper, when it really mattered, as it had last night, her vocabulary was impoverished. It lacked the word *trust*.

Michael Hurzony was a man she took seriously. A decent, gentle human being who she sensed had wanted only to give her pleasure last night. No, she chided herself as she plumped the pillows under her head and lay back again, that was a bit too Pollyanna. The man was a healer, not a saint. He had wanted to bring them both pleasure. But what mattered, what had mattered enough to keep her awake all night, was the realization that if she could not drop her guard for Michael Hurzony, Paul had left her an emotional legacy as permanent as scar tissue and ten times more cruel.

Rachel was up now. Jenny could hear her opening drawers and banging them closed. Making a noisy effort to disturb her mother's rest. She had a right, Jenny thought. Her child's anger was understandable, grounded in events she was still too young to comprehend, let alone control. By two o'clock this afternoon when Jenny would borrow a neighbor's van and drive ten squealing girls to a movie and a pizza parlor in celebration of Rachel's birthday, she knew her child would be happy again. Or at least less unhappy. But between then and now Jenny wished that Rachel had some other person at whom to direct her frustration. A brother or a sister to whom she could go quietly now and share the burden of a less than wonderful mother.

That too was Paul's doing, Jenny believed. Not only had he denied Rachel a father, he had also managed to steal the possibility that she might have a sibling. Jenny would never have another child. Not because of any damage he had done to her body. No, her gynecologist assured her annually that all of her female parts were in splendid working order. She supposed that meant things like uterus, Fallopian tubes — solid parts like that. Trust was an invisible part. A doctor could not be expected to notice that it was missing.

Later that day, Jenny would tell herself that the vision of Paul's dangling Rachel from the fourth-story window of a theatrical stage set had come to her this morning because she was so tired. Because she hadn't slept. Because she was so worried about Nina. Because she was so troubled by David Kalish's increasingly needy demands for attention. Because she was uncertain of her relationship with Michael. Because she was going to make her television debut in two days. Because her mother was senile. Because with all of those things on her mind she had let her defenses down. Why else would that nightmare return to her when she had managed to keep it at bay for a year and a half? It was easy to keep track of it because the last time had been on a holiday — Thanksgiving of the year before last. She had been standing at the floor-to-ceiling windows of the Kalishes' apartment looking out over Central Park.

A man, a tall red-haired man who in no way resembled
Paul, had been chasing a small child who was too bundled
up in a hooded snowsuit for Jenny to notice if the child
was a little boy or a little girl. And although she could
not hear them, she could see from the grinning, clap
-hands delight of the child as he led the man (also gri-
ning) on this merry chase through the playground —
under the swings, quick up the slide, down the slide,
through the bars of the jungle gym — that the man was
an adoring father, the child a happy toddler. So when
the man suddenly caught the child in his arms and in one
terrifying swoop hung him by his knees from the tallest
bar of the jungle gym, Jenny had screamed her surprise,
her terror for the child. The glass of wine had fallen
from her hand, crashing against the Portuguese tiles of
the Kalishes' living-room floor before she had ever seen
that the father still kept a firm grip on the child's back
and that the child was still grinning.

"What happened?" David and Nina had wondered at
once as they moved in to remove the shattered glass at
her feet.

"I don't know," Jenny had answered with embarrassment. Both Minna and Rachel had gathered around
her by now. She could smell the turkey roasting. "It just
slipped out of my hand." It would not do for a woman
just past thirty to tell her friends she had seen a ghost.

She saw it now. Again. On Rachel's birthday. The
white room with the huge white rabbit. The brightly
colored mobile that whirled above the white crib where
Rachel slept. The vision beyond reason, the memory she
prayed to forget.

Year by precious year Jenny counted the time since
that night on Fifty-fourth Street and thanked God that
Rachel had no memory of it. She prayed against what
she knew to be the very real possibility that Rachel
might someday lie on a psychiatrist's couch plumbing
the depths of her unconscious until one day (Jenny

always imagined it to be a very warm day in July, although she could not say why — the actual event had occurred on a rainy night in January) Rachel would bolt upright from the imaginary couch and scream, "Oh my God! I remember! I remember!" That, that imagined possibility that Rachel might one day awaken from the slumber of repressed memory, was Jenny's worst fear. So she prayed against it. Silent prayers in which she bargained with God: if she was a good enough mother, a devoted enough daughter, if she worked hard enough at being both a woman and a human being, Rachel would not remember. Rachel would not be Jenny. Rachel would live free.

In California it was zero hour for Paul Roo, the opening performance of *Pennydance*. The hour of reckoning he believed would toll his future. Much too nervous to remain inside the theater, he paced the sidewalk of a kitschy palm-fronted bar across the street. His body wired with pulsing energy, he shadowboxed an imaginary opponent and then stopped to check his watch.

Unless something unexpected had gone wrong, the final curtain of *Pennydance* would fall in exactly seventeen minutes. Paul's throat ached. In all of the months that he'd been dry he had never felt so sharp a need for a drink as he did in this moment. One drink, one four-ounce shot of scotch, neat, was all he would need to destroy the tension that needled through his spine as he waited.

He abruptly crossed the street, pushed open the heavy brass doors of the theater and took up his post beside the publicity billboard with the life-size silhouette of Jessica Meir, the star of his play. In three minutes the premiere of *Pennydance* would be theatrical history. Obscure theatrical history, Paul cautioned himself as he monitored the adrenaline kicking in, but still a moment that would not come again. He could stand here, out-

140

side the moment, or at its center. The choice was his. He
nodded silently to the usher who soundlessly opened the
interior door to the house, and entered the thick
darkness of the theater.

The scene being played on the stage fifty feet in front
of him was at once as familiar as his own name and as
mysterious as the birth that had proffered it.

He might wonder forever from what dark space he
had dredged these words and wonder beyond that to the
place where he himself had discovered the courage to
record them. What artistic impulse allowed the most
shattering events of his life to be crafted as an entertainment for strangers? To be rewritten, reshaped, recon-
sidered and redistributed with this ending.

They were at a wedding, his parents sitting on either
side of him at the white-clothed table, his father drunk
and stony-eyed as the band played and the bride and
groom danced their first dance. The bride lived in the
apartment across the hall from Paul and his parents. He
was eleven years old and had always thought that she
would marry him were it not for the yelling that could
be heard across the bannister. But now she waltzed in
somebody else's arms. "Love Is a Many Splendored
Thing," the slick orchestra leader in the white dinner
jacket crooned. And now the bandleader was motioning
for all the guests to join the fairytale couple on the
dance floor, and his mother was standing behind his
father's chair whispering in his ear with that faraway
look that came over her when she sat alone and watched
the old movies on television, and his father was not
moving and she was still whispering and he was still not
moving and the dance floor was full of couples whirling
and suddenly there was a crack louder than the orchestra and there was blood on his mother's fancy pink
dress and blood on the white tablecloth and someone
grabbed him and pulled him away, toward the dance
floor, where he wet his pants.

And now it was a play, and Jessica Meir was starring in it for scale salary because she too owed Phil Gruber. Because she too had done time at Glen Crest. Because she had once been a victim, and without Gruber she might have been a victim still. There was no actress Paul could name who could deliver his words better than Jessica Meir. They were the best words Paul had ever written. And the riskiest. With their delivery, he believed, rested the success or failure of *Pennydance*. He wished his mother were alive, her arm light on his shoulder.

He leaned against the cold back wall of the theater and closed his eyes. The music swelled on cue. He could see it all without looking. Jessica was standing down-stage left, her white arms outstretched, her face shining in the pinspot.

"Dance with me," he heard her say. "Just this once, Victor. It won't cost you a penny. You'll owe nothing, I promise. Only dance with me." Her voice was as sure and strong as the words would allow.

Paul opened his eyes in time to see the couple dance and the curtain fall. He heard the music fade and sneak under. For heart-stopping seconds there was the absence of sound that seemed to him as permanent as the earth's silent creation. And then it broke, and the applause thundered with a power that took his breath away, and the cheering rolled and stormed and pounded through the theater, and they were calling his name and Gruber was at his side and the huge arms were propelling him down the aisle.

And then Paul was on the stage. Alone. Blinking against the shimmer of the lights that blinded him and the tears that burned in his eyes. It's possible, Gruber had said. Maybe, it's possible. You can win Rachel back. In the shimmer of lights, Paul saw that it was. He took a bow. The audience seemed to expect it of him. Tomorrow he would call Rachel and ask to see her. And suddenly Gruber was on the stage behind him, pounding his back, and Jessica Meir was crying in his arms and the audience was still standing and whistling and clapping and, yes — he would call Rachel. No maybes.

Jenny had nearly succeeded in falling asleep when the telephone next to her bed rang.

"I'll get it," Rachel yelled. "It's probably someone calling about the party. You don't have to wake up, Mom."

You see, Jenny smiled to herself as she drifted into a dreamless haze, you don't have to wake up, Mom. Little Rachel Sunshine is herself again. Jenny made a half-hearted attempt to straighten out the sheets she had twisted while experiencing the vision, and crawled under the covers. The last thought that crossed her mind before she fell asleep was to wonder what restaurant Steve Burger would take her to afer she went on the air Tuesday night. And whether or not he'd actually pop for the check.

"Mother!"

"Mmmmmm?"

"Mother, wake up!"

"Mmm? Mmm?"

"Mom, wake up! You won't believe this! That was Dad! On the phone! Mom, are you awake?"

"Yes."

"Listen! Daddy just called me. His play? You know, *Pennydance, Pennychance*, whatever it's called — the one with Jessica Meir in it? Well, it's a smash! A great big supercolossal humongous hit out there! Can you believe it? And wait until you hear this — oh Mom, I can't believe it myself! Some big producers want to bring it to New York. You know, like for Broadway! And guess what my birthday present is? I mean from Dad?"

"I can't guess," Jenny said.

"Well, then," Rachel said, bouncing on the bed beside her. "I'll tell you. I get to be his date. For opening night. On Broadway!"

She did three cartwheels across Jenny's bedroom floor and landed on the bed. "I can't believe it!" she squealed as she fell upon her mother and covered her face with wet exuberant kisses. "I just can't believe it! Him and me — on Broadway! Just the two of us!"

PART II

Chapter Thirteen

Over my dead body.

The words had been drumming against the walls of Jenny's head for two days now.

Over my dead body. A relentless pounding that threatened to crack her skull, to tear at the tissue of her brain. To bring on madness.

In the pizza parlor where Rachel blew out her candles and announced to her assembled friends that not only did she have a famous mother, but she was about to have a famous father too, and wasn't she the luckiest twelve-year-old in America . . .

Over my dead body.

In the den on Sunday night while David Kalish installed the video tape recorder, explaining to Rachel as he worked that not only could she run her favorite movies on this birthday present of his, she could also tape her mother's Tuesday-night television appearances.

"And the Emmy awards!" Rachel hooted when he

had the thing hooked up and was playing back tonight's episode of *Sixty Minutes*. "And the Grammys! And the Oscars! And what's the one for the Broadway plays, David?"

"The Tonys."

"Right!" Rachel hooted, "The Tonys! Right, Mom? She had elbowed Jenny with an exaggerated wink. "We can watch the Tonys. Unless, of course, I happen to be actually attending the actual real thing with . . ."

Over my dead body.

"I don't think I heard a thank-you to David for this extravagant gift, Rachel." From Jenny, in a voice not her own.

"I have thanked him about two zillion times, Mom. Haven't I, David? Why do you have to keep sounding like such a mother tonight?"

Over my dead body, Paul. In the supermarket checkout line on Monday morning. In the bank. And all through last night. Louder in the night, louder than any words she had ever spoken, but unmistakably uttered in her own voice.

And now again. *Over my dead body.* You'll have to kill me before I'd let you near Rachel. Before I'd let you see Rachel, before I'd let you lay eyes on her. I wouldn't let you take her as far as I can spit. I wouldn't let you. I'd get a restraining order. A court order, Paul. I'd hire a bodyguard. Six bodyguards.

Tonight, after the show, she would ask Steve Burger if he had any clients who employed bodyguards. It would be three months before Paul came to New York, he had told Rachel. At least that long. She had plenty of time to hire someone. Until then David had agreed to babysit Rachel on Tuesday nights. Readily agreed.

Think about something pleasant, she instructed herself. They were the same instructions the therapist at the women's shelter had given her years ago when the nightmares had still been rending her sleep. When the visions would suddenly appear to haunt her daylight hours. Before time had lulled her into what she now realized was a false sense of security. But that was over now. Now she could see. Now she could understand. As long as he was alive in the world she could take nothing for granted. Nothing could come freely. Not even breathing.

Over my dead body.

"What's that you're saying, Mrs. Roo?" Robin, the makeup man at ATC's New York studios asked as he stood back to gauge the shade of pancake foundation he had just patted over her face and neck. It was a twitch too pale, he decided. It needed warming. "I didn't quite catch that, hon."

Jenny sat perfectly still. Her eyes closed, her hairline and neck swathed in white gauze. Don't call me hon, she thought, as she fought the impulse to open her eyes. "Call me Jenny," she told Robin. "Don't call me Mrs. Roo."

"Well, Jenny honey, it would be better if you didn't talk right now. Not while I'm doing your colors for the first time. Later, sweetie. When we get to know each other and I can do you sort of on automatic pilot, then we'll talk. We'll talk all you want. But right now, hon, I've got two anchors, a weather and a freckled sports waiting and I can't get your tone to come up to save my life. My instructions from Pablo were Honey Porcelain, but that can't be right. You're too pale. If I did you in Honey Porcelain you'd look like something out of *The Midnight Special.* I can't understand it," he said, his own face drawn into a mask of consternation.

Reaching over Jenny's shoulder, he picked up the printed instruction sheet labeled "Jenny Roo — Tuesday Late Only" that lay on the mirrored makeup counter cluttered with bottles and jars of creams and foundations, sponges and brushes of all sizes and shapes and a rainbow palette of eye colors.

"Honey Porcelain. That's what it says here. You don't have a little cold, do you, hon? Maybe a teensy virus that's draining your color? Pablo's almost never wrong."

"No," Jenny whispered, "I'm fine." Her left cheek twitched suddenly. "I don't have a cold." She kept her eyes closed against visions of Paul and Rachel together in a dark theater.

Oh my God! Robin thought as he saw the left side of Jenny's face moved involuntarily. Oh my God! Did they know to shoot her from the right? Were the production people aware of this twitch? Never mind, he thought as he applied Toasted Amber blusher to Jenny's cheekbones. He would tell them if it continued. Probably it was opening-night jitters. Only that. Hadn't he once had a brand-new female co-anchor wet his chair her first night? Was that at CBS Minneapolis or NBC Philadelphia? He couldn't remember. There now. The Toasted Amber was doing its stuff, she was warming up for him now.

"Fabulous eyes," he said. Not just to soothe her nerves, but because it was true. "Luscious lids, Jenny. Positively luscious lids. Plenty of room to play with color. You're going to be sensational tonight, sweetie. I just know it. I always know a winner when I see one. Even with a naked face, I said to myself when you walked in here tonight, even with a naked face this woman is dynamite. I don't have to wait for the ratings. I know a winner when I see one." See, she hadn't twitched at all while he spoke. It was just nerves. No special camera instructions, after all. He really was a genius.

"Can I talk now?" Jenny whispered hoarsely.

"Sure, just puff out your cheeks while you do. That way I can give these terrific cheekbones their due while I contour."

"I do commentary. Do you know that, Robin?" Terrific cheekbones, luscious lids. It really was too much. Opening night on Broadway. Over my dead body. "I'm not auditioning for any chorus line here tonight. I do commentary.''

Goodness, goodness, Robin thought, aren't we just a mess of quivering nerves tonight. God spare me women who take themselves seriously. "Well, of course I know you do commentary. I mean you're a real writer. I read your column in the *Times* regularly. Wouldn't miss it.''

"The *Trib*,'' she corrected tonelessly as he brushed finishing powder over her entire face and neck.

"Well, of course the *Trib*,'' Robin giggled. "Silly me.'' He patted her draped shoulder. "Now if you'll just move over to the next chair, the one to the right, Ceceil will touch up your hair so that it's not quite so stiff in profile. Okay, hon? And I can get to work on Larry here.''

Jenny had been too ridden with anxieties to even notice the entrance of Larry Stone, the Channel Ten anchorman, into the brightly lit makeup room.

"Howdy,'' Stone greeted her as he plopped himself into Robin's chair and stretched his long legs. "How's our brand-new commentator doing tonight?'' he asked amiably. "Any butterflies need taming, send 'em over here. I'll beat 'em into submission.''

Jenny was surprised to see herself smiling in the mirror. All the rumors of the aging glamour boy with an unbridled ego that she'd heard about Stone flew out of her head for this one casually extended kindness. He was not, she noticed, wearing burgundy tonight.

"No. No butterflies,'' Jenny said. "Actually, there were butterflies about an hour ago, but they talked themselves into being caterpillars again and crawled straight back into their cocoons.''

Larry Stone laughed out loud, oblivious to the fact that Jenny could not keep herself from staring at the sight of a rugged male face whose beard was being covered with gauze while pancake makeup was being applied to his skin. "You're a sharp lady, Jennifer Roo,'' Stone said as Robin worked on him. "I hope the

ATC brass upstairs are smart enough to appreciate how much class you're lending to our tired forces. Listen, Jennifer, I just get a lick and a promise from this stud,'' he said as he closed his eyes for Robin's makeup sponge. "Wait up for me, will you? I'd like to run through that intro one more time before air."

They had been through it four times yesterday on the set. There were cue cards, a Teleprompter and a script typed in letters an inch high to cue him. He had been anchoring television news for eleven years, Burger had told her. What could go wrong with a fifteen-second introduction?

Walking down the corridor toward the elevator that would carry them to the Channel Ten news studio, Jenny felt increasingly self-conscious. The only time she had been so made up, so painted, so done, was the day before her wedding when Nina had insisted upon treating her to a full day at Elizabeth Arden. Facial, massage, makeup, hair — the works.

"Listen, Nina," Jenny had argued. "I'm getting married in the woods, not at the Miss America pageant."

Standing beside Larry Stone now, and looking up at his artificially applied ruddiness, she couldn't shake the thought that with their painted faces and their fixed smiles they resembled nothing so much as a pair of Ken and Barbie dolls who had been mismatched for size.

"I read your segment," Stone said as they entered the elevator, his hand lightly on her back. "It's wonderful."

Jenny smiled carefully.

"I'm not just saying that, Jenny. It really is a fine piece of writing. Tight, well paced. Very professional."

Jenny sighed. What had he expected, after all? She'd been writing such pieces for nine years. Maybe she was the Tuesday-night new kid on the block, but that didn't make her a novice. "I'm glad you liked it," she said, holding the fixed smile. "Now, what was it that bothered you about the introduction?"

Stone grinned as the doors opened and they stepped

out of the elevator. The toothy megagrin that network insiders said had won him the anchor spot to begin with. He was the only anchor in New York City who could report the death toll from a five-alarm fire with tears glistening in his blue eyes and segue into a smiling account of a woman being appointed to the Cabinet, without missing a beat in facial expression. The grin did it for him. The grin said, It's okay, folks. This is the news. Good, bad, and ugly. This is life. This is the way it goes. The grin was his facial punctuation, Jenny thought.

"The intro?" Stone said. "Oh that. There's nothing wrong with the intro except maybe it's not as flattering as you really deserve. I just wanted to spend a little extra time with you in case . . ."

"In case what?"

The grin had dissolved into knit eyebrows, earnest concern. "In case you're shaky," he said in a low voice. "The first time out is not a picnic, Jenny. We all know that. We all understand. There's nothing to be ashamed of if this is beginning to feel like aerobic exercise about now." He opened the heavy door to Studio 4D.

Oh hell, Jenny thought. Didn't anyone around here understand that compared to the rest of what was running through her mind tonight, delivering four minutes of television time on the subject of the city's homeless *was* a picnic? She didn't need all this. Not the street-shrink rambling of a makeup artist or the hand-holding of this polished Mr. Nice Guy. She was looking forward to her four minutes. Her material was solid. Her voice was strong in spite of her thoughts about Paul, and she was wearing her good-luck navy-blue pumps. She would do just fine.

It was only when the chilled air of the excessively air-conditioned studio hit her full blast and she approached the blinding lights of the set, that her legs began to quiver. It didn't matter, she thought as she seated herself slowly at the small curvilinear blue desk placed to the left rear of the big white anchor desk. No one would see her legs. The desk, built especially to suit her size, her coloring, and her desire for something both serious and feminine, would hide all that. For all that the viewers could see of her she might as well be wearing a half slip and sneakers with her royal-blue silk blouse and white jacket.

"You look fabulous," Art Kronigsberg, the show's director, whispered as he clipped the small microphone to Jenny's white wool crepe lapel. "Simply fabulous." Clipping on microphones was the job of the floor assistant, not the director, Jenny could see as she looked around at the other people settling into their appointed chairs. This was more special treatment.

"Thank you," she said as Kronigsberg fiddled with her jacket. "Does this mean we're engaged?" she said as she looked down at his hands on her lapel. "Or do we get lavaliered in between?"

"Let's get a voice check," Kronigsberg called to his sound man, ignoring her nervous, schoolgirl joke.

"We already did, boss," someone called out from the dim cavernous space behind the lights. "That's a live mike, Art. Congratulations to the happy couple."

It wasn't much, that joke, but it was enough to break the ice that was beginning to form around Jenny's resolve to "be fine." While the cameramen dollied their cameras into position and the Teleprompter was wheeled up and into view, Jenny observed the easy banter and innocuous jokes that flew about the set. She was dead on with her fraternity-pin joke, she thought. These people, all men except for the floor manager and one young girl in jeans who functioned as Robin's on-set assistant, were probably as close as the members of any Greek-letter society. Twice a night, five nights a week they came together to practice their rituals in this huge cold space in the middle of Manhattan. It wasn't, she decided as she saw the girl fluff powder over Larry Stone's face while he smoked one last cigarette before air time, just the news that brought them together. It wasn't just a job they all shared. No, the Channel Ten News Team, she surmised, was as intimate a jumble of nerves as any initiation ceremony. They got powdered and sprayed together. Their fates were bound in the numbers called ratings. If one fluffed, missed a cue or otherwise came unglued, the others fell as predictably as if they were all joined at the hip.

She would not be part of that joining, she realized as she heard the *Channel Ten News* theme come up and watched, fascinated, as the opening graphics and film montage of New York City rolled on the studio monitor. Tuesday night would not be enough to gain her admittance into this nerve-ridden club. The best she could do here was to function as a weekly court jester.

And then, in the sudden and absolute quiet, the floor manager raised her right arm in a fist and one by one lowered her fingers, a silent countdown to live broadcast.

Now she could hear Larry Stone's voice — not his "howdy how you doin' " voice, but the smooth resonant tones of the anchorman. And she saw in the monitor that the face was not the one she had seen painted, but the one she had seen on her own screen in her own den in her own house.

And there was camera three, the one she had been told in a brief technical rehearsal would be on her, rolling toward her and she saw the red light and she heard Stone say that she was "the nationally famous syndicated columnist for *The New York Trib*" and that he knew how much "you folks" had been looking forward to "our special Tuesday-night Eye on the City segments" and the "unique blend of insight and humor that Jennifer Roo brings to the Channel Ten News Team." And even as she held her eyes steady against the red light and smiled the smile of knowing intelligence that Art Kronigsberg had further described as "ladylike seduction," she was seized by a powerful, almost physical urge to rise at her blue curved desk and holler, "Over my dead body, Paul! Over my dead body!"

She resisted the impulse and began instead to speak the words that she had written, revised, rewritten and finally polished for this moment. In a strong friendly voice that needed no coaching, no entreaties to lightness, she began.

"Good evening, I'm Jennifer Roo, and during the last few months I've done some research on you. Most of you, I've learned, are watching me from home . . . in bed . . . under the covers." On cue the camera pulled back for a long shot of Jenny at her desk. "Here in this television studio there is no bed and there don't seem to be any blankets around either." Now the camera came in for the tight close-up of Jenny's smile. "But the lights are warm here, and the company's good, and if for some reason — a snowstorm, a power failure — I couldn't get home tonight, the thought that I could find shelter here is comforting.

"But for thousands of New Yorkers there are no beds, no blankets, and no shelter tonight. These are the people with no place to go — the homeless, the souls with portable lives . . ."

In the corner of her eye she saw Art Krongisberg beaming and raising his clasped hands in a gesture of triumph.

An hour (to the minute, the second and the millisecond) after the floor manager had signaled ON THE AIR, the red lights went out. The cameraman on camera two picked up his *New York Times* and took off his headset. Art Kronigsberg lit a cigar. Larry Stone fumbled under the anchor desk, got up and crossed the set to where Jenny sat grinning her own grin, and poured a bottle of champage over Jenny's carefully coiffed head.

"Bravo Jenny Roo!" Steve Burger thundered from a folding chair that she had not known was there in the dim light of the back of the studio. "Bravo! Bravo! Bravo!"

"Spare the applause," Jenny said as she stood and looked straight into the merciless lights, her clothes soaked with champagne. "I'm starved, Burger. Where are you taking me to dinner?"

"Any place you want to go," he said as he hugged her.

Chapter Fourteen

"I feel like a kid," Jenny said when she and Burger were seated in the rosy glow of a table at Le Brioneze. "Like it's Prom Night or something and I never want it to end. All hyper and flushed and full of magic."

Burger offered her an indulgent smile. "The next time you make your television debut," he chuckled, "I'll get you a wrist corsage."

Between the first pouring of the wine and the uncorking of the second bottle, Jenny felt the alcohol take hold, spreading a kind of liquid warmth through her tense, tightly held body that made her feel more free, more fluid and more connected to life than she had felt in many days. Since Paul's phone call on Sunday she had felt herself trapped in some dense, gelatinous sea of dread that threatened to drown her. Now, when it was well after midnight in this posh, dimly lit restaurant, and she sat observing her wry dimpled agent, she thought that she might be glimpsing the lifeboat. It was creaky and it probably leaked, but it was out there.

Steve Burger was too old, she had warned herself during the brief crosstown ride from the studio. Too old, too paunchy and too many times married. And furthermore, what made her think that he might be interested in her at all? It had been ages since she had consciously attempted to attract a man; she had probably lost the knack. Certainly he had never given her any encouragement. Bravo, Jenny Roo! Bravo! Bravo! Big fat deal, she told herself. Stroking egos was part of an agent's job. Hand-holding, massaging away insecurity — that's what you paid them their ten percent for. Never mind what terrific deals they brought you. The hugs, Jenny reminded herself as she watched him banter with the maître d'. I pay him ten percent for hugs.

Now, with the wine prickling through her body like a trail of tiny flashing electrodes, she sat back in her chair and brazenly studied Steve Burger's face, tracking clues to his new appeal. Because there was no one else to tell it to, she had been forced to admit it to herself: the excitement she had felt in anticipation of this night had more to do with the possibilities of a leisurely evening spent with Burger than with the brief novelty of being on television.

From the moment Burger had surprised her by offering to host her celebration dinner, the prospect had been her singular diversion.

Burger, for once dressed with the kind of expensive elegance that befitted his stature in media circles, appeared younger and more vital to her than he ever had in the cluttered surroundings of his agency office. But clothes were just window dressing, she decided, thinking vaguely of David Kalish's slavishness to fashion. She leaned forward to examine Burger's eyes as she swallowed the last of the wine in her glass. She believed with the dead Clara Roo — her mother-in-law — that the eyes were the window to the soul. On this measure Burger disappointed her. His eyes were ordinary. No remarkable shade of brown, no flecks of green or gold to catch the candlelight. Nothing special in the eyes, she noted sadly, except the heavy lids and the small pouches underneath that signified overwork. He would make a great Italian character actor, Jenny thought as the waiter refilled her glass. Perfect for the role of the one lonely Italian on the all-Irish detective squad who goes after the mob and ends up collaring his own cousin Nando.

"Do you know what you're missing, Burger?" she interrupted in the middle of his joke about a client of his who was senior White House correspondent for one of the networks.

"What?" he said, ignoring the interruption. "What am I missing, Jennifer?"

"Luscious lids!" she giggled, her fluttery hands upsetting her wineglass.

"Come again?" he said, signaling the sommelier for a fresh glass and a new bottle of the Puligny-Montrachet he had ordered in advance.

"Luscious . . ." she repeated with the breathy Marilyn Monroe voice she had not used since the senior-class variety show at Sarah Lawrence. ". . . lids!" she drained her glass, encouraging the playacting.

"Ah, rats, my darling," he said, trying for Cary Grant but coming up closer to Edward G. Robinson, "you weren't supposed to notice so soon." For a moment he toyed with his silverware. "Jenny," he finally asked in his own deep, cigarette-raspy voice, "what the hell are luscious lids?" His dimples, she decided, were caverns where she might crawl in and hide.

"Oh!" she squealed as if she were still Marilyn and Marilyn had just been pinched unexpectedly. "Oh! I thought you knew, Steven. I thought you knew about *everything!*" She lost Marilyn when she attempted the wide-eyed innocent stare and tried to lick her lips at the same time. She was supposed to be asking him about bodyguards, but God, this was good wine.

It wasn't his mouth either, she decided as she watched him chew on a celery stick. The lips were too thin to be sensual, she thought as she slowly ran her fingertips around the edge of her glass. And dry. Too dry for anything but rough kisses. Damn it! She was doing it again! Fantasizing his kiss. First in Michael's arms, an incident that burned more with embarrassment than with remembered passion, and now again, when she was actually within striking distance if by some miracle he should key into her secret vision and actually reach for her.

Without warning the small, elegant dining room seemed to Jenny to be swaying; the crystal chandelier above their heads to be dipping just a bit. A gentle swaying, in no way menacing. Rather a sensation of being protectively rocked. Sweetly cradled.

"How old are you, anyway?" she blurted. The sexy petulance was gone from her voice now, replaced by something urgent and genuinely needy. "I mean actually."

"Actually," Burger said as he looked nervously around their table, "I'm old enough to know better than to pour you any more of this wine."

"You think I'm drunk!" Jenny shouted in the hushed room.

"No, no, Jennifer." Burger smiled. "You got it all wrong, sweetface. I don't think you're drunk. I'm positive that you're drunk."

"Loose," Jenny said as she tried to meet his level gaze with a lopsided smile of her own. "Not drunk. Just loose."

"Have a dinner roll," Burger said, passing her a silver tray. "You probably didn't eat before the show. Probably you're pouring all this wine into an empty stomach."

"You're so smart, Burger," Jenny whispered right before she passed out across the table. "You really do know everything."

He lived in the same East Side brownstone in which he officed. Jenny hadn't known that about him until she found herself in an ample wood-paneled study whose balcony offered a full view of the offices below.

"It was better when I was poor," Burger was saying as he placed a steaming mug of coffee in her cold hand. "In those days I let the client pick up the tab and I drank the wine."

Jenny sat back on the overstuffed leather sofa and sighed. "I don't know what else to say, Burger. Except that I'm sorry. And terribly embarrassed. And very angry at myself." God, but she sounded ridiculous to herself.

"For what?" Burger said, reaching over from the hassock on which he sat opposite her, to lift a strand of damp hair from her forehead. "You were entitled to a hoot, Jennifer. What do you suppose, Jenny? People just walk in off the street and sit down in front of a TV camera and then they feel nothing when it's over? No charge? No jolt? They feel it, believe me. I know these people. They feel it. And when it's over they feel it, too. The letdown, the decompression, the emptiness."

She sipped slowly at her coffee and fought back tears. Emptiness. He knew about emptiness. Maybe he really did know everything.

"You were terrific tonight, Jenny. The material was solid — visual as hell the way you described those folks sound asleep, curled up in doorways, spread out on park benches clutching everything they owned while they slept."

"Including the benches. Did I say that? Did I say they also clutch the benches?" There were parts of this night that had flown from her. Parts that were, she feared, irretrievable.

"Yes, including the benches. You said that."

"Good," she breathed. She curled her legs up under her. "That's an important part of it. More than squatter's rights, you know. More like staking a claim that even sleep can't threaten. The rest is portable. The shopping bags, the crummy tattered blankets, the layers of smelly cast-off clothing. All that can be moved. But the bench is fixed. If they're lucky it will be there for them the next night. But there are no guarantees." She closed her eyes for a moment, as if she were viewing her own video tape as it had been transmitted to viewers all across the city. "Portable lives," she said softly when she opened her eyes to Burger. "If I had done that piece for print, I would have called it that. 'Portable Lives.' " She reached for a hand-crocheted lap blanket at the end of the sofa and covered her legs with it. Briefly, she wondered who had made the blanket. How many of Burger's clients had ever been up here in the middle of the night?

"Well, whatever you might have labeled it in print, it was terrific for TV. And you delivered it like the pro you are. I was genuinely proud of you." He stood up then, with so obvious an air of businesslike finality that she feared he might actually reach out and shake her hand before ushering her to the door.

"I drank too much," she said sharply, rushing to fill the silence, "because there's more on my plate right now than I can handle." She did not want to be hurried out of this comforting space. Did not want to go home and answer to David Kalish's mother-hen questions: "Jesus, Jenny! It's four o'clock in the morning! I was worried sick! Alone! In the city! No place I could call. Where the hell were you? Didn't you even think about us? About Rachel and me? What were you thinking?"

I was thinking, Jenny imagined herself responding, that I would like to wrap myself up in this blanket and go to sleep for the rest of my life with Burger watching over me.

Burger's voice startled her as he moved to sit beside her on the sofa. "Your friends again? The ones who are splitting up? Didn't I warn you about that? Didn't I tell you to stay out of other people's marriages? That it was a no-win ball game?'' He stood up suddenly, as if to begin the lecture all over again. Or maybe, it occured to Jenny, to talk about his own failed marriages.

"No," Jenny answered, lowering both her voice and her eyes. "It's more than that."

"Your mother?" Burger said as if he were reciting these possibilities from a list all agents were required to memorize before they could sign their first client. Your children? Your lover? Your tennis elbow? Your bank account? Your cocaine habit? What, sweetface?

Sweetface. What did he call the men? Jenny wondered. How much of his time was he forced to dribble away in behalf of other people's problems?

"Do you know what you are, Burger? Do you know what separates you from all the other shine-and-sign agents in this town?"

"No," Burger laughed, aware of the fact that he was being parodied. "What?"

"You're the only one who represents the whole client. The talent, the warts and the craziness too. You're holistic, Burger. You're the first holistic agent in history."

"Great," he said tonelessly. "They'll carve it on my tombstone. I'll get points in Agent Heaven. Now what's the story on your mother?"

Mack. He probably called his male clients Mack.

"It's sweet of you to remember, but it's not my mother. Well, it is, but it isn't. Minna is difficult, no doubt about it, but sooner or later everybody's mother is difficult. Right? I'm doing what I can and I cry a lot on the Second Avenue bus. But it's not my mother." She saw that her coffee cup was nearly empty and looked blankly around the room.

"Rachel?" There was concern in his voice now, Jenny thought. Authentic human concern. She ought to tell him. There was no one else to tell. For that reason alone she ought to tell him.

"Only peripherally."

Burger stood up and paced in front of her, his hands laced behind his back. "Only peripherally? It's after three in the morning, Jenny. Don't give me 'Only peripherally.' I don't play Twenty Questions, but if I had to guess, it wouldn't be vegetable or mineral."

"You'd be wise," Jenny said softly.

"Animal," Burger said, stopping his pacing directly in front of where she sat. "Male variety."

"Bingo!" Jenny's throat ached suddenly. The ache of constriction, the pain that comes when jagged-edged words that need to be spoken are swallowed instead. She mustn't talk about Paul. Not here, not to Burger. Personally, professionally, and in every other way she could think of it would be a mistake. It was too bizarre a story. Too many times she had tried to tell it and been diminished in the process. Too many sessions with counselors, shrinks, and most of all with the critic who lived inside her own head, had ended with dismay, puzzlement and, ultimately, disbelief.

How in God's name had such a strong, talented, happy woman gotten herself into a marriage with so treacherous a man? How could she have stayed with him for so long? How could she have rationalized behavior that she knew with every fiber of her being was abnormal? How? How? It must be that she was stupid. Or too smart. Or too blind. Or too damaged. She did not want to be damaged; for Steve Burger she wanted to be whole. No torn places, no ripped seams.

"Here," he said, passing her a box of tissues from one of the bookshelves that lined the room. "You're crying, Jennifer." As though she were too frozen where she sat to feel the tears. Again, she realized that there was no one else to tell. Nina was gone. David was too needy himself. Her mother bounced in and out of the present as though time were a room with rubber walls. And she could not frighten Rachel. There was no one

else to tell. She wiped her eyes with the tissue and
cleared her throat.

"Do you remember that when I first came to you I
was married?"

"Yes," he answered patiently, "and then a few years
later you were divorced. Right? Around the time of the
first printing of *Natural Ingredients*?"

"Close," Jenny said. "Close to that time."

"A playwright, I think. Unproduced. Peter, Matthew.
A name like one of the apostles."

"Paul."

"Right. Paul."

Burger tried not to look at his watch, tried not to prod
her while she sat silent and still on his sofa. She would
talk when she was ready to talk, not before.

"You don't know why we were divorced," she said,
staring straight ahead into a wall of memory that was
built mostly of secrets. Bricks of avoidance laid with a
mortar of lies.

"No. You never told me and I figured it wasn't my
business. You kept working and your work got better.
There was no reason to know."

Jenny looked up at him and smiled. You kept working. It was like a vault, her work during those years. A
place where she could lock up. A compartment of her
mind that was impenetrable to the world outside. Work
and Rachel, in a safe-deposit box of her own making.

"We were divorced because he abused me," she said
thickly. She had expected that with the speaking of
those words the sky would fall. The earth would open
and she would go pitching head first into a velvet-lined
abyss where the walls were so soft that she would never
know or care to understand where she had fallen. She
would only that she was falling free.

Burger's voice came to her as if through a tunnel.
There was nothing in it to identify this moment, this

place as the site of her fall. "What does that mean, 'he abused me'?"

"He hit me," Jenny said. "He punched me. He threw things at me. He smashed things over my head." Her voice was dry and dead as leaves before they are burned. "He's a batterer. I was his victim." Her eyes never moved as she said it.

Everything Burger had ever wanted to say to someone in pain stuck in his chest. Every joke, every compliment, every word of consolation that he had ever offered to anyone was struck dumb when he looked at Jenny Roo. He moved to hug her, but she held him off.

"After the divorce he moved to California. Rachel was four when he left. He calls her once a week. In seven years I've never heard his voice. They have a code. He fixes it so that she knows when he's calling. I've never heard his voice. Except in my sleep. Except in nightmares. Except when I'm exhausted and I can't sleep. Then I hear him. And see him." All of this, Burger saw, all of this spoken with her eyes so flat and fixed he knew that she must be seeing him now. That that man, that animal, that flesh-and-blood disaster was as real a presence in his own home as he was. Maybe more real.

"Where is he now, Jenny?"

"In California. In California," she repeated as though something inside her head had snapped and the words were reverberating, echoing out of control. "In California. But he's coming back, Burger. He's coming back. Here. To New York. To where Rachel is. To where I thought we were safe. We're not safe, Burger. We're not safe anymore, are we?"

He couldn't listen anymore. He couldn't for one minute longer watch her grow more and more like a stone-eyed zombie, a cold statue of a woman who had begun tonight more alive and aware than anyone he had ever known. He was losing her. She was losing herself.

"No," he said more loudly than he had intended. "No," he whispered again as he pulled her up into the forced comfort of his arms. "No," he told her as he patted her head. "No, Jenny. No, sweetface. You got that wrong. You'll still be safe. Trust me."

Chapter Fifteen

"Sensational," Rachel shouted as she burst through the
front door when Jenny pulled her car into the driveway
the next morning. "Sensational! Awesome! And . . .
poignant, Mom," she gushed as she hugged her mother,
a buttered bagel in one hand and an unfinished book
report in the other. "Truly poignant." It was nearly
eight o'clock as Jenny reached down to pick up the morning newspapers that lay on the front walk.

"Who gave you 'poignant'?" Jenny asked as she
slung an arm over Rachel's shoulder and reached for the
bagel. Burger had provided her with every comfort save
sex and food, and now Jenny was ravenously hungry.

"Everybody," Rachel answered when they were in
the kitchen and Jenny had kicked off her shoes and shed
her wrinkled white jacket. "The entire world. David.
Mrs. Wasserman. Dr. Hurzony. Practically the whole
neighborhood called to say how great you were. The
phone kept ringing until way after midnight. David said

that if we were a telethon, we'd have raised a million dollars. I mean it, Mom. Everybody called. I'm so proud of you! Even your hair looked good. And that makeup! I almost didn't recognize you, you looked so gorgeous.''

Jenny threw a wet dishrag at Rachel and poured herself a brimming glass of orange juice. "I tried to call you, too, Rach, but the line was busy every time. You weren't worried, were you? I mean about my staying out all night.''

"Of course not," Rachel said with what she hoped was an understanding and maternal smile. "You're a big kid, Jennifer. I trust you.''

Role reversal, Jenny thought. I'm the kid and she's the all-knowing, all-forgiving, benevolent mommy. Since Paul had called it seemed that Rachel was taking increased pleasure from playing that particular game. As if a new character had entered the cast of this family drama and all of the existing roles had to be rewritten while he waited in the wings to make his entrance.

"You look so tired, Jennifer. Why don't you lie down for a while before you start to type your column.''

"Oh Jen, forget about the dishes. Just go out and have fun with Dr. Hurzony.''

"Want me to go with you to visit Grandma? I know it's tough on you to go alone.''

Jenny tried to ignore it. The exaggerated concern, the patient, long-suffering tone of voice, and the bemused half-smile that said, "Oh poor Mom, I really do worry about you.''

"How about David?" Jenny said as she rolled up her sleeves and cracked eggs into the skillet. "Was he frantic?''

"Nope. I don't think so. He figured that you and all the other celebrities from Channel Ten were out some-where having a beautiful people party. We made brownies and popcorn. Both in one night. He was terrific.

Sorry, Mom, but nobody worried." Rachel shrugged. "Want some brownies? We saved a few."

Jenny sat down at the kichen table and tried, through the thick layer of fatigue that encased her brain, to figure out how to word her next question without making her fear contagious. From what distance of non-concern must she speak of Paul?

"Sure," she said as she sat down on the kitchen chair and rested her legs on another. "I'll have a brownie. Where's David?" she asked, postponing her real question.

"Still asleep," Rachel said, pouring Jenny a glass of milk to go with her brownie. "Please, Jennifer," Rachel smiled indulgently, "don't ever tell your friends I gave you brownies for breakfast. And by the way, I think your eggs are burning."

"Enough!" Jenny commanded as she stood up to examine the smoking skillet. "I can handle it from here. Hurry up or you'll miss the school bus, Mama Rach."

"I'm not taking the bus today," Rachel said as she sat down at the table and resumed work on her unfinished assignment. "I'm riding my bike."

Jenny's question flew out of her head. Instead it flashed through her consciousness that children who were abducted, children she read about or saw snapshots of on the evening news, were often reported to have been riding bikes when last seen.

"How come?" Jenny asked as lightly as she could considering that the sharply focused image of Paul hiding in the landscaping somewhere along Rachel's route to school refused to dissolve.

"Because it's Bicycle Safety Day," Rachel said without looking up. "Some cop from the Scarsdale Police Department comes over to school today and checks out chains and tires and stuff like that. And if you need a license, you can get it right there at school. I don't need one. Mine's good until next year. Now, if you don't mind, Mother, I need to finish this dumb book report before I leave." Was that petulance in her tone, or exasperation? Jenny couldn't judge.

Never mind which, Jenny told herself. Ask. You need to know. Ask. "Rach? You said everybody called last night. What did that mean, *everybody*?"

Rachel rolled her eyes and put down her pen. "You're really getting off on all this attention, aren't you? I already told you. A whole bunch of neighbors. Mrs. Wasserman. Dr. Hurzony. A few cousins from New Jersey I never even heard of. I wrote down their names next to the phone in the den. That's it."

"Nobody else? Nobody unexpected? Someone you'd never guess would even know about it?" If Paul were in New York sooner rather than later . . .

"Oh my God!" Rachel gulped. "I completely forgot! Nina. Nina called from Chicago. She'll call you again next week. Now I've really got to hustle." She gathered up her work and put it into her notebook, opened the refrigerator to grab her lunch bag, and stuffed it all into the green canvas backpack she strapped around her waist. " 'Bye," she said, kissing Jenny's cheek and examining her skin at the same time. "You really do look tired, Mom. No joke. Why don't you take a nap this morning? And maybe next week, when they put the makeup on you, you should pay attention and learn to do it yourself. See you later," she called as she went out the door.

Jenny tossed the remains of her scorched eggs and half-eaten toast into the garbage disposal and tiptoed up the stairs. Passing the closed door of the hall bathroom, she could hear the sound of rushing water that meant David was already in the shower. She relaxed a little. Through the half-opened door of the extra bedroom across from Rachel's, she could see that his clothes were as neatly aligned on the smoothly made bed as any men's catalogue display.

This room, with its small clock-radio, its consistently empty flower vase, and the badly sagging bookshelves that held old paperback books too good to be discarded but too dog-eared to command space among the enduring hardcover titles that lined one wall of the living room, had been described to her as "the small but charming guest room" when the real-estate agent had first shown Jenny the house.

"I can't imagine who would use it," Jenny had said as she cocked her head into the bare, freshly painted little room. "I mean who might actually sleep here."

The agent, a twitchy divorcee in her early forties who believed that under all that sisterhood crap divorced women shared only the miserable quest for the too few available single men in this world, had eyed Jenny's small lithe body, appraised her naturally curly hair and asked her who the hell she thought she was kidding. "Handy little room," she had said, patting the doorframe and continuing down the hall to extoll the virtues of the master bedroom.

It had been a handy little room, Jenny grudgingly acknowledged as she entered her own bedroom and closed the door behind her. Her mother had slept in it countless times on Sunday nights when Jenny was too tired to drive her back to the city. And in recent years when elderly widows in Minna's Second Avenue apartment building had been mugged and Minna, to use her words, was feeling "briefly rattled," the room was there for her. How much better, Jenny mused as she pulled off the clothes in which she had slept, to feel briefly rattled than to go through life endlessly afraid.

Yes, it was a handy little room. One drawer of the secondhand dresser that stood as solitary mismatched company to the sagging double bed in that room still held a few of Minna's elaborate lacy nightgowns from her years in Macy's lingerie department. A once white bathrobe printed with rosebuds now hung gray and faded from a hook Minna had hammered in herself. Hooks, she had assured Jenny with the nail between her teeth, were the hardware of the fleeting visit. Long-term guests required towel bars and shoe racks. "Two hooks," she had announced as she struck with the hammer, "will suit me fine."

Jenny stripped off her underwear and ran the water for her own shower.

She loved the small windowed shower stall beyond her bedroom. In the apartment on West Fifty-fourth Street there had been only a bathtub and a flimsy plastic curtain to protect her from Paul, and no matter how many locksmiths she paid to secure the bathroom door Paul had still managed to shatter it repeatedly. But this space was different. From the square window that began at eye level she could watch the brightening of the morning sky. From here she could admire the leaves changing in autumn. And here, with no sound save the rush of the water, she could be free to think her own thoughts, make her own discoveries.

"Trust me," Burger had said to her last night, "you're still safe."

"See that, Jenny," she said against the rush of the water, "you're still safe. You're safe — maybe, but you're crazy for sure." Maybe she was being too hard on herself, but the idea that she had, for even one moment, considered Steve Burger as a candidate for romance was so mortifying to her now that instinctively she turned off the water and stood shivering in the full power of discovery so long overdue.

Burger as lover, Jenny thought. Talk about unnatural! She expected that if she were to examine her body right now every inch of her skin might be tinted with a permanent blush. And she knew, in this moment of realization, exactly what Steve Burger was a candidate for — *Daddy*. The benign compassion he had offered her last night was not a lover's shelter; it was the unconditional advocacy and protection of a father.

Perhaps she had known this last night. Perhaps she had only managed to block the thought until now, when she was alone. But sometime this morning, in those unconnected moments when dawn had made the lamplight in Burger's study seem garish and somehow sad, she had awakened on the sofa to find her head in his lap and his hand absently stroking her hair. Burger himself had sat slumped against the back of the sofa, his mouth slack in sleep. She had tried, with as little movement as possible, to reclaim the precious comfort of her own unconsciousness. To hold on for just a moment longer to the forgiving oblivion of sleep. To hold at bay the blurry awareness at the back of her mind.

But now, fully awake and chilled with the self-discovery of how she had managed to deceive herself, there was no place to hide. She wanted a father. A daddy who would stroke her hair and tell her funny stories about snuggling up to the Statue of Liberty. Her own father, the warm flesh-and-blood dragonslayer who had sat on the side of her first real bed, had died too soon. He had explained away the shadows and vanquished the bad dreams of her childhood, but when the real adult monster of Paul threatened her, he was gone.

"This time," he would say if he were here now, "this time I'll get it right. This time I won't die so soon. This time, sweetface, I'll take you to the fireworks and to the Bronx Zoo and Madison Square Garden. And this time I'll be around to screen your boyfriends. And I won't let you marry that snake. This time I'll be there when you need me."

By the time David Kalish knocked at her door she was sound asleep, scudding through a dream in which Larry Stone had tripped on the slippery floor outside Studio C, and, with only minutes to air time, she was being pressed into service as the Channel Ten anchorwoman.

"Hold it!" she kept shouting at Art Kronigsberg as he clipped on her microphone. "I can't do this! I'm not prepared! I'm not a big enough kid yet!"

"Bad dream?" David said as he crossed the carpet and sat down on the edge of Jenny's bed. Jenny grabbed for the covers and sat bolt upright. Later she would remember that as she came crashing out of the dream it was not his voice or his touch that identified David. It was the spicy smell of the men's cologne he used too much of that she recognized. That and the red terrycloth robe she had given him last Christmas.

It looks good on you, she nearly said as she secured the sheets around her body. "Not bad exactly," Jenny said, her voice husky with sleep, "but definitely interesting. Was I loud? Could you hear me shouting?"

David smiled. "No, not loud. But I could see you struggling. Was it about Paul? About his coming here? Rachel told me. Was that your nightmare?"

"No," Jenny said flatly. "Not this time." She rubbed sleep from her eyes. "Rachel told me Nina called last night. What's happening?" She tried very hard not to notice that he was naked under the red robe.

"Not much," he said as he propped a pillow on the empty side of the bed and stretched out on top of the covers beside her.

"What do you mean, 'not much'?" She tried to ignore the fact that at nine o'clock on an ordinary Wednesday morning they were alone in her house, lying on the same bed, each of them wearing almost no clothes, while they talked about an absent woman who was her best friend and his wife.

David rolled over onto his side and leaned on his elbow. "Well, it was after one o'clock when she called. Mostly I think she was surprised to find me here. She was calling you, after all, wanting to know how the broadcast went. She wasn't expecting to talk to me, so it was kind of stiff. Kind of awkward."

Kind of stiff. Kind of awkward. Jenny's muscles

tensed. It was as if with those words he had read her mind on the subject of this moment.

"I hope," Jenny said in a voice aiming for lightness, "that you explained what you were doing here at that hour. That you were babysitting for Rachel." Her eyes sought a crack on the ceiling of her bedroom, a place where she could focus her eyes as David drew slowly nearer.

"I didn't explain anything, Jenny," he said softly. "I played it her way. Sketchy information. Nothing solid. Nothing to hold on to. Let her think what she wants to think," he said in a voice heavy with innuendo.

"You want her to think that we're lovers?" Jenny shot back. Her eyes had left the crack on the ceiling and were now focused clearly on David's face. "I can't believe that! You actually left her with the impression that we're living together? That we're sharing the same bed?"

And she knew then, when he took her face in his hands and kissed her, that in some way she could not explain she had invited that kiss. Not with an inadvertent slip of the tongue. Not by the ironic suggestion that they share the same bed when in fact at this moment they already did. That was not where the invitation had come from. It had come from need. Her need, his need, a mutual longing to connect. To draw from that connection the energy to survive in a world where the currents ran against you as often as they ran with you. It was the sweetest, purest kiss she had known since junior high, but she drew back from it.

"We're friends, David," she said with finality. "We've known each other forever and we're practically family and . . ." She lost her train of thought when he kissed her again.

"I think," she whispered, "you're doing this for all the wrong reasons, my friend."

"I'm doing it," he said, tracing her profile with his

fingertips, "because I want you. Don't try to make it more than it is, Jenny."

I don't have to try, Jenny thought as she rolled onto her stomach. She turned her head away from him on the pillow.

"Listen, David," she said as she stared at the wall, "I think it's possible that you believe that. I think that what we have here may be just an old-fashioned case of horny and homeless. Two cases, in fact." His sigh was so deep that she not only heard his expired breath, she could also feel it on the skin of her bare shoulder. She had wounded him. An unintentional wound, but one she nevertheless regretted.

"For the record, my friend, if I had known you could kiss like that four years ago, I would have stolen you from Nina then. But not now, David. Tempted? Yes. I'd be a liar not to admit that. And I can think of a hundred preludes to sex less wonderful than friendship. But right now I need the friend a whole lot more than I need the lover."

It was a longer speech than she had intended to make, and it was full of murky half-truths, but in explaining it to him she had made it clear to herself.

The silence and stillness on David's side of the bed lasted a long time. Long enough to make Jenny wonder if she hadn't gotten it wrong. Maybe David, with his pure sweet kisses and his confused unconditional need, was exactly the protector she was seeking. Maybe the solution to all her problems was lying right beside her and she was a fool to turn her back on him. Maybe she would write a column on clichés and write the lead paragraph on the one that claimed that the Lord Works in Strange Ways.

"Me too," David said, startling her in the silence. It was a voice so full of resignation that she sensed the mattress sagging as she felt him get off the bed.

"Me too what?"

"Me too needs a friend more than a lover." Jenny drew the first free breath she had taken since he had walked into the room. "But just for the record, Jenny?" David said as he paused with his hand on the doorknob.

"What?"

"Your ex-husband must have been some kind of crazy to let you get away."

Jenny swallowed hard and ignored that. "Will you tell me what Nina said?"

"Nina said she was confused."

Jenny burrowed more deeply under the covers. "What else is new, David," she said as he left the room and closed the door behind him.

Some kind of crazy, Jenny heard again as she prayed for sleep.

Chapter Sixteen

Jenny ignored the ringing telephone outside her study door as she worked against deadline on her column. Her long nap following David's departure had put her behind schedule and she was feeling the pressure. Rachel would get the phone. Since Rachel had been old enough to open a can of chili and take a decent phone message, Jenny had taught her that on Wednesday nights she was on her own until that door opened. Sometimes it opened sooner and sometimes it opened later, but the rule was that it be opened from Jenny's side only. Under no circumstances was she to be interrupted while she worked. So when Rachel barged through the door to tell her that Burger was on the phone, all of her gratitude and affection for the man were lost to irritation. She ought never to have confided in him.

"I'll call him back," Jenny said, waving Rachel away. "And how many times must I tell you that when I'm in here working —"

"It's not *Mister* Burger," Rachel said importantly. "It's somebody else. With the same name. And almost the same voice, except not so tired. What should I tell him?"

Jenny shuffled the pages of copy that lay on her desk, decided she couldn't compete for the Pulitzer every week, and said she would take the call at her desk. "Close the door behind you," she told Rachel as she reached for the phone.

"This is Jenny," she said, beginning a silent word count of her copy. "Who's this?"

"This is Jake Burger," came a voice with no hestiation. "My father is your agent."

"Oh," Jenny said. And then, considering that she had so recently entertained the fantasy of Steve Burger being her own father, she promptly ran out of things to say.

But Jake Burger had a lot to say, and it seemed to Jenny that he couldn't get it out fast enough. "It was my father who suggested that I call you," he began quickly. "Actually he suggested it a long time ago, but I just got around to it. You see, I'm doing this story about print journalists going electronic and he thought that, well, since you're just starting to do electronic, I could sort of catch you at the starting gate. That was his phrase, by the way — 'starting gate' — not mine."

"Slow down, Jack," Jenny said, "I'm not sure I'm following this."

"Jake," said Jake. "Not Jack. A lot of people make that mistake. Try remembering that my name rhymes with fake."

"Oh, I certainly will remember," Jenny said, completing her word count and pushing her copy aside. "Who's this story of yours for, Jake? Who do you work for?" It was unlikely, Jenny thought, that a son of Steve Burger's would be employed by any scandal sheet, but the offspring of successful parents sometimes rebelled in strange ways. And then a thought crossed her mind that was even more unsettling: given his father's clout in the world of media, it was probably some big-time publication that would give her just the national visibility she was so eager to avoid. Either way, she decided, she was going to turn him down.

"I don't work for anybody," Jake Burger said quickly.

"You're a free-lancer?" Jenny asked, her interest momentarily heightened by memories of her own shaky year spent writing on speculation. No contracts, no advances, no security. A lot of query letters and a lot of tuna fish was how she remembered that time. The fact that her time of professional struggle had coincided with the one year of her marriage free of abuse was a memory she chose to forget.

"Not exactly," Jake Burger said. "I'm a graduate student at Columbia Journalism. The story would satisfy a course requirement." It all came out in a stream, as if he had one breath to spend on this information and no more.

"Oh," said Jenny, again searching for words that refused to come.

"Say, didn't my father ever mention any of this to you?" For the first time, Jenny heard less than complete confidence in this person's voice.

"No, he didn't," Jenny said honestly. And then she flashed back to her own student days in journalism school and added, "But I'm lousy at remembering that kind of stuff."

"I'm a fan," Jake said. "A big fan. He must have told you at least that much."

"Of course he did," Jenny lied. All that she knew of Burger's children was what she had seen in the framed snapshots that cluttered his desk along with the apple cores and the big-figure contracts. Two boys and a girl. One blond boy, one redhead with frosty blue eyes, and the daughter whose features were vaguely Oriental.

Each one, Jenny had speculated, the child of a different mother. All of them appearing to be somewhere the ages twelve and fifteen. She wondered briefly if Jake was the blond kid or the redhead and exactly how outdated the photos were.

"Yeah, well, you probably get a lot of requests for interviews. He told me you would probably turn me down."

"I'm not turning you down," Jenny found herself saying.

"Terrific!" Jake said. "How about tomorrow?"

Tomorrow she was planning to visit her mother. Tomorrow she was going to call Nina in Chicago; and since it was evident that David Kalish's offer to stay with Rachel on Tuesday nights was creating more problems than solutions, tomorrow she had also planned to interview a few candidates from the Westchester Agency. An altogether lousy day, tomorrow.

"Tomorrow's fine," she said on impulse. "But it has to be morning."

"No kidding?" His husky voice was suddenly boyish.

"No kidding," Jenny laughed. "Where do we meet?"

"Can you handle Morningside Heights? We could start at my place if the neighborhood doesn't throw you. Columbia's not exactly in Westchester County, you know."

Brassy kid, Jenny thought. "Where's your place?"

"Riverside Drive and One Hundred and Twelfth Street. Not exactly your kind of neighborhood."

"I'm a big girl," Jenny said. "I can handle it."

Slowly circling the blocks around his deteriorating apartment building across the street from Riverside Park, Jenny was convinced that she had made a mistake. A big mistake. Not only were there no available parking places here, she realized as she rechecked the automatic lock button that secured all of her car's doors and windows and closed her sun roof, but an early April heat wave had drawn every junkie and wino normally floating around upper Broadway toward the park today. From Needle Park to Grant's Tomb, they had flocked to the green oasis.

"Spring fever comes to beautiful Morningside Heights," she whispered to herself as a scabrous half-naked man stumbled in front of her car, a brown paper bag clenched in his hand. Ten-thirty in the morning — Whoopee Time! Twice, while she had been stopped for red lights, teenaged boys had whistled and yelled Spanish obscenities while pounding on the hood of her car. If you had half a brain, she scolded herself, you'd get the hell out of his neighborhood, hit the West Side Highway, and go see your mother. A visit with Minna would be lots more fun than this.

On her third pass in front of the address Jake Burger had given her, a massively built young man wearing a purple muscle shirt and white jogging shorts signaled frantically for her to pull over. She looked straight ahead and ignored him. That's it, she told herself, no more. I'm getting out of here. But a double-parked station wagon cut her off before she could get away, and the broad-shouldered jogger was suddenly yelling through her closed window.

"I'm Jake!" he shouted with a huge grin spreading across his wide mouth. "Read my lips! Pull over and let me in!

"I told you parking was tough around here," he said when she released the lock button and let him in. "Didn't you see me waving the first two times you passed?"

"Of course I did," Jenny lied. "I just thought you had missed your float in the April Fool's Parade out here today."

Jake laughed, a much lighter laugh than his father's,

although in person his speaking voice was much as Rachel had described it — almost like Burger's, but not so tired. "There's a blue Toyota pulling out up there. See it? Grab it!"

Maneuvering her car into the space, Jenny got her first look at Jake Burger, albeit a side look. Thick brown hair laced with gold streaks identified him as the blond child in Steve Burger's collection of snapshots. But those photographs had to be at least ten years out of date, she concluded as she cut her wheel a final time and turned off her ignition. The man sitting beside her was no kid. Twenty-six or twenty-seven was what she guessed.

"Gorgeous day," she said dumbly when he came around and opened her door for her — a gesture that surprised her, a chivalry she knew he had not learned from his father. In fact, now that she had a good look at him as they began walking along Riverside Drive, she saw that apart from the brusqueness of the voice he resembled his father not at all. Not from Burger had he acquired those deep-set gray eyes hooded with thick black lashes. Not the high cheekbones or sharply defined jaw either. Whoever his mother is, Jenny thought, she's a looker. Only the broad nose in the middle of Jake's otherwise striking face saved him from prettiness. Jenny imagined that a gifted sculptor had carved that face, and that by the time he came to crafting the nose he had grown tired of delicate chiseling and just roughed it out.

As he gradually slowed his pace to match Jenny's shorter strides, she wondered if Steve Burger had ever had a body to compare with his son's. And if he had, how many client dinners at places like Le Brioneze had ruined it? It was impossible to imagine his aging, pouched face set above all that well-toned and muscled youth walking beside her. And then she quickly looked out toward the river, away from Jake Burger. Physical attraction, even the first vague stirrings of it, made her intensely uneasy.

"Intimacy problems" was what the best-selling pop psychologists called her pattern of withdrawal from men. Occasionally she would stand in bookstores and thumb through such books, thinking that she would like to lead all these easy-answer how-to authors on a tour of every battered-women's shelter in the Western Hemisphere. When they had seen the welts and the bruises, the scars and the lumps, when they begged to be spared the sight of one more wired jaw or burn mark, she would end the tour. Now, she would say to them, go back and write the book that says how to get past all that you have just seen. And when you've done that, send me a copy. And this is how I'd like it inscribed: "For Jenny — who still wants it, but is afraid she'll get it."

Across the street the warm breeze coming off the Hudson River ruffled the trees in the park. Beyond the stone retaining wall at the park's western edge, the river lay like a huge blue gemstone in the brilliant sunlight. If the weather held out, Jenny reminded herself, she could use her theory about good weather lowering the hostility index in New York on the air next Tuesday night. Maybe she would try it out on Jake. She certainly couldn't think of anything else to talk about. Although the silence that hung between them as they walked the blocks toward his apartment seemed to trouble him in no way, she was growing more uneasy with every step.

"How did you recognize me?" she asked too brightly. "I mean when I was driving past."

"From TV," he said.

"Oh." Oh. Oh. Oh. What fascinating conversation you offer, Jenny. I'll bet he just can't wait to do this interview so that he can record a few more of your scintillating and profound ohs, she told herself. But the fact was that she had no idea what she should be saying to this person, or, for that matter, what she was doing in his presence at all. Burger, she told herself. You agreed to this meeting because you owe Burger so much.

Two young black women, their corn-rowed hair braided with elaborate ribbons and feathers, pushed baby carriages toward them. "This is a fascinating neighborhood," Jenny said, seizing the opportunity to fill the silence. "Are those women students, do you suppose? Faculty wives? Members of some neighborhood collective?" The questions came out in a staccato rattle, an audible echo of her nervousness as she walked beside him.

"I really don't know who they are," Jake said when the women were behind them. "Why? Do you want to write about them?"

"No, no. I just wondered." They were crossing 113th Street now. In moments they would be in his apartment. Jenny's palms were damp as she pushed up the sleeves of her white silk shirt. "Listen," she said abruptly, "it's a gorgeous day."

"I know that," Jake said with that wide smile spreading across his face as though he knew a whole lot more. "You already said that."

"Yes, well I guess I did. But what I was thinking was . . . I mean it seems a shame to go hole up indoors with all this free sunshine out here. Maybe we could just cross the street and talk in the park."

"I would need to get my tape recorder," Jake said. "Unless you object to my using one with you."

"No, no. That's fine. Maybe while you go get it, I could walk up to Broadway and find us some grocery store that has cold drinks. My mouth tends to go dry when I talk for long periods of time." And also when I'm shaky, she thought, when I'm nervous.

"Terrific idea!" said Jake. "There's a great deli right around the corner and up the street from my place. Get some sandwiches too. I'll grab a blanket. We'll make a real picnic of it. Here," he said, reaching into the pocket of his shorts and handing her a ten-dollar bill. "Go for broke! Sandwiches, chips, pickles, the works.

I'll meet you in front of my apartment building in ten minutes.''

"What kind of sandwiches?" she asked, raising the ten dollars to her eyes to shield them from the dazzling April sunlight.

"Surprise me," he said as he began walking away. "I'm not fussy," he called over his shoulder as he turned the corner.

She had taken no more than ten steps when the tattooed arm came around her neck and clamped against her mouth. "I ain't fussy neither," the voice in her ear thundered. "Hand over the ten and your pocketbook and you live to be an old lady. Holler and I shred you up like cole slaw." She could smell the wine on his breath, felt its heat in his hand, and against the back of her neck she felt the prick of the knife blade. Her body went limp. Let go, the voice in her head screamed, let go! The money and the pocketbook fell to the pavement when she opened her clenched fists. "Burger!" she screamed as he pushed her to the pavement. "Burger!" She blinked, just blinked, and he was a streak of blue running toward Broadway.

"I can chase him, or I can take care of you," Jake Burger said seconds later when he dropped to his knees beside her. "I'm going to take care of you." Gently, he lifted her trembling body from the sidewalk and carried her away from the curious crowd that had gathered around her. "You've got a scream like a siren, Jennifer Roo," he said, walking slowly to the door of his apartment building. "You could wake the dead in New Jersey." He carried her into the elevator. "Damn it! I never should have let you go alone!"

"It's not your fault," Jenny muttered in a voice so weak she could not identify it as her own. "I said I was a big girl."

"Not that big," Jake said, holding her closer in order

to turn his key in the lock of his apartment door. "Two more steps and I wouldn't have heard you scream. I would already have been inside. Jesus!" There was sweat running down his face as he laid her on the sofa of his sunny sparsely furnished living room.

"I'm fine," Jenny whispered, trying to raise her head. "Really. I'm fine."

"Right," he said as he pressed a cold washcloth to the skin wound on the back of her neck. "Sure you are. That's why your whole body is shaking, right? Because you're fine. That's why your eyes are frozen like twin ice cubes, right? Because you're fine. Ah shit! I never should have let you go alone!" There were tears in his deep-set eyes as he leaned over her and wiped her face with the washcloth. "I'm so sorry. I'm so sorry, Jenny."

Paul used to do that, Jenny thought as she instinctively brushed at his tears. Cry and tell her he was sorry. So sorry. After he hit her. After he threw things. After he made her bleed. She lay back against the sofa and willed her body to release her from the fear that was coursing through her blood, tying knots in her lungs, strangling her heart.

"It's not your fault," she whispered against Jake's face as he bent over her. "This is different. It's not your fault. You didn't mean for this to happen. You didn't try to hurt me."

"Oh no," Jake cried. "Of course not, but if it weren't for me you never would have been in the neighbor —"

"Ssh," Jenny said, closing her eyes. One day at a time, girl, just one day at a time. . . . Things will turn out. . . .

"You're shaking so," Jake said. "Please try to stop, please."

"I'm cold," Jenny said. "That's why I'm shaking. Maybe I'm in shock. I'm so cold."

Gently, so gently that she barely knew that she was being moved, he turned her on her side and tucked a heavy wool lap blanket around her. It was not a replica of the blanket on his father's sofa, but it was crocheted with the same yarns, crafted in the same colors.

"I'll make you warm," he said as he smoothed the blanket over her shoulders. "I want to make you warm."

"I need to believe that," Jenny said.

Jake looked down at her, his body relaxed but his face so drawn with intensity as he stared at her there that a new wave of tremors began in Jenny's legs. And then he crossed the room and sat down in an overstuffed chair and continued to watch her.

"Believe it," said Jake.

Nobody moved.

Chapter Seventeen

Standing naked in front of her dresser, Jenny pawed through her underwear drawer.

"Mom!" Rachel called, coming up the stairs. "I'm leaving!" She came into Jenny's room carrying the bright-yellow duffle bag that her friend Patience had given her for her birthday. "The Wassermans are honking their horn for me in the driveway."

"Okay, kiddo," Jenny said, giving up her search for the perfect bra. "Have a super weekend and be sure to thank the Wassermans for everything."

"I will."

"And, Rachel?"

"What?"

"Promise me you won't pick the fastest horse there. That you won't gallop when everyone else is trotting."

"Mother!" Rachel moaned in her World's Most Exasperated Daughter voice. "It's a *breeding* farm. I already told you that. Saratoga is where they breed these horses, not where they ride them. Only jockeys get to ride them."

"Just be careful, Rach. That's all I'm asking."

"I promise I will," Rachel said. And then, fearing still more maternal warnings, she switched the subject. "What are you going to do while I'm gone?"

"I'm going to be interviewed," Jenny said.

"Like that?" Rachel said, her feathery eyebrows arching. "Naked?"

"It's an in-depth interview," Jenny said with a straight face. But then, seeing the confusion in her child's face, she quickly hugged her and told her that that was just a joke. She was only kidding. Really, she was only going to take advantage of the marvelous spring weather and putter around the garden. "Now scoot," she told Rachel, hugging her one last time. "Have a great spring vacation and stay off the fast ones!"

As soon as she heard the front door slam, Jenny went back to her underwear search. It was a miracle, she told herself as she finally found the lacy powder-blue bra she had bought for the dress she wore to the Kalishes' wedding. A miracle that she should be standing here on a Saturday morning, consciously searching for seductive underwear. A miracle that she was, for the first time in so long, allowing herself healthy sexual fantasies. "Not just allowing," she said to herself as she smoothed on body lotion, "actually summoning them."

Since Jake Burger had ridden with her to her mother's apartment two weeks ago, insisting that she was still a little shaky and ought not to be behind the wheel by herself, she had been living a vivid and fertile dream life. It was as though that portion of her imagination that had been shut down for so long had suddenly been reactivated and, clang! out came fanstasies so ripe and juicy they made her laugh out loud with the joy of their creation. Jenny and Jake on beaches, Jenny and Jake beside mountain streams. Jenny and Jake on the floor of a forest. The smell of pine needles. At the supermarket, she bought a pine-scented room freshener and sprayed it all over her house.

Fantasy, Jenny knew, was a long way from reality, a long safe distance away from actually getting into bed with Jake Burger. But to even think about it, to sit at her desk and imagine it, to crawl into her bed at night and go to sleep pretending he was lying right there beside her, was a small step that felt like a long journey to someone who had been paralyzed for so long.

Yesterday they had lunched together, meeting for the first time since the day she had been mugged. And even in the smoky, raw business atmosphere of The Press Club, she had sensed that the attraction was mutual. Within seconds of his arriving at the table she had reserved, he was examining the back of her neck, running his fingers over the place where the knife blade had grazed her skin. Catastrophe had given birth to a spontaneous intimacy. It would not have surprised her if he had leaned down and kissed the red scratch marks before he sat back down and opened his menu. He hadn't done that, of course, but still it would not have surprised her.

Instead, he sat down and looked around the room. Not the head-popping, celebrity-hunt look around the room that Minna had given this place when Jenny once brought her here, but a quick survey of the surroundings before he turned his gaze directly to Jenny. "Do you come here often?" he asked in a voice so low it seemed to Jenny to vibrate.

"Never," said Jenny.

"Then why today?" Jake had asked. In well-tailored street clothes, with that honey-wheat shock of hair brushed away from his face, he looked older, more substantial somehow.

Jenny smiled. "When I was in journalism school, I

would have sold my soul for a look at this place. I always pictured it as wall-to-wall Sulzbergers. I thought you'd get a kick out of it.''

"I do," Jake had said. "I do get a kick out of it." And then that wide smile took over his face and it seemed perfectly natural that he should reach for her hand. And that she should let him take it.

She had talked to herself the whole way back home. "Not thirty yet," she told herself as she drove. "But closer than I thought. Twenty-seven. Okay, he's twenty-seven. Fine. Twenty-seven." And then she had changed lanes and told herself that it didn't matter how old he was because her clock had stopped with Paul's beatings and she had been in a holding pattern ever since. But any minute now she could really fly. "You see that, Jennifer," she had yelled through her open sun roof, as though there was a Jenny in the sky somewhere who had the courage and the good sense the earthbound Jenny could never quite get cooking at the same temperature. "You see how all those years of arrested development finally pay off!"

By the time he actually rang her front doorbell this morning, she was lotioned and sprayed and buffed and brushed into a shining frenzy. You smell like a goddamn flower shop, she told herself as she tucked her royal-blue silk shirt into her jeans and checked the mirror one last time. The silk-and-jeans combination way of resolving all questions of dress for this day. She had no idea what Jake had planned when he had asked to spend it with her, but she figured that if this shirt had been good enough for the hundreds of thousands of people who had seen her wear it on television, it must be okay. And the jeans would take care of the rest. She readjusted her bra straps one last time and ran down the stairs.

"Here is what I've learned about you since yesterday," he said as he stood on her front porch, the screen door between them. He made no move to come in. He just stood there cataloging her past. "At Sarah Lawrence you were lousy at math and good at everything else. You took the TV job for no good reason except that it was offered to you. The *Trib* syndicate pays you a lot less than you're worth to them, and the American Television Company pays you more than you're worth. And you like expensive restaurants."

"You've been talking to your father, Jake," Jenny interrupted. It made her laugh out loud to hear herself described in this deadpan, Maxwell Smart delivery of his.

"Right! Also, your book is in its fourth printing and all of the royalties are automatically transferred to your managed reserve account. You have a daughter, you're divorced, and you're devoted to your mother." He paused for breath. "And you're a terrific little Miss Fix-it when it comes to other people's problems."

"You have definitely been talking to your father."

"Yes, I have. And it's definitely not enough. I need more. Let me in."

She opened the door, and, as he stood in the center of her living room, if he didn't feel immediately at ease in her home, at least, she saw, he had the good sense not to fake it. "Well," he said, swinging his arms in wide athletic circles as he took in the pristine white area rugs and the collection of crystal animals that lined a tall étagère that was lit at each level, "it's all very complete, isn't it?"

"I'm comfortable here," Jenny said, sitting down on the sofa, "if that's what you mean."

"I mean," he said, glancing from the brass andirons at the fireplace to the small gallery of lithographs and oil paintings that lined the room, "it all seems very finished. Very — permanent."

"I never thought of it that way," she said, standing up to pull dead leaves off the dieffenbachia plant in front of the windows, "but I can understand why you would. Student apartments are not the most settled of spaces."

Jake laughed nervously and ignored the reference to his own life. "I like it here," he said with absolutely no enthusiasm. "Show me the rest."

She walked him straight through the kitchen past the smell of freshly brewed coffee and the homemade banana bread that sat on the counter — a ridiculous advertisement of her modest domestic skills. From just such homey little touches, she decided, his awkwardness grew.

"Come see my garden," she said, heading out the back door. "You want chaos and confusion?" she said as she surveyed the empty clay pots and huge plastic bags of potting mix that made an obstacle course of her small patio. "Here it is. Nature's own."

"What's this?" he called, walking quickly away from her and crossing the patio and the slightly elevated lawn to where a patchwork of red, purple and yellow tulips stood proudly behind a line of lacy white hyacinths. The sun was warm in this corner of the backyard, and last year she had finally gotten the spacing right.

"My bulb patch," Jenny said, coming up behind him.

"Looks pretty good. How come yours are so much healthier-looking than the ones in my window boxes?" he asked with strained politeness. "Mine won't bloom until next month."

"I force them," she said, hoping to provoke interest with irony.

"What?"

"I put them in my refrigerator and that makes them bloom earlier and more profusely."

"Oh," he said, hooking his thumbs into the pockets of his slacks. "I wouldn't have known that." His deep-set eyes, squinting against the sun, seemed to disappear into their sockets. She could not read his face at all out here, but in this place that was to her the closest thing to a sanctuary she had ever created, his voice was full of clumsy pauses and awkward words. Never trust a fantasy, she cautioned herself. Not completely.

"Can we go in now?" he asked after a particularly long silence punctuated only by the sound of two yellow jackets circling the flowers.

"Sure," she said, a little sad that he had turned his back so soon, but more confused by the growing sense of unease that made it hard to believe that just yesterday he had held her hand all through lunch with no awkwardness at all.

"Let's have a picnic!" Jenny said as soon as they were in the house. An unplanned invention to get them away from here, to quickly remove him from all of this suburban domesticity that was either boring him into silence or giving him the creeps. She wasn't sure which, but she knew that banana bread was not the ticket. "We owe ourselves one," she smiled. "Want to go back to Riverside Park and try again?"

"No," Jake said, pouring himself a cup of coffee from the pot on the kitchen counter.

"Central Park?" Jenny suggested. The city was a good idea. He liked the city.

"I don't think so," he said, looking directly at her.

"Want to drive to the country? There's a duck pond not very far from here. I'm long on stale bread. What do you want to do?"

"I want to kiss you," he said, putting his coffee cup on the counter and coming toward her. "First I want to kiss you, and then we can feed flowers to the bumblebees if that's what you want, but first I want to kiss you."

Jenny stood dumbly in the middle of her kitchen and inhaled. "That's fine," she whispered.

"That's fine?" he hollered so loudly that at first she was frightened. "That's fine? I also want to hug you. Is that fine too?'' She wished only that he wouldn't shout.

"Yes," she whispered as she moved into the circle of his arms, "that's fine too."

"Good," he said, lifting her off the ground so that their lips were only inches apart. "I'm glad that's fine. I'm delighted that it's fine." And then he kissed her, a kiss so long and deep, so full of joy and discovery, that the kitchen, the garden, the whole house at 14 Cherry Hill Lane slipped away, and the world went with it. Her tongue traced the fullness of his lips, and she clung to him until he set her back down on the floor.

"Is that how you treat all of your interview subjects?" Jenny said with her arms still around him, her fingers exploring the muscles in his back.

"You just stopped being an interview subject," he said, kissing the top of her head.

"What am I now?"

"Anything you want to be!" Jake said.

He sounded exactly like his father, Jenny thought.

"Can I be Barbara Walters?"

"Sure." He grinned. "But why would you want to be?"

"Oh," Jenny said, standing on tiptoe so that she was tall enough to kiss his broad nose, "so I could ask you a few outrageously personal questions."

"I'm twenty-eight," Jake said. "Let's go feed the ducks."

There was, in the soft easy joy of the day, only one hard place for Jenny — and that place was memory. The place where the warm tingling happiness she felt with Jake touched the cold toxic ground of Paul.

Only his return, Jenny thought as she watched the ducks scramble and fight for the bits of bread she cast upon the water, could spoil her contentment. Was happiness, she wondered as she watched a fierce mallard steal the crumbs from the other ducks, like bread? Was there only so much of it to go around? Did the most ferocious always get there first?

Everything, it seemed to Jenny as she stood in the park with Jake's arm around her, everything she had ever dreamed and worked for and cherished, Paul had threatened. He had made a torture chamber of the home she had labored to create. With wild drunkenness he had attacked the career she worked to make for herself. And what mattered most to her, the child she would lay down her life for, was now his pawn, in a game so treacherous it made her tremble to think of it.

"You're shivering," Jake said as he tightened his hold on her. "Let's go back to the car."

This too, Jenny thought as she rode beside Jake through the streets of Manhattan, when he comes back he could threaten this too. She reached for Jake's hand. No, goddamn it! No! Over her dead body would he steal her happiness. There was no way he could take Rachel. No way he could spoil the perfection of this day. To even think of him now was a sign of her weakness. Bury him, she told herself. Bury him! She turned on the car radio to silence the screams in her head.

"Here's what I learned about you since yesterday," Jenny said as they parked his car, a red Mustang convertible, and headed for the festive sounds of the street fair in Little Italy. It was nearly evening. "You like country-western music, banana bread and William Safire." And then, just to hear how it sounded out loud, she added, "And you're six years younger than I am."

"No wonder you quit reporting and took up features," Jake said as he stopped to buy two sausage-and-pepper hero sandwiches from the street vendor at the corner of Mulberry and Hester streets. "You have no passion for detail. I like Willie and Waylon and that's all. The banana bread is too recently acquired a taste to be called a favorite, and I only like Safire on language. I don't even look at his other stuff."

Jenny stuck her tongue out at him and he took that opportunity to kiss her again. The whole day had flown this way, full of easy kisses and spontaneous hugs and the pretense of an interview.

"Go ahead," Jake said, fanning his mouth against the fiery taste of the hot Italian sausage. "Ask me anything."

"Okay. What were you doing between college and graduate school that you got to be such an old person of twenty-eight before you hit on journalism?"

"Going to law school," Jake said casually as he entered a brightly decorated groceria and Jenny followed. "Two Cokes please, cold if you've got them."

"No kidding?" Jenny said as she popped the tab on her Coke and followed him back out to the street.

"Jenny," he said, placing his can of Coke on the sidewalk and grabbing her shoulders, "I have something very serious to tell you."

"What?" she said, genuinely alarmed by the solemn look on his face and the stern tone of his voice.

"A serious interviewer does not ask a serious question and then respond to the answer with 'No kidding.' You gotta watch that, Jenny, or you'll never make it to network."

"I don't want to make it to network," Jenny said, relaxing. "I don't even want to make it to prime time. What were you doing in law school?"

"What most people were doing," Jake said before he took a long swallow of the Coke. "Becoming a lawyer."

Jenny stoppped walking. "What's a lawyer doing at Columbia Journalism School?"

"Getting ready to work for the FCC. You know something, Jenny? You're a quick study. You're getting better at this question-and-answer stuff all the time."

"Right." Jenny smiled. "Mike Wallace and Oriana

Fallaci are probably quaking in their boots right now."
And then she tossed her uneaten sandwich and her Coke
into the nearest garbage can because a real question occurred to her, so real that she lost her appetite. So real
that she hesitated to ask it. "Why would someone who
wants to work for the Federal Communications Com-
mission want to interview Jennifer Roo? It doesn't
wash, Jake."

"You know," Jake said with that easy grin taking
over his face as he stood opposite her, "I think I
underestimated you. You really could make it as Barbara Walters. You've got that same sneaky interview
technique she has."

"What technique is that?" Jenny asked, momentarily
distracted.

"Oh, you know," Jake said. "She asks three or four
soft easy questions, and then zingo! in for the kill."

"I'm not in for any kill, Jake. I just want to know
why you called me."

"I already told you," Jake said, no longer smiling.
"I'm a fan of yours, I've admired your work for a long
time. And then, when I saw you on television for the
first time, when I actually got a good look at you, I
admired more than your work. So I called my father
and . . ."

Mistake, Jenny thought instantly. A mistake to con-
fide in one's agent. A mistake to tell your agent your
troubles. A mistake to speak to Steve Burger of the
unspeakable. "And then what?" Jenny said, feeling the
irregular heartbeat begin in her chest, the disappointment congeal in her blood.

"And then he gave me your unlisted phone number
and then I called you." The streetlights came on with a
low hissing sound and Jenny could see that he was
straining, that his mouth was drawn tight, that his eyes
were squinched with beseechment.

"What else did your father tell you about me?" Jenny
asked.

The sound of an accordion split the air, a mixture of full-chorded completion and squealing complaint. Behind Jake Jenny saw three strolling musicians, two mandolin players and the accordionist, turn the corner and make Jake their mark. "What else, Jake?"

"Signore, you want something special for the lovely signorina, we play it." The mandolin player who spoke had a gold front tooth that reflected the streetlight.

"Never mind," Jenny said suddenly. "Don't answer that last question. I'd rather not know what he told you."

"He told me everything," Jake said reaching for her. "Play 'Angela Mia,' " he told the musicians.

Chapter Eighteen

"I feel like the Virgin Bride," Jenny whispered to Nina long distance that same night. "You've got to come home just to meet him."

"Maybe I will," Nina laughed. "Do you want to meet my plane?"

"When?" Jenny asked offhandedly. She thought she heard Jake's car in the driveway.

"Tomorrow night."

"Are you serious, Nina?"

"I'm better than serious, I'm pregnant," Nina said. "But you mustn't tell David. I want to tell him myself. If this endometrial treatment works and I carry safely into the fourth month, I'll name the baby after you, Jen. But only if you keep my secret until tomorrow night, big mouth."

"On my honor," Jenny began to say and then she heard the car door slam. "I've got to go, Nina," she whispered. "Jake just came back. That's terrific news, and I've got a lot of news for you too — mostly disaster bulletins — but I've really got to go now!''

"It's after midnight there," Nina said in her sensible voice. "Where did he go at this hour?"

"To a drugstore," Jenny whispered. "Really, I have to hang up now!"

"What's the disaster bulletin?"

"It's about Paul . . . he's coming back to New York." She tried to say it evenly and failed. She could hear Jake's tread on the stairs now.

"Jesus!" Nina breathed. "I'll call you tommorrow night after I get in. David's picking me up. Just tell me one thing — what did your boy wonder go to the drugstore for at this time of night?"

"None of your business!" Jenny told her and hung up. It was not Nina's business to know that she no longer trusted a diaphragm that had not been used in nearly two years.

"You should have seen me," Jake said as he entered the bedroom and tossed an economy-size box of condoms on the bed. "I felt like I was back in high school. Like everyone was watching me." He pulled off his clothes quickly and, ignoring Jenny's gasp at the naked sight of him, went into the bathroom. "I think my voice actually changed when I asked the girl behind the counter for those," he called out to her.

"Did it go up or down?" Jenny called, nervously patting at the lace front of the white spaghetti-strapped nightgown she had purchased after their lunch at The Press Club. She was sweating.

"It went up," he said, walking out of the bathroom with a full erection. "Now where were we before we were interrupted?" He lifted the covers and got into bed beside her, kissing her closed eyes.

"Not this far along," Jenny said, crossing her arms protecively over her breasts. "We still had our clothes on." Her voice was steady, but Jake could feel the tremor in her body.

"That's a beautiful nightgown," he said, pulling the blankets back. "Unfold your arms and let me see it."

"I can't," she whispered. All of the bravado she had felt when she was talking to Nina had fled now that he was back. I want this too much, she told herself. Too much. I'm making too big a deal out of it.

"Of course you can," he said, gently lifting one arm and then the other away from her body and spreading them wide against the bed. "Of course you can." And he sat up and kissed each of the palms of her hands before she could clench them. "How long?" he whispered as he brought this lips to the insides of her elbows. "How long has it been?"

"A lifetime," Jenny said, tears welling behind her closed eyes. "A very long lifetime." She lay perfectly still.

He kissed her eyes and licked at the tears and then he lay back down, leaving space between them.

"Just tell me one thing," Jake said. There was a new resonance in his voice as he lay beside her. Something she hadn't heard before. A heaviness.

"What?"

"Am I moving too fast?"

"No."

"Too slowly?"

"No."

"Well, then tell me what you want me to do."

"I can't," Jenny said.

"Well, then open your eyes at least. I can't have a conversation with a woman who won't even look at me."

"I can't," Jenny whispered.

"Please."

"I can't."

"I thought you wanted this," he said, turning toward

her. "I thought you wanted this enough to have me go out in the middle of the night and drive to the only all-night drugstore in Westchester County and embarrass myself like some overeager teenager so that you could feel safe."

"I do feel safe," Jenny said, forcing herself to open her eyes as she spoke the words.

"Tell me that again," Jake said as he looked at the tears streaming down her face, "when you really mean it."

"I do really mean it," Jenny cried, sitting straight up in bed. "I want to really mean it!"

"Then tell me what to do, for God's sake!" Jake said loudly. "I feel like I'm the one who abused you! I feel like I'm the one who's responsible for those tears! Like I'm the one who's making you shiver right now! Damn it, Jenny. I never hurt you!" He sat up beside her.

"Don't yell at me, Jake," she sobbed as she curled her body into a tight ball. "Please don't yell at me."

Jake ran his hands over his face as if he could massage away frustration. "You know what this was?" he said as he suddenly got out of bed and looked down at her sadly. "An ego trip. A bloody ego trip! For forty-eight hours I've been walking around thinking I was the guy who could break the mold. That if I took it slowly enough with you, if I didn't come on too strong, you'd open up like one of your backyard tulips." He began to pace the room.

"I was wrong," he said, stopping next to the place where she lay. "I was wrong to have called you in the first place. I should have listened to my father. 'Jenny Roo?' my father said to me. 'She's a terrific lady, sure I'll give you her phone number. Only I don't know where you'll find the kid gloves soft enough to handle her.' And then he told me about the ex-husband who beat you, and that the same guy was coming here from Los Angeles pretty soon and that you were very frightened. Very skittish. That this was probably the worst possible time to get to know you. Oh no, I told him. Oh no, I said to my father when he got through warning me away from you. I can handle that. The arrogance!" he said, slapping his forehead. "The unbridled arrogance to think that I could handle that. I can't. I wish that I could," he said wistfully, "but I can't. I'm going to take a shower now and then I'm going to go home."

Jenny lay on the bed and heard the bathroom door close and the shower go on.

"A lifetime," she whispered to herself, as she lay there curled in her white nightgown listening to the rush of water behind the closed door. "Several lifetimes." And she had a sudden flash of what she would look like as a very old woman. Shrunken, dry-fleshed, empty. Rachel would move away, Nina and David would spend Thanksgiving with their grandchildren, and she would be alone. For a lifetime. She got out of bed and wiped her face with tissues. One day at a time was how a lifetime got spent.

She walked carefully to the closed bathroom door and stood facing herself in the full-length mirror that was mounted on the back of it. Slowly, as if watching a stranger in that mirror, she lifted the white nightgown over her head and stood naked in front of the mirror. For all of the redness that rimmed her eyes, she looked surprisingly good to herself. Her flesh was firm and her small breasts were taut in the chilled air of the empty bedroom. She tried to remember what she had looked like when *she* was twenty-eight. How she had worn her hair, how much she had weighed. What she had felt like, what she thought about things. Blank. Nothing came back to her. What had she done on her twenty-eighth birthday? She couldn't remember. She could describe all twelve of her child's birthdays in great detail — the designs on the paper plates, the flavors of the ice cream and cakes, exactly what gift she had given Rachel for which birthday. But she couldn't remember what her own birthday had been like for a single year of the last ten.

And then she thought of Minna, who until this year had always remembered her birthday. First with balloons and cake for breakfast and later with the less flamboyant gestures of the middle-aged — fur-lined gloves, silk scarves, tickets to the ballet. And in more recent years, when she had proudly announced that even a widow living on social security could afford to buy her daughter a birthday present, there came imitation-pearl earrings, paperback books, a spray bottle of some off-brand cologne being featured at the five-and-dime store nearest Minna's apartment. And this year from Minna, nothing. Jenny thought her heart would burst.

She took a deep breath, turned the doorknob and entered the bathroom. It was filled with steam and Jake did not hear her first light tap at the opaque shower door. But she opened it anyway.

"Do you know what Janis Joplin said about freedom?" she yelled above the noise of the water, laying one arm around his soapy neck and closing the shower door with her other hand.

"No," he said, moving her into the hot spray of the shower and soaping her back as though he'd been doing it for years.

"What she said about it," Jenny yelled as she turned around and brought his soapy hands to her breasts, "was that freedom was just another word for nothing left to lose."

"She didn't say that," Jake yelled back. "Kris Kristofferson said that. He wrote the song."

"Yes," Jenny said, reaching for his stiff slippery cock, "but she sang it."

"Very wonderful," Jenny said as she stretched luxuriously and rolled over next to him on the damp sheets. "That's how I feel. Not just a little wonderful, or medium wonderful, but very wonderful."

"I'm very glad," Jake said, running his fingers through the wet curls of her hair. "Very." He lifted his head off the pillow and asked her if she wanted to try it again, this time in bed.

"You mean like grown-ups?" Jenny said as she knelt to straddle him. "Like full-grown men and woman do it?" She had not been astride a man since the earliest times with Paul, and to look down now and see Jake's face smiling up at her, to feel his powerful runner's legs wrapped around her back, made her almost giddy. "I thought you young folks found this conventional kind of thing boring," she said in a high-pitched croaking imitation of feeble old age.

"Yeah, we do," Jake said as he reached up to circle her nipples with his thick fingers. "But we make exceptions for senior citizens."

"That's very kind of you," Jenny said as small bolts of pleasure shot through her breasts, her back, her arms.

"Well," Jake said, continuing to stroke her breasts and moving his thighs more closely around her, "we found that the more unconventional settings created ambulatory problems."

"I'll bet you did," Jenny said, leaning down to kiss away the smile and lick at his shoulders. "Touch me," she whispered as she traced the curve of his ear with her tongue.

"That's another thing," Jake said in his field reporter voice while his hands explored her back, the curve of her waist, the firm swell of her bottom. "We discovered that older people had difficulty with lubrication. Most of them required some sort of preparation to help with the dryness."

"Dryness!" Jenny howled as she guided his hand between her legs. "There's a major oil slick spreading in there!"

"Well," Jake said in his own voice when he felt her wetness and heard the sharp intake of her breath, "that's what makes this sort of study so fascinating. The exceptions."

And then there was no more banter. No more games, and no more pretending that this wasn't the glorious lovemaking that it was.

"I can't believe it!" Jenny cried as his slow gentle thrusting grew more rapid and the heat in her belly threatened to explode. "I can't believe it! I can't believe this is me! I can't believe it!"

"It is you," Jake said as he arched his back and began to quicken their pace. "Believe it."

"You're my miracle!" Jenny roared as the orgasm spilled liquid fire through her body.

"No, Jenny," Jake told her as he thrusted toward his own climax. "Jenny? Jenny! This is . . . real!"

They slept as they lay. Toward morning, Jenny felt the tug of covers being drawn to the other side of the bed and she thought, in that moment of half-sleep, that it was someone else who was taking away her comfort, but then she heard Jake's voice and felt his arms come around her. "Sorry," he mumbled. "We were all tangled up." Jenny fell back to sleep.

"Very wonderful," Jenny said as she watched him come awake the next morning, "and also very hungry." She rolled over and began to nibble at his chest.

"Like for what?" he said, laughing. "Stop it, that tickles."

Very wonderful, a man who wakes up laughing, Jenny thought. "Like for blueberry pancakes," she said, licking at his neck. "Like with a side of bacon," she said with her lips against his shoulder. "And a side of hash browns," she said, falling across him to nibble on his other shoulder.

"I think," Jake said, holding her head between his two big hands, "that I may have created a monster."

"There goes your ego again," Jenny said, kissing his eyes. "You didn't create me, fella. I was a big breakfast eater long before I met you."

"And when was that?"

"About a hundred years ago," Jenny laughed. "Come on, I'll race you to the shower. Loser buys breakfast."

Chapter Nineteen

In those first days of May, Jenny bent to her garden and felt that she too was blooming. That she, like the yellow daffodils with cupped faces, had also spent time in cold hard ground, and that suddenly the air had warmed and the earth had softened.

"Want to hear what your daughter thinks about your new lover?" Nina said after they had shared lunch at Tavern on the Green. Jenny had chosen the restaurant that sat in Central Park for two reasons — because it was lovely and because it was Tuesday. She needed to be in the city to spend the evening with Jake before she went on the air, a broadcast-night habit his father had unwittingly established.

"I already know," Jenny laughed as they came out of the restaurant and stood in the bright sunlight. "She thinks he's a hunk. I heard her tell her friend Patience."

"Want to know what else she thinks?" Nina said as they began to stroll along the cobblestone paths into the park. "She thinks that if I hadn't come back when I did, you and my husband would have danced off into the sunset."

"Clearly a case of overactive prepubescent imagination," Jenny said in a hollow voice.

"Is it?" Nina asked without looking at Jenny as they walked.

"It is," Jenny said firmly. A kiss is not an affair. She was prepared to tell that to Nina now that Jake had taught her the difference. She had no idea what David's version of that morning's events had been, but she knew that if Nina pressed her she had nothing to be ashamed of. "You know how Rachel has always depended upon you and David as surrogate family. She adores the two of you. She'd take you any way she could get you."

"I know that," Nina said softly. "I just wanted to hear you say it."

They walked in easy silence for a while, Nina pausing every now and then to admire babies who slept in carriages or crawled on the warm grass, displaying an interest she had never allowed herself to evidence before.

"If it's boy we're going to name him for David's father," Nina said casually. "But that's another secret you've got to keep. Even from David. He still thinks I want some super-Wasp name like Trent or Morgan. Can you imagine a kid named Trent Kalish?" Nina laughed. "It's almost worse than Patience Wasserman."

Sometime during Nina's treatment in Chicago, Jenny guessed, the doctors had not only protected her pregnancy, they had managed to reconnect her head bone to her heart bone. It was too soon to judge if the connections would hold, if this thoughtful concern for David might be sustained through the adversity of another miscarriage; but for the moment Jenny chose to believe that the woman walking beside her was her friend again. That the blend of self-confidence and humanity that had characterized the old Nina would stick now. It was possible, Jenny thought as she felt the sun's warmth on her back, that Nina had been treated by more than a fertility specialist in Chicago. Maybe she had talked it all out with a very good psychiatrist on North Michigan Avenue. Maybe an ego as strong as Nina's really could transform a self-image that called itself "damaged goods" in March and have it repaired by May. Maybe a healthy pregnancy was the best antidote to maternal ambivalence. Maybe good sense made for the best mending job. Jenny had no clues and she asked very few questions about how Nina had spent her time in Chicago. The job, the treatment, where she had lived were of little consequence. She didn't need to know those things. It was enough to take shelter in the fragile reconstruction of the friendship.

"Well," Nina said as she slowed her steps and turned to face Jenny. "I think it's time."

"For what?" Jenny said, spotting an ice-cream vendor a few yards away. "We just finished lunch. You don't want to gain all the weight in the early part of —"

"For the news about Paul," Nina said as she sat down on a bench nearby and patted the place beside her.

Jenny sighed and reluctantly joined her, facing the sun. "You really want to take a glorious day and flush it down the toilet, Nina? Are you sure you want to do that?"

"No," Nina said, putting on her sunglasses. "But I don't think it's such a hot idea for you to pretend that he's not coming back. For you to keep avoiding the subject."

"I am not avoiding the subject," Jenny said defiantly. "I am positively not avoiding the subject."

"Not much you're not!" Nina said, smiling indulgently. "First you describe the subject to me as a disaster bulletin, and then you spend a four-hour lunch date talking about everything from diaphragms to news programming without ever once mentioning his name.

Disasters do not go away just because nobody talks about them. Haven't you ever heard of disaster preparedness, Jenny? Don't you know what they do in the Bahamas when a hurricane is coming?''

"They tape the windows," Jenny said harshly. "Frankly, I don't think taping my windows will do much good.''

"And neither will pretending Paul's not coming back to New York," Nina said gently.

Jenny looked away. "I know that," she said softly, "but from what Rachel tells me, he's not coming for months. Don't you think I'm entitled to a little springtime, Nina?''

Nina followed Jenny's glance to the bobbing kites in the sky above Central Park and bit her lip. "That's not how I heard it," she said, laying her hand on Jenny's arm.

"How you heard what?''

"Rachel told me he's coming to New York the first week in June." Nina put her arm around Jenny's shoulder.

"I think," Jenny said, stiffening, "that that is only wishful thinking on Rachel's part." Her entire body tensed. "I think that's just another example of Rachel's fertile imagination. I think now that you're going to have a baby her desire to have a complete family of her own is working overtime." She sat on the bench, her palms pressed over her mouth, as if to muffle the scream that was bubbling in her throat now that no more rationalizations would come. "I think," she said, folding her hands tightly in her lap and giving it one last try, "that if he really were coming that soon, Rachel would have told me." Her chin began to quiver and she bit her lip to stop it. Springtime, damn it! Springtime. She had not had a real springtime in years. She was entitled to this one.

"I think she wants to tell you, Jenny," Nina said

quietly, "but she's afraid. She's afraid of what you might do."

"She should be afraid!" Jenny said, standing up and hugging her elbows. "She's got that right!"

She would not, she promised herself, directly accuse Rachel of withholding information. Of betraying her own mother and threatening her own future by her silence. Not yet.

For four days Jenny scrutinized her daughter's behavior, looking for something, anything that would identify her nervousness, give signs of the stress she might be feeling. Nothing but a math test seemed to be troubling Rachel. Jenny listened in on her phone conversations and learned only that her child had a crush on her homeroom teacher, a bear of a man named McWilliams whose frequent hugs of his favorite students (boys and girls) sent shivers through Rachel's body. The knowledge that everyone needed a Burger, someone to hug away the terrors of being alive, was the sum total of knowledge Jenny gleaned from eavesdropping. After four days Jenny was ready to believe that an early-June arrival for Paul was nothing, after all, but a fantasy of Rachel's wishful imagination.

But on the fifth day, the mail brought confirmation of her coldest fears. Even without the Los Angeles return address printed on the envelope, Jenny would have recognized the exaggerated slant and flamboyantly looped style of Paul's handwriting. She opened the brown envelope and unfolded the single page of its contents where she stood, as if to carry it inside the house was too confining. As if by standing there outside on her own front porch she was already poised to flee whatever punishment he might send her.

The letter was typewritten by a machine whose print she did not recognize.

DEAR JENNIFER:

AS RACHEL HAS BY NOW INFORMED YOU, DISCUSSIONS FOR A BROADWAY PRODUCTION OF "PENNYDANCE" (A PROJECT I ASSUME YOU ARE FAMILIAR WITH BY THIS TIME) WILL BRING ME TO NEW YORK THE WEEK OF JUNE 4.

ALTHOUGH I AM WARMED BY OUR DAUGHTER'S HIGH ENTHUSIASM FOR A REUNION (AN EVENT I HAVE LONG HOPED AND WISHED FOR), IN DEFERENCE TO YOU I SUGGEST THAT YOU AND I MEET PRIVATELY FIRST.

AS MOST OF MY MEETINGS WIL BE IN THE THEATER DISTRICT AND I AM TOLD THAT YOU WORK NOT FAR FROM THERE ON TUESDAY NIGHTS, MAY I FURTHER SUGGEST A MEETING IN THAT AREA ON TUES. JUNE 5.

SINCERELY,
Paul

Only the signature was in his own hand.

On first reading, Jenny's impulse was to tear the page apart, to rip it into pieces so small she might toss them into the air and make their landing invisible. Like acid rain, she would later think. Instead, she slowly and deliberately refolded it and carried it into her house.

She sat down on the sofa in her living room and looked around her as if something in the room might give her proof that she was not alone with this news. As if a watercolor still life that hung on the wall might tell her not to be afraid, or a bentwood rocking chair would speak wisdom if she would only listen. She walked through all of the rooms of her house, the letter clutched in her hand, and searched for feeling, for some physical sensation to replace the numbness that was filling her body and overtaking her mind.

In the kitchen, she attempted to pour herself a cup of

coffee, but all that she saw in that room was the sink. She stood immobilized by the memory of the morning when Paul had banged her head against the porcelain sink on West Fifty-fourth Street. She saw that she had spilled the coffee all over the countertop, and left the cup where it was. In the study she sat down at her typewriter, and without inserting paper she turned on the machine and typed every curse word she knew. Abruptly, she hit the off button and climbed the stairs to the second floor. Every window in every room offered the same view — her baby being held by Paul, dangling out an open window.

In the master bedroom she ran her hands over the bed where she had reclaimed her body's right to pleasure with Jake, and discovered that her face was wet with silent tears. There was so much to lose in this house if Paul invaded it.

With quickening anger she went to Rachel's room. There she tore open drawers and shook out books looking for some proof of Paul's return. A letter, a postcard, anything that would corroborate the message she still gripped in her fist. She picked up soft stuffed animals and threw them against the walls, thinking their innocent beaded eyes might harbor secrets. By the time she discovered the locked metal file box in Rachel's dresser drawer, her unfocused suspicions had taken shape. Collusion, that's what was going on here. The sealed box held messages from Paul, an insidious secret correspondence designed to win Rachel's confidence, to winnow her away from Jenny. From the mother who sought only to protect her. It was obvious. He was coming back to get Rachel. To stage not a theatrical production, but a custody battle. Or something worse. An abduction. The successful play was merely his credential for reclaiming her; an opening night on Broadway the dangled carrot. And Rachel, Rachel who had kept all of this locked up, hidden from Jenny, would bite. Oh yes, she would fall for the honeyed language and the languid expression of his eyes. She would listen to his enchanted tales of the palm trees and the movie stars, and the glitter would blind her and she would say, "I want my father. You can have everyone else, I want my father." Jenny screamed. A high-pitched yell of pure frustration so loud it seemed to come from all four corners of the room at once. She sank down on Rachel's bed, her head in her hands, and tried to talk to herself. To resummon the reason his letter had stolen.

At first the words were slurred and would have been unintelligible to any listener. But gradually her voice took on greater distinction. And even if what she was saying did not make complete sense at first, the sound of her own voice gradually brought her back. "One day at a time . . . is how a life gets spent."

Slowly, with all of her concentration shaped to the task, she began to restore order to Rachel's room. She took care to recreate the adolescent priorities that kept girlish underwear folded in preciously neat stacks but let shoes and skirts lie wherever they happened to fall. When she was satisfied that she had left no trace of her rampage, she carried the metal file box out of the room and went downstairs.

She had work to do. Rachel would not arrive home from school for another three hours. That was time enough to gather information that might make a confrontation with an already frightened child unnecessary. Jenny sat down at her desk and dialed the *Trib*. "Research, please," she said when the connection was made.

"This is research," a male voice said. "Mr. Hill speaking."

"Mr. Hill," Jenny said as she numbered the questions she was scribbling on a lined yellow legal pad, "I'd like to speak to Carmen."

Carmen Lopez, if not exactly a friend, was the one researcher at the *Trib* who had never failed her. And perhaps more importantly, Carmen had never bothered to ask why Jenny needed to know things like the ratio of large dogs to small dogs being destroyed by the city's pound annually or what color Marlon Brando's eyes were. Jenny asked for and routinely got such information from Carmen with an efficiency and accuracy that astonished her. Computers, Jenny supposed. Everything in the universe was catalogued somewhere in the *Trib*'s computer networks. Every mystery was solvable, every enigma could be explained if only Carmen Lopez was pressing the right buttons. What time was it when the Potsdam Agreement was signed? Who served the official New York cheesecake? No problem. Just straight answers with no questions asked.

"This is Mrs. Lopez," Jenny heard her voice on the line. Once a year, at Christmas, Jenny made it her business to deliver gifts to those people at the *Trib* who had made themselves indispensable to her. Carmen was at the top of the list. It was not difficult to picture her now, her shiny black hair twisted into an elaborate braid atop her head, her glasses dangling from the chain she wore around her neck. "Who is calling?"

"It's Jennifer Roo, Carmen. I need four items. This afternoon if possible."

"Go," said Carmen. Jenny could see her poised over the console that sprawled in front of her, her fingers arched above the keyboard.

"First," Jenny said authoritatively, "I want anything you've got on a play called" — her eyes scanned the page of Paul's letter — "*Pennydance*. It opened in Los Angeles and seems to be headed for Broadway."

"When did it open?" Carmen asked. "And where?"

"I'm not sure," Jenny said. She cleared her throat. "Try the last three months. If you come up empty, work backward from there."

"Anything special you want on it?"

"No," Jenny answered. "Just anything you've got. Reviews, pictures, magazine pieces. Interviews with the playwright."

"Who is?" Carmen asked matter-of-factly.

"Paul Roo," Jenny said too loudly.

"Spelled the same as your name?" Carmen asked without any change in tone.

"Yes," Jenny said. She licked her lips. Her mouth was getting dry. "Don't forget the West Coast editions of the trade papers. *Variety* and the like on both coasts."

"Of course," Carmen said. "What's next?"

"Next," Jenny said, consulting her notes, "I want to know this city's best agency for providing bodyguards."

"Repeat, please."

"Bodyguards. Personal security guards."

"Got it," Carmen said. "What else?"

"Get me the name of the city's foremost expert in domestic violence."

"What kind? Private? Public? Academic?"

"All kinds," Jenny said. "Carmen, you're terrific."

"I try," said Carmen, nonplussed. "What's next?"

"This is the last one. I want to know the ten most heavily trafficked public spaces in New York City."

"Indoor or outdoor?" Carmen asked.

"Indoor," said Jenny.

"Fine. Let me read it all back to you." She did, flawlessly. "Do you want me to call it in piecemeal or wait until I have the whole lot?"

"One question at a time will be fine," Jenny said. "They're all for different stories, you see. Unrelated columns I happen to be working on simultaneously." It didn't matter to Jenny that Carmen hadn't ever asked why she needed information, never questioned Jenny's purposes. It simply made her feel better to offer this sparse explanation to the woman who asked no questions and provided only answers.

"Okay," said Carmen. "I'll call you back." She hung up.

Planning, taking the ideas that came into her head on such divergent wavelengths and setting them all out in neat little rows to examine their patterns, was not Jenny's way. Not by choice did she operate on instinct, it was just that she was a lousy strategist. The questions she had put to Carmen Lopez had all been born on instinct, a disjointed logic Jenny could not have explained. Maybe when she had the answers she could make a pattern, but not now. Now she sharpened a number-two pencil and began to write notes in the margins of Paul's letter.

He had terrible instincts, Jenny saw as she reread his first paragraph. "As Rachel has by now informed you . . . . a project I assume you are familiar with" — one completely false assumption heaped upon another. She underlined his mistakes with a black felt-tip pen, and in capital letters wrote the word "Arrogant" in the margin. Briefly she wondered whether he had labored for that haughty self-important tone, or whether it had come to be his natural style. What was left on the first paragraph when she finished marking it up was the date of his arrival. There was nothing she could do about that with a felt-tip pen.

The second paragraph was pure Paul. Cruelty couched in pretty language. To refer to Rachel as "our daughter" was an invention in treachery. Jenny had been awarded sole custody of Rachel nine years ago in an uncontested divorce proceeding. At the time she had asked nothing from him and received nothing. There was nothing of his she wanted to share. That was why she had sent back his hundred-dollar check. She did not need to read farther than the words describing his hopes for a reunion to feel the drums begin to beat in her head. On a separate sheet of paper, she quickly wrote another question for Carmen. Who were the five most respected attorneys in the metropolitan area who specialized in custody suits? Who was the best of them all? Was there a woman among them? Within moments, the entire page was covered with penciled questions, some to be fired at Carmen when she called back and some Jenny needed to ask of herself. "A child psychologist for Rachel?" she wrote and underlined. A change in their phone number? Should she buy a gun? Should Rachel stop biking to school and start riding the bus? Should school authorities be notified?

She dialed Jake.

"Do you know how to use a gun?" she asked him.

"Jenny? Is this Jenny?"

"A simple yes or no, Jake. Do you know how to use a gun?"

"What's going on, Jenny?"

"Yes or no, Jake?"

"Yes."

"Will you teach me to use it?"

"No."

Jenny hung up. She threw down her pencil and walked through the house to the backyard.

Leaning against the fence at the back of her property, she could see the whole house. The clean rectilinear shape of it set against the horizon of green trees and blue-gray sky. There were places where the roof needed mending, Jenny saw from here, and the shutters on the second-floor windows needed painting again. It was only a house, after all. Not a sanctuary. Just some red bricks, a little fieldstone and a garden where comfort had bloomed in its season.

Chapter Twenty

"No disrespect or anything, Mom," Rachel said when they faced off across the locked metal file box that sat on the kitchen table, "but I think you're overreacting."

"I don't," said Jenny flatly. "I want you to open the box."

"No," Rachel said with quiet intensity. "It's private."

"So is our trust," Jenny answered, sounding much stronger than she felt. "Open the box."

Rachel scowled, an angry constriction of her small features that made her seem both older and harder than the child she was. "If we have all this private trust," Rachel said, avoiding Jenny's eyes and running her hands protectively over the box, "how come you were snooping around in my drawers? What exactly were you looking for?"

"You're stalling, Rachel. Open the box."

"No!" Rachel cried. "It's private! You can't make

me!'' She grabbed the box from the table and held it tightly in her lap. "I don't go through your drawers! I don't poke around in your personal stuff when you're not here! And I don't listen to your private phone conversations either! You can't make me!''

This was not adolescent obstinance, Jenny saw. This was full-blown determination. And it occurred to her suddenly that if she had no memories of her own father, no recollection of the smell of his skin or the sound of his voice as he read to her aloud — if she had none of that, if all that she had of him could be contained in so small a box, no one could force her to give it up either.

Jenny sat back in her chair and wondered if there was any way on earth she might speak the whole truth without telling the whole tale. A way to make clear to Rachel that her concern was justified, that her fears were grounded in a reality Rachel knew nothing about.

"Suppose," Jenny said as she got up and refilled her coffee cup, her back to her daughter, "you just told me what's in the box.''

"Stuff," Rachel said in a much lower voice.

"What kind of stuff?"

Rachel sighed. "I already told you. Personal stuff.''

"Like what?" Jenny asked, trying to match Rachel's softened tone.

"Six ounces of cocaine and four lids of grass!'' Rachel cried with mock horror. "And my birth control pills!''

It was a nice try, Jenny thought, for a girl who was still waiting for her first period. "Rachel, you know I could have just carried that box off to a locksmith this afternoon. I didn't have to wait for you to come home from school and give you a chance to level with me, to be honest.''

Rachel grimaced and took a few sips of milk from the glass in front of her, one hand still grasping the box. "Feelings," she said as she replaced the glass. "My feelings are in this box.''

"Oh," said Jenny, tripped up in her effort to appeal to Rachel's sense of dignity. Not for a moment had she considered taking the box to a locksmith. The truth was that she had not even searched for the key. She had simply found it and assumed that it contained enchanting letters from an estranged father who was using his most potent weapon, language, to steal the heart of a child. The crime she expected to find evidence for was seduction. "Feelings about what?" Jenny asked as gently as she could.

"What is this, Mother? What are you supposed to be? The FBI? The CIA? I told you it was private and you come back and tell me about trust. Then you tell me about locksmiths. Feelings are private, Mother! Feelings are secrets you keep inside you until they go away. Didn't you ever have a secret? Don't you understand what secrets are?"

Oh my baby, Jenny thought, I could write a book about secrets. And I could teach you the world about feelings that don't go away.

"Rach," Jenny said as she walked around to Rachel's chair and cradled her child's head in her hands, "of course I have secrets. But sometimes, something we think needs to be kept a secret really doesn't. It needs to be told. It needs to come out of the box."

Rachel's body relaxed and her shoulders slumped in Jenny's embrace. "I want to ask a question," Rachel said stolidly.

"Ask," Jenny said. But her breath held.

"Two questions."

"All right. Two questions."

"And you promise that you'll tell the truth?"

"Ask the questions," Jenny said, glad for the fact that Rachel made no move to turn around, to examine her face.

"They're hard questions," Rachel warned. "It's okay that you didn't promise."

Jenny widened her embrace to hold Rachel's

shoulders and felt, beneath her hands, the fragility of youth and of this moment.

"The first one is about Grandma. She keeps getting stranger and stranger, Mom. Is she ever going to get better?"

"No," Jenny said softly. "She'll have some times that are better than other times, but she'll never get better." There was a freedom in telling the truth that emboldened Jenny, that made her break her own rule about never telling a child more than what was asked at the time. She found herself elaborating. "Right now, Rachel, there are no cures for Grandma's disease. But she could live a long time the way she is, and lots of very talented and dedicated scientists are working on senility problems every day."

"Does that mean that when she acts weird it's because she's sick?"

"Yes," Jenny said, choking back the lump that was growing in her throat. "Yes."

"And does it mean that with all of those great minds working on the problem, by the time you're an old lady science will have found a way to hold on to all your marbles?"

For an instant, Jenny glimpsed the mind of her child and wondered how she could have been so insensitive to Rachel's fears. Maybe it was because they were so different from her own, but still, the link between Minna's decline and Rachel's secret fears about her own future was Jenny. And Jenny had missed seeing that. For all of her long, carefully worded explanations of Minna's condition, Jenny had never once addressed the fact that it was not hereditary. She had never assured Rachel that weirdness did not run in her genes, a time-release poison of confusion and bizarre behavior. She did it now.

"Well, that's sure a relief," Rachel said when Jenny had completed her cautious, thoughtful explanation full of learned quotes and statistics drawn from her wide reading on the subject. "I figured that you were already pretty weird and that if you threw in senility I'd be spending my whole life ducking talcum powder."

And real bullets, Jenny thought. From your father. She shook the thought from her head.

"What?" she said. "What's talcum powder got to do with anything?"

"Nothing," Rachel said. "Grandma just likes to play with it. Can I ask my second question now?"

"Sure," Jenny said, surprised that the first had been managed with such dispatch and what seemed to Jenny, success.

"It may be harder than the first one," Rachel said. "Maybe we should take them one a day, like vitamins."

"Never mind, Rachel. Get on with it."

"It's about Dad." Her voice cracked on the third word. "About my father," she amended. *Dad* was what you called him if you could connect him with *Mom*. "Why don't you want me to see him? And remember what I said. You don't have to answer if you don't want to."

I don't want to, said a childlike voice in Jenny's head.

"Maybe you're right, Rachel. Maybe we should take these questions more slowly."

"You want to wait until tomorrow to talk about him?"

"No, no. Let's just take a break for a while. Let's go and get an ice-cream cone or something. What do you say, kiddo?"

"It's almost dinnertime," Rachel said, dejection coating her words. "And I said it was all right if you didn't want to answer that one."

"I will answer that one," Jenny said. "But first I have a question for you. Why didn't you tell me that he was coming here so soon? Why did I have to find out from Nina?"

"You're right!" Rachel said as she suddenly stood up

at the table. "Ice cream is a great idea! What we need here is not dinner, but junk food. Carbohydrates to keep us going."

"Rachel —"

"I'll just go put my box away and you get the car keys and we can —"

"Rachel!"

"Because I was afraid that you would do something."

"Do what?" The light was fading in the kitchen and Jenny wasn't sure she really wanted an answer.

"Something to stop him from coming."

"How could I possibly do that, Rachel?" Jenny asked in a harsh whisper.

"I don't know," Rachel cried. "You're the one with all the great ideas! You're the one who gets paid for coming up with new ones all the time. I'm just a kid! But you would think of something. I know you would."

Yes I would, Jenny told herself as she stood stiff and chilled in her darkening kitchen. You bet I would.

"Let's go and get ice cream," Jenny said.

As she drove back from the ice-cream shop in the co-cooned silence of the car Jenny wondered why, in an effort that was as crucial as mothering, there were no time outs. And no time to pause and collect your thoughts, no moments in which to reshape your strategy.

She inhaled deeply, watching Rachel from the corner of her eye. "Suppose, Rachel, that I asked you not to see him while he was in New York. Suppose I told you that I thought it best if we keep things as they are around here. We have a pretty good life, the two of us. What would you say?"

"I'd say he's my father even if he's not your husband anymore."

Jenny tightened her grip on the wheel. "Suppose I said there were very good reasons why I don't want you to see him."

"You would have to tell me what they were."

"What if I couldn't do that?"

"You would have to."

"What if I couldn't?"

"Oh, you could. Because if you didn't give me a very good reason you know what a kid with my imagination would think? I'd think the worst. And then I might be more afraid of him than I was of you when you started up about that box today."

"I see," said Jenny.

"Oh Mom," Rachel said as she leaned across the seat and kissed Jenny's cheek, "I really hope so." There was such earnestness in Rachel's voice that Jenny could make no reply, but she did make a mental note to call their pediatrician first thing tomorrow morning. The doctor who had treated Rachel for the last five years was a good source of referral to a child psychologist. There was no question in Jenny's mind now about the need for such a person. Maybe, with luck, Rachel wouldn't actually have to go to anyone; maybe the person could just advise Jenny, act as a sort of well-educated interlocutor. The idea of her child actually sitting in the office of a shrink and working backward to the truth about her father made her chest ache as she drove.

"Were you expecting the hunk, or did he just show up?" Rachel asked as they pulled into the driveway behind Jake's red Mustang.

"A little of both," Jenny said as she turned off her ignition. She never should have asked him about a gun. That was just plain stupid. She wanted it only for self-defense. She should have just gone out and bought the thing and asked whoever sold it to her to give her instructions.

"I like him, you know," Rachel was saying. "I really do. I'm really happy for you that Jake . . . that he came into your life."

Came into my life? Came into my life? Where had Rachel picked up that little nugget of soap-opera vernacular? And then it struck Jenny that Rachel's words held no real meaning — they were merely meant as a cue line. It was now Jenny's turn to say, "And I'm so glad that your father has come into your life." Over my dead body.

She watched as Rachel sprang from the car, abandoning all further questions as she ran to the back of the house in search of Jake. She could hear their voices coming from the backyard, and although she could not make out their words, she could smile at the gladsome sound of their animated voices. If she didn't make any more ridiculous mistakes like asking him about a gun, maybe he'd still be there for Rachel when Paul was gone. And she knew, as she sat alone in her car, that to think that she wanted Jake Burger to be a surrogate anything was a lie. "This is real," he had said to her when they made love. And that was what she wanted. Not for him to be a substitute father or a mock-up pal to her daughter, but someone real. Someone whose reality was so undeniable in her life that she was able to turn her back on the nightmare years with Paul and not be afraid of getting hit from behind.

Jake was alone as he came around the privet hedge that bordered the side of Jenny's house. "Rachel let herself in," he said, leaning his elbows on Jenny's opened car window. "Want to get out of the car now and talk to me about guns?"

"No," Jenny said, sighing deeply.

"Then start small," Jake said as he opened the door. "Just get out of the car." His voice was so sober and his gaze so direct, she did as he asked. "A gun?" he said as soon as she stood in front of him. "A gun, Jenny? What's been going on around here? What do you need a gun for?"

"To have," Jenny said carefully. "Just to keep in the house. Just in case."

"Just in case of what?" Jake demanded, slamming the car door behind her.

"I got a letter today," Jenny began as she took his arm and began to walk him down the quiet suburban street, away from where Rachel might hear any of this. "It was from Rachel's father. He's going to be here much sooner than I expected. He's going to be here in three weeks." She pronouced these words with such heaviness that Jake turned to stare at her profile in the twilight, searching her face for more. Surely that was not the whole of it. But Jenny kept walking, her head lowered to the lengthening shadows that fell across the ground.

"I don't think I'm understanding you, Jenny," he said when she spoke no more.

"He wants Rachel," Jenny said without looking up. "He wants to come back and take Rachel."

"He said that in his letter?"

Jenny stuck her hands into the pockets of her jeans. "He called it a reunion," she said in a wooden voice. "What a way that man has with words. *Reunion*. Like it was a Coca-Cola commercial he was planning, not an abduction."

Jake sucked in his breath and stopped walking. "Hold it," he said sharply. "Just hold it right there, Jenny." He stood frozen, his silhouette illuminated by the headlights of a passing car. "Let me just see if I've got this all straight. You're arming yourself with a weapon you haven't the first clue how to use . . . against a man you really don't know anymore, because . . . he wants a reunion with his child?"

"That's wrong!" Jenny cried. "I do know him! Oh, do I know him! And he knows me!" Her voice was rising now, splitting the tranquil night air with its shrill edge of panic. "How he knows me! He knows where all the switches are. Hot, cold, simmer. Even in the dark he could find me. From three thousand miles away he knows how to find my fear. The way to get to me is through Rachel. He knows, Jake! I drew him the diagram. I gave him the blueprints the night I packed her up and we both left him. There are no dead ends on his route, no trapdoors. He's got a straight shot and I'm the one who showed him the way." Although she neither cried nor wailed, there was a sadness in her voice more terrible than tears.

"You were right to do that, Jenny," Jake said. "You were right to leave him." He put his arm around her shoulders, but she shrugged it off.

"Of course I was right. What I got wrong was the timing. I had to wait for him to threaten Rachel before I had the guts to get out. Where was my courage until then?"

For a moment they stood, each of them silent and helpless before that ponderous question. And then it was Jenny was spoke, her voice low and coldly conclusive. "It was nowhere. I used to tell myself that he would change. That I could change him. That success might change him. That he himself spoke of how badly he wished to change. I actually thought that I was being brave by staying. That's what I told myself. But that wasn't true. That wasn't courage. I stayed because I was afraid of what he would do to me if I tried to leave him. I used to sit there, with the icepack held against my head, and tell myself I was a woman of valor. Like Ruth in the Bible. I wasn't. I was a coward."

"You're not a coward, Jenny. You're a victim," Jake said.

"Was," Jenny corrected him quickly. "I *was* a coward. If it makes you feel better to think of me as a victim, go ahead and think that, Jake. But the operative word here is *was*. I was young and I was stupid and I was afraid. But not now. Now I'm a big enough kid to know better." She thought of Rachel, alone in the house she had known today was not a fortress, not a shield, and she told Jake she wanted to go back now.

When they entered the house, Rachel was just hanging up the telephone, writing furiously on a large sheet of notebook paper.

"That was Carmen Lopez," Rachel said. "She was calling you back." There were tears of anger in her eyes and she spoke to Jenny in a voice that sounded as though there were broken glass in her throat. "I think I got most of the message. I got the part about where there are bodyguards for hiring. There are three places, in case you're still interested. And I even spelled them all back to her. And Grand Central Station has the most traffic of anyplace in New York." Not just her voice was quivering now. Her whole body had begun to shake. "But the part about *Pennydance* . . . all those questions you asked her about Paul Roo . . . about lawyers . . . I don't know if I got all that. Maybe . . . Maybe . . ." she said, picking up the wooden kitchen chair in front of her and slamming it against the floor, "maybe since you're such a great snoop . . . you ought to find that out your own damn self!"

Rachel ran out the back door and into the night. It was Jake who ran out after her.

Chapter Twenty-One

Jenny could not concentrate. She tried very hard to focus her attention on what Dr. Liefler was saying about Rachel, but her head was already so swollen with expert opinions and newly acquired information that there seemed no place left to store another word. Words, Jenny thought as she looked at the placid balding man who spoke more of them now. I am strung out on words. Written, spoken, they were all muddled in her head. She could not, in this moment, separate the astonishing words Carmen had handed to her in a print-out this morning at the *Trib*'s offices from the words of the doctor.

Liefler was the only one of the child psychologists referred to her who had agreed to a meeting without pressing the need to treat Rachel directly. "Of course," he had said on the telephone with the same uninflected voice he was speaking in now, a voice Jenny approvingly heard as benign, "I would hope that eventually I could work with the child. But for now I would certainly have no objection to seeing you alone, Mrs. Roo." Jenny agreed at once.

Liefler was speaking now about Vietnam. She tried to relax enough to follow what he was saying. "Do you remember that war at all, Mrs. Roo? I'm sorry," he corrected himself. "I should have said 'Jenny.' Do you remember that, Jenny?"

"Yes, of course I do." But what had Vietnam to do with Rachel? She hadn't yet been born.

"Do you recall, then, the staggering number of men who were listed on the nightly news as 'Missing in Action'?"

"Yes," Jenny said, utterly bewildered by this line of inquiry. "My mother wore an identification bracelet with the name of one of those men on it."

"So did I," said Dr. Liefler.

"My mother's bracelet was for a Marine corporal from Austin, Texas. Damler. Jeremiah Damler was his name," Jenny said. She was amazed to discover that she still held such information in her head and that she offered it so freely now, in this setting.

"And did he come home, your mother's corporal?" Dr. Liefer inquired in his benign voice.

"Yes. Yes, he did. They even corresponded for a while."

Dr. Liefler stood up from behind his desk and looked out at the Manhattan skyline. "I wore a bracelet to remember a boy from Flushing, New York. He did not come home. He is presumed dead, but there is no corpse to prove it." He turned now and studied Jenny's face. Her confusion was visible in the furrow of her brow and the loose way she held her mouth. "His family grieves for him and I grieve for him, but we have no box. His mother, I am told, has a flag. But that is really not enough, is it? We would all rather have the box."

Jenny sat back in her chair and struggled to see the

point. She had written columns about the Vietnam War when the memorial was dedicated in Washington, D.C. She had even met with families like the one he was describing now. But what had this to do with a child who was alive and healthy? With Rachel? The face Jenny turned to the doctor was blank.

Silence filled the room. A silence so dense and viscous that it put Jenny in mind of her own therapy sessions after she had moved out of the women's shelter. "Sometimes, Jenny," her counselor had said to her all of those years ago, "we see the connections and we hear the answers to even the hardest questions, but we are still afraid to speak them."

Jenny looked at her watch, no stranger to the fifty-minute hour that was sliding away while she tried to draw truth from the slippery surface of an anecdote.

"Do you want me to tell you why I think you told that story?" Jenny asked abruptly, "Or do you want to tell me why yourself?"

"I think that you're an intelligent young woman, Jenny. I read your columns and I admire your instincts. I think you might at least take a crack at it."

Jenny bit her thumbnail and looked around the room. It was a comfortable, well-lit room in which most of the space was taken by toys. Dolls, plain and elaborate, were heaped upon the floor, and a brightly colored storage area held shelves full of miniature furniture. Dollhouse furniture. Diminutive beds of all description, some narrow and some wide. Tiny tables and chairs, sofas, fireplaces, bathtubs, and toilets were all available here. There were even miniature paintings to be hung on miniature walls. Jenny's eyes flicked across the rows of toy cars and trucks she assumed Rachel would pay no attention to if she ever came here. And then she turned to the doctor and spoke. Her voice was tentative only in its softness.

"I think that what you're saying is . . . if Rachel is not

allowed to know her father, she will grieve in absentia. She will mourn for him as though there were no box."

"That is certainly possible," Dr. Liefler said.

Boxes, Jenny thought as she waited for him to say more. In the end it all came down to boxes. To storage compartments with straight flat sides that were meant to house secrets too wild and terrible to be contained.

"You described Rachel as a child with a more active imagination than most." Liefler's voice seemed to come to her from a great distance. "If that is so," he said, "and I expect you are a good judge, then I would have some concern for what Rachel imagines to be in that box."

Jenny supposed that what he was saying was that Rachel would fantasize things about Paul that weren't true. Things that might be worse than the truth. But that was not possible, she told the doctor. "Surely, Doctor, in this instance the truth would be more frightening to her than any fantasy."

"Not necessarily," Liefler said. "It is impossible to hypothesize the mind of a child on such matters."

That, Jenny thought, remembering how Rachel's question about Minna had taken her by surprise, was a supposition worth considering. And that was precisely what Liefler seemed to be proposing now as he stood up with an air of finality: that she consider these ideas. Jenny sat back in her chair, refusing to yield.

"I realize that my time is up, Doctor. But I was hoping you might be a bit more supportive of my concerns. The idea that a man who not only beat up on me for years but threatened the life of an innocent child now be allowed access to that child strikes me as insane."

"Has it never occurred to you, Jenny, that he might have changed since you knew him last?" Liefler said as he sat down behind the desk where he kept his appointment book. She knew then, as he watched her expectantly, that if the time ever came for expert testimony in a custody battle, she could not hope to call upon Dr. Frank Liefler to testify on her side.

"Yes, Doctor, I'll admit that such a thought has occurred to me. But I rejected it," she said with a backward glance at the toys scattered behind her. "At about the same time I lost faith in Santa Claus and the Tooth Fairy."

On Fifth Avenue Jenny walked blindly in the direction of Grand Central Station, twenty-two blocks away. Confusion fueled her steps. Oblivious to the hordes of lunchtime pedestrians who strolled the sundrenched avenue, and grasping the large manila envelope that Carmen had given her this morning, she told herself that she was on a mission, some sort of sacred assignment that had been forced upon her by the contents of the envelope.

She had had an opportunity only to give the material a cursory scanning during the short cab ride between the *Trib* and Liefler's office, but it was enough time for her to decide that the man who had written *Pennydance*, the man whom the *Los Angeles Times* critic had called the bravest autobiographical American playwright since Eugene O'Neill, was the same man she had fled in the night years ago. Nothing had changed. Treachery was still treachery, only now it was to be paraded across the stage. Flaunted before strangers. Exhibited to a public who, for the price of admission, would be treated to the three-act horror show that had been private until now.

The envelope contained copies of three different West Coast magazine interviews Paul Roo had granted following the unanimous critical acclaim of his play. Each contained the same vague and self-aggrandizing quote: "Catharsis was a word I had understood only in theatrical terms until I wrote *Pennydance* and experienced it for myself." The rest of the words had blurred on the page by the time the cab had stopped in front of Liefler's office. Except for two: *"Broadway bound."*

"Catharsis," Jenny said aloud as she stood waiting for the stoplight to change at Sixty-fifth Street. "Catharsis my eye! Over my dead body!" Even the I've-seen-it-all-and-there's-nothing-that-could-make-me-look-twice-in-New York cynics who stood at the crowded corner turned to stare at her. When the light changed, people moved away from Jenny Roo very quickly in spite of the fact that several of them recognized her from television.

"That, my dear," said a dowdy middle-aged woman to the flashy-looking girl beside her as they both turned to examine Jenny's path into Central Park, "is the price of celebrity. Starry-eyed aspirers beware."

Change, Jenny thought as she sat down on a park bench and held the envelope against her knees. Wasn't it possible, the psychologist had suggested, that Paul might have changed over the years? After all, he had said in a tone Jenny heard as a lecture, there was some very interesting work being done with men who had no control over their anger. Domestic violence of all kinds was being dealt with by mental-health professionals all across the country. And California in particular was a very active area for such efforts. Child abuse, wife battering, incest — had she no faith in the efforts of dedicated mental-health professionals who were addressing themselves to problems like Paul's right this very moment? Could she not allow for the possibility that given the proper treatment, Paul Roo might have changed? Jenny had been tempted to spit.

"I see why you might hold out that possibility," Jenny had said with forced civility. "It's your stock in trade, Doctor, to change people." He had denied that, saying that it was his stock in trade to help people realize that they were capable of change.

That was a very pretty thought, Jenny allowed as she sat vacantly watching small bare-legged children frolic in the playground area near her bench. A lovely thought that would no doubt warm Dr. Liefler in what she expected would be a very well-endowed old age. Change did not come cheap on Park Avenue. Fleetingly, she wondered what it might cost every time a child who was not free, a child unable to play and grow without demons, crossed Dr. Liefler's threshold and took up one of the miniature beds or chairs. And what, Jenny wondered, ran through the minds of the parents who waited behind his closed door?

Change? Did they believe in change, those people who feared for their children? Did they believe in time's healing powers as well as the doctor's? Or were there some like Jenny, who understood that some dangers had a reality that defied change, that mocked time.

She had tried to explain that to Jake two nights ago, after he had somehow managed to calm Rachel enough to get her to sleep.

"You're a reporter," he had told her as they sat together on the living-room sofa, each of them alert to the slightest sound that might mean Rachel was up and possibly listening. "You're supposed to be trained to look at a situation from all the angles. Can't you open up that tunnel vision for a minute and see that eight years have passed since your divorce? He could have changed."

Ah, Jake, Jenny thought, what could you know? The body I gave to you was healed. You never saw the bruises, you never ran your hands over the swollen places. To him the scars were invisible, she had said.

Jake had only shaken his head and paced the room. "Well, at least offer him an answer," he had urged, picking Paul's letter off the coffee table. "Certainly you can provide him with at least that."

"I will not," she had shouted, forgetting for the moment that Rachel was asleep upstairs, "fuel that fire! I will not respond to the arrogant, self-serving language, and I will not under any circumstances agree to a meeting! Whatever I have to say to him will said by a restraining order that forbids him access to Rachel!"

"You won't get it," Jake had said quietly.

"What?"

"No judge on earth is going to issue an order that keeps a father away from a child he has not seen in nine years. Not when she wants to see him. It won't happen, Jenny."

"What are you talking about, Jake? Of course it will happen! He held her out of an open fourth-story window and threatened to drop her to the ground! Are you crazy? Of course it will happen! Of course I'll get a court order!"

Jake had sat down beside her and put his arm around her shoulder, as much to quiet the hysteria that was creeping into her voice as to offer comfort against the terrifying vision he knew she was seeing. "Jenny? Jenny, remember I'm a lawyer. Trust me on this one. You haven't got a prayer."

"Since when does the FCC require training in family law, Jake? Huh? Since when? Or are you learning all this fascinating theory at Columbia Journalism?" Jenny had retorted.

"Oh Christ, Jenny, give it up! I checked it out with two judges and three divorce attorneys. I didn't make this up. The man has a clean record and he wants to see his kid. You never filed charges against him, you never had him arrested, and he never actually hurt Rachel. You have no case against him."

No case against him? "You're crazy. You really are crazy, Jake! Or else you're just ignorant! Maybe your father didn't tell you the whole story. Maybe he left out that for years I lived with a maniac who tortured me. Who slammed my head against walls. Who pushed me into closets and locked the doors. Who held knives against my throat while he quoted the bloodiest lines from Shakespeare. He could beat me up and recite flawless monologues from Edward Albee at the same time, Jake! Don't you understand the man is a lunatic? Can't you see that Rachel needs protection?" She had been on the edge of tears while saying all this, but the momentum of her righteousness held them back. "Let me tell you a story, Jake. There are dozens like it, but just let me tell you this one." Jake had silently nodded his assent.

"One morning, a few months after I'd gotten the column at the *Trib* and he still could not feel anything but hatred and envy for my success, he woke up hung over. This was before Rachel was born. Anyway, he was fixing himself a Bloody Mary for the hangover, and he was using one of those bottles of premixed stuff that already had the hot stuff in it. But along with the triple shot of vodka, he also added straight Tabasco sauce to give the drink more kick. And I can't remember exactly how it got started, but whatever it was that set him off, he wound up throwing that peppery stuff at my eyes. And of course it burned like hell, and for a few minutes — maybe it was only seconds — I was blind. I couldn't see anything. Nothing. But I could hear him. Oh God, could I hear him! Well, it took me a while to figure out what he was screaming, because usually when he got this way it was unintelligible. Just a string of obscenities. Every awful four-letter word you can imagine a man shouting at a woman, with 'bitch' and 'ballbreaker' thrown in the way some people take a breath to pause when they're angry.

"Anyway, that morning, blinded, it took me longer than usual to figure out what he was hollering. And when I did figure it out, I wished to God that I hadn't. *Lear*. He was screaming lines from Shakespeare's *King Lear* at me. Blindness. King Lear is about blindness. It's the central metaphor of the play, but that's not what he was screaming in that wailing voice of his, that theatrical wail to wake the dead. He was screaming the line Lear himself screams to the Fool: 'Oh, let me not be mad, not mad, sweet heaven! Keep me in temper; I would not be mad!' That's what he's yelling at the wife he has just blinded, at me, at his Fool. *Let me not be mad.*" Jenny stopped her narrative and stood up to face Jake. "Even he knew it, don't you see? Even he could not pretend that he wasn't crazy. Can't you see that, Jake?" It was a plea more than a question, the way she put it. "The court will see that. The court will see that such a man cannot be allowed access to Rachel."

Jake had not responded at once. He had sat silent, looking at his hands for so long that Jenny had time enough to wonder if she had gone too far in telling that story. If in the act of explaining Paul's madness she had somehow exposed the ugly chinks in her own wall of sanity. Advertised in some emotional neon that she too was damaged goods. Jake would not look at her, and when he spoke his voice was so heavy with resignation, Jenny herself was forced to look away.

"It was too many years ago, Jenny. He's been too careful since then. The most a judge will grant you is that there be restrictions on his visitation rights. That they will need to be for designated lengths of time. That he has to give you specific and timely notice of when he is going to see her. Maybe — and this would be the most you could hope for — it would be ordered that his visits with Rachel be supervised. But that's it Jenny. That's the best you could do."

"Those are facts?" Jenny had asked in a voice so weak it was barely heard.

"Those are facts," Jake had said.

Jenny got up from the bench and walked away from the place where the children were playing. A madman was coming to town to see a child who already worried that madness ran in her genes.

At the corner of Fifth Avenue and Seventy-second Street she took a sheet of paper from the manila envelope and crossed the street to a pay phone booth. When the operator came on the line at the law firm she had dialed, she identified herself as Jennifer Roo of the *Trib*, and within seconds she was put through to the man Carmen's research had designated the most knowledgeable child-custody expert in the city — Charles Fox.

"How can I help you, Ms. Roo?" Fox said without hesitation.

It was Jenny's experience that most individuals who held expert knowledge of one sort or another were only too happy to share it with someone whose interest might lead to positive ends. Most spoke freely to a journalist with strong credentials. For some, politicians and celebrities mostly, a positive end was free publicity. For others it was a surprise opportunity to share both the joys and the frustrations of their work with someone who seemed genuinely interested. In all of the years she had been making such cold calls, Jenny had been turned down only twice.

Quickly, Jenny outlined her story. "Of course," she added when she had told him the fictional specific places and dates of her case, "this information is based on a real case, but I would, as always, change the names for purposes of publication." These were truthful words she had spoken hundreds of times, but in this instance the very speaking of them made her throat go dry.

"Of course," repeated Fox. "Well, offhand, I would say your distraught young mother ought not compound her distress by paying unnecessary legal fees. There's not a lawyer in town, including me, who could prevent that man from seeing his child. Not unless he has some sort of criminal record in the state of California."

"He doesn't," Jenny said against the nose of a Fifth Avenue bus grinding its motor outside the phone booth. "I've checked."

"Well, then, it's very clear-cut. There is no way the court might act to prohibit that man from seeing his child. Now, I have several calls waiting, Mrs. Roo. Is there a number where I might call you back and we can continue?"

"Not right now, Mr. Fox," Jenny said, fear speeding up her words. "Just one more question? I'm on deadline here."

"Go ahead."

"In your experience, is it possible that a man who has a history of battering, but has undergone professional treatment for that behaviour, might no longer pose a threat to the child? Or to the mother, for that matter?"

"Well," Mr. Fox said, "most of that treatment is too recent and too sparse to bear evaluation. But my personal conclusion, and this is positively off the record, Ms. Roo, is that only in very special cases is that treatment one hundred percent effective."

"Thank you," Jenny said softly. "That's all I needed to know."

Chapter Twenty-Two

Jenny had walked directly down Fifth Avenue to the Kalishes' duplex apartment.

"I want you to take Rachel for a while," she told Nina and David. "Not forever, just for a while. Please. Just while Paul is here. Once he goes back to California, she can come home."

"Are you crazy?" Nina paced the long living room, shaking out her hair as though she were shaking off the possibility at the same time. "That's a terrible idea, Jenny. This is the first place he'll look for her." She bit her lip and looked meaningfully at David as he leaned against the fireplace with an air of detachment Nina was grateful for. At least someone here was taking the time to think things through. It certainly wasn't Jenny. She had arrived at their apartment door looking like a runaway, some curlyheaded waif in high-heeled shoes. Her hair was disheveled, her skin slick with sweat, and her eyes glittered with the unnatural luster of obsession.

"What about school?" David said as he crossed to where Jenny sat. "How could we get her to school?"

"Oh, that's no problem," Jenny answered quickly. "She's doing so well I can't imagine how missing a few days of the sixth grade would make a difference." There was a forced lightness in that reply, a kind of bubbling giddiness that made Nina wonder if Jenny was high. If, and Nina knew it was preposterous to even harbor the suspicion, her friend Jenny hadn't swallowed something in the last few hours — alcohol, pills, something that was responsible for the way she had arrived. Unannounced, unexpected, unfocused, and clearly unstrung.

"You're right," David said with a silent gesture to Nina, a raised palm, a stop-and-proceed-with-caution sign that Jenny could not interpret. "She is a smart kid, Jenny. No one is challenging that. But business meetings are unpredictable. These Broadway deals can take a lot longer to put together than anyone can predict or plan for. Suppose it turns out that he needs to be in New York for more than a few days. Then what? You wouldn't want her to miss all that school, would you?" Nina nodded her agreement from the post she had taken up near the entrance to the foyer.

Jenny said nothing. She just sat there vaguely observing the strangely awkward behavior of her friends. They seemed to her to be careening around the room like balls in a pinball machine. When Nina stood up, David sat down. When David got up, Nina seemed to jerk herself into a new pose. And both of them kept sneaking looks at their watches. She must have interrupted something here, Jenny guessed. An argument, maybe? Oh no, Jenny thought, please not now. Don't. Please don't go into one of your self-destruction routines now. Don't fall apart on me today.

Nina lit a cigarette from the silver Tiffany box on the coffee table.

"I thought you gave up smoking during the pregnancy," Jenny said blankly.

"That's right," Nina said, crushing out the cigarette. "I did. I was just testing my willpower."

David continued to speak slowly and thoughtfully, but Jenny had stopped trying to listen. She suddenly realized that for David, the quintessential workaholic, just to be sitting around his home at noon on a weekday was very unusual. Something was definitely going on here, but Jenny couldn't figure out what.

"And what about her friends?" David was saying now in that soft reasoned voice Jenny had known for so long. That caring voice. "Who knows what dire results might occur if a day passed without her seeing Patience Wasserman?"

"Exactly," Nina piped in. Again she seemed to be guarding the foyer entrance like some kind of sentinel. "The Patience Deprivation Syndrome could be hazardous to her mental health."

Jokes, Jenny thought to herself. I come to the two people I trust most in the world for crucial advice and I get lousy jokes. Humor, she could now see, was not the panacea she had once thought. She looked at each of them questioningly. "You're her godparents," she said. "If you won't protect her, who will?"

The question was punctuated by the buzzing of the intercom in the Kalishes' foyer. Nina jumped at the sound and looked nervously at David, who checked his watch and then nodded without a word. Jenny watched as Nina moved woodenly to the intercom panel and pressed a button. "Ask him to wait ten minutes and then send him up," she instructed the doorman who waited through the static on the other end of the line. Then she looked helplessly at David and rolled her eyes.

"I'm sorry," Jenny said as she stood to leave. "You obviously have better things to do. I never should have barged in here like this. It was thoughtless. I'll be going now."

"Sit down!" Nina roared, advancing on her small friend with a ferocity that Jenny had not heard or seen since the day she had pressed the small sheet of paper with the telephone number of the women's shelter on it and told her to "use it! Damn it to hell, Jenny, use it!"

"You are being ridiculous, Jennifer! What on earth could be more important to us right now than you?"

"How many times have you been there for us?" David said in a lower voice but with equal fervor. "Huh, Jenny? How many times have Nina or I awakened you from a sound sleep and asked you to solve our crises? To hold our hands? How many, Jenny? How many trips to the hospital in the middle of the night?"

"How many trips on the New Jersey Turnpike, how many trips to the airport?" Nina took over now. "Because we screwed up and expected Jenny Roo to fix it. Expected you to have all the answers. And you know something, my friend, you always do. You always do have the answers. That's why people read your column, that's why they buy your books, and that's why they tune you in on Tuesday nights. Because Jenny Roo has the answers. And because she's always so good about sharing them. So willing to take on everybody's problems. Even when we were kids, Jenny. Got a problem? Go see Jenny. She's good at problems. And now the whole city knows that. But I know more, pal. I see more and I know more. What did you once say to me — that you have been there from the beginning? Well, so have I.

"I watch you with your mother and I want to weep and I see you holding it all together like some kind of Jewish Mother Teresa. Here is suffering, and here is Jennifer Roo. Handling it. Coping with it. Making the best of it. And then I watch you with Rachel and I pray that I can be half the mother to our baby that you are to that kid. She's not just smart, Jenny. She's strong. And who do you think she learned that from? She learned it from her mother. You gave her the answers. Nobody else, Jenny. Just you. Just you had the answers. For as long as I've known you, you have been a one-woman crisis center. Twenty-four hours a day, you've got the answers. Take a break, my friend. Let somebody else have a try at it. Paul is a crisis you can't handle alone, Jenny."

Jenny sat on the sofa, silently twisting the strap of her handbag and wishing that they would stop staring at her like that. Wishing that they might not see the tears welling in her eyes. Wishing that they be spared the sight of her, her body curled tight with pain, her chest heaving with the dry sobs that couldn't be swallowed into silence anymore.

"I love you," Jenny whispered. "I love you both so much," she cried. And then she let the tears and the sobs and every nightmare vision she had locked up for nine years loose in the sunlit living room.

"There are things you don't know," Jenny said between sobs. "Things that nobody knows. He used to send me clippings — newspaper stories about non-custodial fathers who were fighting renewed custody battles to win back their children. Some were even about fathers who kidnapped their own kids. They were never signed and there was never a return address on the envelopes, but every so often I would open the mailbox and in among the bills and the fan mail and the junk, there would be one of these stories. And I would be terrified. For years I worried about what would happen if Rachel ever opened the mail before I did. About two years ago, those mailings stopped. And I began to breathe easier. But three months ago the mailings started again. The stories are different now. They're reports of men who use the courts to win the kids." She stopped, gasping for enough air to go on with this.

"When that phone rings on Sundays — the two-rings-and-call-back signal he has with Rachel — I have to stuff my fingers in my mouth to keep from screaming while she talks to him. For nine years, I have been reading the literature on battered women. There are ten cartons of research material hidden in my garage. There's not a day that I sit down at my typewriter and don't think about writing about it. But I don't. Not a word. I sit there knowing there are thousands, maybe millions of women who need to know what I could tell them, and I don't dare to do it.

"I write about the weather and the stray dogs and the Equal Rights Amendment, and once a year I do a column about Valentine's Day. Or New Year's Eve. Or the assassination of Martin Luther King, Jr. And every time I do that one, the one on the Reverend King, I ask myself the same question. I see him, I sit at the typewriter and I see him on that August morning standing at the podium with the Washington Monument in front of him and the Lincoln Memorial behind him, his arms outstretched to heaven, all those thousands of people on the Ellipse looking to him for the answers, and I hear him speak the words, and I ask myself, When will I be free? Great God Almighty, when will I be free at last? And then I write about something else — about bee-keepers in Brooklyn or people who sleep on the streets — and I tell myself, One day at a time. And that's how I try to take it. Only some days are harder than others, you know."

David and Nina looked at Jenny and then looked at each other. It seemed to them that she had said it all, in the letting go the room had been filled with demons too long caged to take notice of what they might say now. For a long while they each stayed where they were and kept their own silences. Each of them hearing those words again, each of them wishing they might give Jenny her freedom and knowing that they could not.

"David," Nina said, breaking the silence with a hushed voice. "Let me stay with Jenny. Maybe you'd better go down to the lobby and see about our guest."

"Sure," David said, his own voice lowered. And then, sensing that funereal tones would never get her any closer to freedom, that the voice Jenny herself had spoken in had been remarkably clear, almost strong, he said quite loudly, "Shall I have Jake come up or should we wait a while?"

"Jake!" Jenny hollered like someone who was coming out of a dream. "Is that who's been waiting all this time? Jake! What in God's name is he doing here?" No wonder they had been skittering around the room, edgy as caged birds since her arrival.

"He called us a few nights ago and told us he was worried about you since you have been talking about guns," Nina said, "and he supposed that we were too. We asked him to stop by." Nina sighed, a sigh in which relief and expectation were inseparable.

Ah no, Jenny thought, seeing the true extent of the damage she had done by letting her demons loose, by dropping her guard. When had she stopped telling herself to toughen up? When had she invited the people who loved her most to come forward and stand in the contaminated circle of her fear?

For so long she had kept it all inside herself, building barriers of competence, humor — a face to meet the faces. Guarding her pain and her terror as if they were some deadly chemicals. Worried that if her feelings were to spill, Rachel might be poisoned. But it was bigger than that now, she realized. Nina, Jake, David — they were all tainted by her. How could she have let that happen?

"I'm sorry," Jenny said, abashed by the inadequacy of those words. "I never meant for you to worry. I didn't mean to cause you this. And I won't do it anymore, Nina," she said as she stood up. "I'm an adult human being and it's time I behaved like one."

She picked up the manila envelope that lay on the sofa and turned toward the foyer.

"Jenny," Nina said, quickly rising and going after her, "please. Please let us help."

"It's okay," Jenny said, hugging her friend. "I'll be just fine. Don't get up. I know my way out."

Her voice, Nina thought, had never sounded more hollow.

"What a good surprise!" Jake's face broke into a wide grin as Jenny exited the elevator and put on her sunglasses. "Jenny?" he called. His grin faded to confusion as she walked straight across the lobby without stopping.

"Jenny? Aren't you staying for lunch?"

"Oh Jake," she said as if she had just noticed that he was there. "I'm sorry that I can't. I'm in a desperate hurry. But you'll enjoy the Kalishes, I'm sure. They're lovely people."

She strode directly past him and out into the dazzling sunlight on Fifth Avenue.

He followed her for sixteen blocks, careful to keep his distance, cautiously marking time at stoplights so that he would not catch up with her. He had no wish for a confrontation. His only objective was to see that in her obviously distracted state no harm came to her. The memory of her being mugged was too fresh in his mind for him to put aside the notion that she needed his protection.

At Fifty-eighth Street, he saw her enter the ground-level car showrooms of the General Motors Building and decided that among the shiny new Oldsmobiles and the convertible-topped Pontiacs she was safe. He hailed a cab and went back to the Kalishes' apartment.

Funny, he thought as he passed the smiling doorman who seemed to recognize him by now, she had never mentioned that she was interested in a new car.

On the twenty-fourth floor of the General Motors Building there was a public-relations firm named Waller and Epson. They handled the account for an artificial sweetener Jenny was interested in for purposes of a television segment. She had been to these offices twice in recent weeks. Art Kronigsberg had loved the idea. "And now here's Jenny Roo with a few well-chosen words on sweetness . . ."

"Hi, Stephanie," Jenny said, trying, oh God, trying to smile as she approached the blond receptionist she remembered as being very free with the comforts of coffee, office space, and goodwill so dear to any working reporter's heart. "I need to ask a favor, Steph."

"Anything," Stephanie said, taking note of Jenny's abstracted expression.

"Can I borrow an office for a few minutes? I'm late and I need to make a phone call. A rather lengthy and private phone call. Could you —"

"Of course," Stephanie broke in. "Everybody's at lunch around here anyway. Want one with a window? A corner? You can take your pick."

"It doesn't matter," Jenny said as she followed Stephanie down the thickly carpeted corridor, through the labyrinthine path framed by deserted offices.

"Here," Stephanie said, pausing before an opened door no different from several they had already passed. "Use this one, it's Mrs. Thorn's. She takes takes care of all her own plants. Aren't they wonderful?" Stephanie gestured to a particular hardy ficus tree whose leafy branches draped across the wall.

"They certainly are," Jenny said tonelessly.

"Okay, well, take your time, now. Mrs. Thorn is on

vacation and I'm sure she wouldn't mind. Can I bring you some coffee or something?"

"No, thank you. I just need the phone."

"And the privacy." Stephanie winked as she closed the door.

Jenny sat down behind the large maple desk that belonged to a stranger and stared at the telephone. It was right, she thought. It was fitting that she do this in a stranger's place. A stranger who took care of her own plants. She picked up the receiver and began to dial, all the while picturing her own garden at home. The garden in whose soil she had found the closest thing to peace she had ever known. The number was ringing now. She ran her hand over the trunk of the ficus tree behind her and felt its rough and irregular surface.

"Hello?" the voice on the other end said.

"Paul? This is Jenny. I'm coming to Los Angeles."

Chapter Twenty-Three

She told them all the same fabricated story — that she was going off for two days to do a television piece on a gathering of expatriate New Yorkers who were now living in California. The huge party in Los Angeles, she explained, had been an annual event for the last ten years. On the West Coast it was a widely covered media event, but the New York press had virtually ignored it. Until now.

The program director at Jenny's station was hooked on the notion that the one truly appreciative audience for this event were the New Yorkers who hadn't left. The folks who hadn't bought into the sunshine dream. The diehard natives still fighting the traffic, still hanging on to their subway straps, and still trying to avoid stepping in dogshit. What would warm their loyal hearts more than to see that those who had left were so lonesome for the Big Apple that they had to come together in the grand ballroom of the Century Plaza Hotel once a year just to cry on each other's shoulders? It was a great story, she told Nina and David, her mother and Irma, Rachel and Jake. They were even sending her out there with a camera crew, she said. She would be gone only two days.

When would the piece actually go on the air? Nina wanted to know when Jenny stopped by to apologize for her curt exit two days earlier and asked if she and David would look after Rachel while she was gone.

"Oh, I don't know exactly when they'll air it," Jenny had lied, "but their plan is to shoot enough tape to cover any contingency."

"What does that mean, any contingency?" Nina had wanted to know.

"Well," Jenny had replied, "if I were in charge of programming, I'd hang on to that piece of tape until it could win the most hearts for Channel Ten. Say, about mid-January, the first truly debilitating snowstorm? You know. Juxtapose pictures of the bottled-up Long Island Expressway with long shots of the California palm trees and then come in close on the tearful faces of the transplanted New Yorkers who fall apart just thinking about how many years it's been since they've seen the Christmas tree at Rockefeller Center. That's how I would do it."

"Too bad you're not the programming director," Nina had said. "That's damn clever."

Well, maybe it was clever and maybe it wasn't, Jenny thought as she stuffed her toiletries into the soft compartment of the hanging bag she intended to carry on Flight 83 to Los Angeles. What mattered was that they had believed the story. And if it wasn't the most inventive tale she had told in all the years she had been living off her wits, it was certainly the most important, she thought.

Driving to the airport, she supposed that it was the part about the minicam crew that had convinced them.

It never occurred to any of the people who would surely have tried to stop her if they had known the truth that the American Television Company had an affiliate station in Los Angeles. And that the station would furnish her with everything she needed: a field director, a cameraman and a sound technician. But none of them was savvy enough about television production to have figured that out. And the idea that she would be traveling with a crew had made them all think she was safe.

"Will you see my father in Los Angeles?" only Rachel had asked. And even then it was asked casually, as Rachel had watched Jenny gather her scant wardrobe for the trip she said would take two days.

"Of course not," Jenny had said, the pain of lying to her child masked by her feigned interest in the *New York Times* weather page. "I'll be on much too tight a schedule. And besides, he'll be here in New York in ten days or so."

"Eight days," Rachel had corrected. "He'll be here in eight days."

"Okay, eight days," Jenny had said from behind the newspaper page. "Oh shoot, it's really hot there," she had said, throwing down the paper and heading back to her closet. "I better just pack lightweight cottons."

That had been the only serious questioning she had been subjected to.

Well, Jenny reminded herself as she parked in the cavernous garage at Kennedy Airport, maybe not. There was Burger too. Both Burgers really, the father and the son. Jake had offered to drive her to the airport, an offer she of course had to refuse lest he wonder where her traveling companions were.

She had spent the first few moments of their time together last night apologizing for her rudeness in the Kalishes' lobby and the next few talking him out of driving her to the airport. For the rest of the evening she had tried to put her mind on hold and just let her body take over. But Jake wouldn't let her. His lovemaking was tender, but there was a hurried quality in the way he touched her that made her edgy. "There's something on my mind," he had told her as she lay curled tightly against him in his Riverside Drive apartment. They had just dropped Rachel off at the Kalishes'. "Something I've been thinking about ever since that incident at David and Nina's. And by the way, they're as delighted as I am that you seem to be less troubled about what's-his-name coming to New York over the past few days."

"Paul," Jenny had said against Jake's chest. "His name is Paul."

"Anyway, that's not what I need to tell you. What I need to tell you is something you may not like."

"What's that?" Jenny asked, her teeth beginning to ache, her jaw stiffening.

"Well, the other day when you walked straight past me and out onto Fifth Avenue, I followed you. Wait! Give me a chance to explain. I know you think you're a big girl. And I do, too. But you were so obviously not yourself that day, so clearly distracted, that I thought to myself you were a terrific target for every loony-tune in the park that day. And I figured that maybe a relationship as promising as ours could survive one mugging, but two would be pushing it."

Jenny sighed and felt relief spread through her body. "I'm not angry, Jake. I'm touched. Really," she said, kissing him and then suddenly breaking away from his embrace. "Why didn't you ever catch up when you were following me? Why didn't you just walk up to me and tell me I was a jerk and that —"

"Because I know you're not a jerk and I thought the idea that I could follow you would be somehow demeaning to you and —" She silenced him with another kiss, and then she asked how long he had followed her.

"Until the GM Building," he said. He didn't seem to notice that these words raised goosebumps on her skin.

"I figured that you were safe among all those revolving American-made Firebirds and Regals."

"You stopped following me at Fifty-eighth Street?"

"That's right. And then I want back to the Kalishes'. They really are good people; you were right. But that's not all that's been on my mind."

Now, Jenny had thought as she lay beside him, now is where it all comes apart. "What else in on your mind?" she asked, aiming for lightness.

"Well, you know my father is somebody else who's been pretty worried about you, and I've been filling him in right along. And leave it to old Burger, when I told him about your looking at new cars, he came up with a terrific plan."

"What terrific plan?" Jenny had breathed.

"For your meeting with Paul. I mean you are going to have to meet with him, aren't you? Eventually. Sooner or later."

"Yes," Jenny said, "sooner or later."

"Well, that's where my dad's idea came in. He thinks you should meet with him in some very public place. Someplace where he wouldn't think of harming you. You can probably imagine his voice saying this better than mind. 'Listen, kid,' he says to me, 'you tell her that's a perfect place to meet him, the GM Building. Ask her what harm can he do her there. What's the guy going to pull in a car showroom? The worst he could do is slam her fingers in the door of a brand-new Cutlass Supreme. And tell her to take somebody with her. There's nothing more natural than taking a friend along when you're shopping new cars. It's normal as hell. And listen, Jake,' he says to me, 'why don't you be the friend?'"

Jenny lay still and saw Steve Burger's face behind her closed eyes. The pouched eyes, the thin dry lips. And she could hear him on the night she had spent in his townhouse. The night she had laid it all out for him, told him she wasn't safe anymore. No, sweetface, he had told her, you got that wrong. And he had sent Jake to make sure that she had gotten it wrong. That she would be safe.

"So? It's really not such a bad plan. What do you think?" Jake had asked.

"I don't know right now," she had said. "I'll think about it tomorrow. On the plane."

"Do that," he had said as he got up and began dressing. "I'm going to take you home now. You've got an early flight and you can use the sleep." He kissed her one last time. "And one more thing, big-shot reporter. There are muggers in California too. That fantastic a place it's not. Take care of yourself."

"I will," she had promised him. Her fingernails dug into the blanket she pulled around her.

She had lain awake most of the night thinking of all the things she had not told him. Fragments of thoughts and intuitions she would like to have shared with him, but knew she couldn't. Her conversation with Liefler — what would Jake have made of that? If he or David or Nina had heard that story about men missing in action in Vietnam would they have been drawn to the same conclusion? Would any one of them have been capable of telling Jenny that her child was in mourning? She doubted it.

They were all, as Jake had said, good people. Lovely people. And better than that, she knew that they were her friends. And even if they weren't perfect — even if David Kalish was never free of his father's ghost and Nina was bound by the conviction that her worth was in her womb — they cared about her. Even Steve Burger, with his cockamamie plan for the automobile showroom and his failed marriages, wanted only what was good for her.

In one way or another, she had told Nina, we are all

damaged goods. Eventually, she might live in the moment when Jake turned in a certain light and his flaws were revealed too. Maybe one day, when the sky turned dark and a storm threatened danger, he would lock her up in a new kind of box. Then the concern for her safety that now flattered and warmed her could come to seem overbearing. Maybe even smothering. But not yet, she reminded herself. Not yet.

Boarding the airplane, her fingers icy as she handed her ticket to the flight attendant and located her seat, she knew that if he were with her now he would have questioned the soundness of her plan. Even without knowing what that plan was, he would probably be dragging her off the plane if all he knew was that her sole objective in Los Angeles was to see Paul Roo. She herself, having heard the expert opinions, having been subtly but unmistakably warned away from the expectation that time and success could change a man like Paul, was full of doubts. What was she doing on this flight? What faulty self-destructive impulse had made her believe that good might come from rattling the tiger's cage?

The attorney, Fox, had been straightforward in his scepticism of "cures," rehabilitation or any other hopeful change occurring in the lives of men who couldn't keep their anger under control. Men whose anger escalated into violence. Batterers. But he had been equally clear in explaining that she had no case. That she couldn't keep Paul away. The best she could hope to accomplish was a delay, ugly court battles that he would win in the end. Fox had been a dead end.

For months now she had been trying to do battle against the realities of dead ends. All of this time, through denial and postponement, she had gone about life as if she were waiting for an invasion. She had felt it in her bed, in her garden, in Rachel's room. Driving her car, sitting in a movie theater, taking her mother to a restaurant for lunch, she had known that no place was safe. The entire city, she had felt as she had walked along Fifth Avenue the other day, seemed to be changing. Threatened by Paul's arrival. The world for Jenny had been polluted by the invisible and most invasive toxin of all — fear. And no expert or well-meaning friend had been able to offer an antidote. She was meant to wait for zero hour, unsupported by law, and armed with no weapon while time clogged.

She could not do that.

As the plane's engines roared and it sped down the runway for takeoff, Jenny gripped the arms of her seat and remembered something she was supposed to have learned a long, long time ago.

Her mother and father had rented a small house on Cape Cod for two weeks in August. The house, a cottage really, was in a town they had never visited, West Dennis. But Jenny's father had a map provided by the real-estate agent. She had been six, maybe seven at the time, and she remembered now that as they turned off the Cape Highway and the light waned, the landmarks — a dairy store, a particular church driveway that her father had written on the margins of the map — had grown invisible. They drove in circles. Her parents could no longer suppress the pent-up frustrations of having driven long hours through terrible traffic, choked by heat and humidity, only to find themselves lost in the dark.

"Bernie, you fool!" her mother had shouted uncharacteristically. "We've been down three dead-end roads! We're driving in circles! We've gone past it! At least twice we've gone past it. I'm looking at the map. I know what I'm talking about! Poindexter Road is over there!"

"There is no road over there, Minna," her father had shouted back while Jenny cringed in the blackness of the back seat. "Maybe I should pull over. Maybe you would like to drive."

"With pleasure," her mother had said, and shortly

they had exchanged places. Minna, an infrequent and less than accomplished driver, was now behind the wheel. She threw the car into reverse, made a U-turn through someone's dark front yard and shot off across two vacant lots marked "No Trespassing." When she came to a perilous halt in front of the sign for Poindexter Road, she turned off the motor too quickly and, while the car engine knocked against the offenses she had committed against it, she spoke. Minna, who never drove again while Jenny's father was still alive, turned to the back seat and said, "Jennifer, try to remember this. When every road is a dead end, you have only two choices. You can go back to where you started or you can make a new road."

Jenny watched the city disappear through the clouds. "Ladies and gentlemen, the captain had turned off the Fasten Seat Belt sign. You are free to walk about the cabin and . . ."

Jenny unfastened her seat belt and went to the lavatory at the back of the plane. In that cramped space she tried to swallow a tranquilizer that had been prescribed by her dentist for an extraction done four years ago. The pill was probably long past its effectiveness date, Jenny thought as she cupped water in her palms. But it was the best she could do, she figured as she tossed back the small white pill. Maybe the tranquilizer would help her to relax. She was making a new road to a place she could not name. She needed all the help she could get.

On the airplane Jenny slept and dreamed Paul's death. She had seen him assassinated while he sat in the theater watching his own play performed. During the second act someone in the upper balcony of the Helen Hayes Theatre had fired two shots in the back of Paul's head and he had fallen dead across Rachel's lap. His blood was all over Rachel's dress. The blue velvet one, the dress Nina and David had given her for Christmas.

The dreamed assassin was faceless and of indeterminate sex. In the floating, distilled vision of dream the only details that were fixed with clarity were that Paul was dead with Rachel sitting beside him wearing a blue dress. At the Helen Hayes Theatre. Jenny was most certain of this last detail, the theater.

Chapter Twenty-Four

As Paul lay sleepless in his damp and rumpled bed, his mind and his body tossed and turned in anticipation of Jenny's arrival.

In the too-bright kitchen of his small rented house he brewed a pot of coffee and watched the clock count down the hours, trying to hold back the memories that murdered sleep. He failed now, as he had failed so many times before. Memory came to him as it always did, in painful spasms of recognition.

Soon after the strangely silent divorce from Jenny, Paul Roo had packed up his few belongings and sought refuge from his demons. In California he would make a new beginning. In Los Angeles, where he knew no one, he would not hurt anyone, he had promised himself. His inheritance money paid for the move and the setting up of a small apartment. He thought at the time that this was a fitting use of the money from his father's estate. A positive step. A proper one.

He rewrote *Hillside* and he stopped drinking. He took up racquetball and swam daily laps at the West Hollywood YMCA. And then he met Pamela Fanchell, a redheaded acting hopeful who had recently quit law school to follow her star. She wore two diamond studs in her right ear and told him his plays were brilliant. He fell in love with her and wrote two new plays within the year. She moved into his apartment on Mariposa and they began to talk about his writing a play for her, a drama so stunning it would launch two careers in one bold stroke. They spoke, in whispered voices, of marriage. He began to write her play.

And then, on a steamy night in July, he went out to have the pages of Act One xeroxed and returned to discover her in their bed with a reporter from *Variety*. After the reporter left he broke Pamela Fanchell's jaw. She did not press charges, he paid her medical bills with his dead father's money, and he saw that the demons were still with him. Like so many others who sought refuge from their private devils by traveling to the light and the promise of the merciful western sky, he realized he'd been outfoxed: the demons had been stowaways on the same voyage. His demons were trickier, craftier, stronger than he was. Six weeks later he awakened in Pamela's sweat-soaked bed in Venice, California, and stared into the narrowed eyes of two veteran Los Angeles County cops.

"Paul Joshua Roo?" the taller of the two uniforms had stated matter-of-factly. Paul had been too wasted to answer. The best that he could do without setting off the alarm bells triggered to ring in his brain was to blink. His mouth and his throat felt as though they were caked and crusted with dry sand. There was no way he could speak past that. Not without gagging.

The smaller cop, a black man with wiry white hair and a barrel chest, had snapped the yellowing window shade in the cramped, airless room and flashed his badge off the midday sunlight so that it stabbed Paul's eyes, blinding him for the moment. "L.A.P.D., Mr. Roo," the smaller cop spit at him. "You're under arrest, my man. Assault and battery. Get the hell off the bed, Mr. Roo, and put on some clothes. You're coming downtown. Do it now!"

Paul did not think he would be one of those writers whose talents came into perverse bloom when he was locked up behind bars; he had lost control when he was arrested. What would happen to Paul Roo next was not a matter to be left to the fertile imagination of a miscreant; it was the court's decision.

At his arraignment the court took one look at Paul's pure-white record of no previous arrests or complaints in the state of California and granted him pretrial diversion: thirty-two hours of work for the Los Angeles County Department of Parks and Recreation before his trial date in five weeks "and the court will deem this never to have occurred, Mr. Roo," the judge declared dryly.

"And, Mr. Roo, while you are out there emptying the waste containers in the parks and pulling the chewing gum off the benches, I want you to give serious consideration to Ms. Fanchell's head injuries. You gave her a concussion, but you could have blinded her. Or made her deaf. Or worse, Mr. Roo. So while you take that pickstick in your hand to keep Los Angeles beautiful for the next few weeks, I want you to think hard on where you got the crazy notion that it's all right for a man to beat up on a woman. It's not all right, Mr. Roo. Now get the hell out of my courtroom and I'll see you in five weeks." The judge pointedly took off his glasses and looked away from Paul. "Next case."

Score one more for the demons, Paul had thought as he left the courtroom. Never mind what his clean record said; he knew he belonged in jail.

"I congratulate you, sir," had come a smooth resonant

voice from behind him as he had descended the stairs of the courthouse. "I'd be pleased to buy you a drink in honor of your legal victory."

Fuck you, Jack, Paul thought as he whirled to confront the man. But the words slid away when he saw who it was who had a hand on his elbow.

"Arthur Coleman," the man said, removing his arthritically bent right hand from Paul's sleeve and extending it in introduction. "I'm —"

"I know who you are!" Paul had grimaced, ignoring the outstretched hand. "You're Pamela Fanchell's criminal-law professor. My hotshot public defender picked you right out when you walked into the courtroom. Shoved your whole glorious career down my throat while we waited to be called. Forgive me if I don't bow. Now if you'll excuse me, Professor, I don't want a drink! And I sure don't want your patronizing sarcasm! So just fuck off and let me go home."

But the harsh words had not impressed Coleman. "Okay, no drink. And no sarcasm. And I'll do the best that I can to keep a lid on the patronization. How about a cup of coffee?"

By three o'clock that afternoon, Paul was into Arthur Coleman for six cups of coffee, two grilled-cheese sandwiches and a whole lot more.

After the first two cups of coffee — swallowed in silence, but producing the desired effect of calming Paul's shredded nerves — Coleman had leaned across the Formica luncheonette table and asked simply, "Ever do it before?"

"What?" Paul had said, his hand trembling as he held the cup. Hot coffee dribbled down his chin. What the hell was he doing here with his victim's renowned legal counsel picking up the tab?

"Abuse a woman," Coleman said matter-of-factly. His pouched eyes held steady on Paul's chin. "Ever beat up somebody you loved?"

Paul had stood up so quickly that he knocked the coffee cup over. Mopping at his pants with paper napkins, he hissed at Coleman, "Listen, Jack, I'm grateful for the coffee and the silent companionship, but this is not the courtroom! We left the courtroom! And this is not the classroom either, Professor, so take the wily cross-examination tactics and go dazzle your students! I'm going home!"

"Sit down, young man," Arthur Coleman had ordered. "You are embarrassing yourself. Waitress, bring a fresh cup of coffee and a menu for my friend here."

"I am not your friend!" Paul had shouted as he grabbed the table and lowered himself into the chair. "Get that straight, Professor. I have all the friends I can use, thank you very much. I don't need a friend who's out to nail me."

"Out to nail you? What gives you such a strange notion?"

Paul ran his hands through his rumpled hair and longed for a shower, sleep, another life. "You think that's a strange notion? Listen, Professor, you walk into the courtroom carrying Pamela Fanchell's brief and exit holding my arm. What would you deduce? Just answer me that and then I'll be on my way."

"I have a weakness for victims," Arthur Coleman had said without a trace of irony. "It's obvious I can't help Pamela. Maybe I can help you."

"With what?" Paul had asked as his coffee was set on the table. "What is it you think I need help with, O wise and beneficient counsel?"

"Would you like to order a sandwich while the waitress is here? I think you're a batterer, Paul," Coleman said without the slightest change in tone, without missing a beat. "I think you've done this before, and I'm afraid you'll do it again."

The waitress had taken two long steps away from the table and asked if they would like to order.

"What makes you think that?" Paul had asked. All of his concentration was focused on getting the coffee cup to his lips without spilling it.

"Let's keep the diet bland for a while, shall we?" Coleman had said, turning slightly in his chair to ignore Paul's reaction to his supposition. He addressed the waitress instead. "Grilled cheese on white for my friend. A Rueben on dark rye for me. Thank you, miss." He smiled politely, dismissing the slack-jawed waitress, who could not resist a nervous over-the-shoulder glance at Paul. "Two things make me think that. One, I have a special interest in domestic violence, and two, you didn't deny it the first time you had the chance. Which may work for you or against you, depending upon the help you get."

"Help! You think I need help? Look out that window, Professor. You see that beat-up old van parked a hundred yards from the courthouse? The one that has a banner that says 'Jesus Saves' on its side? Well, try to commit this to memory, *my friend*. Law professors teach law. Playwrights write plays; Waitresses wait on customers, and Jesus saves. Got that?"

"I know someone very good," Arthur Coleman had said evenly. "Someone I think you'd get on well with."

"Get on well with!" Paul had exploded. *"Someone very good!* You sit here jerking me around like I'm a kid who believes in the Tooth Fairy, and for the price of a cup of coffee you hustle me for some shrink pal of yours. I can't believe it! I knew there were sleaze artists hanging around courtrooms, but I thought they were personal-injury types, ambulance chasers. I didn't think to check under your silky academic robes, Professor, to take a peek at what they were covering. But now that I have, let me save you the trouble. Give it up, Coleman. I eat shrinks for breakfast!"

Only when he looked across the table and saw with what satisfaction Arthur Coleman stirred sugar into his coffee did Paul realize too late how much damage he had done himself with that fierce speech, with that damning admission that he had a habit of abusing women.

"I'll bet you do, sir," Coleman had said with a benign smile lighting his flushed old face. "I'll bet you do. But let's forget breakfast for the moment, shall we? Here comes lunch."

The buttery grilled-cheese sandwich that the nervous young waitress cautiously set down in front of him was the first solid food Paul had seen since his arrest nearly thirty-six hours before. There was a part of him that wanted to swallow it whole, that wanted melted cheese and buttered bread to fill every empty place that hurt, to stop up all the cracks in his crumbling façade. His mother had done that with food, he recalled as he took a small tentative bite of the sandwich. Used it to fill the need and the aching silence and the disintegrating structure of her family's life. She grated carrots against time, and it came out a cake. "Chocolate is cake," Paul's father used to say, "carrots is for rabbits. Feed it to the kid." She ran her Mixmaster over the sounds of rages and it came out angel-food cake.

She had served Paul the cake and the ice-cold milk late at night, after his father had gone to bed. And she would smile as she watched him eat, a smile so full of pleasure it had made her plain features seem mysteriously transformed. When she looked at Paul her face was, for the instant, lovely. He tried to picture her smiling when his father was in the kitchen, and failed. He took larger bites of the grilled-cheese sandwich and tasted the salt of his own tears.

"The man's name is Philip Gruber," Coleman had said, quietly breaking the silence. "This is his phone number."

It was nearly daybreak, and the coffeepot was already cold as Paul thought back to that first meeting with Gruber.

Dr. Phillip Gruber had welcomed Paul to his private office at Glen Crest with a single word.

"Jockshit," Gruber had said, dismissing the wall of shelved trophies in his office and beckoning Paul to an overstuffed easy chair and hassock. The chair sat opposite a desk that was a shambles of books and files and dried-up apple cores. There was no couch in the room, Paul noted, his eyes still drawn to the trophy case. "Want to know the truth?" Gruber was saying. "All that stuff just embarrasses the hell out of me, but it cuts through a lot of horse manure with patients who think machismo is cast in bronze. And that's a fact." When he smiled, the big face fell into soft folds that announced how hard he must work to keep the massive body from going to fat. He did that now, just sat behind the disaster area of his desk and smiled.

The old Buddha routine, Paul thought as he sat down opposite him in the indicated chair. The old sit-back, smile-as-if-there-is-no-secret-in-the-universe-you're-not-privy-to, and collect-your-gold-at-the-end-of-the-hour routine.

"How'd you happen to run into old Arthur?" Gruber had asked as he leaned back into his oversize worn leather desk chair and continued to beam that good-ole-boy grin straight into Paul's teeth. "How'd the two of you happen to link up?"

You damned phony, Paul wanted to say, you bloody well know how we got linked up.

"I decked his favorite student with a flowerpot," Paul said directly into Gruber's smile. Blank. He hoped that his clean-shaven face was blank. Hoped that he got points for shooting straight past any denial.

"How'd you happen to do that?" Gruber had asked. His smile had disappeared, but his tone remained just as exasperatingly neutral as if he were asking how Paul managed to part his hair on the right.

"Simple," Paul had said, aiming for the same easy tone. "She threw me out of her bed, acted stupid and then insulted my profession." Paul took Gruber's silence as approbation for his no-nonsense account of the event. See that, Doc, he wanted to say, no pretty language. No theatrical flourish. Just exactly what happened.

Gruber sat forward and leaned his ham-block elbows on the desk. "Good answer, Paul. Straight, fast, and probably accurate. But you got the question wrong, partner. What you just told me explains why you got angry at a woman. But it doesn't say diddly-squat about why you smashed her head." Gruber wasn't smiling anymore.

Paul had breathed slowly and tried to count his exhalations. Somebody else with a wall full of worthless credentials had tried to teach him that technique. He couldn't remember now who it was. His breathing was audibly uneven. "I just told you, Dr. Gruber. The woman was someone who couldn't even handle her own life. One day she was quitting law school to act, and the next day she was going to be the female F. Lee Bailey. And do you know who she took all that indecision out one? Me, that's who. She damn near drove me crazy with all that indecision. Believe me, Gruber, she had it coming."

"Whoa!" Gruber had bellowed. "Back up there, partner. Let's get this straight right up front. What you did to that woman is against the law. There's no law against getting angry, everyone gets angry. But there is a law against assault. Guys who commit assault against women, guys who beat up on their wives, or their lovers, or their mothers, or their sisters, don't win popularity contests, you know. Not even when they tell how it went down as straight as you did. Mostly, if their victims have enough guts to leave them and bring charges, they wind up in jail. And that's a fact. Now let's try it again. Same question. Only this time don't tell me why she made you angry; this time tell me how you happened to smash her over the head with a flowerpot."

Paul had curled his fingers around the arms of the easy chair. He could feel the wale of the corduroy upholstery material underneath his fingernails as he gripped it. His face flushed. "I had a lot to drink that night. I guess I lost control."

Gruber had pressed his meaty palms together and leaned into them, so that his mouth was covered. Paul couldn't tell if he was smiling again, but judging from the cold cast of his eyes he doubted it.

"That happen very frequently?" Gruber had asked, laying his hands on the desk. For the first time since he had crossed the threshold of this office, Paul was reminded by that terse question that he was in the presence of a psychiatrist who was taking his history.

"Which?" Paul had said, a smile of his own forming. "Drinking a lot or losing control?"

Gruber had stood up and turned his back on Paul, studying something in the landscape outside his window. "I don't take too well to cute, Paul. You ought to know that right off."

"That's okay," Paul had said, his eyes hard on the big man's back. "I don't do cute."

Gruber hadn't moved. "Coleman told me you went to college. Somewhere in the Midwest, if I remember right?"

"That's right. Northwestern University. School of Speech. That's where I got my training in theater."

"Do you know what obfuscation means, Paul?"

"Of course I do," Paul had answered, irritation coating every word.

"Well, I don't take too much to that either," Gruber had said dryly. He turned around and faced Paul, the puddled face drawn into a mask of sobriety. "If you and I are going to get anywhere, partner, you're going to have to give up the shadowboxing. What do you say?"

Chapter Twenty-Five

The lone man who stood chain-smoking at the otherwise deserted arrival gate now was indeed Paul Roo, but he wondered if Jenny would know that. He had arrived at the airport a full two hours before her flight was due to land, and with each successive trip to the men's room he had furtively examined his face in the mirror and become more and more convinced that she would not recognize him.

There was nothing in his reflected image to foster such an idea. No perceivable thinning of his hair, no slackness in his jaw, nothing in his face to make profound declaration of the nine years that had passed since they had last seen each other. Like his premature arrival at the airport, the notion that she would not know him was born wholly of anxiety. In fact, the face in the mirror more closely resembled the clear-eyed young playwright she had met in Vermont than the debauched husband she had walked out on in New

York. He supposed it was giving up the booze that had accomplished that.

"You'll see," the bright-eyed psychiatric social worker who headed the detoxification program at Glen Crest had told him on the day he was admitted, weeks before he ever got to meet the famous Dr. Gruber. "Not only will giving up alcohol make you feel better. You'll even look better, Mr. Roo."

"Listen hot-shot," Paul had retorted, "I'm here to get dry, not to win any beauty contests. And furthermore, there's something else you ought to know about me. I spread shrinks like you on toast and eat them for breakfast."

Remembering that day, the man in the mirror smiled, and Paul saw that he looked even better when he smiled than he did when he posed his face in that expression of earnestness he had been practicing ever since Jenny's call. He tried that pose again now, and evaluated it in front of the mirror. The slightly widened eyes, the firm set of the mouth. It was good, he thought, it was the appropriate expression. Then he tried the smile again, but now that it was forced he thought it was less successful. Besides, he told himself, he hated precurtain revisions. Last-minute changes were the sure sign of a faltering production. If you had a good script, Paul believed, you stuck with it. He thought he had a good script. Once more he readjusted the knot in the subdued rep tie he had chosen for today.

He had dressed for this meeting as if he were auditioning for a part in one of his own plays. His first inclination had been to play it with throwaway chic. After all, he was a success in California. He could cut it in jeans, gold chains and a polo shirt. *Pennydance* had given him the credentials. No longer was he asked only to the gatherings of Los Angeles theater people who poured the white wine that was always easier to refuse than the hard stuff; now he was invited to the real thing — the Hollywood parties. Where everything was gorgeous. Where the lawns were groomed and the bodies were lean and tan and the food and the drugs were catered by people who knew what they were doing. People who put their arms around him, walked him out to the multilevel swimming pools and asked him to write screenplays.

"So far I'm uncommitted," he told Phil Gruber when the psychiatrist, who kept reminding him that he was also one of the chief financial backers of *Pennydance*, complained. Hollywood was a jellied sea of temptation that Gruber tried to warn Paul away from. If the Broadway production of *Pennydance* was a hit, Gruber kept saying, Paul could turn his back on "all that low-down, coked-up glittershit" and have the playwriting career he had dreamed about all his life.

"You said that to me, partner. Remember? About three months into our sessions, about the same time you loosened up and started to really talk about the violence. You said, 'Doc' — you were still calling me Doc back then — 'all my life I have wanted to write plays. That's what I dream about.' Well, this is no time to go plugging into a substitute dream. It's not my habit to remind you of what went down in those sessions, but it seems to me you once broke a woman's jaw because she made the honest mistake of assuming that a New York writer who had relocated to L.A. must certainly have moved here to write movies. You don't want to write movies, partner. You don't want no runner-up dreams."

"I'm just keeping my options open," Paul kept telling him. "That's all it is, Gruber, just options. And besides, don't you think when Rachel comes out here she'll get a bang out of meeting a few movie stars? Hmm? Who do you think a twelve-year-old kid would rather be introduced to when she comes out here, Sir Lawrence Olivier or John Travolta?"

"If she comes out here, Paul. If." Gruber had quickly corrected him. "There are no guarantees."

Paul winced just recalling the words. *No guarantees.* If he said it once, Gruber must have said it a thousand times since the opening night of *Pennydance.* And even long before that. Paul had first heard those words from Gruber in what was to have been their last session at Glen Crest. From that day forward Paul Roo was supposed to visit Dr. Gruber just once a week in his West Hollywood private office. Maybe it was that, the changed arrangements that were meant to signify Paul's progress in therapy, that had given him the courage to finally bring up the subject of Rachel.

"My daughter," Paul had said tentatively on that morning eighteen months ago. "I'd like to talk about my daughter," Gruber had offered him only the Texas Buddha face in response to that statement.

"I want her back, Gruber. When this is all over, when I have no more guts left to spill, when I can pass whatever test you throw at me that says Paul Roo is okay, he can control his furies now, I want her back. Hear me? For nine years, ever since the night Jenny packed her up and took her away, all that I have had of that child is the sound of her voice on the long-distance line once a week and the view of how her penmanship improves year by year as she signs my Father's Day cards. I want more, Gruber. I want to be her father."

Paul's face clenched as he walked out of the men's room and back to the still-empty arrival gate, thinking of what Gruber had answered to that.

"Hell of a speech, partner," Gruber had said quietly. "One hell of a soliloquy."

"You son of a bitch!" Paul had exploded. "You shrink-a-dink-son-of-a-bitch! Do you think I made that up? Do you actually think that's a speech I sat down at my typewriter and crafted? Listen, partner! I have been walking through this door every Monday, Tuesday and Thursday for the last six months! And I haven't had a drink in I can't count how long. And I have written a goddamn wonderful play in the meantime. And for what it's worth, pal, I came here on my own! Not like some of these guys who get sent here by the courts. I wasn't charged, no judge diverted me here. Nobody said you go get your head shrunk by Philip Gruber or we lock you up and throw away the key. You didn't call me, buddy, I called you! I had a choice!''

"Yes," Gruber had said mildly, "you did. And that means you went through here a whole lot quicker and stronger than the ones who are ordered here. The ones whose parole officers I keep checking in with. But don't kid yourself, Paul. You were lucky. You had a lenient judge who gave you public service diversion and wiped your record clean. If someone else had been sitting on the bench that day you might have had no more choice than a steer in slaughtering season. So let me set you straight, Paul, just in case the rolling lawns and the carpeted halls around this place have got you confused. When it comes to battering, when it comes to men who commit violence against women and children, I'm no different from the Los Angeles County Jail. With or without the bars on the windows, my job is to stop the violence. You got that?"

Paul had nodded quick agreement.

"Quit nodding, partner, because right now you don't know what the hell I'm talking about here. But you will. I promise you, you will. You'll walk out of here today feeling as though it's Graduation Day and you got top honors. But it isn't Graduation Day, Paul. Not yet. You're not even close to final exams. Sure, you've learned the lessons. You're a quick study. And I think you know how to deal with the physical cues to your anger. And most important, I believe you truly do understand that you alone are responsible for what you do — that it's not the women who create the setting for violence, it's your failure to control your anger.

"I get to where I want to heave every time a guy swaggers in here and tells me, 'Doc, she asked for it. She had it coming.' Bullcrap! There's not a woman alive — I don't care what she did or what she said, or who you think she's screwing behind your back — who's 'got it coming.' Not when 'it' is violence. Not when 'it' is against the law. Now, you walk out of here today and you remember that. Because there's a world full of women out there and some of them, sure as we're born, are going to make you angry. Because that's just the way it is with human creatures. They love and they hate and sometimes they do both at the same time. What I'm saying to you, partner, is that when one of those women makes you angry, then it's final-exam time. Then it's the test. Now you're talking about your daughter, right? Suppose she makes you angry. Kids can do that, you know. Suppose you show up after all these years and she just spits in your eye. How are you going to handle that?''

"Is that what you think will happen?" Paul had asked, gripping the sides of his chair.

"I don't know what will happen," Gruber had replied. "I'm just asking how you would control your anger if it did.''

"I don't know," Paul had said. "I really don't know.''

"Well, then you just take the next thirty seconds and think about it, partner. Because it's exactly as you said. You have choices. Now let me ask it plain — what do you mean when you say, 'I want my child?' ''

It had taken Paul a long time to answer that question, and when he did the words had come in a rush. "I don't know what I mean. Whatever the law will allow. Whatever her mother will agree to. Whatever Rachel wants. Jesus, Gruber, I would settle for an hour in Griffith Park. An ice-cream soda and a Steven Spielberg flick. A thousand games of Pacman at the video arcade of her choice. What do I know? Maybe Jenny's got her so brainwashed by now that she would be happier to spend a year locked up with Attila the Hun than two weeks with me in the summer. All I want is for you to say that it's possible. Not tomorrow, or next week, or even next year. Just somewhere down the road, that it's possible. It would give me a kind of goal, Gruber. Does that make sense?''

''Of course,'' Gruber had said. ''Of course it makes sense. But that's a very long road we're looking down, partner. Long road, thorny road, a road full of twists and sharp turns.''

''But it is possible?'' Paul had asked again. ''Just tell me if it's *possible?*''

''Maybe,'' Gruber had said, standing up to signify the end of the session. ''Maybe it's possible. No guarantees, partner.''

He had been saying it all along. He was still staying it last night when he had met Paul outside the Burgess Theater, where *Pennydance* was playing to a full house.

''Why did Jenny say she was coming?'' Gruber asked as they walked down the street, away from the theater. ''And did she say if she got your letter?''

''She got it,'' Paul said.

''Well, then it doesn't quite make sense to me,'' Gruber said. ''She knows you're going to be there in a few days. What's the point of her getting on an airplane and flying all this way when she could see you in New York next week? That doesn't strike me as very efficient use of her time.''

''Efficiency was never my ex-wife's strong suit,'' Paul had answered. ''She gets it all done, I gather, but on some wavelength only she is tuned into. Frankly, Gruber, it amazes me that a woman like Jenny has managed to survive in this life, let alone accomplish anything.''

Gruber let that pass, chalking it off to nerves. ''Maybe she's got business out here?'' he had suggested.

''Maybe.''

''Maybe she's got family to see.''

"No one I ever knew about," Paul said dryly.

"Well, then it's probably business. Didn't you tell me she's doing television now?"

"That's what Rachel says."

"Well, then," Gruber had said, pointing into the distance, "there lies Burbank. She's probably here on business. What, exactly, did she say?"

"That she had to come to California. Those were her words — *had to*. She gave me her flight number and her arrival time and asked if I would meet her plane. I was too surprised to say anything but yes, and by the time I thought to ask about Rachel she had already hung up. I'll tell you what I think, though. I think she's coming to check me out. I think she needs to see where I live and how I live and whether or not Rachel would fit in out here. I think she may visit my bank and my landlord, and it wouldn't surprise me if she were at the theater tomorrow night counting heads, tallying up the receipts. And I hope she does. Because the more she looks for dirt, the cleaner she's going to see that I am."

Gruber had paused and put his hand on Paul's arm. "No one would like to agree to that more than I," he said. "But I'm going to have to say it again — there are no guarantees."

And because there were no guarantees, Paul had left the jeans and the gold chains on the floor of his bedroom today and instead had worn the crisp white shirt, the subtle tie and the dark-blue linen blazer. Successful, such a costume would announce. Substantial! Reliable! Trustworthy! Credentialed! Look at that expensive haircut! Get a load of that confident smile! The man's a casting director's dream. Perfect for the part of Rachel's redeemed father.

Check that face, he had thought as he shaved for the second time this morning. Heavy-bearded men, men like himself, were villains in the eyes of the world. They looked guilty even when they were innocent, he believed.

Blameless heroes were cast with smooth-cheeked men. Running his hands over his reddened skin this morning, he was sure that given the opportunity, he could play the hero. But now, as the arrival time of Jenny's flight drew nearer, and the waiting area began to fill with other people who were meeting passengers aboard Flight 83 from New York's Kennedy International Airport, he wasn't nearly so certain. He didn't even know what she was coming for, let alone how long she was staying.

He rubbed his wet palms together and looked around the rows of seats where a dozen or so people were now waiting. Randomly, he chose a few of those people and decided to try out the smile of greeting he had practiced in the men's room.

On his first try his mouth twitched and a man in a three-piece suit ignored him. A seated white-haired woman wearing a lavender dress quickly looked away when he smiled at her, and she self-consciously opened a newspaper that lay folded on her lap. One more try, Paul thought, surveying the group. Just one more. In the corner of the waiting area he spotted a small boy, no more than three, who was fitfully pulling at his mother's earrings as she held him up to the huge glass windows where he could watch the behemoth jets as they moved to and from the gates.

"Stop it, Scotty," the mother said irritably, grabbing for her ear. "That hurts! Now just hold still and look out the window for Grandma's plane." The child fidgeted in her arms as Paul walked toward them flashing the practiced smile.

"Hiya," he said in the friendliest voice he could summon, "I bet your grandma is going to be very happy to see you, Scotty." The child spit at him.

Jesus, Paul thought as he quickly turned his back on the pair and headed out of the waiting area to the long corridor of the terminal building. Jesus! He tried to recapture the control, the practiced composure he had worked so hard to establish for this meeting by counting his inhalations and exhalations as he strode the corridor, but the child had blown it all away. Every word he had rehearsed for his speech to Jenny flew from his head now. Every emotional nuance he had contrived to display in the first moments of their meetings was forgotten. Damn kid! He should have known better than to have auditioned for some stranger's ill-mannered brat!

He struggled to run through the script once more before Jenny's flight pulled to the gate and it would be too late. The black wall clocks that hung at intervals as he walked the long corridor seemed to be mocking him. Earnestness, he instructed himself. Calm earnestness. That was the ticket. Animated cordiality was what he was meant to greet her with, nothing bolder. No broad impassioned speeches, and, above all else — no sheepish self-effacement. He would not beg, he would not crawl, and he would not demean himself. He didn't need to, he told himself as he mindlessly entered the gift shop at the end of the corridor. He wasn't asking her for the moon and the stars. He was asking her for the right to know his child, and that was an entitlement neither blood nor malice could deny. He stood at the gift-shop cash register and paid for breath mints to coat the sour taste in his mouth.

"Anything else?" the girl behind the register asked.

"These," Paul said, impulsively grabbing the blue stuffed kitten and an "I love L.A." tee shirt from a shelf. Great, he congratulated himself as the girl put his purchases into a bag and ran for the gate. Positively inspired, this last-minute selection of props. A stuffed animal and a tee shirt. Perfect. That was exactly the kind of stuff a real father would buy for his kid. Just clutching the bag as he ran made him feel that he had the part locked up.

You've got it made, he told himself as he lit a cigarette and then put a breath mint into his mouth.

Jenny's plane was at the gate.

Chapter Twenty-Six

She saw him first, and she told herself that was good. Good that as she stepped out of the jetway and into the bustling airport the first impression was hers. Good that she could read his face before he could know hers. He stood, leaning against a window, his face illuminated by the hazy late-morning sunlight. Quickly he turned his back to the stream of arriving passengers. Not for him, Jenny saw, the boisterous family reunions and the silent rapturous embraces of lovers restored safely to one another by the arrival of this flight. No, not for Paul. He held himself apart. Not for him, Jenny thought, to witness the young army sergeant falling into the arms of his blond acned girlfriend, or the grandmother who could not find enough places to kiss on the face of her bewildered grandchild. She wondered, seeing him stand off by himself that way, clutching some paper sack, how he might think to greet Rachel. And then, slowly, as if with great consideration, he turned from the window and met her eyes with his own.

Once, while trying to write a stage direction for one of his plays, he had come to Jenny seeking advice for a character he wanted to smile in a certain way before a line of dialogue was spoken. A broad smile, Jenny had suggested. No, he had told her, that was not it. A cunning smile, she had offered. No, that was wrong, too. "I need a smile from that actor to communicate more than mere happiness. It has to express both confidence and beseechment. How do I write that into a simple stage direction for the actor?"

"Tell him," Jenny had said, "to smile as though his life depended on it."

That was the smile with which Paul approached her now. She wondered, as he walked slowly toward her, how much time he had spent rehearsing it.

"You look good, Jenny," he said, stopping just far enough away from her to dispel any notion that he might touch her. "You really do look good."

She wanted to tell him that he looked lousy, that his skin was raw and lined and that when he offered her an intensified version of that phony smile the V-shaped squint lines that formed between his eyes made him look like a failed used-car salesman. She wanted to tear out his black eyes as they roamed her body as if he still held some residual right of possession. And she wanted, more than anything, to tell him that she wished that he were dead. Not in the way that she had dreamed it. Not with Rachel at his side. But, as in the dream, she wished that his death might come quickly. Before he could prepare a speech or a smile to meet it. That would not happen, she told herself as he stood prattling on about how much, how very much he thought her new short hairdo flattered her face, enhanced the eyes he had never been able to forget. Stuff it! she wanted to shout at him. Take this oily badly contrived monologue and wipe your lying eyes with it!

"What are you carrying in that bag, Paul?" she asked, nodding in the direction of his hand. These were the first words she had spoken directly to him in nine years and she was surprised by how evenly she said them.

"Oh, this?" Paul said nonchalantly while his smile widened with delight in seeing that his props were so well serving his intended purpose. "This," Paul said, raising the bag in his hand, "is for Rachel."

"Lovely," Jenny said as she snatched the bag from his hand before he could protest. "I'm sure she'll be grateful." She fought the impulse to examine the contents of the bag right now, where she stood. It was enough that the bag was in her hand now, not his.

"Hey, no," Paul said, calling back the smile that had faded briefly, "let me carry that. And your travel bag too," he said, reaching for the fold-over bag she carried over her arm.

"No," she said flatly. "I will carry it."

"Okay," Paul shrugged. "You carry the stuff. If you need to win that badly, Jennifer, okay. Just like returning the birthday check. You win."

"I don't need to win anything," Jenny said as she looked around the waiting area and saw that the crowd had left and they were suddenly alone. "It's just a very light bag and I can manage it myself." She turned and began to walk quickly down the long crowded corridor, Paul at her side.

"Where can I take you?" he said, reaching into his pocket and dangling car keys. "What would you like to see while you're in town?"

"Nothing," Jenny said without slowing her pace. "I'm taking a return flight back to New York in exactly two hours. I haven't come to tour Los Angeles, Paul. I don't need to see the back lot at Universal Studios or the homes of the movie stars. I came to talk to you, and we can do that right here."

On the list provided by Carmen Lopez Jenny had learned that the New York airports were among the most heavily trafficked areas in the city. There was no reason to believe that this wasn't also true of Los Angeles. The airport was as public a place as any, as protected a setting as she might hope for.

"I suppose you would prefer the cocktail lounge to the coffee shop," she said, trying to keep her voice neutral. She had not risen at dawn this morning and traveled three thousand miles in order to make judgments. Her judgments were already made. She had come all of this way simply to deliver them.

"The coffee shop will be fine," Paul said against the accelerated heartbeat and pulse rate he had been trained to perceive as warning signals. He tried now to heed the warnings. "There's a fairly decent coffee shop on the lower level. But there really are much nicer places to talk, Jenny. And they're not all that far. I could get you back in plenty of time for your flight."

"I am not leaving the airport," she said as she stepped onto the escalator beside him. And he saw then, in the way she held her head as she spoke, in the way she planted her feet for the ride down, that there was nothing in the script that he had gotten wrong, there was nothing he had said or done that was a mistake; only this — that somehow he had misjudged his audience.

As he stood to let Jenny be seated first in the artificial light of the coffee shop, she allowed herself to look at him, really look at him, for the first time. She thought that if she were ever to tell anyone about this meeting, and she doubted that she would, it would be David and Nina, if only because she would enjoy hearing them laugh out loud at the description of Paul's costume she would share with them.

"Remember those floppy hats of his, and the worn-out tennis shoes he was so devoted to?" she would tell them. "Well, you should see him now! Brooks Brothers by way of Rodeo Drive!" She saw, too, that he was smaller than she remembered. Perhaps it was the recent experience of Jake's muscled solidity that accounted for this perception, but she could have sworn all these years that Paul was taller. When Rachel complained that she was among the "shrimpiest" of the kids in her class, Jenny had always assumed that it was her own small stature that was accountable. She saw now that this wasn't true. Paul was no giant, either. And it wasn't only that, the size. There was, in the cast of his eyes, something of the sparkle she admired in Rachel's eyes. And even the ears. The ears set closely against Rachel's head — one of the first things she had admired when holding her as a newborn — were the ears set against Paul's head. She looked away.

They ordered coffee when the waitress came. "That it?" the woman said, her pencil poised for more. "No lunch?"

"I ate on the plane," Jenny lied. "But you go ahead, Paul . . ."

"Just coffee," he said, lighting a cigarette, and belatedly offering her the pack.

"No, thank you. I quit five years ago." She liked being able to tell him that. "Um, ma'am, on second thought I'll have a steak sandwich, medium rare, on a hard roll. And french fries."

In some long-ago column she had written about labor-management negotiations she had learned that the men who smoked cigars during those long mediating sessions sometimes did it because the cigars offered them respite from the struggle at the bargaining table. "You see, girlie," one of those labour chiefs had confided to her, 'if you got something between your teeth to suck on or chew on, you don't have to answer the other guy so fast. You got time to think.' If Paul's cigarettes could provide him with that advantage, why not supply her own? So what if she had no appetite. She would chew very slowly, think very carefully.

"How's your mother doing?" Paul asked as the

waitress set down their coffee cups and noisily laid down their silverware. "Is she still knocking them dead at Herald Square? Still the queen of Macy's Lingerie Department?"

Jenny took a small sip of her coffee, and then a larger swallow, inviting it to burn her throat. "My mother quit her job four years ago," she said tonelessly. "She's senile, Paul. She turns on gas burners and then walks out of the kitchen because she doesn't remember that she did it, let alone why. She gets up in the middle of the night and goes to the supermarket in her nightgown. The police bring her home and she does it again the next night."

"What about West River?" Paul offered. "Can't your friend David get her a place there? I would think that with all of his connections . . ."

"She won't go," Jenny said tersely. "She's a New Yorker to her bones. West River is in New Jersey. To Minna, New Jersey is another way of saying death. I can't put her there. Or anywhere else, for that matter. I can't just turn her over to some pasty-faced white coats and wait for her to die."

Enough, Jenny warned herself. His mother died at West River. Stop. That's enough.

"I'm sorry," Paul began to say, "I truly —"

"I'm sure you are," Jenny said, remembering that his own mother had been buried in New Jersey and that at the unveiling of Clara Roo's memorial stone she had stood by herself at the grave. Paul had not come. How sorry, Jenny wondered briefly, could he be? "Look, Paul, I didn't come all of this way to talk about mothers. I came to —"

"I know that," Paul said. "But I really am sorry. I always liked Minna. She was a true original and I admired that."

"She's still an original," Jenny said coldly. "And there was a time when she was equally fond of you."

Jenny laughed, a bitter ironic laugh that made Paul wince. "The fact is that she has forgotten why she hated you and now she asks for you all of the time."

"That must be very difficult for you," Paul said with a heavy voice. And Jenny saw in the way he averted his eyes that this too was a line he had rehearsed. Perhaps not to be delivered in exactly this context, more likely to be spoken in behalf of her struggles as a single parent, but definitely rehearsed.

"I deal with it," Jenny said matter-of-factly. And then, in order that he not trap her again on the unsteady ground of sentiment, she reached for the file folder she carried in a pocket of her hanging bag and took out the press clippings about *Pennydance* she had brought with her. "Tell me about these," she said, spreading the pages over the table between them. "Tell me about your play, your *autobiographical* play."

Paul fingered the clippings that lay on the table and smiled, a small smile that Jenny thought was almost spontaneous.

"This is funny, you know," Paul said. "I mean your cutting out my rave reviews and carrying them around with you. I used to fantasize that. I never had any of the more typical male fantasies when I asked you to marry me. I never visualized you cooking my meals or ironing my shirts. Nothing like that. But I did hope that someday you would do this," he said, running his hand over the newsprint. "I would like you see it, *Pennydance*. I wish that you would at least consider staying here long enough to see one performance. I always valued your opin —"

"No! But I will see it, Paul. I intend to see it. Opening night on Broadway." She saw with what impact that remark registered in the sudden twist of his mouth, the blood that rushed to his face. That face, the one that was about to erupt into rage, was the face she saw in her dreams. In her nightmares.

The waitress set a platter in front of her, and Jenny's eyes found escape in the food for which she had no taste. With trembling hands she lifted the steak sandwich to her mouth and bit into it. When she looked up at Paul his face was still flushed, but his features had settled into an expression less fearsome.

"I suppose you know that if *Pennydance* does have a Broadway opening, I have asked Rachel to attend it with me," he said.

"She mentioned it," Jenny said as lightly as she could.

"Did she also mention how eager she is for that to happen?" Paul asked, leaning across the table and searching Jenny's face.

Jenny chewed her sandwich and salted her french fries and considered telling him an outright lie. No, she imagined herself saying to him. On the contrary, Rachel had absolutely no interest in seeing you on Broadway or anywhere else on this planet, Paul. Rachel thinks you're dead. Rachel thinks you abandoned her. Rachel remembers what you did to her. Over my dead body will you see her. "I know that possibility is very appealing to a twelve-year-old girl," Jenny said as she forced herself to swallow. "But I will not permit her to attend an opening-night performance with you."

"Why not?" Paul demanded fiercely.

She had been a fool to throw away the clippings he had mailed her over the years, she now saw. If she had saved them, she might have built a case.

"Because," Jenny said, feeling the fear in her belly congeal like the grease on her platter, "I screen all of Rachel's cultural activities."

"Really?" Paul said, his thick brows arching with bemusement. "How very wonderful. What does that mean, Jenny? That you pay terribly close attention to the Parental Guidance ratings on films?" Jenny nodded without looking at him. "And do you also preview her video tapes? Do you also accompany her to public libraries and select what she reads? And I wonder, do you also drape yourself in one of Kalideoscope's fur pieces and go sit at Madison Square Garden to check out the Ice Capades before you take her to that! What does that mean, Jenny!"

Jenny took refuge in the food. She would not, no matter how loudly he threatened to cause a scene here, sink to his bait. With great absorption she lifted her steak knife and cut away the gristle on her meat. "It means that I care about the influences in Rachel's life. All of them," she said, daring to look him in the eye. There was nothing of Rachel in his face now, she saw. No real resemblance after all.

"Certainly you care," he said, tracing the rim of his coffee cup with quick compulsive circles. "Of course you care. I wouldn't have expected less." His voice was quieter now, weighted only by the effort it cost him to control his words. He had been right in guessing why she had come to Los Angeles. She was here to check him out as she would a movie or a play or a new school friend for Rachel. There was, in that maternal concern, much to be admired. And had he not promised himself that he would not pander, he might have told that to her now. Perhaps later, when he had persuaded her to stay long enough to see his home, to meet his friends, to actually give him a fair audition, he would tell her.

"You know, Jenny," he said in a voice so uncharacteristically quiet that it frightened her more than any shout, "it makes me angry that you won't give me a real chance. That you won't spend the time to give me a real opportunity to show you who I am now. It makes me angry that you don't trust me."

In nothing that he had said before this could she more clearly perceive practice.

"They taught you to say that, didn't they?"

"What?"

"That I make you angry. It's some kind of exercise,

isn't it? Some kind of warning signal they schooled you in at that place. You were in an institution, Paul. Don't try to deny it, I did research!''

"It's how I feel, Jenny," Paul said with widened eyes. "Angry is how I feel. The only thing learned in what I just said to you is that I didn't accuse you of making me angry. I didn't say, 'You, Jenny, you make me angry.' And yes, they did teach me that.'' He gripped the edges of the table and leaned toward her. "Taking responsibility for my anger is what I have spent the last two years of my life learning.''

"Was it hard?" Jenny asked without thinking.

"It wasn't any piece of cake, I can tell you. I've had ten flops that were less painful than this success.''

"What success?" Jenny asked, pushing the platter away from her, creating a kind of barrier with it on the table between them.

"Jenny, my God! Aren't you paying attention? Can't you hear what I'm saying? Do you actually think that if I were the same man you walked out on I'd have the balls or . . . or the inclination to come to you like this? To write you a letter asking permission? Permission to see my own kid?''

"I won't give it," Jenny said in the voice she had prepared for this moment. A voice that came through clenched teeth now.

Paul pushed his chair back and looked at his shoes. He had had them shined twice while he waited for her plane to arrive. And he had shaved twice, and he had a rented house in Malibu and he had friends and he had written a great play. So what if he had written it at Glen Crest? So what if Gruber was always waiting in the wings to pick his brain and examine the debris? So what! For what it was worth, his admission to Glen Crest had been voluntary. He ought to tell her that.

His silence was a cue, and Jenny took it. "Tell me," she said, summoning the question whose possible answer might strike her into muteness, "exactly what is *autobiographical* about your play?'' her voice quavered as she pronounced the word. It was the question among all those others that had plundered her sanity since he had written to her, the question that she needed most to articulate. "The reviews," she said, tentatively touching the clippings that lay between them, "are vague about details of the plot."

"The violence," Paul answered with an ease that astonished her. He lit another cigarette and blew out the match. "The violence is autobiographical. Oh, there's a lot of trivial stuff drawn from my own life, too. Familiar objects that became props, minor characters — little things that I hung on to that made the writing come easier, I guess. But it's the violence that shapes it all. It's the anger that makes it work."

Jenny's mouth fell open, but it seemed as if no air could reach her lungs. It was true, her worst fears were about to come true. *Pennydance* was the public unveiling of private misery. In a dark theater Rachel would sit among strangers and learn the terrible secrets Jenny had struggled to keep. In as little time as it would take to perform three acts, Rachel would witness all of the cruelty and despair she had spent years trying to shield her from.

"How could you?" Jenny demanded, scraping her chair back and away from him. "How could you! How could you take something so wretched, so full of pain . . . and craft it as some sort of entertainment! How could you, Paul! How could you sell tickets to pain?"

He tried to respond, tried to frame an answer, but she cut him off. "Did you never once think of what this would do to Rachel? Did you, Paul? Forget about me. What about Rachel? What about that blameless child you're so bent on reclaiming? Did it never cross your sick mind what this play of yours would do to her? My God, Paul! If you had actually let her fall to the ground four stories below, you couldn't have done more damage to her than this play of yours will do. I can't believe it! That you would actually write about us, that you would go ahead and expose —"

"Hold it right there!" Paul cried, grabbing Jenny's hands as she began to claw at her own face. "I haven't written what you think. *Pennydance* is not about us! It's about me! Not you, and not Rachel. The violence in my play isn't what I did to you or what I almost did to Rachel. Jenny! I thought you knew that. It's about the violence I lived with as a child. The beatings I saw my father give my mother. The beatings he gave me. Oh Christ, Jenny, the play ends when I'm only fourteen years old! I thought you knew that." His voice lowered now, nearly a whisper. "What Rachel will learn if she sees my play is that she had a grandfather who could not control his demons and a grandmother who was too bound by custom and culture to run away from him. Or maybe," he said, lowering his wet eyes, "my mother just didn't have your courage, Jenny. My father had to be dead and in his grave before she could be free. You made your own freedom. I wish . . . God knows how I wish, that I could have made mine. Sooner." He released Jenny's hands and wiped at his eyes. "I thought you knew."

"No," Jenny said softly. "No. I didn't know." And an image flashed in her mind. The garage. All those boxes. Those boxes of research materials on family violence. On battering. On wife abuse. Child abuse. The carefully stored statistics. The documentation. All of those printed words that lay moldering. Words that said what he had just told her. That the victims of abuse, the children who had suffered the violence in one generation, were many times more likely to inflict it in the next. Words. Expert opinions stored in boxes in the garage. "I didn't know, Paul," she repeated.

"Then stay, Jenny," Paul said. "Stay tonight and see the play."

"I will see the play," Jenny said, struggling to hold on to the resolve she had arrived with. But all that she could see was sweet, gentle Clara Roo, Paul's mother. A woman she had loved. A woman she thought she had known. All these years she had seen people — Clara, Paul, even herself — in a certain light, and now the light had changed. Shifted in some unalterable way that she needed time to adjust to. "But not tonight, Paul. I will see it in New York, I promise. I need some time."

"Okay," Paul said. "I regret that decision, but I can understand it."

"Good," Jenny said. "Let's talk about Rachel." There were words she too had rehearsed for this meeting, but, with the bomb Paul had just dropped, her words, like his, had been imploded. "You start."

"Well," he said, moving in his chair to face her, "there are some more things you ought to know. First of all, I want to see Rachel. I want to be with her. And she tells me that she wants the same things. Look at me, Jenny! I can't take back the things I did to you. I can't pretend any more than you can that those things didn't happen. But maybe I ought to remind you of something — I never hurt Rachel."

And suddenly the words came back to Jenny. The words and the resolve. "Paul, you held her out of a fourth-story window and you threatened to let go of her. Maybe you ought to be reminded of *that!*"

"I have been, I have been reminded. More times than I can tell you."

"Not enough!" Jenny whispered harshly. "Not enough times!"

"How many times is enough times, Jenny? How long before you come out of the tunnel long enough to see that it's daylight?"

"That's a beauty, Paul! Really! You ought to write that one down before it gets away," she laughed.

"You're right," he said, with his surprise visible on his face. "That is a great line." He smiled at her.

"What are you smiling about?" Jenny said,

straightening in her chair. Still wary, still poised for the blow she was sure would come.

"I'm just thinking that it's probably the best speech I've delivered yet today, and it's the only one I didn't rehearse." He laughed out loud and continued to smile at her.

A real smile, Jenny thought. An ad-libbed smile.

"Listen," Paul was saying calmly. "I know how this will end. I know what the law will allow. I will win, Jenny. I can use my attorney, and I will if I have to — but I would much rather do it with your approval."

"I have attorneys, too, you know," Jenny said, thinking of Jake.

"I would be surprised if you didn't," Paul said. "But I can't imagine what good it would do Rachel to have to endure a legal battle. She would have to be wounded in the crossfire."

"Can't you speak in something other than extended metaphors?" Jenny said, shaking her head. "Battles. Crossfire. It really does threaten your credibility when you talk that way."

Paul smiled. "I'll work on it. How's this? Let's try to work this out by ourselves. Let's try to make this as safe for Rachel as we can."

Jenny looked up at him and saw only his face, no masks. "How many times did you rehearse that one, Paul? It's got a nice parental ring."

"Zero." Paul grinned. "Zero times."

Jenny looked at her watch. "My plane leaves in forty-five minutes. How fast can you negotiate?"

"Try me," Paul said.

He lit another cigarette. Jenny went to work on her french fries.

Chapter Twenty-Seven

On her return flight, Jenny stretched across four seats on the nearly empty jumbo jet, and methodically went over the list of demands she had scribbled before she fell asleep on her inbound flight. Only one of them did not provide her with the satisfaction of placing a check mark beside it — the amount of advance notice Paul must provide before he could visit with Rachel. She had asked for five weeks.

"That is impossible," he had said. "My life is settled now, but that doesn't mean it's computer programmed. Regardless of what happens to *Pennydance*, I'm going to continue to live in California. It's impossible to know that far in advance when I'll be in New York. Give me a break on that one, will you? I've already said yes to everything else."

It was true. The entire negotiating session had taken less than twenty minutes. Jenny had been astonished to rise from the table in the coffee shop and discover that she had nearly a half hour before her flight would depart. She had used the time to call Rachel. It was still early enough on Saturday to catch the Kalishes at home.

"Surprise, Rach!" Jenny had said as she stood at the pay phone and watched Paul walk away. "My story didn't pan out too well, something about the hotel's fire regulations. I don't exactly understand —"

"You mean there are so many homesick New Yorkers out there they couldn't fit them all into the one room?" Rachel hooted.

"Something like that," Jenny had answered, suppressing her smile as Paul walked away. "Anyway, I'll be home tonight, sugar. In time to watch *The Midnight Special* with you."

There had been no immediate response from Rachel, and Jenny had stood wondering what the long silence meant, whether or not Rachel was pleased. It seemed to her that no matter how acquiescent Paul had been on each of her terms, she had just this moment let loose the sole claim to Rachel's affections. Was she lost to her this quickly?

"Mother?" Rachel said in that tone of voice that suggested hard words were about to be delivered. "We were sort of planning a party here. David and Nina and Jake and me. We've got about three zillion pounds of the best junk food you ever saw and we were kind of planning to watch *The Midnight Special* on David's giant screen TV. Do you think you could come here?"

Jenny sighed. "No problem, Rach. I'll come straight from the airport. You tell the others." She had nearly said goodbye when she suddenly realized it would be a lot easier to say this on the telephone than to look into Rachel's eyes and speak the words. "Say, Rachel? Guess who I ran into at the airport out here?"

"Who?"

"Your father."

"You did! Really? What was he like? Was he different? Was he nice to you? How did he look?" A stream of such ravenous questions, a voice so full of hunger that Jenny flashed on news photographs she had seen of children starving in far-off places. Children who appeared to be in mourning.

"He has a nice smile," Jenny said, looking over her shoulder.

"Yeah, but what was he like, Mom? What was he really like?"

"Rachel, you're going to see him in seven days. I think you can decide that for yourself."

"Six days," Rachel corrected.

"Right. Six days. I'll see you tonight, kiddo. I love you."

"I love you too," Rachel said. "And Mom? You don't have to bring me anything. You weren't there long enough."

You got that wrong, sweetface, Jenny thought as she looked at the paper sack on the seat beside her now.

She had a head full of second thoughts, and five and a half hours to let them assault her. To ask herself if she hadn't been crazy to make this trip, to agree to let Paul spend even one hour in Westchester County with Rachel this week. Even with the party of her choice in attendance.

"I hope you're not planning to ring in some big gorilla on me," Paul had said in agreeing to supervised visitation. "At least in the first visits."

"No." Jenny had smiled, thinking of David Kalish. "Only a small gorilla."

Maybe she had been wrong, Jenny thought as the captain announced that they had reached a cruising altitude of thirty-three thousand feet and passengers were now free to move about the aisles, but it seemed to her that decisions made and flown from had a built-in irreversibility factor; no message in a bottle could call them back from this altitude. Probably Nina, who had flown her own doubts to Chicago, would understand that.

She had accomplished what she had come to do, she

believed. She had flown and touched ground. And even though the ground she had landed on was Paul's, it was she who had made the rules. She who had handed him the decisions he would have to live with now. There was part of her that savored the victory in that, a part that believed no court could have meted out stricter judgments. But what if they were the wrong judgments? It wasn't as if she could push open the window of the airplane and yell down that she had made a mistake, that she wanted more time to rethink those judgments. She would get that opportunity, Jenny knew, the same way everybody else did. One day at a time. In the meantime she unfastened her seat belt and crossed over to the empty aisle seat where she could freely admire the endless expanse of blue.

The best thing about the sky, she thought, was that there were no dead ends in it.

Maybe she would write a column about that.

She never wrote that piece. In the days that followed her return from Los Angeles she thought a good deal about the sky and about how, since her meeting with Paul, she had been flying through it on instruments. He had scrambled her radar somehow; the screen on which she had carefully reviewed the past for so many years had gone blank, and no new image had yet emerged to replace the one that Paul had erased. She sat at her desk scanning the copy for her Tuesday-night television segment and thinking that she really needed to get busy. Paul was due to arrive in three days. There were arrangements to be made. If she still wanted David Kalish to act as Rachel's bodyguard for that first visit, she had better pick up the telephone and ask. There were times now, since her return, when she forgot that only she knew what had transpired in Los Angeles. Momentary lapses when she could not recall the details of her cover story about the Los Angeles reunion of expatriate New Yorkers. Questions posed by Nina that she couldn't answer. Things she wanted to say to Rachel that she simply could not bring herself to speak.

She had thought for so long that the only thing she needed to teach Rachel about her father was caution, and although that was still true, Jenny now knew that more than just warning signals were there for Rachel. She pushed the copy aside and turned off the typewriter. She would go through the mail she had been ignoring since her return and then she would call Jake and Nina and David and invite them to dinner tonight. And after Rachel was asleep she would tell them all what had really happened in California. And pray for their understanding.

But where could she begin to explain how that meeting with Paul had changed her? With what words? What words could convey this feeling that since Los Angeles she had energy to burn? Not nervous energy, not the urge to clean out closets or go on a pruning rampage or hide in the garden, but the physical sensation that there was new strength flowing through her body. She tried to give it a name, this feeling, and failed.

As a child, she had suffered a sore throat that had become pneumonia. Minna had nursed her through long, gloomy winter days with honeyed tea and spoonfuls of cheery-flavored penicillin. During the nights of chest-racked coughing and fever that had made her nearly delirious, her father had sat on the edge of her bed and told her how things were made. Between the spasms of coughing, and the cold washcloths applied to her burning forehead, he explained about steel mills and assembly lines. And food colorings. How do they made a skyscraper, Papa? she would ask. And he would tell her. From the cornerstone to the topping off, he would tell her all he knew. She had missed seven weeks of school that winter, and it was spring before she had her full strength back. But when she returned to school she felt no sense of loss. She had learned so much in those weeks!

That was how she felt now, as if she were slowly regaining her strength after a long illness. There was an exhilaration in that, a feeling that it was all right to climb on the monkey bars again, to run full tilt in all of the races. But still, it was too soon. The world was not yet again in clear focus, it still seemed to tilt just a little.

It was the tilt, the intuition that for the first time in so many years her life was approaching the center, but not quite there yet, that made it hard to explain. For between the moments of pure sensate joy there would come the sadness. The unbidden tears, the inexplicable weight on her heart, the tightening of her throat. And suddenly, everything was off center.

"Mom? Mother? Are you all right?" Rachel asked her this morning as Jenny spread peanut butter on Rachel's lunch-bag sandwich. "You look like you're going to cry." And then, with Rachel's small hand patting her back for comfort, Jenny had freed the dry sobs in her throat and cried out loud.

"Mom, Mommy? What's wrong? Please tell me what's wrong." Rachel's warm cheek pressed against Jenny's tear-streaked face. "Mother. If it's about Dad coming, it's okay. I don't have to see him. I can live without him. Mom?" Rachel was wearing the "I Love L.A." tee shirt from Paul. It was too big, but not by much.

"No!" Jenny had cried, pulling Rachel closer. "No, no, baby, it's not about Dad. Of course you're going to see him! I want you to see him! Oh my baby it's not about Dad!" She tried to wipe at her eyes, but Rachel's hand was already on her face, patting the tears away.

"It's about Grandma, isn't it?" Rachel said in a cold little voice that mocked the brimming of her own hazel eyes. "Isn't it?"

"No," Jenny said, her hand stroking Rachel's hair. "No, sweetheart. It's something I can't explain." There was no lie to that, Jenny knew, but to see the pain that such an admission brought to Rachel was more than she could bear. "Well, in a way it's about Grandma, but not Grandma Minna, Rach. It's about Grandma Clara."

Rachel's eyes widened and her mouth fell open. "You made that up! I don't even remember Grandma Clara! You made that up just so I would feel better. Mommy, tell me the truth, didn't you make that up?"

Or maybe she just didn't have your courage, Jenny.

"No," Jenny said, her voice more even now, her voice sounding more like a mother's voice, calm and centered. "I didn't make that up." And she knew then that it was true. That the inexplicable tears and the undiagnosed pain she had carried back from California were a kind of mourning. For Clara Roo, for herself, for every woman who had ever cowered or ducked or held the scalding-hot secret of abuse from the world. And with the unleashing of grief so long delayed, so long held behind the steel curtain, Jenny knew what she must do. As soon as Rachel left for school, she would begin.

"Come on," Jenny said, "let's go wash our faces, spread a little peanut butter, and get you off to school."

Rachel looked at her quizzically. "You're sure it's about Grandma Clara?"

"I'm sure," Jenny said running water in the sink.

"I guess seeing Dad made you think about her after all this time, huh?" Rachel said as she stood beside Jenny at the kitchen sink, the two of them splashing water against their tear-streaked faces.

"That's right," Jenny said, struck by the naked reasoning of Rachel's twelve-year-old vision.

"So in a way, I guess, it really was about Dad." It was a question as much as a conclusion the way she said it.

"In a way," Jenny said. "You could say that."

"I am saying that," Rachel said, looking her mother squarely in the eye.

God bless this child, Jenny prayed, seeing the determination in her child's face. This free brave child.

"So? What's the . . . what do you call it — the bottom line? Do I see him or not?"

"You see him!" Jenny said, hugging Rachel hard. "You absolutely, positively, no question about it see him!"

"Good," Rachel said simply. "Because now I believe you. Before I wasn't sure."

Chapter Twenty-Eight

Rachel went off to school smiling, but five minutes after she had hugged Jenny goodbye and slammed the kitchen door behind her she was back knocking at the front door.

"I just wanted to check," she said simply as she studied Jenny's face in the morning sunlight. "There were two things I didn't ask you because I was afraid to."

"And you came back to ask them now?" Jenny said softly.

"That's right."

"I'm still here," Jenny said, reaching for her child. "Ask."

Rachel buried her head against Jenny's shoulder. "Did Nina lose another baby?" she whispered hoarsely.

"Oh no, sugar! Nina just visited the doctor yesterday. She's in great shape and the baby is fine, too." She could feel the subtle slump in Rachel's body, the small release of tension. "What's the second thing you want to ask?"

"I don't want to ask it," Rachel said, her voice muffled against Jenny's bathrobe, "I need to ask it."

Give me strength, Jenny prayed. And give strength to my child.

"Did you and Jake break up? Is that why you were crying?" And then Rachel was sobbing, her body heaving against Jenny in convulsive thrusts. "Because . . . because if you did," Rachel choked, "that would really . . . that would really kill me!"

"Look at me," Jenny said, feeling the tilt in her child's world, and cherishing the stability of Jake's presence in her own. "Jake and I are terrific. Better than ever."

"Really?" Rachel said, pulling back to get a better look at Jenny's face while she spoke.

"Really."

"Honestly?"

"Honestly."

"Good. Your cheeks are dry. I believe you." and within seconds Rachel was back on her bike, swiping at her tears and shouting over her shoulder. "Have a great day, Mom! And don't get weird any more! Okay?"

"Okay," Jenny called after her.

And then she went to work.

The first thing she did after dressing in her oldest jeans and her most tattered sweatshirt was to climb on top of the Toyota and change the overhead light bulb in the garage. The dismal glow of forty watts suddenly became the dazzling light of two hundred. For this work, Jenny thought, there must be no dimness. Then she backed the car out of the driveway and parked it on the street. Back in the garage, she set up a folding table and a lawn chair that had once belonged to Minna. Briefly, she considered bringing the coffeepot out from the kitchen and plugging it in out here, but the search for an extension cord would only slow her down. There were ten small cartons of material on battered women set against the side wall of the garage. Coffee could wait.

As she worked through the years of accumulated newspaper stories, magazine reports, scholarly journals and books, some of the information came back to her as if she had filed it only yesterday. The case studies, the individual stories were especially vivid. Especially easy to recall.

The woman in Indianapolis whose husband was being considered for a seat on the appellate court and threatened to kill her if she made public the facts of his abuse. The woman's name was Marie, and Marie kept a diary. The broken wrist, the boiling water — all of it was in the diary the police found with her body.

Odette. Odette from Memphis, Tennessee, who had scars up and down her back from where he had cut her before she found shelter at the Treetop House. Odette stayed four nights that first time and then she went back home. And this time he cut her face. She went back to Treetop House for three weeks, long enough to write a volume of poetry that Jenny realized, scanning its pages, she had memorized. And then she went home and shot him dead with a twenty-two at close range. While her children watched.

The report from the Independent Task Force on Family Violence. Four hundred and twelve pages of documentation that made Jenny's head ache with its fine-print recommendations.

A *Time* magazine cover story. September, 1983.

Nearly six million wives will be abused by their husbands in any one year. . . .

Or maybe my mother just didn't have your courage, Jenny.

Two thousand to four thousand women are beaten to death annually. . . .

Violence. The violence is autobiographical.

Of the women who seek assistance, nearly eight percent cannot be accommodated by existing shelters. . . .

There are four cartons of research material hidden in my garage. There's not a day that I sit down at my typewriter and don't think about writing about it. But I don't. I sit there knowing there are thousands of women who need to know what I could tell them, but I don't dare.

Twenty-five to forty percent of wife beaters are child abusers. . . .

Words. Words on the page. Or words to be spoken? That was the only decision Jenny needed to make as she dug into the last carton. Should she tell her story in print or on television?

"Words are power," Paul had once told her. In the early days. The days before they were married. The days before the abuse. Her words, he had said, because they were written, because they could be read and reread and understood again and again, had an influence far beyond those of any playwright. "My words do not even exist in time until they are spoken by an actor. And once they are spoken, they vanish with the breath that gives them voice. You, dear Jenny, write with indelible ink and I write with the wind."

Print. She would do it in print.

But as she was replacing the last carton in the corner of the garage, and wiping sweat from her eyes, Rachel came riding her bike up the driveway and straight into the garage.

"What's going on? It's about a hundred degrees today," she said, panting and pulling her tee shirt away from her perspiration-soaked body. "What are you doing out here in the Sad Corner?"

"The what?" Jenny said, blinking the sweat from her eyes.

"The Sad Corner. God, it's bright in here."

"Say that again," Jenny said, suddenly aware that she had worked straight through the day without a break. "About the Sad Corner."

Rachel squinted against the light of the new bulb. "Once, when David was staying with me, I asked him if he knew what was in all those sealed-up cartons you kept stored in here. And he said that that was your Sad Corner. That was where you kept all the stuff you wanted to write about, except it was too sad."

"Come inside," Jenny said, heading for the air-conditioned comfort of the house. "We need to talk."

"Mother . . ." Rachel said, hanging on to her handlebars, "this isn't going to be weird, is it?"

"No," Jenny said, feeling the sweat drip under her clothes. "Tough. It's going to be tough. And confusing at first. And painful. But it isn't going to be weird. Let's go in."

"Okay," Rachel said when they were in the kitchen and she had stripped down to her underwear and poured herself and Jenny huge glasses of cold lemonade. "Talk."

Jenny held the icy mug of lemonade to her head and leaned against the kitchen counter.

"David was right about the Sad Corner, Rachel," she began. "There are things in those boxes that I need to write about. Things I wish that I could have written before now."

"You're going to write a column about sad stuff?"

"Yes," Jenny answered softly.

Rachel thought of the locked gray metal file box she kept in her room. "I hide my sad stuff, too," she said, offering what she could.

Jenny nodded.

"Will it be a sad column? I mean, sometimes you write about sad things and you make people laugh at the same time. Will this be like one of those or will it be completely sad?"

Jenny wiped her brow. "I'm not sure, Rach, but a lot of people might think so. The only thing I know is that it will be hard to write. Maybe the hardest column I've ever written. For sure the most important."

"What if it's too hard?" Rachel wondered. "What if it's as hard as . . . as algebra, say?"

"Well, then I'll just have to keep working at it," Jenny said.

"Are you going to cry when you write it?"

"Maybe," Jenny said. "Probably."

"You're crying now," Rachel said solemnly.

"That's okay. It's good that I'm crying. It's good that I'm doing this."

"Are you going to do it now? Write it, I mean."

"No," Jenny said, struggling for composure, for mother-calm. "Not right now."

"Why not?" There was a wariness in her child's voice that made Jenny shiver. Because, she thought, I will cry when I do it, and you, my precious baby, have seen enough of tears. Because there will be anger when I do it, and you have known enough of anger. Because when I go into that workroom and close the door behind you, you will not bear witness.

For in that instant of watching Rachel fold the tee shirt that had been Paul's gift, Jenny thought of her own father. The feel of his beard bristling soft against her skin when he carried her home from the fireworks display. The shape of his head as she watched from the back seat as he drove. The warm place he left in her bed when he sat on its edge to kiss her good night. Was he good, her father? Was he as good a man as she remembered? There was no way to know, Jenny realized. Her time with him had been too brief, so foreshortened by his early death that all Jenny had of her father was golden foreground, studded wtih small jewels of memory that glittered in the intense light he had cast upon her childhood. But Rachel, Rachel had no such memories. She had known no such moments with Paul. And whether or not he was now capable of providing them, that too was an unknown.

Only this was certain — Rachel wanted her father. Wanted the mysterious stranger on the other end of the long-distance line to be someone real. Someone who would leave a warm space on the edge of her bed. Someone she could freely call *Dad* as he tucked her in at night. Until that connection was tested in a fair test, Jenny knew that the column must wait. Such strong words would hold until Rachel was a big enough kid to handle them. Maybe that would be six months from now, and maybe it would be six years, but eventually that time would come. One day at a time.

"Well, then, when are you going to write it?" Rachel prodded.

There's a time and a place for everything, Jenny's father used to say, and she knew that this was not the time. The right time was after Paul was gone. After Rachel had had the chance to get to know him on his own terms.

"Not today, Rach, but soon." For already the first words of the column were locking into her head. *Nearly six million women will be abused by their husbands or lovers this year.* And the last words were coming right behind. *Trust me. I was one of them.* "Very soon, Rachel. I will write it very soon."

"And then what?" Rachel wanted to know as she swallowed the last of her lemonade and chewed on an ice cube. "What comes after the hard part?"

The hardest part, Jenny thought. "After that I will show you what I have written and then you'll tell me if you think it should be printed or not."

Rachel considered this. "What if I say no? What if I say that it shouldn't be printed? That it's too sad or something."

"Then we'll tear it up together," Jenny said. "And then we'll talk some more."

"Yes, and then what?" Rachel needed to know. "If it's so important, you'll write it again, won't you?"

She's not just smart, Jenny. She's strong. And who do you think she learned that from? She learned it from her mother.

It was Nina who had said that.

"Yes," Jenny said calmly, "I will write it again. And if it's still wrong, if you think it's still wrong, I'll write it again. And again. And maybe I'll have to cry again, I don't know. But I'll work on it until you think I've gotten it right."

"You would do that?" Rachel asked incredulously. "You actually think that my opinion matters so much? That I'm so important?"

"Rachel," Jenny said, her heart swelling with a rush of pure love, "I don't think so, baby. I know so."

Rachel studied the clock that hung on the kitchen wall above the sink. "Well, okay, then," she said. "Let me know when you need me."

Thank you to those who listened, taught, read and believed: Andrew Bundy, Ruth Benz, Jean Peterson, Arthur Bodin, Judy Gibbs, Edwin Shulman, Dan Thomas, Jags Powar, Patty Detroit, Claudia Hevel.

And my boundless love and gratitude to the in-house stalwarts: Neill, Adam and Todd.

HERE IS YOUR CHANCE TO ORDER SOME OF OUR BEST

HISTORICAL ROMANCES

BY SOME OF YOUR FAVORITE AUTHORS

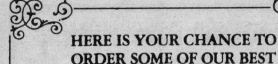